Praise for
Guardians of the Desert

"An absorbing story, a unique world, and fascinating characters. Leona Wisoker is definitely a writer to watch!"
—Tamora Pierce

"Compelling characters and a colorful setting make this a satisfactory multivolume fantasy."
—*Library Journal*

"For its complexity, intriguing story, and (as in the first volume) for its characters I find totally fascinating, I heartily recommend *Guardians of the Desert*."
—*SF Revu*

"A storyteller with a good deal of promise. Give this one a try."
— CJ Cherryh

"Sturdy, engaging, confidently-written—*Guardians of the Desert* is all any fan could have hoped for in a sequel. The delightful Ms. Wisoker is now two for two."
—C.J. Henderson

Children of the Desert

series

by Leona Wisoker

Book One: Secrets of the Sands

Book Two: Guardians of the Desert

Guardians of the Desert

Leona Wisoker

Copyright © 2010 by Leona Wisoker
Interior map by Ari Warner Copyright © 2009
Cover illustration Copyright © 2010 by Aaron Miller
Cover design by Rachael Murasaki Ish

First Trade Edition—published 2011
Printed in the United States and the United Kingdom

MERCURY RETROGRADE PRESS
6025 Sandy Springs Circle
Suite 320
Atlanta, Georgia 30328

www.MercuryRetrogradePress.com

Library of Congress Cataloging-in-Publication Data

Wisoker, Leona.
  Guardians of the desert / Leona Wisoker. -- 1st trade ed.
    p. cm. -- (Children of the desert ; 2)
  Summary: "The second of an epic fantasy series with a desert setting, about the relationship between humanity and an ancient, mysterious race"--Provided by publisher.
  ISBN 978-1-936427-02-4 (alk. paper)
  I. Title.
  PS3623.I847G83 2010
  813'.6--dc22
                                    2010052947

Dedication

This book is dedicated to all the librarians who are trying to do more and more with less and less, every day. I would not have begun reading fantasy fiction without the guidance of a librarian; I certainly would not have begun writing it. I owe a great debt to the public library system: one beyond repaying.

To librarians everywhere, I say: Never doubt that you are appreciated; by me, at least, you are deeply loved.

Acknowledgments

Writing well is *not* a solitary art; I could not have produced this book without the support of dozens of people. My husband has never stopped believing in my ability to overcome any obstacle; and I, not wanting to disappoint him, have scaled mountains I never would have dared try otherwise. My parents have cheered me on unceasingly. My siblings, extended family, and friends have all been supportive beyond my wildest dreams. I must offer a deep bow to the exceptional trio of Chris Addotta, Amy Smith, and Ame Morris, all of whom not only served as the best beta-reader group I could have asked for, but have also helped me staff convention tables, fed me when I was ill, and made me laugh when I was cranky. Chris Addotta created the calendars and the complex game of chabi. I *truly* could not have gotten through Book Two without these three wonderful ladies! Another specific and sincere bow goes to Coyote Run; their music has kept me going through late-night editing rampages, online conference discussions, and long-distance drives. It would have taken me twice as long to finish this book without their tremendous and contagious energy driving me on. And I was blessed, once more, with magnificent cover artwork: I am humbly grateful to Aaron Miller for working with us to produce such perfection.

Many more names deserve mention: Allen Wold (the best writing mentor I have yet encountered), Edward Morris (proflic past the point of insanity), Zachary Steele (just insane—in a good way), John Adcox (an amazing writer and friend); the list is a long and diverse one, and includes the staff and volunteers of several conventions: MarsCon, RavenCon, Wicked Faire, BaltiCon, Faerie Escape Atlanta, CapClave, and DarkoverCon. Then there is Steven Savage, whose book *Fan to Pro* serves as a constant nudge for me to aim ever higher; Beau Carr of The William & Mary College Bookstore, who set me up with my first-ever bookstore book signing and was gracious enough to invite me back several times; Debbie and Brian of Mystic Moon in Norfolk, who invited me in for a signing that proved to be the most welcoming experience I had all year; all the blurbers for the first book (especially C.J. Henderson, who was not afraid to tell me about the soft spots in *Secrets of the Sands*—gotta love that honesty! It helped me improve Book Two immeasurably); Rick Starets, from whom I learned a great deal about showmanship; Ari Warner, whose maps continue to illuminate my fictional world; and last but by far not the least, all the fantastic librarians who added my book to their catalogs. I know I have left out names worthy of notice, and I apologize; but I simply do not have room for all the thank you notes, and must pick and choose from the very top of the list.

Above all, I must go down on one knee to my publisher and editor, Barbara Friend Ish of Mercury Retrograde Press: for pushing me to go ever deeper, to take more risks, and for leading the waltz out of my comfort zone into a place where I could grow as a writer. You would not be holding this book in your hands without her expert and dedicated guidance, and I salute her with all my heart.

Table of Reference Material

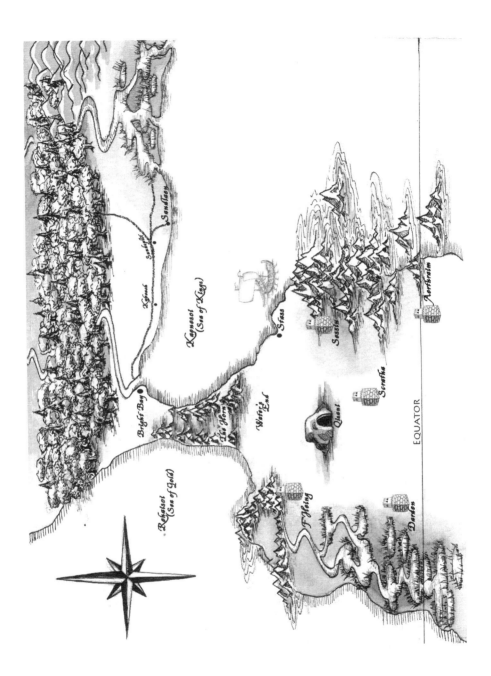

Royal Library Map no. 123:
The Southlands and Southern Kingdom

To Lord Oruen, greetings from Lord Cafad Scratha, Regent-Head of Scratha Fortress:

As by now you must know that I disregarded your instruction to travel north as your Researcher, some explanation is in order. First let me assure you that the assignment has not been abandoned completely; my former servant, Idisio, has agreed to continue the work. While he is, of course, not yet the scholar or possessed of the level of learning you may have desired in a Researcher, still he learns quickly and has a sharp eye. I hold every confidence that he will perform sufficiently for your needs.

His companions, one Deiq of Stass and one Lord Alyea Peysimun, are traveling with him due to an unusual combination of circumstances, and only part of that tale is rightfully mine to tell. They may or may not share their own influences on the situation with you, and thus my account of how I come to be resident at Scratha Fortress and a former street-thief has taken on your assignment of chronicling the northlands must necessarily remain incomplete.

As briefly as possible, then: during my initial travel eastward with Idisio along the Coast Road, I passed through each village along that main road and made certain notes, as follows: Kybeach, the closest village upon Bright Bay borders, is a small and unpleasant town which is breeding a remarkable amount of resentment and squalor. The residents are sullen and hostile, and the heavy stamp of Northern Church abuse lies clear on every face. Their main industry seems to have been that of gerho breeding, headed by one Asti Lashnar; Ninnic and Mezarak were apparently far fonder of dining on gerho than you, Lord Oruen, have proven to be. Your dismissal of gerho from your kitchen has put a catastrophic strain on Kybeach as a whole and the merchant Lashnar in particular. I strongly recommend extending a hand to this village; as close as it stands against Bright Bay, I feel you can ill afford the villagers' resentment to grow any further or even to remain at its current, dangerous level.

Moving on from Kybeach, we traveled to Obein. The difference between the two is distinct: Obein is tidy and cheerful, resilient and even prosperous in the wake of recent events. Their residents are merchants and craftspeople, farmers and innkeepers; altogether a higher class of folk, with much less fear or harm in their souls than even the happiest person in Kybeach. I am at a loss to explain this distinction, except to note that the swamp stench of Kybeach and the distance of Obein, along with the clear preference of merchants to pause at the farther station to arrange themselves preparatory to arriving in Bright Bay, has given the two villages a very different spirit.

From Kybeach we moved on to Sandsplit and there encountered the surprises that turned me to the southlands. Your missive, for one, caught up with me there; and I will pause in my narrative for a moment to note that if you aimed to enrage me with that note, you certainly succeeded. With the passage of time since that day, my temper has cooled somewhat, and I now believe your attempt to inform *me of proceeding matters held no intention of malice; rather an astounding level of ignorance you can ill afford if you expect to deal with the desert Families and win their respect to any degree. Sending a young northern woman with no ties to, nor understanding of, the southlands along with one of your so-called "Hidden"—who are known, every one, to all those involved in southland politics, as spies and assassins—and your preferred advisor, a man as well known to be* hask, *traitor to his chosen faith and banned from the southlands; in short, choosing this combination of ambassadors to hold Scratha Fortress in my absence was a catastrophically poor one. It may take you years to recover from the consequences of this one decision, although I recognize that you had no way to know the intricacies of the situation.*

I will thank you, however, for your warning that Pieas Sessin had left to hunt me, and for the information that he was disowned and disgraced. Although you clearly expected him to follow our false trail west to the Stone Islands, still your very timely information quite possibly saved my life and that of my then-servant, Idisio: Pieas Sessin caught up with me in Sandsplit Village. Your warning gave me a chance to prepare, and he fled rather than face me.

A troubling piece of information also came to light during my stay in Sandsplit; a northern man has taken over one of the local inns. He claims a southerner came to his home city of Stecatr and offered a trade of one inn for another; offered, in fact, a high enough price for the northerner's inn that the man leapt at the chance and promptly moved south to claim his new business. While this may seem a trivial matter, I see a worrisome possibility inherent in the matter; given Stecatr's position, both geographically and politically, I suggest you look into this to see if other southerners are pursuing such trades. An influx of northerners into the Coastal Road area could severely unbalance matters ranging from trade to local culture, as would a similar flood of southerners, whether kingdom or Family, into the conservative northlands.

Returning to my narrative: I chose, after reading your missive, to abandon the task of King's Researcher in favor of returning to Scratha Fortress, considering the dangerous game you had set into motion more important to rectify than was completing your assignment. The horses you had loaned me I left in the care of a local merchant named Yuer; he may return them or not, as he pleases. That matter you must take up directly with Yuer himself.

My notes on Sandlaen Port, from whence we departed by ship, must wait for another time, as they are largely irrelevant to this section of the tale. I will admit that in order to speed our travels and avoid inconvenient arguments with you, Idisio and I stayed below while the ship restocked its supplies in Bright Bay, and I instructed captain and crew to keep mute as to our presence.

Our arrival at Agyaer Port and our climb up the long Wall Stair are similarly irrelevant to your concerns, save to note that I sent out multiple missives of my own during that time, calling for a Conclave to be held at Scratha Fortress. As noted above, I knew your choice of ambassadors would spark deep problems and decided it most appropriate to summon an official, recorded gathering to address that issue and one other: that of Pieas Sessin's disgraceful behavior, long overdue for formal recognition.

Our travels to Scratha Fortress are likewise irrelevant to you at this time. Upon arrival at the Fortress, then: among the arrived Family representatives were Alyea and Pieas himself; the former accompanied by Deiq of Stass and the latter under the protection of another Family. Sorting out both matters ended with Lord Alyea's investment as a full desert lord and the death of Pieas Sessin, ironically as part of Lord Alyea's investment. That part of the story, as I intimated above, is not properly mine to address. I suggest you speak with Lord Alyea herself regarding the matter, and if possible with Deiq of Stass.

I have chosen to remain at Scratha Fortress for the foreseeable future; I have come to see your advice to rebuild my Family rather than continue a wandering search for vengeance to be, after all, wise words. I am sending Idisio, as mentioned previously, to complete your initial errand; he will take on the name of Gerau Sa'adenit in his writings, so as to provide a seamless transition in the annals of history. Please render him the same assistance and courtesies you would have shown to me. He has proven himself, in our travels, to be exceptionally bright and, once removed from his initial immoral life, quite reasonable in his ethics as well. He holds the full support of Scratha Family and is to be treated as a noble of our line at the very least.

Rest assured that Scratha Fortress considers you an ally and will provide what it may to assist you during your time of leadership. A formal ambassador shall be appointed to your court as soon as I have trained one to my satisfaction; that ambassador will speak further with you, at that time, on matters of trade and other agreements.

Meanwhile, I enclose the first of several missives to come, providing an account of southland politics and history which you may find useful in avoiding egregious errors in the future. As a matter of policy, the desert Families have not provided this information to northern kings; you yourself must admit that the majority of the last few kings have not been particularly safe to entrust with any real knowledge. As examples I present Ninnic, who almost destroyed your kingdom in his madness; Mezarak, similarly if less strongly afflicted; and Dusty Rose, the king who not only brought a street whore into his court circle, but following her death took on her moniker as a way to honor her memory, shortly thereafter dying himself of the same foul rot which had taken his beloved streetwalker. This last king is still commemorated in bawdy songs sung by rough sailors. I would in passing suggest you lift the ban on such songs, as execution seems a harsh punishment for a bit of satirical commentary on what was, unarguably, an asinine moment in the history of your kingdom.

As you, however, seem relatively sane and reasonably intelligent, I entrust you with this knowledge—not lightly, as the other Families are sure to be annoyed with me for defying their collective decision to dole out only what they feel you need to know—but with the certainty that if you are left in ignorance you will once again stick your foot in a pie of the type which is baked in no oven.

I close this letter with gratitude for your assistance and with hopes for a future in which we will both speak honestly and plainly to one another, and use our alliance for the mutual benefit of our respective realms.

May the gods watch over you and smooth your path with their breath, and lead you into the brightest of possible futures.

Lord Cafad Scratha
Regent-Head of Scratha Family
Scratha Fortress

A Discussion of
Desert Family Structure, Leadership,
and
Hereditary Positions

(excerpt)

Each Family has its own distinct and unique command structure which has evolved, over the years, to best suit its specialties, ethos, and location. Many kingdom residents mistake one as representative of the whole, but this is absolutely not the case. For example, Scratha Family and Aerthraim Family are both matrilineal; however, Scratha was founded with female leadership and has continued that line ever since, meaning that the numainiae, the proper (plural) title for a female Scratha Head of Family, trace their descent back in one unbroken line to the First numaina.

Aerthraim Family, in contrast, began with an open heredity pattern, meaning that any qualified direct descendant of their leader could be selected by that leader as successor; since the Split, their leadership structure has morphed into various and increasingly bizarre variations, the most recent of which is a strict matrilineal, insular form. Their current title for their female Head of Family is mahadrae, which roughly translates as chosen mother of the free people. This strange designation has ruffled a few feathers throughout the other Families for some years now, as you might imagine, since it implies that while the Aerthraim are free, the rest of us are bound and chained slaves to some inimical force. The fact that the Aerthraim have also refused to allow any desert lords to swear service to their Family name adds in a troubling and strongly offensive element to this perception.

Such are the subtleties of the world you stepped into when you sent Alyea south to hold Scratha Fortress in your name, Lord Oruen; your advisors have taught you poorly if the above is entirely news to you.

From the collection
Letters to a Northern King of Merit
penned by Lord Cafad Scratha during the reign of King Oruen

Chapter One

Song filtered through the air of Scratha Fortress. Deiq lay on his back, watching dust particles drift through the air, and focused his attention on the chant. It came from the other end of the Fortress: Alyea's hearing would probably never get sharp enough to hear that far, but for Deiq it was a simple matter of screening out all other noises along the way.

The song clarified: tenor and soprano voices, male and female, wove across a rattling beat from at least three different *shabacas*, and a piping cactus-flute warbled the main theme:

Iii-naa tarren . . . iii-nas lalien . . . iii-be salalae . . . .

The accents and inflections marked the singers as servants rather than nobles. Deiq smiled at the ceiling, reflecting that a thousand years ago there would have been only a jacau-drum beat behind the song, and the singers would have been the leading men of the tribe.

The chant had run very differently back then: *Itna tarnen, itnas talien, itnabe shalla: We empty ourselves into the gods, the gods pour themselves into us, glory be to the gods.* Time had changed both pronunciation and meaning; the modern understanding of the old paean was closer to *We serve the gods, the gods smile on us, we survive under the glory of the gods.*

Which said a lot about how much humanity had changed since the ha'reye first emerged from their seclusion . . . and how little humans still understood of what they had agreed to.

These were dangerous thoughts with a full ha'reye beneath the Fortress and a restless, newly bound desert lord pacing around. Deiq distracted himself for a few moments by focusing his vision narrowly enough to track a single dust mote dancing along its erratic path, then widened his vision to take in the entire room without moving his eyes.

Beside him, Alyea sighed deeply: he blinked back to human-normal vision in case she woke. She rolled closer; he moved an arm and let her tuck in against his side, his mouth quirking in a tired smile. Humans were so damn *vulnerable* . . . and so *stupid* at times. Even though he'd promised to protect and guide her, that left a lot of room for interpretation.

He wouldn't take that leeway, of course; but Alyea didn't even understand that it existed.

Not that she'd had much choice about his presence while she slept. She needed rest before the Conclave, and he wasn't about to leave her alone again. Besides, the other options for companionship were as welcome as letting an asp-jacau chew his arm off.

He watched her sleep, reflecting how much more pleasant she was to look at than the grimly suspicious stares of the other desert lords. Her dark hair was half undone from the sensible top-knot that kept desert heat from soaking the back of one's neck with a continual layer of sweat. Deiq had bound his own hair in a simple tail; perspiring rarely became an issue for him. Alyea's light clothing, however, already sported several tell-tale dark patches. In true summer it wouldn't have been so bad, but the weather had begun edging towards the rainy season, and the ambient humidity was climbing rapidly.

Deiq set his fingertips against Alyea's temple and gently soothed her body temperature down until the rank sweat-smell faded. She sighed and rolled away again, one arm stretching up over her head and her lithe body twisting like a cat's; his hands itched to touch her again, with much more than fingertip pressure this time.

How many times before this have you fallen in love? she'd asked earlier, not understanding at all; and he hadn't been able to bring himself to explain. She'd looked so *hopeful*, her dark eyes lit with an intensity he'd seen before; she was still young enough to be romantic, in spite of her insistence that roses wouldn't mean anything to her.

He sighed and kept his hands to himself. That would just complicate matters, at the moment. After the disaster her second blood trial had become, she needed extra time to heal—and not just physically.

So let Alyea think he was in love with her for now. Humans needed that kind of security, and it didn't really matter. She'd figure it out eventually. Until then, it was pleasant to have her quiet, innocent trust resting against the edges of his mind.

He knew it wouldn't last. It never did.

Eyes half-shut, he watched the dust of decades swirl through shafts of reflected sunlight and listened to the song being sung at the other end of the Fortress.

Joyfully accepting servitude to invisible forces: how could humans think that way? How could they not *understand*?

A sucking weariness passed through Deiq's entire body for a moment, hazing his vision around the edges; then the haze turned golden, and he felt an immense *presence* thrust into his mind.

You fight what you are, the Scratha ha'rethe said. *Why? Why do you spend so much time thinking about the humans? Why do you bother? At the least, you could have the dignity to focus on those who choose to serve, instead of the* tharr.

The invisible ones, that meant: the commoners, the ordinary ones whose existence normally didn't even register with the ha'reye. People like Alyea, before her trials; like Meer.

Deiq shut his eyes, grimacing, and blocked memory so quickly he barely knew he was doing it himself. The ha'rethe stirred restlessly, its golden stare intensifying.

Something troubles you.

Nothing important, Deiq said, infusing his reply with a deliberate boredom. *Just remembering one of the more amusing tharr.*

Not amusing at all; but he didn't want the ha'rethe to pry.

You waste your time on this, the ha'rethe said, drawn in the direction he'd hoped for. *Those who do not serve do not matter.*

It was the old argument, and one he'd never resolved with any of the ha'reye or ha'ra'hain.

He repressed a sigh, and answered, *Don't they all serve, in the end?*

You indulge in foolishness. The golden haze faded away with the suggestion of an annoyed head-shake. Deiq let out a long, quiet breath, feeling as though a dangerous precipice had just smoothed out into relatively stable terrain.

Brooding would only attract the ha'rethe's attention again, and draw them into an argument Deiq preferred to avoid, so he gently nudged Alyea's shoulder with a bent knuckle to wake her. She rolled towards him as she opened her eyes; the movement put her right up against him, her dark stare inches from his face. The moment hung and stretched; he stayed very still, as though to avoid startling a wild creature.

At last Alyea blinked, awareness dawning in her expression, and scooted hurriedly away from him. "How long have I—?"

"Almost time for Conclave," he said, sitting up and looking away to give her some sense of privacy. Her withdrawal wasn't surprising; it was a matter of instinct for any human to back away from close contact with a ha'ra'ha. Desert lords trained themselves to overcome that instinct, which only proved how damned stupid humans could be.

A faint burning ache passed across his chest.

He shut down that emotion-laden line of thought before he attracted the ha'rethe's attention again. *Foolishness,* it had scolded; not the first time he'd been faced with that accusation, and it wouldn't be the last.

He manufactured a pleasant expression for Alyea's benefit and suggested, "Let's go get some food before Conclave starts."

That trivial normality relaxed her vague disquiet instantly. As he let her lead the way to the kitchens of Scratha Fortress, he held back a sigh at how simple maneuvering a human, even a desert lord, always was; and only then realized that he'd hoped Alyea, somehow, would be different.

Chapter Two

The two largest rooms in Scratha Fortress, by far, were the formal dining hall and the *teuthin*, which Deiq translated as *meeting place*.

"Bit more complicated than that, of course," he added as he walked with Alyea through the quiet corridors towards the Conclave. Servants moved about in groups, discussing in low voices how to allocate tasks; Alyea recognized the scene as typical of an influx of wholly new staff as yet unaccustomed to working together.

She'd seen it at home twice: once after her father died, when her mother had inexplicably swept out the old servants and replaced them with almost all new; and again after her whipping, as though to deter such betrayals in the future. Or perhaps Lady Peysimun simply couldn't stand having servants who had watched her daughter being publicly whipped and humiliated.

Alyea had never asked; had never wanted her suspicions confirmed. Her mother could be remarkably shallow at times.

Deiq's quiet, velvet voice brought her out of brooding.

"A *teuthin* is by implication any neutral ground, where grievances are either set aside or resolved without violence. It's a place where everyone's status is the same, where all voices can be heard and even the poorest commoner has the right to speak his mind freely to the lords of his land. I believe there's even a story or two about a commoner so impressing the gathered lords that he was adopted into a desert Family on the spot . . . It's the sort of legend that humans seem to love hearing."

Deiq seemed completely unselfconscious about referring to himself as nonhuman—at least when they were alone. In mixed company, around those who might not know his background, he tended to pass himself off in roles of *rich merchant* or *mysterious quasi-noble*.

She thought about how long he'd been concealing his nature, wondered who else knew the truth about him, and mused how lonely it must be to lie to everyone he met.

He glanced at her, an odd sideways motion filled with amusement.

"Very few, to answer one of your questions," he said, a smile tugging at his thin lips. "All the Fortress Heads know what I am, and the loremasters, of course; but even most of the desert lords you'll meet don't need to know that I'm anything but a rich merchant or—" the amusement in his voice deepened: "—mysterious quasi-noble. Thank you; I do like that phrase."

Alyea blinked, taken aback at how easily he could read her, and tried to cover her thoughts more securely. She had to stop walking to concentrate, and Deiq paused as well, the smile still on his face as he watched her efforts.

Noise scratched at her inner ear: the murmur of someone talking in a near-by room. A moment later her pulse overrode the distant voice, then faded away. She shook her head, hard, as though that could secure her hearing in one range. It seemed to help; her hearing stabilized long enough for her to construct a mental image of walls around her mind.

"Better," Deiq said at last. "Good enough for most of the desert lords you'll encounter. But why does it even bother you in the first place? I'm your guardian, Alyea; I'm not going to hurt you."

She shook her head, not sure how to answer, and started walking again. He stayed by her side, dark and sober now, and let the moment pass.

The teuthin of Scratha Fortress was round and dominated by an enormous circular table crafted from black hardwood. The table's thick layer of varnish caught and refracted orange evening sunlight, swirling it into the illumination cast by the lamps: large versions of the smokeless green-oil lamps she'd seen at the Qisani during her second blood trial. Rough grey stone lay in great slabs underfoot and tapestries covered the pale stone walls, each hanging representing one of the Families gathered around the table.

The Scratha Family banner, hung behind Lord Scratha's chair, depicted a bright green lizard perched on a wide-leaved plant, its thick tail seeming to merge into the ground with the central stalk. Alyea admired the fine stitching and bright colors, wondering whether the plant and the designs meant anything.

"The plant is desert ginger," Deiq murmured in her ear as they sat down. He ignored her sharp glare and went on, "The lizard represents subtlety and sharp perception; the ginger relates that to the heart and spirit. The color green ties it into life. Now here's something interesting: see the angle formed by the tail and the leaves? If you traced that out, you'd find the symbol for a desert animal called a groundhog; that symbolizes community. Putting this banner up says that Scratha's intentions are to draw the community around the table together and promote understanding among the desert Families. It's the banner Scratha has almost always used at Conclaves."

She tried to attend to what he was saying, but a dull feeling of resentment crawled along her spine. He just reached into her head and pulled out whatever he felt like listening to, and she had no such option; it made her feel exposed, and vulnerable, and afraid at a gut level that went past rational thought. Something about the way he looked at her, sometimes, reminded her of a snake about to strike, or a hawk ready to stoop on its prey; and despite his assurances that he wouldn't hurt her, she couldn't bring herself to fully trust his intentions.

He lies, Chacerly had said with decades of pain in his voice. *You can't trust him.*

Not that Chac had proved trustworthy; he'd be going home with the Darden contingent, if she understood matters correctly. Meaning Micru could be traveling with Sessin . . . and Micru, while more respectful, had still treated Deiq with a wary reserve. The way the other desert lords regarded Deiq suggested their mistrust ran just as deep.

And she'd agreed to let Deiq be her guide for the next *year*. She bit her lip and tried not to think about it, hoping Deiq hadn't already heard her. But if he had, he made no sign; his dark gaze moved from the faces at the table to the tapestries on the walls.

Deiq said, in a barely audible voice aimed for her ear alone, "I'm not entirely sure Scratha knows what his own banner means. Much less some of the others displayed here today."

His gaze rested on the banner over Lord Evkit's head: against a background of dark and light green stripes, a great horned owl stared to the left, wings partially spread. Beside it, facing the opposite direction, a badger crouched, mouth slightly open in a ferocious snarl. The feathery leaves and heads of angelica plants in full bloom were picked out in detail in each corner of the banner, using fine white thread.

A troubled expression settled on Deiq's face, but before he could say anything more, Lord Scratha rose from his chair and began to speak.

"I declare this Conclave open; the required number of Family representatives are in attendance, and time has been given for all to arrive, rest, and arrange themselves in readiness. Are there any protests as to the opening of this Conclave?"

No voice offered argument.

"Very well." Scratha nodded to the servants waiting by the four sets of massive metal doors set at equal intervals around the room; they turned and began tugging the doors shut, leaving the room in the process. "Let the understanding of the south, the responsibility of the west, the wisdom of the north, all come together and merge with the new beginnings of the east to inform and ease this gathering."

As he named each direction, another door clanged shut. He didn't look towards the sound, his gaze fixed on nothing in particular and his tone vaguely impatient, as though he found the ritual tiresome and meaningless.

A few dark frowns appeared on faces around the table, but nobody protested. Deiq's troubled expression remained, and he crossed his arms as he watched the remainder of the Scratha lord's invocation. Alyea took the opportunity to study the other lords around the table.

While everyone around the table wore fine clothing, it tended towards a simple cut and presentation. Scratha and Lord Evkit were the only exceptions; both had woven their hair into dozens of thin, bead-laced braids, and Scratha's forearm bracelets were the most intricate Alyea had ever seen. Rather than flexible strips wound around the arm, as most of the southern bracelets seemed to be, several of Scratha's bracelets extended a finger's-width above the skin, supported by a rigid metal frame; they gave the man a barbaric, intimidating appearance.

"This Conclave," Scratha said, once the formalities were over, "has already begun on something of an . . . unusual note." He made no move to sit; his gaze slid to Lord Evkit.

The diminutive teyanin lord's chair seemed subtly higher-seated than Alyea's own, as though to tactfully minimize the height disparities. A thoughtful move, and one that allowed the dour Lord Evkit to glower back at Lord Scratha with no loss of dignity.

The brooding Scratha stare moved to settle on Alyea; a hard flush rose to her face. She almost dropped her gaze, but Deiq hissed wordlessly, the sound just audible; it was enough to stiffen her back and lent her the courage to return a glare of her own.

The faintest hint of a smile touched Scratha's mouth; he nodded fractionally, then swept his gaze around the table, assessing. Thirteen people stared back, waiting: Deiq, Idisio, Alyea, Gria, and nine desert lords from various Families.

While they had all been introduced during the formalities, the only names to stick in Alyea's mind were the ones she already knew: Irrio, Azaniari, Faer, Rest, and Rowe. The others blurred together in her head, and she couldn't recall the proper formula for titles.

Was it "Lord Darden" only in formal settings, or every time? Did she have the right, as an equal, to call him "Lord Irrio," or was that only appropriate in casual settings? And how much leeway would she be given before they expected her to be letter-perfect on all of it?

She remembered Chacerly's words about the teyanain, as they passed through the Horn: *Given that you're surrounded by men who do know better, that leeway will be very short.*

She drew in a long, calming breath against sudden panic. Would Deiq's presence at her side give her more or less rope? She suspected she wouldn't know until it jerked taut.

"A Conclave begun with a plot revealed and a death chosen isn't what I expected when I called you all together," Lord Scratha said. "Normally that sort of thing happens at the end of a Conclave."

A few smiles rose and faded as swiftly.

"As the last surviving member of Scratha Family, I had the authority to call and rule these proceedings," he said, then dropped a quick glance to Gria, seated to his left.

At their first meeting, Alyea had been jarred by the contrast between Gria's southern appearance and nasal northern accent. The girl's dark hair and almond skin had led Alyea to suspect that Gria held a strong southern lineage; the truth had proven even more interesting. Now, as Gria sat straight-backed and quiet in flowing white and ruby silks, hair elaborately arranged and braided with precious beadwork strands, and feathery earrings dangling to each side of her narrow face, no doubt remained. She looked like a desert Family *s'a-kaensa*—king's daughter—although Alyea knew such a mixing of terms would likely outrage most of the men sitting at the Conclave table. Desert Families had leaders, lords, or a dozen other terms meaning the same thing; but never kings: and thus, no kings' daughters.

Lord Scratha kept his gaze on Gria as he went on, "As the last *male* survivor, I do not hold that authority. Gria has been confirmed, by means of certain privileged tests, to hold a pure female bloodline, and thus to be a direct descendant, of a notable Scratha line. She holds the right to cancel these proceedings, should she choose. Due to the unusual circumstances and her own admitted unreadiness to lead Scratha Family, I have asked to be allowed to act in her stead at this Conclave. Gria, do you grant me this authority?"

Alyea thought the girl looked far from ready to do anything but crawl back into bed and sleep for a tenday. But she answered with a clear voice and no sign of strain, meeting the eyes of each Family representative in turn as she spoke:

"I grant Lord Cafad Scratha the authority to hold and preside over this Conclave, out of full willingness on my part and in no way compelled, bribed, or enticed."

As she caught Alyea's eye, a faint, bitter smile touched Gria's mouth for a moment, and Alyea blinked back sudden tears. She wondered if Gria felt grateful that Alyea had intervened and probably saved her from a lifetime of humiliation at Lord Evkit's hands, or blamed Alyea, with typical adolescent idiocy, for the entire situation. Gods knew her "mother", Sela, still seemed to hold Alyea responsible for the fiasco their foolish wedding expedition had become.

Gria's gaze moved on, flinching away from the small teyanin lord further down the table. Evkit blinked languidly and showed no offense at the slight; Alyea couldn't help glancing at Gria's hands and forearms, still swathed in bandages where the *ugren* cuffs once rested. Whether or not Evkit had ordered the permanent slave-cuffs put on Gria and her "mother", Sela—still a matter of dispute—it would likely be a long time before Gria felt comfortable in the presence of any teyanin.

"Are there any arguments with this transfer of authority?" Scratha demanded, his own gaze turning fierce as he stared directly at Evkit.

The teyanin lord shook his head mutely, lips tight, and nobody else spoke in protest.

"Then I officially take charge of and open this Conclave. Before beginning to discuss our various concerns, I have an announcement of concern to all here. I know you arrived from outside sources due to Scratha Fortress being shut and emptied, and I know you expect to leave through the hidden ways under this fortress, now that I am bound and the ha'rethe protector is awake. But I tell you this: the ways have been shut."

A startled incomprehension appeared on every face. Alyea blinked, even more baffled; what were *the ways*? This wasn't the time to ask; hopefully it would come clear with time and context.

"The ways are shut," Lord Scratha repeated, his back straight and his expression uncompromising. "You may not travel to or from my lands using the hidden ways unless I permit it. And I will not grant that permission to *any* of you."

He glared at Evkit in particular as he spoke.

Evkit jerked forward, hands splayed on the table and a dark flush spreading across his face, and shouted something in a language Alyea didn't know. Most of the other lords around the table looked shocked and appalled; Gria blinked as though not understanding the fuss and Idisio, sitting beside Deiq, merely looked vaguely puzzled.

"Kindly keep it in the *kaenoz* tongue, for those who don't understand," Lord Azaniari interrupted, frowning at Evkit. "We've more outsiders than usual at this Conclave."

Evkit drew a deep breath and said through his teeth, "You *cannot* close the ways! That is *beyond* your authority!"

"It's *my* damn land," Scratha answered. "I can do any damn thing I like."

Evkit shifted as though to stand; cast a sullen glance at the floor and bared his teeth at Scratha instead.

"Let's not start shedding blood *this* early," someone said acerbically, and smiles flickered around the table again. "Certainly starting off with a bang," another voice murmured.

"Easy, Evkit," said Lord Faer, who was seated beside Evkit. He reached out, not quite putting his hand on the teyanin lord's shoulder. "Scratha, really, that's unmannerly—"

"I don't care for what you call manners these days," Scratha snapped. "My family was slaughtered by assassins that came through those passages. I've the right, and the need, so don't you wave *unmannerly* in my face, Faer!"

A silent flicker of something Alyea couldn't name went around the table. It felt, in that moment, as though everyone were trying very hard *not* to look at one another; she blinked hard and dismissed the thought as the product of nervous imagination.

"The teyanain have always had passage-right—" Irrio objected.

Scratha's hawk-glare turned on the Darden lord.

"Yes," he said, "let's talk about the teyanain's infamous *passage-right*, shall we? And their guardianship of the hidden ways. And the death of my *entire godsdamned family*."

By the last words, his gaze was fixed on Evkit, and the teyanin lord, heedless of dignity, had climbed atop his chair to glare at the tall Scratha lord.

"*Say it*," Evkit invited, his lips writhing into a ferocious snarl. "Say accusation; say! I love to hear this."

"So you can declare blood feud on my family and muddy the issue past all recognition or sense?" Scratha bellowed, the veins in his neck standing out and his face nearly black with fury. "Not godsdamned *likely*, you little *ta-karne*!"

Alyea felt scarcely able to breathe through the tension cresting in the room. Several other desert lords rose to their feet, clearly unsure whether to physically intervene or let events play out.

Deiq showed no such hesitation. He stood and in one smooth movement leapt onto the table itself, stamping both his feet loudly.

"*Stop,*" he said; and while his volume remained low, the command, along with his leap, drew every eye to him. "That's enough, my lords. With all due respect: that's enough. You *cannot* afford to lose your tempers with a full ha'rethe below you. *You*—" He turned to point at Lord Scratha. "You most of all. So *stop it.*"

He turned in a slow circle, looking down at each lord in turn, then sprang to the floor as lithely as he'd ascended and took his seat amid utter silence.

"What would Conclave be without everyone losing their tempers?" someone said a bit shakily, obviously attempting to make a joke out of the moment; it fell flat.

Deiq didn't even smile. "Other places," he said, "fine. But not here. *Not here.*"

Evkit, Alyea noticed, had lowered himself into his seat once more. He studied Deiq with a speculative, narrow-eyed stare, seemingly unsurprised by the ha'ra'ha's pronouncement.

"I suggest, Lord Scratha," Deiq said, his tone still level, "that if you cannot discuss that particular matter *calmly,* you drop it altogether for the moment."

Scratha's face flushed dangerously again; Deiq met his stare without flinching.

After a moment Scratha straightened and said, in a reasonably steady voice, "Lord Evkit. During my travels, I saw marks on the hidden ways that indicated, to me, that the teyanain had left directions on which tunnels led to Bright Bay, the Wall, and Scratha Fortress, among others. Can you explain why the teyanain, who should know such things by heart, felt the need to mark out such spots in *kaenic?*"

Evkit studied Scratha, his gaze thoughtful; he passed a slow glance around the table, then said, flatly, "No. No can explain."

Scratha made a choked sound and clenched his hands, dropping his chin to his chest and glaring at the teyanin lord. After a visible struggle to keep from bellowing, he said, rather hoarsely, "Lord Evkit. As host of this gathering, I have the authority to *require* an answer."

"No can explain," Evkit repeated stubbornly. "Without knowing answer, no answer to give."

Deiq's eyebrows lowered into a dark frown, and he regarded the teyanin lord with deep suspicion but made no open protest.

"You claim you don't know why those marks were made?" Scratha demanded, incredulous and openly disbelieving.

"No answer to give," Evkit said, crossing his arms and sitting back in his seat. He caught Deiq's hard stare and shrugged, pursing his lips as though amused.

"Can you *guess?*" someone else said, sounding exasperated; Evkit shook his head, obdurate.

"No guess at such important answer. Not fair to Scratha, no? But I say again: teyanain not kill Scratha Family. Not one drop, not one hair, not one wound. We not kill."

"I think that's the best you're going to get, Scratha," Lord Rowe murmured, his face puckered in deep worry.

Scratha drew in a deep breath, let it out, and said, "Then can *anyone* at this table answer the question of *who—*"

"Don't ask that," Deiq cut in swiftly, on his feet faster than Alyea had ever seen him move before and his face closer to white than she'd thought it could go. She felt an icy chill dribble down her spine, and her bladder felt overfull for a moment.

"Move on to something *else,* Lord Scratha. *Right now.*"

Everyone stared at Deiq as though he'd gone completely mad. He glared them down, defiant and unapologetic; a sensation like being brushed gently by the very tip of a powerful wing on a down-beat shivered through her. The assembled lords clearly caught the full buffeting power: questions and protests died unspoken, and one by one they dropped gazes to the table or looked away.

Scratha drew in another deep breath, swallowed hard, and looked down at the parchment in front of him. "The matter of Pieas Sessin has been settled," he said thickly, flicking a glance at Rowe. "His name was cleared in full by his honorable behavior during Lord Alyea's blood trial."

After another long beat of silence, Rowe shifted in his seat, his frown moving from Deiq to Scratha, and said, "You should have waited on me, Scratha. You knew I was on my way; I should have been here!"

Deiq let out an almost inaudible sigh and sank back into his seat. Alyea realized, astonished, that Deiq's hands were *shaking.* She murmured, "What just—"

"Later," he whispered back. "Much later. Please."

Alyea nodded, a chill writhing up her back; *You can't trust him* ran through the hindside of her mind. Deiq tilted a darkly sardonic stare at her, and she suspected he'd heard the thought this time. To avoid looking at him, she forced herself to focus on Scratha's answer.

"At the time of the trial," Scratha said with careful precision, "I did *not* know you were on your way, Lord Rowe."

"You bloody well knew a Conclave would bring a Sessin representative!" Rowe snapped, leaning forward, hands resting against the table edge as if ready to push himself to his feet. The backs of his hands were decorated with swirling lines that appeared to extend up under his long sleeves. Alyea wondered if the bright blue color of the ink had a different significance than the red, black, or green designs other lords displayed. "Don't play idiot with me, Scratha!"

Deiq didn't react; Alyea shot him a worried glance and he whispered greyly, "Posturing."

Scratha matched glares with the portly Sessin lord. "Pieas Sessin admitted to a number of serious indiscretions in front of a full desert lord, a ha'ra'ha, and a Callen. I'd prefer to avoid relating the details."

Rowe's face settled into grim lines.

"The misdeeds he confessed," Scratha went on steadily, "would have been cause for dishonorable execution on the spot. The witnesses constituted a legitimate triad of judges. I allowed Pieas the mercy of an honorable resolution because he seemed. . . ." Scratha paused, an odd expression crossing his thin face, then finished, "seemed honestly repentant."

With a sudden flash of understanding, Alyea remembered Pieas's plea to Scratha: *My lord, give her another chance. I've never seen Nissa so heartbroken before. Don't hold her to blame for my sins.* She wondered if that, more than anything else Pieas had said during her final blood trial, had earned the wayward Sessin an honorable death.

She also wondered if she'd ever truly be at peace over killing Pieas. At the thought, the room seemed to rock slightly, and Deiq's hand closed tightly around her arm.

"Don't," he said in her ear; she swallowed hard and redirected her thoughts back to the moment with a fierce effort. The room steadied. Deiq released his grip and returned to sitting with his arms crossed, a faint frown seemingly etched into his stern features.

"I see," Rowe said, and slumped in his chair, his anger visibly draining away. "I didn't know that. I thought . . . You've made no secret of how you hate my family. . . . "

The last words seemed to blur and drawl with honeyed, weary slowness; Alyea blinked hard, and the long pauses snapped back into focus.

Rowe's voice now sounded tart, not tired. "And considering how you treated Nissa. . . ."

Scratha winced, then seemed embarrassed at showing a reaction. "That had nothing to do with my decision," he said a bit roughly. "Are you going to call challenge on me, then, Lord Rowe, over Nissa? Or bring it up as a Council matter?"

He waited, his long hands clenched into fists, knuckles barely touching the table. The array of ebony and silver beads on the ornate bracelets climbing from wrist to elbow on each arm rattled and hissed; Scratha glanced at them, his frown deepening, and flattened his hands out to rest on the table, quieting the noise.

Rowe studied the tall Scratha lord, a faint frown creasing his forehead. "No," he said at last. "She wouldn't thank me for getting involved."

Scratha let out a hard breath and relaxed, although his expression remained grim. "Thank you, Lord Rowe," he said.

The Sessin lord nodded and looked down at his hands, still frowning, as if regretting his decision.

"The question of Pieas Sessin does, however, bring us to another matter of Conclave business," Lord Faer said. "The investment of Lord Alyea."

As if he'd been waiting for that, Evkit sat up straight. "Challenge," he said before anyone else could speak. "Irregular trials, invalid process. I challenge."

Alyea's stomach contracted. Scratha shot her a hard stare and shook his head slightly, as if warning her to stay quiet; and nobody else seemed to react, as though this were simply more posturing on Evkit's part.

"She bears all three marks," Faer pointed out.

"Bribed," Evkit said baldly.

A shocked hiss sounded around the table, indifference evaporating; so this wasn't routine political maneuvering. Alyea glanced at Deiq; his face remained serene, his arms folded across his chest.

"You're accusing Callen of accepting bribes?" Lord Rowe demanded.

Evkit pointed at Deiq, the motion made threatening by the angular black lines that ran from his fingertips to just below his elbows. "He make arrangements," the teyanin lord declared. "Who will argue with ha'ra'ha? He is too powerful."

Everyone turned to look at the tall ha'ra'ha sitting beside Alyea.

Deiq blinked lazily and said, "She passed all the trials by her own wits and strength."

"All three trials, in less than two tendays?" Irrio said. He narrowed his eyes at Alyea, a half-smile on his lips. "Impressive, given that preparing for each trial normally takes years."

Azaniari raised her eyebrows and stared hard at Lord Irrio. "*Does* it, now?" she said. Irrio flicked a hand in an apologetic motion.

Aerthraim-Darden, Alyea remembered; the woman claimed two Families. Through marriage, obviously; and Irrio represented Darden, which meant Azaniari's home Family had to be Aerthraim.

Now, *that* was a story she'd be interested in hearing one day.

Deiq spoke, and Alyea blinked back to the moment, wondering why she kept drifting; it seemed as though everything were moving so slowly, the conversations interminably drawn-out and the speech patterns drawling, ambling, boring.

"It does make one wonder about people who need all that preparation," Deiq said amiably, then glanced at Alyea and added, "If you doubt me, my lords, just *look* at her; she's barely listening half the time. You've all seen that look on new lords before."

Alyea stiffened as every eye suddenly turned to her, squinting and intense. "Thanks a lot," she muttered; Deiq just grinned.

Scratha cut in, after a sharp glare at Deiq. "*I'll* speak to the legality of her trials. The Scratha Fortress ha'rethe upholds her claim. Are there any *valid* challenges remaining to Lord Alyea's investment?"

"What Family blood does she intend to claim?" Rowe asked.

Scratha nodded at Alyea, granting her permission to speak; she cleared her throat and said, "None. As far as I know I'm not directly related to any of the desert Families."

Expressions around the table ranged from Deiq's smug smile to Rowe's thunderstruck gape.

"Good gods, Deiq," Lord Rest of Eshan Family said, speaking for the first time. He sounded utterly shocked. "You put an *independent* through the trials? Are you *mad*?"

"I can't believe she survived," Rowe said, looking at Alyea with a new respect. "I thought she was some desert lord's by-blow, raised north to avoid scandal!"

Deiq sat quietly, expression bland, hands folded in front of him on the table.

"No," Alyea said, torn between amusement and annoyance at both the assumption and their insistence on speaking of her in the third person. "As far as I know, my family have all been tidily chasing northerns for bed-partners over the past five generations."

Deiq leaned back in his chair and roared with laughter, although Alyea didn't think the comment that funny. Several of the desert lords, including

Scratha, grinned openly; the remaining tension in the room dissolved like smoke in a strong wind.

"You do have a way with words, young lady," Faer murmured, smiling. "Tidily chasing, indeed." He shook his head.

Deiq faded into chuckles and then into a wide grin. Watching his eyes, Alyea caught a calculating glint as he looked round the table, and realized his over-loud laughter had been a deliberate manuever.

He tilted a sideways glance at her; seeing her regard, he pursed his lips and took on a bland expression.

Don't trust him . . . Chac might be right.

"Well," Rowe said, "that still leaves the question, doesn't it? If you don't claim Family blood, then you'll have to apply to be accepted into a Family, and there's not many who would take anyone outside their bloodline."

"There's Aerthraim," Rest said, looking towards Lord Azaniari.

Several people snorted; Azaniari, expressionless, met Rest's gaze levelly and said nothing. After a bare heartbeat, Rest dropped his stare to the table, looking rather chastened.

"Don't be dense," Faer said. "They don't have desert lords at all."

"Excuse me?" Irrio said, nodding towards Azaniari. "They don't?"

"I stopped considering myself a member of Aerthraim Family a long time ago, Lord Irrio," Azaniari cut in without hesitation. "And I believe they still return the feeling. I *asked* not to be introduced as Aerthraim at this Conclave." She cut a sharp stare at Scratha, who lifted one shoulder in a tiny, unapologetic shrug.

"What you *consider yourself* isn't the question," Irrio responded, frowning at her. Alyea thought he seemed disproportionately miffed over the slight to her status. "Legally, like it or not, you are considered an Aerthraim desert lord, representing Aerthraim Family at this Conclave."

Azaniari flicked a hand and shook her head as though warning Irrio to let it drop. Her ornately beaded earrings, shaped like dangling feathers, chinkled and swayed with the movement.

"In any case, Lord Faer is correct that Aerthraim Family wouldn't take Alyea in as a desert lord," Azaniari said, "so that's not an option, either. Lord Scratha, do you have any ideas?"

Everyone looked up the table at Scratha, but Alyea spoke first. "It doesn't matter. I'm not going to apply to anyone. You called it right; I'm an independent. I don't need to join any desert Family."

Azaniari smiled as though deeply amused by a private joke.

"That's ludicrous," Faer protested. "You can't do that!"

"Why not?" Alyea said. "I'm going back north after this Conclave, and I've no real intent of returning. I don't see any need to live south of the Horn."

Rest quavered, "But nobody's *told* you?"

"Told me what?" Alyea glanced around the table, noting that Scratha looked faintly embarrassed. Nobody seemed inclined to speak; even Deiq dropped his stare to his hands and avoided her eyes. *"What?"*

Deiq cleared his throat. Without lifting his gaze, he said, "Desert lords don't like to travel far from their fortresses. They don't like losing contact with their Family—protector."

Alyea wondered if that tiny hesitation meant anything other than a momentary search for the right word; wondered why he hadn't simply said *ha'rethe*. But the conversation went on without pause, and she let the question go for the moment.

"It's like going *deaf*," Rest said violently. "Blind. Mute. You can't *feel* anything."

"At least if you travel to another Family fortress you have courtesy-rights," Rowe added, his plump face creasing in distressed lines. "The local ha'rethe honors you as a lord. But if you go beyond any ha'rethe's range . . . it's horrible." He shuddered.

Idisio's expression shifted to startled understanding; although what he'd suddenly seen clearly, Alyea had no idea. Probably something to do with the time he'd spent traveling in Scratha's company.

Alyea protested, "But Lord Azaniari—and Eredion! And Lord Scratha spent plenty of time in Bright Bay."

"Well, Bright Bay's about as far as you can go and still have any sight," Rowe said. He glanced at Azaniari.

The thin, elderly woman shrugged. "It's peaceful, living outside the range," she said. "I've enjoyed it, actually." She smiled at Alyea. "It's not as bad as they make out," she added gently. "They're spoiled, that's all."

Irrio shot her a hard stare, and Alyea thought she saw a flicker of something tormented in the man's eyes; but it passed too quickly to be sure.

Scratha snorted. "It's not fun," he said. "I rode from Bright Bay to Sandlaen Port and thought I was losing my mind. Nobody warned *me*." He shot a hard glare around the table again.

"Nobody thought you'd be mad enough to ride past Bright Bay," Faer said with surprising acerbity. "Why would we warn you? We never think of it ourselves."

"I'm sure I'll be fine," Alyea said. "I do have family of my own in Bright Bay, you know. I can represent Peysimun Family." The notion startled her even as she said it, but felt right in a way she had no words for.

"You *can't*," Rest said, the quaver firming into anger. "Even if you can endure the discomfort, the politics won't allow it! A desert lord for a northern family? Let you wander around the northlands with no obligations to the south at all? Madness!"

"Rather like what I've done for years," Scratha noted dryly.

"Not at all!" Rest snapped. "You're part of a proper southern Family! You always knew you had a reputation, a community, a responsibility! She's. . . ." He waved a hand in the air. "It's impossible. Her family has no idea how to handle a desert lord. They'd ruin her, or she'd ruin them. You'll have to take her in, Scratha."

"I don't *have* to do anything," Scratha said. He leaned back in his chair and seemed to be enjoying the moment. "If you recall, I had nothing at all to do with Lord Alyea taking the trials. I wasn't consulted, advised, or involved in any way. So no *have to* attaches to me." He steepled his fingers under his chin and looked at Alyea. "Do you intend to apply to me, Lord Alyea, for membership in Scratha Family?" His tone, while utterly courteous, still held enough ice to warn her what the answer needed to be.

"I do not," Alyea said firmly. "I have no interest in being a part of any desert Family." *Especially not Scratha*, she carefully held silent; saw the glitter in Scratha's eyes and knew he understood.

"Oruen will be terribly disappointed to hear that," Irrio said. "Didn't he send you down here to take control of Scratha Fortress? And you're really going to trot back empty-handed? How remarkable."

"My original charge," she said carefully, with a quick look to Scratha's stony expression, "involved responsibility for the fortress during Lord Scratha's absence."

"Good gods, don't get this started again," Faer cut in. "Irrio, don't be an ass. We don't need to go into the regrettable misunderstandings involved in Lord Scratha's absence. It's sorted out. The man's here; he's bound; the issue's over and settled."

"Not quite over," Irrio observed. "There's the matter of an heir. Or lack thereof." He smirked.

Gria's face went from white to red to white again; and Scratha stood, leaning forward to rest his fisted hands on the table. Before either one could say anything, Azaniari said in a loud, heavily-tried voice, "Knock it *off*, you two. Get back to the question at hand, which is Lord Alyea's investment. There's no law that she has to be part of a desert Family. Sit *down*, Cafad." She smacked the desert lord's taut arm with one hand, sparing him only a brief glare; Alyea glimpsed a small sepia design inked on the palm of her hand. "And Irrio, quit needling him. You know that isn't a valid Council issue to raise right now."

Alyea had to smile; Azaniari sounded like a mother scolding two quarreling children.

"No law," Faer said with evident relief as Scratha sank slowly back into his chair and Irrio dropped his glare to his hands, "but is it entirely wise?"

"Wise or unwise, what we have is what sits before us," Azaniari said crisply. "We can't force Lord Alyea to be a part of a desert Family, and there's no legal reason to deny her investment. Call it, my lords, and have done! Raise a legitimate objection or welcome her as a desert lord." She slapped her right hand down on the table in front of her, palm down, and aimed a severe stare around the table.

After a moment, one by one, each desert lord copied her motion, most of them looking severely disgruntled about it. Evkit, Alyea noted, actually seemed amused about something. That worried her; she trusted Evkit even less than she trusted Deiq.

"That's over with, then," Azaniari said cheerfully, winking at Alyea. "Let's finish the remaining business and move on to my favorite part: the after-Conclave feast."

"Sounds good, but I think I'll pass on the coffee this time," Alyea said dryly, and was rewarded with a round of relaxed laughter. Even Evkit pulled a pained face and joined in with a brief chuckle.

"Well done," Deiq murmured as talk turned to relatively minor matters needing rulings. "But watch Evkit—he's got something in mind. I don't like that look on his face."

"You sound like Chacerly," she sighed. "He would have said the same thing."

"That's because he's no fool," Deiq said. "When a teyanin smiles, you count your fingers and toes to see what's missing; when a teyanin lord smiles, you check to see if your throat's been cut. And as this one's *the* lord of the teyanain, he's doing far too much smiling for my comfort."

Chapter Three

Eredion knew the dead woman.

Even though he'd sent her to her death years before, her face, laughter, and scent remained in his memory, as clear as his knowledge of northern family trees, as enduring as the echo of Rosin Weatherweaver's laughter.

Eredion put his torch into a nearby holder and knelt by the long-cold remains, noting the lack of decay and scavenger damage; the creature that killed her hadn't liked anything, not even natural processes, touching its toys.

In what little fairness Eredion felt able to extend, it hadn't actually *intended* to kill her. It had only wanted . . . to make friends. To play. Unfortunately, its understanding of *play* came from Rosin Weatherweaver.

If a ha'ra'ha couldn't resist Rosin's manipulations, what chance did a simple desert lord have? But Eredion didn't—couldn't—accept that excuse.

I could have walked away. I could have exiled myself, risked being disowned, let someone else stand there and stare into that horrible grin every damn day. . . .

No. I chose to stay because I was afraid who they might send to replace me . . . and what would happen if I wasn't there to at least try to rein in the madness.

But would Kallia thank me for that? I doubt it.

He began reaching out to close her bulging eyes; stopped and sat back on his heels with a dry bark of self-disgust. *I could have saved her. She wouldn't even have come to Rosin's attention if not for me.* He shut his eyes, but that only made the pressure of bitter memory and self-recrimination worse.

Damn me, if I'm not already, for this alone. Oh, Kallia. . . .

He sucked in a breath through his teeth, focusing on the taste of the moldy, rot-filled air, then forced himself to stretch out his hand again. As soon as his trembling fingertips brushed the dank flesh, it exploded like a puffball mushroom gone to spore, flinging long-repressed rot and mold in all directions—including across Eredion's face.

He coughed and spat, his eyes hot and watery. The thick mask secured across the lower half of his face blocked most of the evil mucus, but he had to rinse his eyes out with a precious handful of water from his flask before his vision cleared.

"Little enough revenge," he muttered at last, looking down at what remained of her face.

With a deep sigh, he began to recite prayers: one for cleansing a tormented soul, one beseeching forgiveness for wrongs done, and an invocation of all three gods in their proper aspects, to guide and bless the dead wanderer into the proper realm.

This was his fourteenth such recitation this morning.

Far overhead, the palace bells began to count off another hour towards noon: far too many of which, like the bodies in these dank catacombs, remained.

By noon, Eredion gathered nearly enough human remains to fill the charnel-cart. Mostly he found piles of bones, many chewed—he felt a surge of nausea every time he found another one like that—but some entire, and even stacked in elaborate patterns, as though the creature had *played* with them.

Eredion hated dismantling those. The bone sculptures emanated a slick, oily aura that had nothing to do with tactile senses; but once he overcame revulsion and picked them respectfully apart, chanting prayers of cleansing as he worked, the remains lost that grotesque awfulness and became simply dead bone.

Even the air felt cleaner afterwards, which made moving on easier.

Still, by the time the Palace bells rang the noon hour, his head ached as though a thousand blacksmiths hammered at his skull, the inside of his mouth tasted like the leftovers of a four-day drunk, and he wanted to get the hells out of the catacombs.

He'd bring the charnel-cart to the grave keeper; she would do her own prayers and ceremonies and burn the day's recovered remains on the giant graveyard slab, and then Eredion could go take a nice hot bath and get very, very drunk for the rest of the day.

And not think about having to come back tomorrow, and the day after, and the day after.

His attention fixed dreamily on that bath—and the drinking—he reached out to open a plain black metal door and found the latch secured by a huge padlock looped through sturdy metal bars welded to the door itself. It wasn't too unusual for a door in the catacombs to be locked; it only meant that the person behind that door had once held value to Rosin.

But nobody had opened that door for months. Only Eredion dared enter, laboring day after day to remove the worst of the gory hell as part of his self-imposed penance. Bit by bit, he had found and opened the secret passages, the secret rooms; but Eredion knew his ignorance kept him moving through the catacombs far too slowly.

If anyone had breathed behind this door when Rosin died, they wouldn't be doing so now.

Eredion raised the sledgehammer, guilt and frustration surging like fire into his muscles, and shattered the padlock with one gigantic blow.

As the door sagged open, shaken free by the tremors of his attack, the darkness within flowed out, enveloping Eredion in a cloak lined with a thousand tearing claws.

He caught a brief glimpse of a tormented, grey-eyed stare; then an all-too-familiar pain racked through every nerve in his body.

Oh, gods, not again! Eredion thought hazily.

The floor came up under him and consciousness, mercifully, fled.

Chapter Four

As late-afternoon light filled the room for the second time since the doors closed, the assembly scraped back chairs and rose to its collective feet. Alyea stood, repressing a deep sigh of gratitude; their only relief over the last two days had been brief meals and the inevitable follow-up to that. But even then nobody left the room; to her utter astonishment, servants brought in a series of large chamber-pots and screens, closed off half the room, and removed the stinking pots when everyone had taken a turn.

She found it the most outrageously humiliating moment she'd experienced in a long time, but everyone else seemed to take it for granted, and she hadn't dared complain. No point marking herself even more the outsider than she already was. Still, it took a real effort of concentration to not only endure her own turn, but to listen to the unapologetic grunts, farts, and pissing of the other desert lords. And even the aroma-sticks the servants waved through the room in the wake of the chamber-pots had only layered one stench over another.

Alyea wanted to flee the room, suck in lungfuls of fresh air, go huddle in a hot bath, and *sleep* for a tenday. She couldn't believe she'd just stayed awake for two straight days. Just one more item everyone around her seemed to regard as completely normal; she wanted to sit and think it all through, make sense of the madness she'd stepped into.

But the teuthin doors hadn't opened just yet, and nobody was moving to do anything about that.

Evkit cleared his throat. The sound brought apprehensive silence and a host of wary stares; the little teyanin lord seemed supremely smug about something.

"Let me be first to welcome Lord Alyea," he said, and bowed deeply. "And first to extend invitation to visit my lands as honored guest, take pick of my devoted *kathain*. And my fortress fully stocked," he added with a smiling glance at Scratha. "I invite Lord Alyea remain long as desire, and enjoy my hospitality."

Alyea drew a deep breath, considering for only a moment, then said, "I'd be pleased to accept, Lord Evkit. Thank you for the invitation." She decided against asking what *kathain* meant; it was probably just the southern term for a personal servant.

"Then I give further offer of escort," Evkit said, his smile widening. "We both go in same direction; why not travel together? Safety in numbers. I would not allow honored guest come to harm on way to my lands. That would be intolerable discourtesy."

Alyea didn't need to hear Deiq's small choking noise, or turn to check Scratha's expression, to know she'd just been backed into a corner. And worse, the teyanin lord had just secured his right to stay until Alyea left.

She held her shoulders still against a shrug and her mouth relaxed with an effort.

"I'm honored, my lord," she said, a bitter taste on her tongue.

"The honor mine," Evkit shot back, his grin threatening to split his head in two, and left the room without looking back. Irrio followed, almost on his heels, clearly unhappy about something.

Servants hurried into the room, opening the other doors from the inside, and began clearing away the debris of two days of often-heated discussions.

Deiq muttered, "I *told* you to watch him."

"What was I supposed to do?" Alyea demanded.

"There's ways of putting an answer *off*."

"Not against that one, there isn't," Lord Rest said unexpectedly. "She did the best she could, Deiq. You're acting like her mother. Go find a *kathain* to play with and leave Lord Alyea be."

Deiq's face darkened.

"Can we at least clear the meeting room before you start a fight, Lord Rest?" Azaniari asked tartly. "And a meal would be nice, along with a drink or ten. I think you'd get along famously after that. Besides, I think Lord Alyea can answer against Deiq's attentions herself; if not, she's a damn poor desert lord."

"Hells," Rest snorted, and stomped out of the room.

Alyea shot the old woman a grateful glance. Azaniari nodded, acknowledging, then took Scratha's arm and urged him from the room.

"Food, my lords," she called over her shoulder in a light sing-song, as if coaxing a group of stubborn farm animals. "Fooo-oood. Food, food. This way, my lords. . . ."

Alyea put a hand over her mouth to stifle a giggle. The servants went about their tasks, blank-faced, ignoring everything around them unless it stepped into their paths.

Beside her, Deiq shook his head, looking bemused. He said quietly, "She'll have Scratha back as a major power in less than five years if she stays helping him."

"I hope she does," Alyea said impulsively. "I like her, and I like Lord

Scratha. He's a good man."

He slanted an unreadable glance her way and said only, "Mm."

Regarding Common Misunderstandings

(excerpt)

As the Northern Church has gone well out of its way in recent years to paint the desert Families as not only barbaric but cruel, a few of their common charges ought to be dismissed up front, to avoid tainting any discussion of southern holy days and celebrations.

No desert Family has ever offered human sacrifice to any god, demon, or combination thereof; this charge is perhaps the most understandable error, as several of our own historical records use the term "sacrifice" in regards to the blood trials, and death is a very real risk in a true trial. This topic, however, could take up several books in its full explanation; so for now I must ask you to simply accept my reassurance that never has a screaming virgin—of either gender—been dragged to a bloodied altar and disemboweled as a gift to the gods. If time, politics, and wisdom permit, I shall go into this further at a later date.

Neither do we dance naked round great fires and invoke demon-spirits upon the northlands; nor do we castrate young boys and train them into demon-warriors. None of our women has ever given birth to a three-headed goat, and the milk we feed our children comes from their mothers, not pregnant horses, goats, or (one of the oddest charges I have found) snakes. (How in the world one would milk a pregnant snake I have no idea, and certainly no desire to find out.)

These distortions, and many others, of course have a fragment of truth. Great fires are built on many occasions to celebrate both holy days and seasonal celebrations; just as they are in the north, although I understand the Church has always attempted to suborn or destroy such rituals. Northern priests are called s'iope: beloved of the gods; ours are named, simply, Callen, and each chooses his or her path and which of the three gods to serve. The Callen of Comos do indeed castrate themselves, but only men over a certain age are allowed to do so, and only at an advanced level of devotion; they claim it helps free them of distractions and allows them to focus on the voice of Comos as conveyed by the wind spirits.

Women, before you ask, may also choose the path of Comos. But rather than being subjected to a physical alteration, they are required to remain sequestered within a community of their peers until they have ceased having their moon cycles; then they are allowed the higher training and may once more travel freely in the world.

Goat milk is indeed a staple of the dahass, *the loose and masterless tribes that still wander through the southlands; and to be perfectly frank I believe these tribes may have sparked many of the wilder rumors that have spread through the north. Only when they cross a Family boundary do they owe any respect to anyone but themselves; and much of the south still remains unclaimed, uncharted, and wild.*

And snakes, pregnant or otherwise, are quite tasty; barring only the mi-

cru, the tiny black and tan viper, which holds venom not only in its mouth but throughout its entire body, making it a poor snack for predators. As you do not care for gerho, I doubt you would find even the best snake meat to your taste; they are very similar.

From the collection
Letters to a Northern King of Merit
penned by Lord Cafad Scratha during the reign of King Oruen

Chapter Five

The borrowed servants had, with the uncanny intuition of servants everywhere, ferreted out a number of long-hidden decorations that Scratha, by his expression, had likely never seen. Deiq watched the lean Scratha lord with amusement as the man tried—and failed—to hide his reaction every time he focused on another unearthed antique proudly displayed in his great hall.

Deiq sympathized; to his eye, humans always insisted on putting out the gaudiest possible decorations during feasts. But this wasn't as bad as it could have been; at Sessin Fortress, everything was coated with bits of glass and mirror, resulting in a glittering display that inevitably gave him a headache.

Scratha, at least, had always leaned towards the minimalist. Their figurines were largely carved of rock and left vague, in contrast to the explicit detail Darden and F'Heing enjoyed.

A Conclave feast, however, demanded honoring the gifts collected from other Families over the years. So there was a glittering monstrosity from Sessin, and a distinctly male-female wood carving from Darden, which the servants had done their best to at least place discreetly; a slightly less explicit cast-metal male statue from F'Heing, and an elaborate bead and feather headpiece from Aerthraim Family. The most useful item was the cups from which they drank: distinctly teyanain-crafted, with the odd marbled translucence only found in rock from the Horn.

No doubt some of the other decorations came from the lesser Families, but Deiq wasn't familiar enough with their patterns to place those accurately. He thought the series of long, narrow tapestries, showing mountain goats climbing a ridge towards a single red dream-flower, might be from Toscin, but he couldn't be sure.

He wished Idisio had come to the after-Conclave feast. He'd have liked to see the younger ha'ra'ha's expression on seeing the Darden statuette. Alyea didn't even seem to notice it, and she wasn't alone; few humans besides Lord Scratha even glanced at the decorations. Their attentions, as always, stayed on their own pre-dinner maneuvering; and the main focus this time was on Alyea.

Deiq wasn't surprised. She was the newest desert lord, and her ignorance made her vulnerable. They would see her as a new, rich resource for their damned games and political manipulations. He'd seen this before, hundreds of times; seen it go well, seen it go deadly sour. Alyea seemed to be handling the attention with grace, even given her limited knowledge of southern custom. Still, he stayed close by her side, hoping his presence would deter the worst of the attempts to use her.

"Tell me about Peysimun Family," Lord Rest said, his manner that of a comfortable old uncle, and pressed another drink on Alyea. "I don't think I've ever had any dealings with them before."

"What would you like to know, Lord Rest?" Alyea said with remarkable composure. "That's a rather broad question."

She sipped at her drink. Deiq, watching out of the corner of his eye, saw her swallow much less than she appeared to, and relaxed slightly. She was no fool about that, at least; even though her tolerance seemed high, the liquor served to desert lords tended to be rather stronger than ordinary.

"True," Lord Rest said, chuckling at himself. "Very true, that. How about your specialties, then?"

Alyea blinked, looking off-balance; Deiq cut in smoothly.

"Lord Rest, the northern noble families don't work quite the same way southern ones do," he said, inflection implying that Lord Rest was rather dense to not know.

Rest shot Deiq a sharp glare; he'd known, all right. He'd meant to make Alyea sound stupid. Deiq smiled back, letting a little extra tooth into the expression, and Lord Rest abruptly saw someone across the room he just *had* to talk to. With profuse apologies, he hurried away.

Alyea flashed a frown at Deiq, plainly not understanding; he lifted his eyebrows in bland response.

"Are you going to ruin every conversation I get into?" she demanded in a low voice.

Deiq blinked lazily, resisting the urge to say something nasty in return. The sharp hearing of desert lords meant that at least three other people nearby had picked up on that comment, including Evkit.

"Possibly," he said instead, and lifted his gaze to meet the amused glances being aimed their way; the watchers looked away hastily. Alyea caught the subtle attention shift, and her frown deepened.

"Deiq," she started; he looked down at her, *willing* her to just shut up before she made an even worse mistake. She stuttered, her face flushing, and went reluctantly quiet.

You're not the only one with sharp hearing, he tried to tell her without speaking aloud; a thickly muffled sensation met the attempt, and he withdrew, repressing a sigh. Women seemed to open to that aspect of their new abilities later than men, and with more difficulty.

He couldn't resist looking up and around to find Azaniari in the crowd; she was seated on a small couch, listening patiently as Gria rattled on with great animation, no doubt over something trivial. As though feeling his attention, the apparently old woman—and *there* was a story, all in itself—glanced up. Meeting his gaze, she gave a tired mouth-quirk that could have meant anything, then returned to Gria's babbling.

Beside him, Alyea stirred, her annoyance pushing aside the temporary hold on her mouth. "Deiq," she said, "I need to make allies here. I need to talk to people. And you're not helping with that damned glower. I can handle this; let me be!"

He looked down at her for a long moment, well aware of ears perking nearby, and found no answer that wouldn't make the situation even worse. Let her make her own damn mistakes, then; maybe she'd grasp her ignorance before she landed in an ugly mess.

"I'll be over there," he said at last, nodding to a pillar a few feet away. "Just glance over if you need me."

Leaning against the pillar, admonishing himself to wait patiently, he watched the crowd descend upon her, swirling her away. Her bright laughter rang out across the room.

Nobody came to talk to him; and nobody glanced his way, not even once.

Chapter Six

Thankfully, Deiq remained quiet for the rest of the evening. Even through dinner, sitting next to her with his dark gaze moving around the table, he said little to nothing. Nobody else seemed particularly interested in speaking to him, either; by the end of the meal, Alyea felt a reluctant sense of guilt over ignoring him for so long.

As the last plates were cleared away, and coffee trays were wheeled in, she turned her smile his way and said, lightly, "I think I'll skip the coffee this time."

He regarded her with a strange expression and said, "Probably a good idea."

A servant placed small cups in front of them. Alyea quickly turned hers upside-down, offering the servant a regretful smile. He nodded and poured steaming black liquid into Deiq's cup, then moved on. A moment later, another servant placed a full cup of a liquid almost as black in front of Alyea, removing the upside-down cup.

She regarded the drink with caution, then glanced at Deiq for help. He was smiling: but it was a strange, dark expression that shifted his lean face into starker planes.

"It's tea," he said quietly. "From the smell, I'm guessing F'Heing red bush, prepared *thopuh* style."

"Very good," Lord Ondio F'Heing said from across the table. His smile reminded Alyea of a cat about to pounce on something small. The severe cut and dark colors of his clothing heightened the menace of his expression. "Do you know what region and year the batch is from?"

One of the strange green-oil lamps nearby flickered and began to gutter; a servant quickly moved to turn up the wick. Renewed light washed across the area, and Alyea repressed a sigh of relief, only then realizing that the increasing dimness had been bothering her for some time. Her shoulders relaxed.

Deiq regarded Lord Ondio for a long moment, then said, "I haven't studied F'Heing teas extensively, I'm afraid."

Ondio's smirk widened. "So there *is* something you don't know."

"But," Deiq interrupted, "given that red bush *thopuh*-style teas were only made for a hundred years before a combination of a volcano exploding, a plague, and political shift destroyed the plantations and the skilled workers; given that *thopuh* tea grows more valuable with age; and given that I'm doubting F'Heing would give out its most valuable stores to Lord Scratha at the moment; given all that, I'm guessing this comes from the Sta region of the F'Heing Mountains, and that it was packed within the five years previous to the Sta plantation's destruction."

The room went completely silent. Ondio looked as though he'd bitten into a sour fruit when he'd been expecting a delicacy. Alyea's shoulders went tight again; she drew a deep breath and forced herself to relax.

"Indeed," Ondio said through his teeth, then forced a laugh in an obvious attempt to sound unaffected. He cast a quick look to the head of the table, where Lord Scratha sat watching, expression hawk-intent. "You're wrong, of course. We only give out properly precious gifts. We would never insult—"

"Of course," Deiq said, voice and manner bored, as though the entire conversation no longer interested him. "I did say I haven't studied the matter extensively."

Ondio's jaw clenched. He shot a poisonous glare at Deiq, then rose. "If I may be excused," he muttered, offering a short bow to Scratha. At his host's nod, he left the room hurriedly.

Scratha's mouth creased in a faint smile. He nodded briefly to Deiq, then went back to his interrupted conversation.

"I can't tell if that was outrageously rude or well-played," Alyea said in an undertone.

"I know," Deiq said, as quietly. "That's why you ought to be keeping *your* mouth shut right now." He met her glare with a mild, indifferent expression.

"I haven't done that badly so far," she snapped.

He raised an eyebrow and said nothing in return. She jerked her gaze away, seething with the impulse to slap him, then remembered a conversation with Chac: *I've been crashing about like a horse in a glass shop*, she'd said, and he'd given her the same dry eyebrow-lift Deiq had just offered.

She drew in a deep, quiet breath and shut her eyes for a moment; looked up to find Deiq's dark stare turned elsewhere.

"Yes, you have been," he said, the words directed at her, but his attention apparently on Evkit's low-voiced discussion with Irrio. "We'll talk about it after dinner, if you like."

She swallowed back another surge of indignation and just nodded, somehow knowing he'd pick up on the silent agreement.

Picking up her cup of tea, she took a tentative sip. The aroma reminded her of smoky pine, and the taste was heavy and thick with burnt overtones.

It wasn't entirely unpleasant, and she took a second sip, astonished at how it seemed to coat the inside of her mouth and yet melted away instantly into a lingering memory of taste.

"Thopuh tea," Deiq said, returning his attention to her at last, "is a remarkable accident. The F'Heing enclave area, from which all their trading ships sail, originally belonged to another Family entirely."

A few heads turned sharply, and spines stiffened. Scratha looked down the table at Deiq again, an amused expression crossing his face.

"It's a story most of the desert Families don't like to think about," Deiq went on as though nobody else existed in the room.

"Much less hear at a Conclave dinner table," someone said acerbically.

"At least Lord Ondio's left the room," someone else muttered.

Alyea was too fascinated by the darkly amused glint in Deiq's eyes to look for the identity of the speakers; she felt captured, enthralled, like a rabbit facing a snake. He was making a point, one that he damn well knew would infuriate most if not all of the gathering, and he didn't care.

Her mother would be screeching with fury at the breach of etiquette. Insulting guests at her table was absolutely forbidden, whatever their crimes. But Scratha made no effort to stop Deiq's story.

"F'Heing Family lands had no ocean access," Deiq continued. "The Family that once occupied that space was called Tehay. They were relatively peaceful: fishermen, tea-growers, coffee-growers, farmers. But they were stubborn; wouldn't allow outsiders into their lands, wouldn't teach anyone their ways, wouldn't allow trade posts or even roads through their lands. No outsider ships landing at their docks, and so on. They kept access to their lands very controlled. Rather like the teyanain."

He glanced at Evkit, who was studiously examining the coffee grounds at the bottom of his empty cup, a ferocious scowl on his dark face.

"F'Heing—and other Families—tried many ways to breach that isolationist attitude. Some tried for marriage—"

Someone closer to the head of the table made a thick, protesting noise.

"Others tried bribes—"

"Damn it, Deiq!"

"Not that I'm *naming* anyone, mind you," Deiq retorted without lifting his gaze from Alyea's face. "But if you'd like to step up to the admission yourself, feel free."

Heavy silence.

"As it turned out, nothing worked," Deiq said after a few moments, the amused tilt returning to his eyebrows. "Until F'Heing Family decided they'd had enough of *subtle* and went in for *direct assault*. It just so happened that the tea farmers were in the middle of harvest at the time. Hoping they wouldn't have to lose the whole harvest, they force-dried the newly plucked tea leaves over pine fires, packed them into tight blocks, and buried the blocks before they retreated farther up into the mountains."

He paused, and his gaze finally left Alyea and swept the table. Nobody spoke. Few met his stare.

"The invaders found the buried blocks of tea before they found the farmers. They tried the tea, and decided they liked it more than the lighter tea the farmers usually produced, and dubbed it *thopuh* — blood of victory — tea. They hunted down the fugitive tea-farmers, forced them to explain the method of making this new tea, and then killed them all."

Alyea swallowed hard, the silence in the room beginning to hurt her ears. She cast an uneasy glance around the table and saw, without surprise, that almost every face had an ugly expression now. Gria looked appalled; Azni studied her coffee cup, frowning. Only Scratha seemed to share Deiq's mild amusement over the story.

Alyea resisted the urge to shake her head or kick Deiq under the table, knowing the former would make her look like a fool and the latter would have no effect at all. She suspected that her efforts to win allies at the pre-dinner gathering were being destroyed, and wondered if that were part of Deiq's intent in telling this grossly offensive story.

"Thopuh tea quickly became the most expensive, and desirable, tea in the southlands; and F'Heing never suffered any reprisals from the other Families for the attack," Deiq finished. His gaze flicked to the head of the table. "Not even from —"

"That's enough," Scratha said, his tone mild but his gaze darkening.

Deiq inclined his head and tossed back his entire cup of coffee in one swallow, then turned it over before any of the nearby servers could refill it.

"I'm grateful for your indulgence, Lord Scratha," he said easily, splaying his large hands palm-up on the table. "I seem to be losing my manners from lack of sleep."

"It's been a long two days," Scratha said, and waved to the waiting servants. "I suggest we all retire early. Many of you have a long road to travel in the morning."

As the servants came forward, ever-so-politely lifting away empty cups and offering subtle prompts to finish full ones, Alyea stared at Deiq, still unable to believe his gall.

He met her stare with a placid expression. Before either of them could say anything, a servant dressed in the brown and grey of guest-quarters staff instead of the black and grey of dining-hall staff approached.

"Lord Peysimun, I'll take you to your rooms, if you're ready to retire," the dumpy woman said in a thick southern accent, hands folded across her broad stomach. Alyea noticed the servant was missing the tips of two fingers on her left hand, and only realized she was staring when the woman shifted her hands to hide left under right.

"Sorry," Alyea muttered, feeling her entire face heat up, and looked away hurriedly. "I know the way —"

"Your room has changed, Lord Peysimun," the servant interrupted, no trace of discomfort on her broad features. "You have new status, get new room."

"What? But I —"

Deiq's hand closed around her elbow; he used the other in a "wait a moment" motion to the servant, then leaned in close to speak in Alyea's ear.

"You weren't officially accepted as Lord Peysimun until you were confirmed by Conclave. And you're the only desert lord besides Azni being *given* a room, in case you didn't realize; everyone else is camping outside the walls. So smile and say thank you, damn it!"

Alyea forced her mouth into a smile. "Thank you," she said to the servant, and stood, shaking her arm free from Deiq's grip. "I'm honored." She turned, caught Lord Scratha's eye, then bowed deeply; he nodded, looking distantly amused once more.

Alyea followed the plump servant out of the dining hall without looking back, well aware that Deiq trailed a matter of steps behind her. She wished she could just tell him to go somewhere else, but knew he would just give her that abstracted, sardonic stare and ignore the request completely.

Chapter Seven

Alyea's new room was considerably more luxurious than the last. Two rooms, in fact, and a side room for the kathain—six of whom stood lined up with their handler, patiently awaiting approval.

Deiq repressed a groan. He'd forgotten about this particular tradition, and hadn't thought to warn Alyea about it. Her expression, as she stared at the waiting group, told him she had no idea what she was looking at; she probably thought they were just servants.

"Kathain for your approval, Lord Peysimun," said the handler, a stringy old man with a large black birthmark on the side of his face and several missing teeth. "As many as you feel the need for tonight."

The missing teeth turned the handler's smile into a leer, and Deiq saw Alyea's expression change rapidly as she grasped the implications.

Deiq laid a hand casually on her shoulder and dug his thumbnail into the fleshy part. She shot him a furious glare.

"Three," he murmured, almost subvocalizing. "Pick three, with thanks, and send the rest away. *Do it.*"

He heard a tiny grinding sound as she clamped her teeth tightly together. For a moment he thought she might refuse; then she forced a strained smile and turned her attention to studying the offered kathain.

Two women, and four men; the youngest was perhaps fifteen and the oldest almost thirty. None exceptional, either in beauty or ugliness; a statement all its own, but not one Alyea would understand how to interpret. And none were dressed provocatively, not here: at F'Heing they would have been presented nude; at Sessin, bedecked with glittering finery. But Scratha had always preferred to present their kathain soberly dressed in the same earth tones as the curtains and linens. No doubt the closet in the kathain room already had a full stock of varied outfits to suit any taste.

After a thoughtful inspection, Alyea indicated the two women and the youngest boy. Deiq held back a grin at that mistake: she clearly expected that those choices would remove actual sex from the table, and perhaps leave the chosen kathain as mere cleaning-servants. And he suspected that she'd chosen the boy more to keep him from being "used" elsewhere than by any particular interest in him.

Some of her northern assumptions were going to be *amusing* to remove. . . .

The handler flicked Deiq an appraising glance, then bowed and with a few polite phrases retreated from the room with those not chosen. The remaining kathain bowed and stood quietly waiting.

"You can rest for the night," Deiq told them once the door of the outer room closed behind the departing group. "I can handle Lord Peysimun's needs for the moment."

They nodded, expressionless, and went to their room. Alyea began to make a sound similar to a pot coming to a boil; Deiq turned, caught her arm, and forcefully hustled her through the outer room and into the bedroom, shoving the door shut behind them.

"Horse in a glass shop," he said before she could speak. "It's a traditional courtesy—"

"That boy is younger than I am!"

"He's no younger than you were when Oruen took you to bed," he said.

Her face darkened, then whitened, and she looked away, clenching her hands.

"That was *different*," she said.

"Because you had noble rank?"

"Because I had a *choice!*"

"So do the kathain. That boy is here because he *wants* to be. It's an honor. Certainly more of an honor than being a night of fun for an unmarried man twice your age is, north to south."

Her head jerked up; she glared at him with hot outrage.

"Look at what is, not what you want to be," he said without remorse. "That boy probably knows more about sex than your average whore. I told you: desert lords *change* after the trials. Kathain are part of every desert lord's staff. They fill that need—"

"They won't damn well fill mine—"

"You think you'll have a *choice?*"

She tilted her chin, all ignorant northern arrogance; he tried another approach.

"Alyea," he said, more patiently, "there's a lot you still don't understand, and I'm *trying* to teach you."

"By pissing off all the desert lords you can reach?" she demanded.

Deiq repressed a sigh, realizing she was referring to the incident at dinner. She'd completely missed the point of his story. He'd intended to show her what kind of people she was dealing with now, and pass along a warning that her northern notions of politics weren't going to do her any good here. But all she'd seen was what northerns would consider a severe breach of etiquette. He wasn't even sure she'd listened to the contents of the tale itself.

He restrained himself to observing, "Doesn't matter if they get mad at *me*; they already hate my guts."

She turned away, paced a few steps, flung herself back around to glare at him. "You're making this impossible," she snapped.

"I've saved you from at least three major political blunders tonight," he returned, allowing irritation into his voice this time. "Lord Rest was angling to make you look like a fool, and I turned it around on him. If you'd hesitated another moment over being walked to your room, you'd have implied you didn't find the change to your satisfaction, or the servant offensive, or any of a hundred other inflections you didn't even realize you were conveying. And if you'd refused the kathain gift you'd have been slapping Lord Scratha in the face. You have *no* damn idea what you're doing!"

She turned away again, and sat on the far edge of the wide bed, her head hanging. In the silence came a distinct moan; Alyea stiffened and snapped back to her feet, whirling round with an expression of astonished horror on her face.

Deiq held up a hand to keep her from bolting into the other room. "They're fine," he told her, his irritation fading into genuine amusement. Time for her first lesson on the southern reality, apparently. "They're practicing."

"They're—" Her face turned a greenish shade. "That's *disgusting.*"

"It's practical," he said, and moved forward, worried that she was about to faint. "It's their job, Alyea." He gathered her into his arms; she leaned against him, shuddering with revulsion.

Another loud, gasping moan came from the kathain room.

"And I think they're probably showing off a bit," Deiq said into Alyea's hair, grinning. "To show they're ready for you."

Gods knew *he* was, and the kathain's display wasn't helping any; but Alyea wasn't showing any interest at all. He breathed through his nose and tried to keep his hands from wandering.

"*Gods.*" She broke away from him and put her hands over her ears as though that might help.

Relenting, he soothed the air around her until she couldn't hear the increasingly enthusiastic noises from the kathain, then gently nudged her into curling up on the bed. With a sigh, he settled down beside her, arm's reach away, and eased her into sleep without further conversation.

Talking could wait for now. But as he leaned back against the wall, he wished he could block his own hearing as simply, or take advantage of the kathain's enthusiasm himself.

"This is going to be a *very* long year," he muttered. "And I'm a godsdamned fool."

Something feathered against his mind, a tickling sensation he recognized instantly: someone was looking for him. A moment's concentration yielded an image of Idisio slipping from his room, disquiet filling his mind.

Deiq sighed, looking down at the sleeping desert lord; for there to be any chance of a coherent conversation with the younger ha'ra'ha, their meeting needed to be held away from this room, and he could tell by Idisio's aggrieved energy that whatever was going on should be dealt with now.

Crossing the room, he paused in the doorway, fingers resting lightly against the frame, and considered for a moment. Ward the inner room against intrusion, or the outer? Outer, he decided, and moved to the outer door of the suite. He laid his fingers against that frame and mentally traced a meandering, complex design along the edges of the door. A faint golden shimmer washed over the surface of the door, then disappeared.

Deiq nodded to himself and slipped from the room.

Nobody would cross the threshold now, not without a serious helping of determination and even then not without alerting him to the attempt. It was the best protection he could give her at the moment. But the kathain could easily gain access to her room, and on realizing that he'd left, probably *would*; it was something of a status prize to be the first of a new desert lord's kathain.

That encounter would teach her more than words about the reality of her new life, and might actually make her *listen* for once when Deiq tried to explain things to her. He just hoped she wouldn't hurt the kathain too badly in the process.

He intercepted Idisio three hallways over.

"Deiq! I was looking for you; I have to talk—"

"I know," Deiq said patiently, and steered the younger ha'ra'ha to a nearby courtyard, trying to block out the strong musk of recent and enthusiastic sex. He really wished Idisio had taken the time for a sponge bath, at the least; at the moment it was not a smell he wanted pressed into his nostrils.

"Riss is—"

"Hold on." Deiq waved Idisio quiet. He stood still, listening with care, but found no trace of watchers within hearing range. Reassured of that much privacy, at least, he walked unhurriedly to each archway and watch-hole, lacing them with wards to turn away any visitors. Turning to survey the courtyard, he decided darkness didn't suit his mood at the moment, and reached out to three of the five oil lamps; the freshly saturated wicks flared into white life immediately.

Satisfied, he walked back to stand in front of Idisio.

"Now. What is it?"

Idisio's wide grey eyes held a faintly dazed look. "What did you just do? I saw . . . *shimmers* . . . and you didn't even *touch* the lamps!"

"Wards, to ensure our privacy," Deiq said. "They're fairly simple, as is igniting a ready wick. I'll teach you. But first, what do you need to talk to me about?"

Idisio glanced around the courtyard, up at the overarching spread of stars against a black sky, then around again, with an increasing attitude of discomfort.

"Riss heard . . . some gossip," he said at last. "From the servants. About . . . ha'ra'hain. And . . . desert lords. And their . . . interests. Ehh . . . needs." He almost squirmed with embarrassment on the last word.

Deiq rubbed the bridge of his nose, glad he hadn't allowed Idisio to reach Alyea's new suite. "Mmph. I take it she's upset."

"Just a bit." The dryness was an attempt to hide a deep discomfort. "Is it true? I mean, I don't . . . I don't *feel* that . . . I mean, it's great, but it's not, you know, a, a *need* . . . and she's worried about. . . ." Apparently unable to continue, his face a deep crimson, he looked away, hunching his shoulders.

"Worried about being enough for you," Deiq supplied, and sat down on a stone bench with a sigh. "She won't be, Idisio."

Idisio jerked a protesting stare up at Deiq, then away again, his blush somehow managing to deepen. Deiq regarded him with amusement; he'd never seen another ha'ra'ha blush so easily and violently.

"You're leaving soon," Deiq pointed out. "And you'll be gone years, at best. Even a young human male would have difficulty staying faithful under those circumstances, Idisio. For a ha'ra'ha growing into his strength . . . it's impossible."

Idisio turned in place, paced a few steps, then turned to face Deiq again. "Are you saying I'm—" His voice broke. "Some kind of animal? That I won't be able to control—"

Deiq blinked and reared back, astounded. "*What?* Gods, no!"

"Then I *could* wait. If I wanted to."

Deiq stared, utterly bemused. He hadn't even considered that concept until he was over two hundred years past Idisio's current age. He blurted, "Why in the hells would you *want* to?"

Idisio opened and shut his mouth a few times, apparently at a loss for an answer.

Deiq drew a long breath and said, as reasonably as he could, "Idisio. You've known her less than a month."

"So?" Belligerence lined Idisio's jaw now; Deiq resisted the impulse to roll his eyes.

He tried a different tack. "Idisio, you're not human. You're not going to have a human life span. By the time you start to slow down, Riss's grandchildren will probably be long in their graves. And you'll drive yourself completely crazy if you try to hold to human notions of faithfulness. It's too damn *difficult* for us."

"Have you tried?" Idisio challenged.

Deiq set his teeth in his tongue, counted to fifteen, then said, steadily, "Yes. Several times over the years. It never works out well in the end."

He tried not to think about the promise he'd made regarding Alyea. The challenge issued by the Qisani ha'reye had seemed deceptively simple: *Stay only by her side, as though locked into the human concept of marriage.* He'd accepted, like a newborn fool, forgetting all the times he'd failed at self-assigned versions of that task in the past.

He'd thought it would be *different* with Alyea, gods help him. Somehow, he'd thought that she might turn to him out of true interest, not compulsion alone. He *wanted* it to be different, and it was; she showed no compulsion yet, but no interest either.

Deiq had stuck himself in the hells' own corner.

Foolishness. Yes . . . and with a high price attached to failure this time.

Or return to us, and remain with us, for a span of at least a hundred human years.

And then there was the question of whether the Qisani ha'reye had tried to stack the deck on that deal, as the human saying went, with their *thorough* approach. Deiq shut his eyes for a moment, blocking that memory before Scratha ha'rethe could notice his distress and rouse again; if Meer was a topic fraught with danger, the bloody disaster that Alyea's second trial had turned into was ten times more so.

"Why didn't it work out? What happened?" Idisio demanded.

"That's a fairly personal, and rude, question," Deiq remarked cooly.

Idisio shrugged and faced him, rebellious as any young human male could be: squinting, lips pursed, hands on hips. "How am I supposed to understand, if you don't explain?"

Deiq snorted, amused by the ridiculous stance and expression, and said, "All right. I'll indulge you the once, and tell you about Onsia. She was in her thirties at the time, and thought me a rich merchant. She'd been through two other husbands, both sailors, both dead; they'd worked on my ships, as it happened. We met at the land-remembrance ceremonies, and liked each other; she liked the notion that I wouldn't be going out on the ships, and I liked that she wasn't entirely innocent about men, as was the fashion for women at the time."

"So you liked her because she was a good fuck. Great." Idisio scowled as though disgusted over such a shallow attitude.

Deiq regarded Idisio with strained patience. "No," he said. "You're obviously too young to understand that part of it. Never mind. We got along well for a while; she wasn't worried over reputation and wasn't looking for a permanent relationship. Then her children started pressuring her to formalize the arrangement. She dropped a few hints, and I decided it was worth a try; I'd never bothered with marriage before, and I was curious to see what it was like."

"You married her because you were *curious*? Not because you loved her?"

Deiq shook his head slowly; Idisio's expression hardened into deep distaste.

"You were raised in a very different place and time, Idisio," Deiq said before the young ha'ra'ha could say something monumentally stupid. "It wasn't important to Onsia whether I loved her. Not after two husbands. She wanted someone to put food on the table. Which I did."

"So what went wrong, then, if it was so perfect?"

Deiq bit his tongue against an urge to slap Idisio back to sense. Granted, Idisio was upset over Riss, and bewildered by the sudden changes in his life; but there was no need for him to be *this* stupid. How had he survived a day with Cafad Scratha, let alone earned the man's respect?

Idisio glanced up and caught Deiq's expression. The color washed out of his face, and he seemed to shrink into himself. "I'm sorry," he said, barely audible. "Everything's just upside-down right now. I didn't mean it to come out like that."

Pale and miserable, the younger ha'ra'ha resembled the starving street-child he had once been: it was impossible to be angry with such a woeful countenance. Deiq was impressed by how quickly Idisio had been able to call that expression up; no wonder Scratha had never been able to throw a real temper tantrum around him.

"I'm sorry," Idisio said, ducking his head to stare at the floor. "Please, tell me the rest of it."

"Stop that," Deiq said. "I'm not Scratha."

Idisio stayed still for a moment, as though thinking about that; then slowly straightened, not quite looking Deiq in the face.

Deiq smiled, genuinely amused, and said, "As it turned out, Onsia *did* take all the marriage vows seriously: especially the one about monogamy. I didn't expect that. I thought all she wanted was security, and I didn't mind that; but at the time I wasn't inclined to restrict myself to one partner—"

Idisio's face wrinkled into a stern frown.

"Don't judge," Deiq said before Idisio could speak. "And I did try. To see if I could. But in the end, I couldn't; wouldn't, if you prefer."

He'd almost wrecked more than one of his carefully-arranged alliances while trying to hold to Onsia's demands, but Idisio wasn't likely to understand that, either.

Idisio chewed his lower lip, visibly restraining more rude comments. "So you left her?"

"Yes. With enough money to keep food on the table for the rest of her life, and some for her children."

"But you never really cared about her?"

"I wouldn't say that. She was a good woman."

"Did she love you?"

"I doubt it. She was also very practical."

Idisio shook his head and began pacing, muttering to himself; at last he turned and said, "So what do I say? What do I *tell* her? She's been crying. . . ."

Deiq grimaced. "Of course she is," he said under his breath. The entire conversation abruptly annoyed him; Idisio was far too young to be tangling himself up over a human he'd met just over a tenday ago. And his questions about *love* and *caring* were all human, and juvenile at that. "Tell her whatever will make her happy, Idisio."

Idisio's grey eyes widened in shock. "That's cold!"

"That's *reality*," Deiq shot back, standing.

An uneasy shiver ran across his back. He closed his eyes, seeking out whatever had provoked that reaction. It only took a moment to see that Alyea had woken, and was *not* happy about something. *Three guesses what*, Deiq thought, but didn't smile; Idisio could only take that expression personally at this point.

He spoke without really paying attention to his own words: "Stop *worrying* about her so much, Idisio. She's young, and lonely, and latched onto you as the closest thing to a kind hand she's met lately; but you'll likely forget about her within a tenday after we leave. Now, if you'll excuse me—"

He flicked a hand to release the wards, then stepped sideways, pulling on the shimmering power of the ha'rethe below their feet as he would pull on a rope. A moment later he emerged into the outer room of Alyea's suite.

All three kathain bolted out of the inner room a breath later, their expressions sullen and offended; spared him a brief glance, then dove into their room without pausing.

Deiq pursed his lips against a wide grin, forced a sober expression, and went in to explain.

Chapter Eight

Alyea woke to someone breathing in her ear and hands—more than two—wandering over her body with far too much intimacy. Aqeyva-trained reflexes cut in; she shoved in one direction, kicked in another, then twisted around into a compact crouch atop the bed.

Blinking sleep from her eyes, she followed the sounds of multiple thuds and yelps of aggrieved complaint to find the three kathain sprawled on the floor around the low bed. They stared at her as though unsure whether to be upset or shocked at the rejection. The strange white light of the oil lamps spaced around the room drew slanted almost-shadows across their expressions, making the entire moment surreal.

Her initial rush of panic slid into anger. "What the *hells*!" she blurted.

Then another detail came clear: they were all naked, and had been well on the way to removing her clothes.

She yanked her garments back into place and snapped, "How *dare* you!"

Their stares turned to bewilderment. They glanced at each other, then slowly climbed to their feet and moved into a huddle, the boy in the center. She couldn't help staring at him; the dark gloss of his skin and the muscle beneath were far more adult than the still-soft angles of his face and hairless body admitted.

Her gaze moved sideways, taking in darker striations along the lower stomach of the woman to the right and her equally hairless body: they had all been shaved. Even the hair of their heads was cropped shorter than any she'd yet seen in the southlands; when presented, they'd been wearing *wigs*.

"Lord," the younger woman said, dropping to her knees. "We not please?"

Her pale blue eyes anxious, she slid her hands under her breasts as though offering them up for appraisal.

Alyea just stared, at a loss for words. The youngest woman had the lightest skin and most delicate build of the three, along with ash-blonde hair.

"What are you *doing* here?" Alyea blurted. "You're *northern!*"

The young woman stared at her, uncomprehending. "I am yours, Lord," she said. Her hands slowly moved from her chest, sliding down her stomach. "You want?"

Alyea choked off her first response: *Hells, no!* She couldn't figure out how to get out of this without offending some stupid southern custom, and found herself wishing Deiq were around. He'd know how to sort this out.

Then it occurred to her that he'd probably left her alone on purpose, to force her to deal with this on her own: it was exactly the manipulative sort of thing he *did*. Anger began to simmer again.

Mistaking her hesitation for interest, the kathain began to smile. The older woman dropped to her knees and reached for the boy's groin with hands and mouth; the boy tilted his head and arched his back in near-theatrical appreciation.

"Oh, gods," Alyea breathed, horrified, and found she didn't care about offending custom any longer. "No. No! That's enough. Get out. Out!"

They scrambled to their feet, bewilderment returning to their expressions, and retreated a few steps.

"Out! *Out!*" She found herself on her feet, a heavy wooden bowl in her hand, with no memory of having grabbed it from the side table. She raised it to throw, too angry to consider common sense; their expressions went sullen, and they bolted from the room without further argument.

She threw the bowl anyway, just to relieve her too-tight nerves. It hit the wall by the door as Deiq stepped into the room. The bowl cracked into three splintered pieces; he ducked just in time to avoid the fragments.

Her fury turned scorching at the sight of his ever-smug face. Untrustworthy, manipulative, deceitful *bastard*—

"*Out!*"

"Alyea!"

His expression was honestly shocked. She took a savage satisfaction in that, and threw a thick-walled glass vase. This time he snaked out a hand and caught it, wincing a little.

"You'll run out of objects soon enough," he observed, his dark humor returning, and set the glass vase carefully aside on the floor.

She glared at him. "Get out," she said again, low in the back of her throat, as near to a growl as she'd ever come. "I will *not* talk to you right now. And take *them*—" She pointed a shaking finger towards the outer room. "Take them with you! I've had enough. *Enough!*"

He studied her face for a long, intense moment, as though judging her sincerity; Alyea gave him back the most menacing glare she could summon.

"You have a great deal to learn," he said at last, clearly disapproving.

"Well, that won't happen tonight!"

"Obviously," he remarked. With a shrug that came as much from his eyebrows as any shoulder movement, he retreated from the room. She stood still, listening; heard him, low-voiced and entirely too calm, urging the kathain from their quarters out into the hallway.

The door shut behind them. In the silent relief of being alone at last, she dropped to sprawl across the rumpled bed and promptly burst into tears.

Desert Pride, Honor, and Death

(excerpt)

Another area in which the southlands differ dangerously from the kingdom is in the matter of death. Take, for example, Pieas Sessin's death. One accustomed to northern ways might think that his uncle, Lord Eredion Sessin, would be furious; that Lord Eredion might set out to exact vengeance upon Lord Alyea. This is absolutely not the case. In fact, if you were so crass as to ask him directly—which I strongly, most strongly, Lord Oruen, advise against doing—more on that advice shortly—but should you speak with Lord Eredion regarding the matter, I am quite sure he would express honest relief.

Pieas Sessin acted the wastrel and fool for some time, shaming his Family despite all attempts to recall him or redirect his overfull energies. Therefore, his life, at the time of his final encounter with Lord Alyea, was of far less value than his death. Pieas understood this and knelt as sacrifice, offering no resistance whatsoever. I can speak to this: I witnessed it myself. Pieas chose to end his life in the service of a ritual which cleared his name and any prior shame to his Family immediately and irreversibly; so now, the only public words you will hear regarding Pieas Sessin will be positive ones, and any who publicly challenge that memory may find themselves, in turn, challenged to a blood-right duel.

Few northerners can grasp this concept. You will probably not fully grasp the treason I commit merely by explaining this on a durable medium which, no doubt, you will save and store in your library. Others than you may one day read it, which doubles and even quadruples my offense, as I have no control over what these potential readers may do upon understanding that the official history of Pieas Sessin, as it is even now being penned by Sessin Family loremasters, to be so highly glossed as to perpetuate a fiction upon the ignorant. This is why speaking directly to Eredion regarding the crimes of Pieas would be, now, highly inappropriate and display only your terrible ignorance.

I am not myself afraid of the wrath of the other Families; but for your own sake, I would advise against aggravating the southern loremasters if you can possibly avoid it. They are a stronger force than you can possibly understand at this point, and you can ill afford their collective ire. So hide these letters well, and let not a hint regarding the source of your new knowledge slip from your lips until you are thoroughly and unmistakably secure not only in your own recollection of the words in these letters, but in your position as leader of the northern kingdom as well.

From the collection
Letters to a Northern King of Merit
penned by Lord Cafad Scratha during the reign of King Oruen

Chapter Nine

Spread out around Scratha Fortress was a landscape of opposites: great rocky ridges covered in scrub flattened out into desolate sandy patches dotted with spindly devil-trees, gigantic desert-sage bushes, and a dozen varieties of cacti. A few areas of thicker growth spread improbable splotches of green against a bleak landscape of brown.

"I thought it would all be sand," Idisio said in a muted voice.

They stood looking down at Scratha lands from the highest point of the fortress, the great—and, as yet, empty—Watchtower. Deiq tried to remember the last time he'd stood this high above the ground and studied such a large sweep of land at one time; the only place he could think of was the Northern Church Tower in Bright Bay.

But this was not the place to brood over the memories that roused; he turned his attention to Idisio's comment instead, pleased that at least Idisio's overly emotional attitude of the night before had disappeared.

"Hardly," he said. "Only the deep stretches of the central desert are sand, and even there you'll find some growth and rock."

He fell silent, thinking of what those sands covered, and sighed.

"And ruins," Idisio said.

Deiq jerked a startled glance at the younger ha'ra'ha, wondering if he'd broadcast his thoughts accidentally. "What?"

"Well, it's a standard in every desert story, isn't it?" Idisio seemed to be watching a great red-tailed eagle soar on the rising dawn breeze. "The ancient city, buried under the sands. And then there's a wanderer who stumbles into it, and finds a trapped spirit, and talks to it . . . and there's usually some sort of treasure involved. Or a quest. Or something."

Deiq stared, speechless. At last he managed, "It is? Really?"

Idisio laughed. Dawn light edged his smooth, fair skin with a golden tint and caught greenish highlights from his grey eyes. "You never heard any of those tales?"

Deiq shook his head slowly, fascinated. "Tell me one."

Idisio shot him a dry sideways stare, suddenly seeming mature beyond his years. "Stalling?"

"No more than you are."

Idisio shrugged again, his gaze going distant. "At least Riss didn't throw anything at *my* head."

Deiq shook his head but didn't correct the misunderstanding; he wasn't avoiding Alyea out of fear, but irritation. Smoothing out the incident with the kathain handler and Lord Scratha had taken some delicate maneuvering. If Alyea threw something at him, he was likely to throw it back, rather harder, just at the moment. But explaining all that to Idisio would probably spark another argument about relative morality.

At last Idisio said, "Mmm . . . all right. Got one. I'm no bard, mind you. But there's one story I've always liked. . . ."

In the dead wastes of the kingdom-that-was lies a crypt; a grave, from the days when stone was worked with tools that cut through granite as though it were only clotted milk, and the bodies of even the common-born were buried entire, rather than set into bone-boxes or ground up for fertilizer. In those days, beautiful trees raised their arms to the sky, and water moved freely across the surface of the land, laughing and sparkling like rivers of liquid blue diamonds; the air-spirits walked in bodies of gold, and the earth was cool and black with life.

In those days, there was a leader, a kaen, a man of surpassing strength and virility, with many women attending to his every desire. And it came to pass that the one thing he most desired, he could not have; no woman quickened with his seed. He had no children, for all his many wives, and while he put this woman and that woman aside, at last he was forced to admit the fault lay within himself.

Deiq's stomach tightened, and he shut his eyes. It *would* have to be *this* story. Unwanted, an image of the city rose in his mind: sunlight gilding the great striped arches with tones of honey and apricot; white, gauzy draperies fluttering in a breeze. A nightsinger warbling outside his guest-room window, the scent of *ravann* oil and the light scrape of salt scattered over smooth skin as he passed his palm across—he blinked hard and stopped the memory there, before it cut any deeper.

Idisio went on more slowly. His voice broke and steadied a few times as he tried different pitches before finding one that worked.

This troubled the kaen mightily, as well it might. His lands, rich as they were, would quickly be torn apart by his three younger brothers, all of whom desired to lead after the kaen passed from this world, and none of whom were competent to do so. The kaen summoned healers and wise men from all over the lands, and consulted seers and mystics until his head swam from all the incomprehensible things they told him. At last, befuddled and angrier than ever, he sent them all away, no closer to a course of action that would gain him legitimate children; and he went out to walk his lands with a hood over his face and his leadership staff and chain left behind.

This was a common thing, you must understand, that the kaen did such a thing; while his advisors spoke against it, still he went walkabout often. His subjects were accustomed to treating all strangers with courtesy in case such a visitor turned out to be their kaen in disguise, and the kaen was accustomed to being received with great courtesy everywhere he went, with or without his marks of leadership.

Deiq found himself smiling. Idisio's delivery managed to capture the kaen's pompous arrogance perfectly. More than one kaen had taken that approach; some from paranoia, some from a strange desire to be ordinary for a few moments. Deiq thought it a stupid custom. The kaens never had understood the burden they placed on their subjects with their wanderings, and never wanted to listen to him on the matter, either.

Thank the gods that at least Oruen hadn't taken such a notion into his head yet; Chac had done *some* good with his biased teaching.

Idisio drew a deep breath. His eyes slid half-shut, and he went on, the last traces of uncertainty leaving his voice:

So you can imagine the kaen's surprise when he stopped at a well near the center of his lands and was rudely pushed aside by a fat old man.

"No drinking here today!" the fat man declared. "I've claimed this well for mine, and you shan't have any!"

"This is a public well," the kaen pointed out, amused by what he took to be a madman; for the fat man's eyes had a glaze never seen in one wholly rational.

"Not any longer!" said the fat man. "It's mine now. And the only way you'll drink from it is if you come to me with your firstborn child."

Now the kaen began to grow angry. "You have no such authority," he said. "Step aside, before you go to the guards!"

"If you touch me," said the man, "this well shall instantly go dry, and your entire lands, O kaen, will then go as dry as your loins."

Deiq repressed a sigh. An old, fat man? Time distorted history in strange ways. And the story itself was, not surprisingly, going far off the track already. Maybe that was a mercy.

The kaen stood up straight and put his hood back.

"How do you know who I am?" he demanded.

"Never mind that," the man said. "None shall drink from this well, until you come to me with your firstborn child." He smiled, and it was a thing of terrible evil, that smile.

Terrible evil? Deiq suspected the Northern Church had meddled with the story at some point. It didn't sound like anything from the southern religions; they tended to avoid notions of absolute good and evil.

The "firstborn child" part was accurate enough, if badly twisted; it *hadn't* been his fault, damn it! But then, he hadn't been old and fat, either. He tried—

and failed—to find amusement in that.

If only the kaen had *listened* . . . If only Deiq himself hadn't been such a fool.

He shook off sour memory and tried to listen to the story as nothing more than an amusing fiction.

"How dare you!" raged the kaen, and losing his temper, laid hands on the man to thrash him for such impudence. Upon the moment he touched the fat man's sleeve, the entire of the man within the robes disappeared, and the kaen was left holding only a greasy, ragged scrap of cloth.

A strange sucking sound came from the well, and the kaen rushed over to look; and indeed, all the water drained as though a great plug had been pulled, and within two breaths only black mud remained at the bottom. A great wailing went up from all around him, as the other wells, rivers, lakes, and fountains all vanished the same way and with the same speed; and the kaen stood aghast at what his pride had caused.

Deiq's amusement faded. He wanted to stop the tale there; but that would mean explaining why it bothered him.

The vivid image of all life draining from the once-glorious city brought back the rush of guilt he had felt, standing in the ruins years later. The kaen had been a fool, and a proud one, but his people hadn't deserved to suffer any more than the people of Bright Bay deserved what Rosin Weatherweaver and Ninnic had handed out.

If Idisio had found the story about Onsia damning, he'd react even more poorly to the truth of this tale; and once more, Scratha Fortress wasn't the place for the argument.

Deiq pursed his lips and stayed silent as Idisio continued. The young ha'ra'ha's eyes were fully shut now, his thin hands moving in great descriptive swoops.

For all the rest of his days the kaen sought to find some word of the fat man, to trace down his identity; and just as ardently sought to produce a child, submitting to every indignity and procedure his healers and sages heaped upon him. Both efforts were to no avail, and he died younger than his father had, and was buried in a great crypt in the center of his lands.

His people tried, as the lands dried around them, to draw the favor of the gods back upon them. They held great ceremonies begging for forgiveness. They sacrificed animals, criminals, even young children in an effort to appease the angry gods. Nothing worked, and at last they left the barren land, carrying all they owned on their backs and in carts. Some went north, and some went west; some east, and some south.

From that scattering came the desert Families. The great central desert remains empty to this day, but for the restless ghost of the old kaen: still looking for some way to produce an heir, to find that evil fat man, and to return his lands to their former lush glory.

Deiq said nothing for a long moment, staring out at the western horizon. His eyes blurred with tears; not at Idisio's revisionist story, but at the memory of how beautiful that city had been, and how broken it had become. Regardless of whose mistake had been the deciding factor, in the end, the kaen's ghost would never find any peace from the disaster he'd brought on his city—and neither would Deiq.

He cleared his throat and said, thickly, "And you *like* this story, do you?"

"Well," Idisio said, "it stuck in my mind, anyway." He grinned, then took a sharp look at Deiq's face. "Deiq?"

"Never mind," Deiq said, and rubbed an arm over his eyes briskly. "Just remembering. That story's nowhere near accurate."

"You mean there really is a city out there under the sands? And you were *there* when it fell?" Idisio's eyes went as round and almost as pale as a full moon.

Deiq shook his head and didn't answer. When Idisio opened his mouth to press the question, Deiq made a curt gesture with one hand to indicate the subject closed, and Idisio subsided, a keen glint in his grey eyes that warned the topic would come up again.

There would be time to talk about it later. Deiq closed his eyes, suddenly weary. Once they cleared Scratha lands, maybe . . . He had a lot to talk about with both Idisio and Alyea, and almost none of it could safely be said within these walls.

"Let's go see what's left of the armory," Deiq said at last. Idisio, malleable as any young human male, perked up immediately, and they left the wide roof of the outlook post without looking back.

Chapter Ten

Lord Azaniari's suite had oddly colored walls. Where most of the fortress was a plain, drab grey or brown stone, here the blandness was punctuated by a random series of pale yellow blocks. It was attractively done, and made the room more serene. The dawn light tumbling through ceiling tubes overhead and through the great, deep-silled windows glowed against those bricks.

Alyea glanced up at the ceiling tubes, awed yet again; the Northern Church had destroyed all such mysteries as "heathen, heretic, demonic devices". They seemed entirely common in the southlands, however. All the subtle sophistications she encountered here made a lifetime of believing the southlands barbaric seem painfully ignorant.

Nothing but sand and savages, her mother had sniffed, time and again; and the Northern Church certainly painted everything south of the Horn as brutal, dim, and dangerous.

Dangerous, at least, Alyea still agreed with.

She cradled the simple white teacup in her hands and held it out for Lord Azaniari—or "Azni," as she insisted on being called in private—to refill, then sat back in her chair, sighing.

"This is all so damn complicated," Alyea said, abandoning courtesy.

Azni smiled. "You'll get used to it." She tucked her feet up under her as she curled sideways in her wide, overstuffed chair, a northern-style piece of furniture unearthed from storage.

Alyea resisted the impulse to do the same. She needed to keep every shred of dignity she could manage right now. It was all very well for Azni to play casual. Alyea's mood was just too sour at the moment.

She sipped the dark tea, catching the familiar aroma and smoky taste of thopuh, and grimaced at the memory of Deiq's outrageous behavior the night before.

"Last night," she said, lifting her cup slightly. Azni smiled, apparently understanding.

"I've always been fond of thopuh tea," Azni said quietly, turning her cup in her hands. "And the story behind it *is* interesting, if rather embarrassing."

"How does he get away with such rudeness?" Alyea burst out, leaning forward. "He's *impossible!*"

Azni lifted a thin eyebrow. "He's an elder ha'ra'ha," she pointed out. "He could ask Lord Scratha to bend over if he liked."

Alyea stared, mouth open at that bluntness, feeling shock rush a wave of color to her face.

"Oh, Alyea," Azni sighed, leaning forward to refill her cup. "You haven't the slightest idea yet what you're dealing with here, do you? You're still thinking in northern terms."

She shook the sturdy white teapot gently, then whistled, short and sharp. A plump servant came in from a side room and removed the empty pot without speaking.

"Deiq's been getting away with much worse than that dinner tale for many years," Azni said. "The rules are different for him. Mainly because he doesn't *care*. I admit a reluctant admiration for that. I used to be like that. . . ." She pursed her lips, frowning, and shook her head.

The servant returned and set the teapot down; Azni leaned forward and tilted the small lid sideways. Steam spilled out, braiding up into the still air, and the thick scent of thopuh tea filled the room.

"But Deiq, he's not as bad as he could be," Azni said, sitting back and watching the steam. "And he's not as cold as he was, a few years ago. Something happened, along the way, to shake him badly. He's changing, and that in itself is astonishing. And a bit dangerous. Ha'ra'hain don't change their minds easily." She lifted her gaze to Alyea. "And he is right, you know. Kathain are fairly well essential in the first few months of a desert lord's new life."

"Did *you*—" Alyea stopped short, biting her lip, and looked away.

"Of course," the elderly woman said serenely. "About ten a day, in the beginning, if I recall; and later, there was Regav. . . ." Her voice faltered, then steadied. "He was a desert lord too, so that . . . was enough. And then . . . it stopped being an issue."

Alyea looked up in time to see Azni make an impatient motion with one hand, as though to push away the past.

"Never mind," Azni said, and leaned forward to fuss with the angle of the lid for a few moments. At last she sat back in her chair again and sighed. "You won't be feeling the effects yet, I suppose. It took me a tenday or two once the final trial ended, I believe; but then, my final trial took months, not days. Unlike you, I stayed in isolation through the birth of my. . . ."

Her voice faded; eyes filling with sudden tears, she pressed the back of one hand against her mouth.

"Lord Azni," Alyea said, feeling horribly inadequate. "I'm so sorry."

"Never mind," Azni said again, wiping her eyes clear. "Done is done. And that was a long time ago."

Her determined attempt at brushing aside the past was denied by the shadow of an old, deep pain in her eyes. Clearly, she still hurt over giving away her first child; but courtesy forbade pressing the point. Azni was an elder, and of superior rank; Alyea had no right to explore painful areas just to get answers.

Alyea looked down at her cup, frowning, and turned it round slowly. Somehow, the child she'd given hadn't seemed real until now. She had barely experienced the pregnancy, after all, before the ha'rethe took it from her.

When there's as little time as you had, she remembered Deiq explaining, *they have to take more. To sustain the child.* And he'd expressed doubt as to whether she'd ever be able to have children again . . . She might have given away her only child.

"High price to pay," she muttered, and only realized she'd spoken aloud when Azni answered:

"Yes. But it's done, and we live with it." Looking as though she didn't believe her own words, Azni cleared her throat and took several sips of tea; an uncomfortable silence hung for a few breaths.

"Will I ever see. . . ." Alyea couldn't finish the question aloud, but Azni seemed to understand.

"I haven't," Azni said. "I don't know of many who have. And many of the children from blood trials don't survive, if I understand correctly. That's why we're not drowning in ha'ra'hain and their offspring. The ones who do survive tend to stay with their ha'reye parents."

She paused, as though she might say more; shook her head and went back to staring at her teacup with a brooding expression.

"Why is Deiq walking around in human society, then?"

"Ask him, not me," Azni said a touch curtly. "And I believe I'd like to be alone now."

"Of course, Lord Azaniari," Alyea said reflexively, setting her cup down and standing. "Gods hold—"

Azni didn't look up, and her voice was tart as she said, "Lord Alyea, I find polite formalities rather empty. And I've long hated that blessing, as I don't believe in the Three, the Four, or any other nonsense religion. So please—just go."

Alyea swallowed hard, bowed, and retreated as hastily as was decent; but Lord Azni's bleak expression haunted her steps for quite some time.

Chapter Eleven

Each Head of Family put his or her own mark on a fortress. The few times Deiq had seen, first-hand, a Family's transition of leadership, he'd observed the rearrangements with intense curiosity. This unusual situation was the most interesting he'd ever seen; the staff were all temporary, loaned from the various Families attending the hastily-convened Conclave. Lord Scratha, rightfully, had little trust in most of them.

The presence of a northern-raised *numaina* altered a number of the standard arrangements, right down to what was being prepared in the kitchens and what furniture was being hauled out from under dropcloths and dustjackets.

Lord Scratha's study served as the hub of the change. The furnishings were distinctively northern now: a wide-seated wooden slat-backed chair behind a massive blackwood desk, fronted by two thickly upholstered northern chairs—in which sat Alyea and Idisio—and two southern-style kneeling chairs. Drab brown, thick curtains had been replaced with equally thick white drapes, through which streamed intense afternoon light but little heat. Deiq nodded to himself, recognizing the work of Bright Bay weavers; another sign that Scratha Fortress would have much closer ties to northern merchants under Cafad Scratha than it had ever held before.

Given Cafad Scratha's obsessive nature, if he took it into his head to pursue that angle, Sessin Family might find themselves facing serious competition for the post of "king's favorite" in short order; and what an interesting situation *that* would create, after the years of animosity between the two Families.

Putting that thought aside for the moment, Deiq leaned against the wall by the door, arms crossed, and raised an eyebrow at Lord Scratha, who sat behind the heavy blackwood desk with an expression of strained patience.

"He's on his way," Deiq said. Everyone turned to stare at him. Alyea and Idisio looked puzzled; Scratha's scowl deepened.

"Damned games," Scratha muttered.

"You'd do the same," Deiq observed, then cocked his head, listening to the faint patter of someone walking quietly down the flagstones of the corridor nearby. "Here he is."

Scratha smoothed his expression into pleasant blandness just before his *s'e-kath*—what northerns would call his personal manservant, although with rather more duties than northerns usually assigned—opened the door to announce the arrival of Lord Evkit. The teyanin lord walked into the room with a serene expression and no trace of apology in his manner. He slid a blank stare across Deiq, bowed to Lord Scratha and Alyea, then climbed onto one of the kneeling chairs without a word.

Scratha drew in an audible breath, glanced down at the floor; let out the air in a long hiss. "Lord Evkit," he said with commendable courtesy. "Thank you for coming."

"Lord Scratha," Evkit answered promptly, then sat still as stone, patient as death.

Scratha glanced at Deiq, as though seeking advice.

Let it go, Deiq advised, pleased that the man had at least asked before opening his mouth to rebuke Evkit for tardiness. Scratha might just grow into a good leader after all.

Scratha let out another long breath, returned his attention to the three in front of him, and said evenly, "I called you here to discuss your departure, my lords." He dipped his head in an inclusive nod to Idisio, who squirmed uncomfortably in his chair.

Alyea might be deaf still, but Idisio, at least, Deiq could reach as he would a desert lord. *Damn it, sit up straight*, he sent. *You're his equal, even his superior, don't you dare cringe like that!*

Idisio jerked in his seat and almost turned to stare at Deiq; caught himself at the last moment and managed to stiffen his spine a little. Deiq restrained a sigh. Teaching Idisio to let go of his human, street-thief upbringing was clearly going to be as difficult as convincing Alyea to abandon her northern protocols.

Scratha blandly ignored the young ha'ra'ha's discomfort and observed, "My *s'e-kath* tells me that our other guests have cleared Scratha borders, and that only the teyanain remain at the gates. He also tells me that the rainy season is due to hit this area in a matter of days." He folded his hands together on the desk before him. "I do not have the resources to host you through the coming months. So I have to ask, rather bluntly, when you plan on departing."

His gaze settled on Lord Evkit, and his mouth twisted a little. The tiny motion made it clear *resources* had little to do with his question.

"My people ready to leave at Lord Alyea's word," Lord Evkit said, just as blandly.

Deiq didn't need to see Alyea's face to know she was deeply annoyed at being backed into a corner once again. He wished he could speak to her as he had Idisio, to offer some guidance; and he knew Scratha and Evkit expected him to be doing just that. Any mistakes she made would be laid at his feet; something else he hadn't gotten around to really explaining. But right now, she probably wouldn't have listened anyway.

Without hesitation, as though she'd already been thinking on the same question, Alyea said, "Would tomorrow morning suit, Lord Scratha? Lord Evkit?"

"Absolute," Evkit said. Lord Scratha nodded.

"Excellent," Alyea said briskly. "I'll meet you outside the gates an hour before dawn, then, Lord Evkit."

Exactly the answer—and, more importantly, the *attitude*—Deiq would have advised himself. He smiled, pleased and a bit bemused. Alyea, like all new desert lords, wavered between old and new habits seemingly at random. He found himself looking forward to the day she finally settled into her new life—the day, by implication, that he could move on and be free of his obligation to this stubborn northern.

His amusement faded, his mood darkening. In the back of his mind, he heard the accusation again: *Foolishness.* And his own tart remarks to Idisio: *You're not human. Stop thinking that way . . . it's too damn frustrating for us.*

Raising his head, he found Evkit had left the kneeling chair and was staring straight at him.

"You travel also?" Evkit inquired, black eyes grinning in an expressionless face.

"Yes," Deiq said tightly, then realized what he'd admitted to the sharp-eyed teyanin lord in that instant.

Damn it, he thought, exasperated at his own clumsiness. He should have indicated boredom, even amusement, over the notion; made it seem as though he was ambling alongside for his own purposes, or that the entire trip was somehow his idea, not Alyea's. Instead, his tense reply only confirmed Evkit's suspicions that Deiq followed Alyea's lead, not the other way around.

Evkit's mouth spread into a smug grin. "I look forward to," he said, bowed, and left the room.

Deiq looked up to find Alyea frowning at him, clearly puzzled, while Scratha's frown held much more understanding.

But Scratha said only, "Deiq, I'd like your thoughts on the supplies you'll be needing, if you please," then busied himself spreading maps over the vast surface of his desk.

Diverted, Alyea and Idisio moved to study the maps. Deiq took a moment to compose his temper and banish the lingering whisper of *damn it* and *foolishness*, then followed suit.

Chapter Twelve

Of all the rooms in the sprawling fortress, Alyea liked the small dining room best. Suitable for a dozen or fewer, the room was much cozier than the vast formal dining hall. A rough, dark red plaster covered the walls; in this windowless chamber, the only light came from hanging candles and large green-oil lamps set in alcoves around the room.

The table sat low, intended for cushions rather than the higher northern seats. Gria looked completely at home, perched cross-legged and barefoot on a thick blue cushion; she had dressed in informal, desert-style, loose silk pants and an equally flowing top. Her hair, bound back into a combination topknot-braid, gave her the air of someone who had spent a lifetime in the desert. She unabashedly reached and leaned to grab from the baskets of flatbread or to scoop more rice into her *tibi*, the shallow, oval eating bowl most southerners carried with them as a matter of course.

Scratha probably had a supply of much finer dishes; for some reason he'd opted to set out humble, wooden traveler's tools this time. Alyea wondered if that was an oblique comment on the morning's planned departure.

In sharp contrast to Gria, Sela sat stiff and rigid atop three stacked cushions, her knees locked tightly together under the formal, tight-skirted northern dress and the *tibi* balanced precariously on one knee. Now and again she shifted uncomfortably, then quickly put a hand to the cushion, as though afraid that small movement would tip her over.

Riss, sitting on Gria's other side, wore an outfit that matched Gria's in all but color; hers was a deep, shimmering red. The two girls chattered together in low voices, occasionally breaking into shared laughter, and ignored everyone else in the room. It was visibly aggravating Sela, who shot several poisonous glares at her niece and cleared her throat multiple times, without any noticeable effect.

Lord Scratha seemed content to let everyone be for the moment. He ate quietly, his eyes fixed on his food. Idisio and Deiq, likewise, sat without speaking, eating without haste, their attention on their own thoughts.

Alyea felt herself relax into the quiet of the room, the undemanding, ordinary nature of the meal. Dinners at home weren't usually this peaceful. Her mother always seemed to be nagging about Alyea making suitable connections or why she wasn't attending some event or other at court; after all, she and Oruen were so *close*. . . .

Her mother would be incensed by Alyea not only having a child out of lawful marriage but then giving the child away. The roof might not survive the explosion when she found out that might be Alyea's *only* child. . . .

Alyea stifled a sigh just in time, and was actually grateful for the distraction when Sela spoke.

"My lord Scratha," she said, her fingers tight around the almost-untouched bowl of rice and flatbread on her knee. "There are a few—"

"I'm not your lord, Sela," Scratha interrupted, his dark stare coming back from wherever he'd been wandering in thought and focusing sharply on the northern woman. "You haven't sworn yourself over to Scratha Family. Or did you intend to?"

Sela's face flushed a startling crimson color; she hesitated as though unsure how to answer.

"No," Scratha said, rescuing her from confusion, "I don't expect you will, and there's no reason for you to do so. You're not part of the direct bloodline. You're welcome to stay for a time, but I see no value in swearing you into the family."

Sela's face cooled, taking on a harder cast at that unsubtle snub.

Before she could say anything, Scratha added, "But in any case, in this informal of a setting, please, call me Cafad."

Riss broke off her conversation with Gria, her attention on Scratha now. "Could you explain that?" she asked, just as Sela opened her mouth again. "The naming conventions in the south, I mean. I'm a bit muddled about them."

Idisio's expression changed to puzzlement, and he began to say something. Stopping short, he cut an aggrieved glance at Deiq, as though the older ha'ra'ha had kicked him under the table.

Scratha's mouth moved in the faintest of smiles. "Of course," he said gravely. "Calling someone 'my lord', in the north, is a basic phrase of respect. In the south, however, using the possessive 'my' indicates that you have sworn service to that man or Family. So, 'my lord Scratha' would mean you *serve* Scratha, or me personally, depending on modifiers I won't get into."

"How about *my lady*?" Gria asked, her dark eyes lit with a sly mischief.

Scratha shook his head. "That's almost wholly a northern term, and meaningless here," he said. "You are *numaina*, not *Lady*; a Scratha noblewoman is one of several variants of *numaina*. A servant is one of several variants of the term *kathain*; *s'e-kath*, as with Seg—" He tilted his chin to indicate a tall man standing against the wall nearby.

Alyea had been trying not to stare at the indicated man ever since they sat down; he displayed the rich darkness of the deepest southern coloring variations—and almost translucently light blue eyes. She'd never seen anything like it. The combination of height and coloring, set against those strange eyes, drew her attention repeatedly. And the way he stood so very still and watched the room with total focus told her that Seg was definitely more than just a servant, whatever Scratha claimed.

Scratha continued: "*S'a-dinne kath*, as the dining servants; *s'a-kathalle*, as the cleaning staff."

"*S'a*," Gria said, seeming truly interested this time. "That's women, right? So only women can serve meals? I've seen male servants about the dining hall."

"That gets a bit tricky," Scratha admitted. "There are a few instances where the desert tongue assigns gender to items or actions, where the northern tongue has no such concept. A servant is simply a servant, in Bright Bay; but the concept of serving, in the southern language, is female. A servant's actual gender doesn't have to match their job title. So *s'a-dinne kath* covers all dining hall servants; men, women, children, and neuter. Of course, you can break it apart and modify it to *s'e-dinne kath, s'ii*, and so on; but that's not common, and really only used for exceptional servants, as a designation of honor."

Sela's eyes glazed. She prodded listlessly at her rice, clearly not listening to the lecture. Scratha's gaze flicked to her, and his smile widened a notch; he nodded at Riss and Gria as though to say *thank you*.

"You look tired, Sela," he said aloud. "I'll have Seg take you back to your quarters."

Alert, the tall servant stepped away from the wall and moved to stand by Sela.

"What?" the northern woman said, startling upright. "Oh! Excuse me, I—"

Her jerky movement set the cushions under her skewing. A frantic grab to keep herself stable was unfortunately made with the hand holding the bowl, and the rim of the *tibi* cracked upwards against the lip of the table.

Rice sprayed up into the air and scattered across Sela, the cushions, and Gria; the latter ducked and burst into laughter. Sela, her face crimson once more, scrambled to her feet, seeming caught between equally humiliating urges to curse aloud or to burst into tears. She settled for cuffing Gria sharply on the side of the head.

Or tried to; Seg's hand shot out and caught her wrist, turning the blow aside. Seg's other hand latched on to Sela's elbow, and with apparently minimal effort on Seg's part, Sela stumbled into a sharp turn and several steps away from the table.

"I think perhaps *nu-s'a* Sela is feeling tired and needs to retire for the night," Seg said in a serene, clear bass. "My apologies, Lords. I will escort her." He kept moving as he spoke, and had Sela at the doorway and out of the room before the final word died from the air.

Alyea turned an astonished glance to Scratha. The man sat very still, a grave expression on his face and no trace of humor in his eyes. Gria, her grin wavering into a more uncertain expression, glanced around as though seeking an explanation of what had just happened.

"I'll have another talk with her," Scratha said quietly, apparently to the room at large.

"I don't understand," Gria said, her uncertainty folding into sterner, sulkier lines. She brushed rice from her shirt, picking at clinging pieces with a frown of distaste.

Scratha put his hand over his eyes, his lips thinning. "Riss."

"Right," the former stable hand said briskly, rising. She urged Gria from the room without further comment.

An odd expression crossed Idisio's face; he looked, for just a moment, relieved. Glancing away hurriedly before the young ha'ra'ha caught her staring, she found Scratha's gaze directly on her.

"Do *you* understand, Lord Alyea?" Scratha inquired.

Alyea barely stopped a stammered, witless reply from emerging; but it only took a moment to see what the answer had to be. She drew a long breath and said, evenly, "Gria is Head of Scratha. It's inappropriate for anyone to smack her like a child being scolded."

"Good," Scratha said, his fierce expression gentling. He flicked a glance to Deiq, then to Idisio. "Riss will be fine, Idisio. She's learning fast, and I'll keep her busy."

Idisio's face flared as brightly as Sela's had. He stood hurriedly and muttered apologies, then almost bolted from the room.

"Touchy," Deiq said lazily. "He'll grow out of that." He smiled and stood, subtly urging Alyea to her feet at the same time. "Good evening, Lord Scratha."

Alyea didn't resist. Something about the inexplicably darkening expression on Lord Scratha's face sent chills up her spine.

She found herself *very* glad they were leaving in the morning.

Chapter Thirteen

Pre-dawn, the dying sliver of the Healer's Moon was barely visible against a dense freckling of equally pale stars. Deiq tilted his head and scanned the sky, tracing constellations humans stopped tracking hundreds of years ago; many overlapped the new. The left paw and head of the Old Tiger now formed the chest and spear of the Hunter; the right wing of the Parrot was now seen by mankind as part of the Endless Fountain.

No doubt the Northern Church had declared even more alterations, with their own distorted pantheon in mind. Deiq had never bothered going north long enough to learn such minor matters. Exploring the differences might be an interesting pastime on the road, however, and he could use the original star-stories as a way of teaching Idisio about the *real* history of the world they walked through.

Slightly cheered, he returned his attention to the teyanain camp before him; what remained of it. Evkit's grand tent, which had replaced the temporary *shall* offered to Alyea days ago, was as always the last to be broken down.

Three *athain* were taking great care with the folding and packing of the sturdy, silky material and deceptively slender poles.

Athain. Not ordinary servants, but teyanain spirit-walkers. In travel clothes, the only signs of their sworn calling were the peculiar triple-split braids hanging from just behind their right ears. Deiq was careful not to stare, not to show how much it disturbed him that Evkit had athain breaking down his tent. Either Evkit held his own holy men in a dangerous contempt—not likely—or there was something special about the tent itself . . . something that couldn't be trusted to ordinary hands.

Deiq itched to wander closer and sniff out any traces of several dangerous substances, most of which were strictly forbidden anywhere on the land of an active ha'rethe; knew he'd never get close enough without risking a rapid descent into open violence.

The teyanain took their privacy *seriously*. Deiq wouldn't get anywhere near that tent or the chest it was being stored in, not for the entire of the journey back to the Horn. He knew better than to even look at it for too long.

If he'd known Evkit had three athain with him, he'd never have agreed to this madness. Ordinary travel with the teyanain was one thing, but three athain took it to an entirely new and much more dangerous level.

One athain, two athain, clee; a children's song from long before Alyea had been born. *Clee, clee, all we three; clee, claw, into the maw . . .* largely nonsense, as all children's songs were, but drawn from a real fear and a real danger.

Too late to back out now.

Alyea, meanwhile, sat sipping thopuh tea with Lord Evkit, each sitting on a large, flat boulder dragged, centuries ago, to serve as seats for visitors camping outside the gates. Deiq inhaled the rich, tarry aroma and smiled; Evkit, at least, was serving the real thing.

Deiq could almost see the centuries the block sat on a back shelf of a small tea shop, while wars and negotiations raged by outside, soldiers and merchants and whores taking their turns amusing themselves in the main and side rooms; could hear the rattle of stone dice and goat-ivory telling-chips, the slap of seer-cards and the laughter of a woman well-amused by her company of the night. . . .

He sighed, opening eyes he hadn't realized he'd closed. Evkit's tent was completely stowed away, and the teacups were being collected, Alyea and Evkit rising gravely to their feet and bowing to each other. Time to move on, then.

"That was wonderful tea," Alyea said, coming to stand beside Deiq. Her face held a glow of warmth and inner satisfaction. He blinked hard, forcing himself to stay in human-vision although he ached to see that glow tracing its way through her entire being in snaky, seductive spirals and swirls. "You should have tried some."

He blinked again, lazily, and said, "I've had it. I could smell it. One's as good as the other, for me." He offered a dry smile, knowing she'd think the self-mocking expression to be aimed at her; and as expected, she flushed a little and turned away.

"Idisio, *you* should have tried it," she said to the younger ha'ra'ha, as though determined to make the point to *somebody*. Idisio shook his head, expression grim.

"I won't drink anything offered by a hand I don't trust," he said in a low voice, then glanced around apprehensively.

"Nobody heard," Deiq assured him. "You did it right."

Idisio relaxed noticeably and let out a soft breath.

Evkit turned from a quiet discussion with his athain and motioned the three forward.

"We go," he said. "Shoes all in packs? Good. Barefoot always best, you trust me on that, you will see. Escort around you, yes? Walk in middle, no harm come to you. Hai, we move slow at first, then fast; you keep up, or you are carry. Hot sun, hot land; teyanain not stop, not afraid. You have water? Good. Drink little sips, but drink often, and tell when skin empty. We give more."

"Don't you need the water yourselves?" Alyea protested.

Evkit grinned, a sharp white flash of teeth. "We teyanain," he said. "We carry water for you, and we find water along way for us. We all have water, all for you; ask, ask, when empty, we give. No shame, you not teyanain." His dark stare moved to Deiq. "*You, though, you not need.*"

Deiq shook his head without speaking, all too aware of Alyea's intent stare. Trust Evkit to start out the trip by highlighting their differences. And by pointing out that the teyanain wouldn't be offering Deiq water, Evkit was, more subtly, putting him on notice: *You're not our ally, and we are not yours.* Sharing water served as an unspoken bond when going out into the deep desert lands they had to cross.

Just the first of many small repercussions from allowing Evkit to sense that Alyea had the lead role at the moment. There would be more; and Deiq would have to endure them, because any attempt now to put himself back into the dominant position would earn the hostility of the teyanain they traveled with.

He returned a blank stare to Evkit's mocking grin, refusing to give the bastard the satisfaction of a reaction. After a moment the teyanain lord turned away and yipped out orders. Nine teyanain guards took up places just outside arm's reach, three each to left, right, and rear. The three athain stood two full arm's lengths farther out, again to left, right, and rear; Evkit took the lead spot, some distance ahead of the party.

Servants laden with packs, panniers, and carry-poles settled into rougher lines behind; then everyone in the lead group stood perfectly still.

Alyea settled her pack on her shoulders again, fidgeting rather than truly needing to adjust the weight. Deiq stood still, knowing what was coming and unable to think of any way to warn her that wouldn't interrupt the moment. The best he could risk offering was a carefully directed murmur: "*Aqeyva.*"

She jerked a little, and then seemed to understand. Her breathing deepened and her nervous twitching calmed. Idisio seemed to have grasped it on his own; he was doing a creditable impression of a lightly-breathing statue.

Deiq felt pressure growing in his ears and swallowed, clenching his jaw to redistribute the tension. Knowing it for a useless attempt didn't stop the reflex. His ears popped, then filled again immediately. He worked his jaw three more times before managing to control his own instinctive twitching.

He found the small noises of the servants in the rear group tremendously distracting. They weren't trained to this discipline, and had no way to know what they were doing interrupted his focus a hundred times a breath. He blinked, slow and lazy, and forced himself to forget they existed for the moment.

Gods, he hated traveling with the teyanain. And he'd only ever walked in a group with one athain before, not a full *clee*; he began to suspect that he would have a shattering headache by the end of the day. He cut his eyes to the side to check Idisio, but the younger ha'ra'ha seemed perfectly calm, his eyes half-closed and hazed with almost-trance.

At last Deiq managed, knowing himself the last holdout, to master his breathing and ease his pulse into a matching rhythm with Alyea's. A moment later he felt the dizzying shift over into being *one breathing creature with many legs.*

It was a tremendous risk, a vulnerable moment no other living ha'ra'ha, and certainly no other First-Born, would ever have allowed—he discounted Idisio as too young and inexperienced to truly understand the implications of what was happening. But Deiq had no choice but to submit. To travel in a full clee there was no room for individualism. He had to let the athain lead the dance, or they wouldn't travel a step; and under the dual pressure of protecting Alyea and keeping his own standing among the teyanain, he couldn't back out.

Dimly, he heard the athain howl their travel-welcome; a long, yipping ululation that seemed to go on and on and on—but then things *blurred*, and Deiq realized that his body had begun moving.

There was no space left for fear, no space left for thought. The *clee* was moving, and nothing else mattered. The chill of the dawn moved into a scorching heat. Deiq adjusted his own temperature reflexively, soothed Alyea's body to a reasonable warmth, nudged Idisio's ragged breathing easy. He felt the athain working similarly with the warriors at each corner of the group, which now appeared to his altered perception as a diamond rather than a square arrangement.

The tight hold of the *clee* loosened in spots, now that they had everyone moving in synchrony. Deiq found himself able to think again, and prodded about to be sure the athain hadn't pried where they weren't welcome. But they'd politely—and honorably—restricted themselves to controlling the motor centers, and left memory and mind alone; he relaxed into their grip a little more, relieved.

If he'd wanted to, he could have taken sips from his waterskin. He could sense Alyea moving, with intense caution, to do just that at intervals.

On occasion the *clee* broke out into variations on the travel-song, meaning they'd found some obstacle ahead: possibly a snake, or a desert-scorpion nest. The athain never allowed that perception to filter into the guest-circle; whatever the issue, it disappeared under the hurricane-swirl of energies being channeled through Evkit and out ahead of them.

Deiq wondered what Alyea saw; wondered if she realized she was in the midst of an honor not one in a thousand desert lords ever received. A full *clee*! It was the stuff of legends, and Deiq had seen some of those legends in true life. Even the most exaggerated-sounding tales didn't miss the truth by much.

The teyanain, as they often boasted, were *different*.

And gods, was he glad of that; and, just as strongly, glad that he rarely needed to deal with them, let alone travel with them. But he was grateful that Alyea was experiencing this for herself. While similar to what he'd done for her during their initial walk to Scratha Fortress from the Qisani, this was an entirely different flavor of compulsion, and one she would only benefit from knowing about.

She ought to come out of the clee-trance tonight with the much better understanding of just how godsdamned dangerous the teyanain were, at least; and that would make the next few days significantly easier on Deiq. She'd start listening to him again, and once she did that he could arrange a parting of ways with the teyanain, one that wouldn't result in a disastrous, generations-long feud.

Gods. The word tumbled over itself in the haze, and he almost laughed. For all that he used the terms and cant freely as any human, he'd never believed in the human gods. He knew what humans had worshiped before the emergence of the ha'reye, and it bore no resemblance at all to the Three, or even the Four; although, amusingly, the latter was probably closer.

The travel-end howl rose, fractured, rose and fractured, and once more; shaking everyone out of the trance and into themselves again. Deiq dropped to his knees, unable to stop himself. His whole body vibrated in belated protest of the compulsion, and a reddish haze laced the corners of his vision. He shut his eyes and dropped his chin to his chest, wrapping his arms around himself, and fought to rein in his hoarse breathing.

Violence crested and faded inside him. Again. Again.

"Hai, ha'ra'ha," Evkit said, close at hand. "Drink."

Deiq blinked, testing vision; blinked again, feeling as though sand scraped inside his eyelids, then looked up into Evkit's dark, sober stare.

"You drink," Evkit repeated, shaking a waterskin in front of Deiq's face. Seeing that he had Deiq's attention, he upended it and squirted a brief stream into his own mouth, then offered it to Deiq again. "You drink."

Deiq very slowly unwrapped his arms from the fierce hug around his own ribs and closed the fingers of one hand around the waterskin. It scratched against his fingers; he could feel an inner bag sliding against the outer, roughhide covering.

He paused another moment to look at Evkit and raise an eyebrow to be sure. The teyanain lord nodded and said, "You do well, ha'ra'ha. Desert truce."

Deiq's hand tightened reflexively around the skin, and he took a long drink to hide the slight convulsion of relief. The water hit the back of his dry throat like a blessing from the gods he'd just been thinking he didn't believe in. He swallowed and coughed, took another drink, then handed back the waterskin with a deep nod of thanks.

Evkit returned the nod and moved on, squatting to offer water to Alyea. On her hands and knees, she looked something like an exhausted asp-jacau; her head hung, her breathing came in harsh pants. Deiq let them be. Evkit had already named Alyea *guest,* he wouldn't hurt her at this point.

He looked for Idisio, expecting to see the younger ha'ra'ha in similar if not greater distress; but Idisio sat calmly cross-legged on the sand, eyes clear and bright, sipping from his own waterskin and watching Evkit tend to Alyea.

Idisio glanced up at Deiq, as though sensing the attention, and his mouth quirked a little. Late afternoon sun caught against his light brown hair, raising glimmering arrays of color. His skin, unlike Alyea's, hardly showed any darkening from the day's journey. Another day's travel under the hot sun and Alyea could begin passing for a full southerner; Idisio, as ha'ra'ha, could stand naked under a desert noon heat for days and not darken significantly unless he wanted to. Just one more detail Deiq needed to explain. He put it aside for later, hoping he'd remember.

But the younger ha'ra'ha didn't even seem *tired* from the long march; that part, Deiq didn't understand at all.

"It's just an aqeyva trance," Idisio said, accurately reading Deiq's expression. "I've been practicing those a lot lately. It's not so hard to do it while moving."

Deiq blinked, his pride stinging at being outdone so easily by a lesser ha'ra'ha; and found himself wondering if, after all, a hundred years with the Qisani ha'reye was such a high price to pay for walking away from this arrangement.

He'd never thought of himself as *old* before, and he didn't like it one bit.

Chapter Fourteen

After sunset, the desert, moonless, became *black*; and cold. The teyanain servants had each produced a number of thick fire-coals from their packs, then gathered a surprising amount of deadwood from the nearby brush. The resulting blaze largely chased away both the shadows and the chill air, and the circle of *shalls* set up around the campfire seemed to trap the heat.

Alyea sat cross-legged on a mat, a heavy shawl wrapped around her torso, socks over a layer of salve on her feet. She kept her hands wrapped around a hot cup of thopuh, and shivered from nerves as much as from residual cold.

"That was slow?" she said, and heard it come out more caustic than intended. Apologizing would do no good, not in this company. She tilted her chin instead and directed a flinty stare at Evkit.

He grinned, his light shirt and breeches serving another reminder to Alyea that she wasn't nearly his match. She thought, sourly, that he didn't even seem tired from the day's long march. If anything, he seemed refreshed, as though the impossibly long trek had somehow given him energy, not wiped it out.

He laughed, not in the least offended by her snappishness, and said, "But that was slow, Lord Alyea. We go much faster tomorrow."

She stared at him in open disbelief. Beside her, Deiq made a soft noise, an almost-chuckle.

"My feet are *raw*," Alyea protested.

"Salve help," Evkit said, still grinning. "And you desert lord now. You heal fast. Tomorrow, you be fine. And then you have—" He lifted one foot out, waggled it briefly. "You have hard skin."

"Callus," Deiq murmured.

"Yes. Callus. So you not hurt so bad tomorrow night."

Alyea barely stopped herself from saying *That's not possible*. Apparently she wasn't beyond being shocked by anything these people said or did, after all. She glanced down at her one visible foot—cross-legged, the other was tucked up under the opposite thigh—and wiggled her toes thoughtfully. It didn't feel quite as raw as it had at the end of the day's march; still, she wasn't inclined to peel off the covering to see the current state of the damaged flesh.

Deiq said nothing, his gaze on the fire-pit. Shadow seemed to gather under his eyes and in the hollows of his ears and neck, moving just slightly off the rhythm of the flame-cast shadows around them.

Alyea blinked and shook her head to dispel the illusion. From the other side of the fire-pit, Evkit's grin widened.

"How far did we travel today?" she asked abruptly.

"No more than Qisani," Evkit answered.

Alyea frowned, and Deiq clarified, not looking away from the fire: "Due west from Scratha Fortress, about fifty miles."

"Tomorrow we go fast," Evkit said, and stood. "Tomorrow we go double."

"*Double?*" Alyea said involuntarily. Deiq shut his eyes, a muscle twitching in his cheek.

"Good sleep," Evkit said, and turned away. Alyea watched him climb into his *shall*, and found herself yawning.

"Gods," she murmured, setting the cup of tea down on the mat in front of her. Almost immediately, a servant snagged it up and away. Another servant stepped close, as though to help her to her feet.

Deiq, glancing up, flicked a hand in peremptory dismissal. The waiting servant bowed and moved away without protest, and Deiq went back to watching the dancing flames.

One by one, everyone else retired for the evening. Deiq and Alyea sat alone by the fire, save for one servant and the fire-tender. Alyea sat quietly, staring into the fire, and let the tension of the day relax from her muscles.

At last, feeling the pressure of being watched, she looked to her right and found Deiq looking at her, his eyes glinting with tiny reflected flames. It gave him an uncannily demonic aspect, and she repressed a shiver. His mouth twisted into his usual sardonic smile; she knew he'd been reading her thoughts again.

She said, low-voiced but sharp, "Stop that!"

"Wasn't," he said economically. "Your face said it. I still scare you."

"Do you blame me?" she retorted.

His gaze flickered to the surrounding tents, to the fire-tender, the now-drowsing servant, and back to her.

"No," he said, one eyebrow tilting, and grinned with more real humor. "But *I'm* not what you ought to be scared of right now." Again his gaze made the rounds of the camp.

She bit her tongue, well aware that the quiet only made voices carry more clearly, and thought through her reply before speaking.

"Of all the things that worry me just now," she said, "you're not nearly at the top of the list."

"I won't hurt you," he said, his stare turning oddly intense; she had the feeling that he was saying more than she really understood at the moment. Then he shook his head, the dry smile returning, and the shivery heat faded from his gaze.

"I know," she answered, not at all sure she believed her own words—or his.

An Explanation Of Commerce

(excerpt)

We come at last to the matter of commerce, that which remains within the southlands and that which moves beyond the borders to cross kingdom soil. As might be expected, the supplying of a large, well-populated stone fortress set in the midst of wasteland is a tremendous endeavor, and over the years an intricate web of agreements and alliances has formed between the major and minor Families to ease the process.

Deiq of Stass has actually been a severely disruptive influence on that network. His Farms, improbably, flourish, turning miles of wasteland into terraced and raised gardens of astounding fecundity. His farmers form a strange collective, working, regardless of gender, to their capacities and strengths, and receiving shares of the profits from their labors. There are, for example, designated merchants, who handle the selling of the produce; cooks, who turn the produce into various jams, jellies, pickles, and other long-store items; field hands, who labor to coax the most from their green charges.

Strangest of all, if I understand correctly, each of these is seen as equal and paid accordingly. A merchant shares the profit at the same rate as that of the field hand, who may have no understanding of money but is skilled at picking out the healthiest seedlings and bringing them to top yield, which the merchant is hopeless to achieve.

The Farms are independent of any other political entity or Family; they do not owe their first crop to Sessin, for example. They sell equally to all, and hold the same price regardless of status or volume. Only geographical distance affects the cost, such that in local areas and the southern ports of Agyaer, Stass, Port Sand, and Terhe the prices are far lower than when the goods arrive at your kingdom ports of Bright Bay and Sandlaen, and higher yet if sent to the independent city of Kismo in the north. The Farms only concern themselves with sale to those primary ports; the Stone Islands seem to hold no interest to their trading goals, and their merchants rarely if ever go there.

The Farms only exist along the eastern coast, and there are four of them to my current, certain knowledge. Another is rumored to exist high in the mountains between Agyaer and Terhe Ports. What items of interest could possibly grow in so inhospitable a territory is beyond my comprehension, so the rumor is most likely just that: an amusing fiction.

The prior arrangement, which still exists along the western coast south of the Horn, involved Families working very hard to create and protect the secret of an essential crop or staple item. F'Heing, for example, in the fertile crescent of land protected by the Jagged Mountains, has established rice farms, wheat fields, bean crops, and even enormous, exotically colored flowers, seedlings of which are routinely shipped north and sell for outrageous prices. Thrifty farmers, I believe, save the seeds from the matured seedlings and try desperately to coax them into life the following season, with sharply limited success.

The Jagged Mountains, incidentally, contain the secret home of the famed "F'Heing Ridge Mountain Coffee", which no doubt you have heard of and perhaps even tasted. This variant of the bronze-leaved high mountain coffee bush produces a superior bean which, when roasted under the (also secret) F'Heing-developed process, is sought after by coffee experts and gourmets throughout your kingdom and the southlands.

That F'Heing is also noted for some of the more troubling drugs circulating throughout our shared world is not surprising, especially after the advent of the east coast Farms cut heavily into some of their staple sales. If, in your drive to cut these drugs from your kingdom, you offend F'Heing Family, you run the very real risk of F'Heing ships refusing to bring rice, grain, and beans to Bright Bay. This may sound minor, especially with the aforementioned Farms, as well as Arason, serving as prime sources for wheat, corn, and beans, but I suggest checking with your stores-master and merchant guilds on the ratios of who supplies what.

In my understanding, Arason sells most of its produce north of the line of the Great Forest, and very little volume trickles down the long road to Bright Bay. Likewise, the southland Farms pass out their produce mainly south of the Horn, with little of it reaching Bright Bay and Sandlaen Port. I am told that the farms local to Bright Bay barely produce enough, some years, to feed a hundred people besides themselves; the soil has been overworked and is becoming, frankly, exhausted. The farmers of the F'Heing enclave, meanwhile, can load their abundant produce onto a fast ship and be at your docks within two days of harvest.

A satisfactory alliance with F'Heing Family, then, is critical to the survival of your giant city.

A common saying in the southlands may be germane here: Nothing is ever simple. So it is with politics; so it is with trade. Remember that, and perhaps you will be the first northlands king in some time to hand down the throne to a legitimate child of your line.

From the collection
Letters to a Northern King of Merit
penned by Lord Cafad Scratha during the reign of King Oruen

Chapter Fifteen

Deiq sat outside the *shall* the teyanain had provided for Alyea, disinclined to crowd into the small space with her; all too aware that the sleepy nodding of the night-servant and the blank stare of the fire-tender were shams intended to make outsiders careless.

Idisio, still bound to human habits, had gone to sleep. Deiq, older and more rooted in his other heritage, rarely bothered. The deep sleep at Scratha Fortress had been the most vulnerability he'd allowed himself in years, and he'd only risked it because of the presence of a full ha'rethe—which was a mixed blessing. While ha'reye protected their own, they also had a tendency to consider those they protected to literally be theirs—as a human might own a cow.

Deiq had been careful to give Scratha ha'rethe no reason to breach courtesy and pry through his mind while he slept. Ha'reye were, by nature, essentially lazy; intruding into even a ha'ra'hain mind took more attention than they cared to spare for a trivial curiosity or amusement. Lately Deiq had been more grateful for that than he cared to admit.

He sat on neutral land now, a place unclaimed by any ha'ra'ha or ha'rethe. Here it was safer to brood over things he didn't want to share. Not completely safe; not with three athain nearby. But the day's labor had been a drain on even them, and he could feel them resting in deep, restorative trance-sleeps. Lord Evkit's presence burred against Deiq's perceptions as the teyanin lord slowly dispersed the gathered energies he'd been channeling all day and settled to sleep.

At last, the entire camp save Deiq, the fire-tender, and the night-servant were in true resting mode. Only then was it finally safe to *think*, for the first time in days. To calculate, based on the direction they'd taken, the speed Evkit had announced, and the games the teyanain liked to play, where they were headed. Out of ten different routes Evkit might have chosen across the deep desert, Deiq suspected he knew where they'd be at the end of tomorrow's march.

Evkit knew about the ruins.

Deiq stared into the dark, remembering translucent white draperies and apricot walls, grand hallways and seductive scents; remembering a black glare filled with hatred and the pride that shattered an entire city.

He knew what the ha'reye would say, what they *had* said, at the time: *Those who choose not to serve are not worthy of our protection.*

But those you don't protect aren't going to want to serve, he thought; and wished he'd understood that concept much, much sooner.

Chapter Sixteen

The soles of Alyea's feet were, as promised, whole and unmarked by the time Deiq shook her awake in the grey pre-morning. Her feet had even regained their former calluses, which last night had been worn away to raw skin. She ran her hands over the rough flesh, shaking her head slowly in disbelief; looked up to find Deiq watching her with a strange smile on his dark face.

He made no comment, however, just handed her a cup of thopuh and a tibi of morning-rice, which differed from the evening meal only by having bits of cooked dove egg scattered across the top and the addition of desert-sage to the flavorings.

As she ate, the teyanain broke down the *shalls* and methodically wiped away all traces of their presence. Even the fire pit was well-buried by the time she finished eating.

Knowing what to expect this time made falling into the walking-trance easier, although it laid an uneasy shiver along her spine that walking from the Qisani to Scratha Fortress with Deiq hadn't provoked. Instead of the glorious wonder of seeing everything at once, she felt as though the athain had wrapped her up in a protective cocoon and were carrying her along on a wave of nearly inaudible chanting.

With her vision blurred, she had no real notion of her surroundings, which also disturbed her; but Deiq made no protest, and according to her understanding of the teyanain, they were bound to treat her safety as paramount while she was their guest.

Heat flared and swirled around her, and a growing heat seared across the bottoms of her feet, racing up her legs, then as swiftly dispersing. She wondered what her feet would look like tonight; it seemed impossible that they could be unharmed after walking a hundred miles in less than twelve hours. But to heal overnight from the state her feet had been in was also impossible. She set worry aside and tried to relax into the flow of the day's travel.

At last the warbling howl of the travel-ending chant broke the haze, and she staggered a step, then another; felt Deiq's hand close around her arm, swinging her to stand against him. She grabbed him for support and leaned into his warmth for a few breaths. When her balance settled, she let go and stepped back, blinking hard. At least she hadn't dropped to her knees this time. Perhaps next time she wouldn't even stumble.

She turned to look at their new surroundings, and forgot everything else for a long, stunned moment.

Great arches lofted overhead in staggered ranks, segments of interior walls left bizarrely exposed by the almost complete destruction of the outer ones. Bright red and white stripes endured, somewhat faded now, on the tops of each archway, and the pillars that still stood were as broad around as massive oaks. Intricate carvings wound up each cracked pillar from ground to archway topping: scripts in a language she'd never seen intermingled with detailed images of flowers, fountains, and birds.

The ground underfoot, sandy, dusty, and damaged, still showed a few tiles of what had once been a magnificently designed floor. A cracked black granite orb lay some distance away, its polish dulled by centuries of sandstorms. Fragments of a chunky white granite pedestal were scattered like stone petals around the dark globe.

Alyea took in a deep breath of hot, dry air, inhaling the smell of neglect and abandonment; of death and decay. No birds sang here; not even a lizard scurried through the lengthening evening shadows. And nothing grew. *Nothing.* Not so much as the deceptively dead-looking sticks of plants waiting for the next rain. It seemed as though nothing ever grew here, and no rain ever fell.

Her throat burned with the lack of moisture in the air. She took a cautious sip of water, looking at her companions. The teyanain guards had fanned out, prowling through the ruins around them, clearly checking for danger in this lifeless place; the athain stood still, regarding their surroundings with weary blankness. Evkit studied the destruction with a faint smile that sent unexpected shivers up Alyea's back; and Deiq squinted, tight-lipped, with an expression of utter loathing that broadened her nervous shiver into a wide ribbon of worry.

Idisio stood quietly, eyes closed, head cocked a little as though listening.

"We camp here tonight," Evkit said, bizarrely cheerful.

Deiq cast him a dark glare. "Of course we are," he growled. "Of course you *would.*" He turned and stalked away before anyone could answer.

Evkit's smile widened. He nodded as though pleased with himself and made a sweeping gesture that managed to include Idisio and Alyea.

"Come," he said. "I show you, while daylight lasts. Then we eat."

Alyea blinked, caught against the urge to go after Deiq, and opened her mouth to refuse. Just then, Idisio opened his eyes; something in his expression stopped her words cold in her throat.

"I'll go with him," he said quietly, not quite looking at her. "By your grace, lord Evkit." With as little ceremony as Deiq had shown, he turned and trotted after the older ha'ra'ha.

Evkit seemed unoffended and unsurprised. He bowed gravely to Alyea and repeated, "You come. I show you."

Seeing no politic alternative, and trusting that Deiq wouldn't have walked away if she'd been in real danger from Lord Evkit, she shrugged assent. As she followed the little teyanin lord into the ruins, she realized that her feet and legs, as promised, felt no more sore than they would have after a brisk walk from her palace apartment to the throne room.

"This place," Evkit said, apparently not in the least disconcerted by having to look up at her as he spoke, "was once as Bright Bay. Central. King-city, yes? Life, trade, large." He gestured around broadly.

"What happened?"

"Humans said *no* to ha'reye."

Alyea stopped short, unable to believe that bald statement, and stared down at the teyanin lord, horror-struck. *"What?"*

Evkit hopped lithely atop a crumbled section of wall and stood eye-to-eye with her. "Ha'rethe dying. Ha'rethe say, give me child, last child, to rule over city after ha'rethe death. Lords of city choose the one to go to ha'rethe; the chosen one refuses."

He turned half-away from Alyea, his dark gaze sober as he looked around the ruins. A shiver ran down Alyea's spine: would her child one day rule over the Qisani? And if so, would she ever know?

Evkit went on, "No time left for another choice. The chosen already sworn, ceremony already begin. But she refuse, and she do worse: she try attack ha'rethe when it come for her."

The silence hung, deepening like the purple twilight descending over the ruins. Alyea tried to imagine having the presence of mind to do such a thing; she remembered being utterly bewildered and overwhelmed. Such a thing almost had to be planned in advance. She looked around at the ruins and swallowed hard.

"This first true human city," Evkit said softly. She could barely see him now. "And first to fall. Ha'reye not friends, Lord Alyea. Never friends. And ha'ra'hain not allies."

"Was this . . . the Split?" Alyea asked. Her dry throat snagged on the words; she took a sip of water and repeated the question more clearly.

"Part of," Evkit agreed. "The Split not one thing, not one event. It many years of many problems, some human stupid, some ha'reye stupid. All disaster in the end."

"Deiq knows this place," she said suddenly, unsure how she knew, but certain all the same that the dark loathing in his stare spoke of personal memories.

"Yes," Evkit said.

Implication shuddered through her; she couldn't breathe for a moment. "Then he's . . . *old.*" Her mind refused to tally how many years ago the Split had been: too large a number for ready translation into years of age.

Evkit let out a little yip of amused surprise. "You not know that already?"

"I thought . . . maybe a hundred years."

Again, a muffled yip.

She said, feeling the need to defend herself, "He said Lord Eredion was his father. And Eredion can't be *that* old!"

Dead silence. "Eredion not Deiq father," Evkit said eventually. "Deiq alive long before Eredion born. He lie to you, Lord Alyea. Big, big lie."

"Why would he lie to me about that?" she demanded, a familiar simmering resentment climbing her spine.

A huffing yip; the teyanain chuckle. "He ha'ra'ha," Evkit said. "They breathe, they lie. All same. You no trust anything a ha'ra'ha say, not ever. You count your fingers after dealing with one, and touch them to be sure it not illusion they still attached."

Alyea let out a harsh chuckle of her own. Deiq had said the same thing about dealing with Lord Evkit. She almost asked *And what lies are you telling?*; finally kept her mouth shut, aware that Evkit's amicability could change to blinding rage at any moment.

"Dinner," Evkit said succinctly. Alyea heard him climbing down from his perch.

She turned, only then realizing that the fast-arriving desert night left her blind. The only light came from the stars, and the air had acquired a distinctly dangerous chill.

"I can't—Lord Evkit?"

Silence.

She stood still, sudden terror swamping her; her breath hitched in her throat once, twice, before she controlled it. "Lord Evkit? I can't see."

"I know," Deiq said from behind her; she yelped, spinning to face him, and lost her footing on a loose rock. His hands grasped her upper arms, holding her steady and keeping her upright. A fierce warmth burned through her, banishing the chill.

"He just *abandoned* me," she blurted, fear melting into a blurry anger.

"No," Deiq said. "He knew I was here." His hands loosened, but didn't fall away; she welcomed the contact as her only point of reference in the blackness.

"This isn't a game!" she snapped, glaring at the vague silhouette of his head.

He made a soft, amused noise and turned her, moving to stand shoulder to shoulder with her.

"Look up," he directed.

Unwillingly, she tilted her head to stare at the overarching spray of stars, picking out constellations almost reflexively. The Fountain had always been her favorite, because of the stories associated with it: the many ways the southern kings battled the demons to keep their water flowing. The tales were filled with wit and trickery, treachery and danger, and had set in her mind indelible images of great stone cities with striped archways—

She blinked, hard, and lowered her gaze to stare into the darkness around her again.

"Many stories come from this place," Deiq said. "Some of them even resemble the truth."

"Did you hear Evkit telling me the story of this place?"

"Yes." His tone, mordantly amused, said *Of course.*

"Is that true?"

"More or less."

"And you were—"

"Leave that for another time. Let's go get some dinner," he suggested.

She opened her mouth to protest, to demand the rest of the story; then found herself at a loss for words and suddenly aware that she *was* hungry.

Deiq's grip on her upper arm tightened. He let out a small sigh, then turned her around and steered her through the maze of broken stonework to the small teyanain campsite.

Chapter Seventeen

Teyanain trail food never sat right in Deiq's stomach; this time, the offering was stale flatbread soaked in boiled goat milk and a side of fermented black beans. Alyea's nose wrinkled, but she had the sense not to protest or to hesitate about eating; Idisio showed no discomfort over the smell or appearance. Deiq gagged down a few bites, then handed the rest off to Idisio without comment.

The smell of the camp, from the food to the rank sweat of a day's hard travel, suddenly felt like a thick slop in his nostrils. He stood and walked out into the dark beyond the firelight. Once far enough away that he could breathe again, he put his back to one of the few remaining upright pillars and studied the stars, a vast, irritated restlessness stirring in his muscles. He wanted to move, but didn't dare go too far from Alyea; and right now, walking off his frustration would take him miles from camp in short order.

Some time later, he felt Idisio approaching. Not inclined to talk, he allowed himself a small grunt of acknowledgment.

"Everyone's settled," Idisio said quietly, and perched on a chunk of overturned column.

"Good for them," Deiq said, glaring out into the dark, and wished Idisio had stayed in camp; he wasn't in the mood for inanely pointless statements.

Idisio scuffed a foot lightly across the litter of stone chips on the ground. "I've never been able to see so well on a moonless night before," he said. "It's strange."

Not as stupid a comment; worth answering, at least. "You're growing into your heritage," Deiq said. "Over the next twenty or thirty years, you'll see more changes." He tilted his head and looked up at the constellations overhead, thinking about his intention of teaching Idisio the old stories; but surrounded by the ghosts of his failures, he couldn't bring himself to care enough.

"How come I thought I was human all my life?"

"Because that's how you were raised," Deiq said, impatience returning. "If you'd been raised by a family of ducks you'd have thought yourself a mallard."

"Really?" The startlement in Idisio's voice was a sharp reminder of his youth and inexperience.

"No," Deiq said heavily. "It's an allegory." He stalked a few paces away to relieve his frustration; humans didn't understand such things, and Idisio had been raised with human blinders. Deiq didn't have the patience at the moment to strip them away.

"Don't you mean metaphor?" Idisio said from behind him, not moving to follow. Deiq stopped and turned around slowly, annoyance melting into a mild interest.

"No," he said. "There's an old tale I'm referring to. Allegory."

Idisio hopped off his crumbling seat and came over to stand beside Deiq. "Show me the well?"

Deiq blinked, taken aback. "The well?"

"From the story I told you."

"I told you that story wasn't any good. It's distorted."

"But any big city needs wells," Idisio pointed out. "And ha'reye like water. And you told Alyea that Evkit's story was reasonably accurate. So whatever happened, was near a well."

Deiq stared at the younger ha'ra'ha's night-blurred features, astounded at the sharp reasoning; perhaps Idisio didn't suffer from human blinders quite as much as Deiq had thought. And he shouldn't have been able to eavesdrop without alerting Deiq.

He settled for saying, "I didn't know you were nearby, hearing all that."

"I'm good at sneaking around," Idisio said with some pride.

"Apparently so." Deiq let out a long breath, debating whether to warn the younger of how rude he'd been, and how dangerous stalking an adult ha'ra'ha was; decided Idisio already knew, and didn't care. The boy was brash and arrogant, just like Deiq himself at that age.

I'm not old, damn it. I'm not! He's just too damned young, that's all.

Deiq pushed aside that line of thought and turned to stare over the ruins, gathering his bearings.

"All right. This way."

Sunlight poured through enormous stone arches painted with vivid red and white stripes. The floor beneath was thick whitestone tile, cool under bare feet even on the hottest day of the year. Walls were sparse, more dividing sections than true barriers; the staggered archways led from the lush gardens to the luxurious throne room with little visual interference.

Fine draperies of handwoven silk, laced with threads of silver and gold, hung between the pillars in the throne room, providing some privacy but allowing the inter-

mittent wind to wander through unchecked. Sunlight seemed to bounce from every surface; the white underfoot, the drapery threads, the massive, gem-bedecked throne on which the kaen sat, draped in shimmering cloth and watching Deiq's slow approach.

Sunlight failed to light the kaen's face, which was shadowed and harsh, pitted from a childhood bout of sun-pox. His deep-set black eyes glared unforgivingly.

"Ha'inn," the kaen said, but the word was a curse, not an honor. "Come for my other daughter? Or perhaps for my only son?"

Deiq blinked away from sun-flooded memory into midnight darkness, and realized he'd gripped the low wall in front of him so hard the stone was beginning to crumble under his fingers. He let go gingerly; a few small fragments skittered to the ground with a hissing rattle.

"This was the well," he said aloud, smoothing his palm gently over the wall in silent apology to the innocent stone. "The central well of the city. This is where the seers and wise men and priests came to commune with the gods . . . and with the ha'reye."

"Plural?" Idisio said beside him.

Deiq decided he'd *definitely* have to stop thinking of the younger ha'ra'ha as ignorant. "There was only one here," he said, "but back then, there were so many more of them . . . speaking to one might as well have been speaking to all. It was . . . like a net. Tug on one, the rest feel it. Now there's too much space between. . . ."

He stopped, pursing his lips; none of this was news to the teyanain, but still, no point risking the conversation moving into areas they might not know about. He wasn't stupid enough to think he'd sense one listening nearby; today's teyanain had an uncanny ability to hide from *other*-vision when they wanted to.

"So what really happened?" Idisio asked, trailing his own fingers across the well-wall surface.

"I was an idiot," Deiq said, and sighed. "I didn't see it that way at the time, but I made a bad mistake, and upset the kaen; and he passed that anger on to his son. It didn't help that the son turned out sterile. . . ."

In the back of his mind, he remembered the young kaen's rage: *Lift your curse!* he'd demanded. Deiq had shaken his head, over and over, trying to explain the condition had nothing to do with their mutual antagonism, and couldn't be so simply cured. Not surprisingly, the young man hadn't believed him. . . .

"He thought I'd done something to stop him from fathering children," Deiq said after the memories subsided enough to allow him speech again. "He swore he'd have his revenge on me. I tried to tell him it wasn't my doing. He wouldn't listen."

Although he could have done a better job of explaining, in retrospect: arrogant, temperamental, and powerful, flushed with youth and surety, Deiq had seen humans with only a fraction less contempt than his parent ha'rethe. He'd made mistake after mistake and seen it all as human idiocy rather than his own rashness.

"He threatened to refuse the annual gifting if I would not give him back the ability to father a child," Deiq said, his voice thickening in his throat. "I told him the death of his city would be on his own head, and I left."

"Left the room?" Idisio's tone said he knew better.

"The area. I didn't come back for two hundred years, and by that time the city was long since destroyed, and the land barren."

Heavy silence hung around them for a long time. At last Idisio said, shakily, "You knew that would happen?"

"Yes. I warned him, and he said I was lying to him, as ha'ra'hain always lie. I got angry, so I walked out . . . and kept going."

It had been so much more complicated than that, of course. But explaining years of built-up tension in a midnight discussion to a younger ha'ra'ha who had no idea how things had been back then wasn't realistic. Maybe as they traveled, he'd be able to tell bits and pieces of the painful story, and make Idisio understand; but Deiq felt he had reached the limit of what he could talk about at the moment.

"You could have stopped it," Idisio said, his tone filled with accusation.

Deiq stood silent, looking back through memory at the proud folk he'd been dealing with; at the prickly pride he himself had nursed at the time; at the many, many misunderstandings that had lain among the humans, the ha'reye, and the half-breeds—most of which still stood to this day.

"Maybe," he said at last. "I don't really know."

"But you didn't even *care*, did you?"

Deiq blinked, rage rising fast and hard; he gripped the wall again. It crumbled sharply under his fingers, and he let the pebbly bits fall, rattling, to the ground. Some fell into the well itself, and landed not far down; the sands of a thousand years clogged the funnel.

Idisio backed up several hasty steps, and Deiq felt the younger's fear rising as sharply as his own anger. A red haze began to haunt the edges of his vision.

"Go back to camp, Idisio," Deiq said through his teeth. "*Slowly.*"

Idisio took a startled, bounding step, then froze, breathless, as Deiq whipped around.

"Slowly, Idisio," Deiq breathed. The pulse in his temples overcame all sound, all sense; and the red haze was closing in. "*Slowly.*"

Idisio edged a cautious step further away, another, and another. Deiq forced himself to turn around and stare into the blackness of what had once been a massive well. He fixed his thoughts on what the buckets had looked like: larger than a man, they had been hauled up throughout the day by an ingenious winch system only the Aerthraim understood today.

At last Idisio and his jagged, provocative fear moved out of range, and Deiq let out a shaky breath; desperately hoping none of the teyanain had been around to see *that*, and wishing, not for the first time in his life, that he could find solace in prayer.

Chapter Eighteen

As the grey dawn warmed into a rich spray of orange and red across the horizon, Alyea realized the teyanain weren't assembling into a traveling configuration. Instead, they seemed to be packing up in a much more leisurely fashion than usual, and the athain sat in a triangle, heads bowed, chanting under their breath. Watching them, Alyea was irresistibly reminded of musicians practicing before a performance.

She shot Deiq a worried look. He lifted a shoulder, but the lines around his eyes were tight, and he said little as they waited. At last, everything loaded and packed away, Lord Evkit waved to them.

"Follow," he said, grinning. "We go."

Alyea cast a quick glance at the sun, already nearly free of the horizon and well on its way to heating up the desert around them. She said, tentatively, "Are we traveling far today, Lord Evkit?"

"Very far," he said, his grin settling into smug lines. Deiq gave a short bark of astonishment.

"That's not *possible*," he said, but Evkit cut him off:

"No, ha'inn, you no spoil surprise," Evkit snapped, pointing a stern finger.

Deiq shook his head, a dark frown wrinkling his face, but said nothing. Evkit waved again, beckoning them forward; Deiq nodded curtly to Alyea's dubious glance. She bit back questions, but his evident startlement had laid a cold chill of fear down her spine that didn't dissipate as they began walking.

They filed through the ruins at the head of a tidy column of teyanain guards, athain, and packbearers. Idisio's usual, brightly curious gaze seemed dimmed this morning, and he stared more ahead or at his feet than around at their surroundings; he refused to look directly at Deiq.

Deciding to stay out of whatever was going on between those two, Alyea looked around as they walked. The great archways they'd camped among fell behind them, and the walls became thicker and less damaged; almost as though the palace had been the center of whatever disaster struck this place.

At last they reached a building that seemed nearly whole: pale walls with wide, rounded openings curved about one massive central chamber, the roof pierced by nine symmetrical, almond-shaped openings, two of which had crumbled together into one irregular, gaping hole.

Standing just outside one of the archways, Alyea could see that the floor had once been richly laid with an intricate mosaic of blue, red, black and white tiles. Many of the tiles had been pried free of their settings, and the few remaining pieces only hinted at the overall design.

"Blue tiles," Evkit said, following Alyea's glance to the floor, "have ground in sacred stone, blessing-stone, what northerns call lapis. White is finest marble ground in with finest god-milk stone, what you call chalcedony. Red had rubies, black had jet, sometimes even black sapphire. All sacred, all great value. Most go with refugees fleeing city. Some go to looters, but not many."

He bared small teeth in a humorless grin.

"Teyanain guard this city. This *ours*. We not like looters." He looked at Deiq, as though expecting a challenge to his ownership claim; the ha'ra'ha just stared back, expressionless. Evkit shrugged, his grin fading into a faintly disappointed scowl, and returned his attention to Alyea. "This was temple of city, the place for all to worship. Old gods, these. Before Three, before Four. Strong gods." His scowl turned to a smirk again. "Not nice gods. Liked sacrifices."

"Human?" Alyea said, one eye on Deiq, whose expression was rapidly darkening.

"Sometimes," Evkit said. "Not always death, though. Sometimes just—"

"Lord Evkit," Deiq said flatly. "Are you going to talk us to tears, or are we moving on at some point?"

Evkit grinned, as smug as Alyea had ever seen him. "Of course we go," he said, and motioned to the athain.

The three athain knelt, each before a different archway, murmuring what sounded like prayers. Then they stood, one by one, and walked directly into the temple. Reaching the center of the room, each athain simply vanished, between one step and the next; Alyea let out a startled yelp.

Idisio and Deiq had identical grim expressions, but showed no surprise.

"I go now," Evkit said. "See, you safe. You come next, ha'ra'ha—" he nodded to Deiq. "Then you, younger, and then the Lord Alyea. Order of honor, yes? Then the rest come through. Move quickly, door not open for long."

Deiq scowled in black outrage for just a moment; then shook his head and went back to looking grim.

Evkit grinned and strutted out into the center of the room, vanishing as had the athain.

Deiq drew in a deep breath and glanced around at the waiting teyanain. He put a hand on Alyea's shoulder for just a moment, then walked forward and disappeared. Idisio made a faint, choked sound, and his gaze darted around as though he might try to run; then his back stiffened and he marched forward, tight-lipped.

The remaining teyanain all took one tiny step forward; the message was clear. Alyea fiercely blocked out fear and walked into the ancient temple before thoughts of how insane this was could stop her.

She passed from chill to cold and back into a damp heat in less than a breath; took a sideways step, not quite a stagger. Someone caught her arm and pulled her aside. Something about the warmth and size of the hand told her it was Deiq; she let him direct her without protest.

Blinking eyes clear of a strange haze, she looked around. Stone walls mottled with grey-black patterns rose into a dome overhead. The floor felt gritty, and glancing down, she saw it was covered with a light scattering of sand, seeming more as though it had been tracked in than spread deliberately.

The air felt odd: overpoweringly humid after the desiccated ruins, and hard to breathe. Idisio stood, ashen-faced, not far away. Deiq stood behind her, his hands on her shoulders and his warmth unpleasantly intense against her back.

Lord Evkit and a handful of other teyanain stood before them, and the look in the teyanain lord's eyes drenched Alyea in sudden cold sweat. She felt Deiq's hands tighten on her shoulders, a low growl building in his throat.

"Welcome, Lord Alyea," Evkit said, bowing and flourishing out one hand. As he straightened, Alyea bit back a gasp at the transformation. All pleasantness had disappeared: now Evkit's eyes held a murderous glare. Hatred changed his entire face from amiably wrinkled to demonically furrowed.

Deiq's grip moved to just above her elbows. He almost lifted her out of the way, the growl emerging, then started forward. Before he completed the first stride, the air filled with a white dust. Alyea felt hands latch onto her from behind and draw her back, clear of the forming cloud.

With a choking cough, Idisio staggered and collapsed. Deiq let out an ear-bruising bellow and flung himself at Evkit, hands reaching for the teyanin lord's throat. Alyea delivered a neat back-kick that should have connected with a knee—or, given typical teyanin stature, something even more sensitive—and found herself kicking empty air instead. Off-balance, she would have fallen but for the firm grip of teyanain seemingly all around her now. Glancing reflexively towards Deiq, she stopped struggling, too fascinated by what was happening to pay attention to freeing herself.

Deiq fought with his eyes shut, lashing out with hands, feet, and a speed and viciousness that shocked her. Evkit had withdrawn well out of range, and the teyanain fighters surrounding the ha'ra'ha grinned as they danced clear by mere hairs. They seemed to regard this as nothing but a game, an elaborate dance with bizarre rules.

At last one of Deiq's blows connected solidly, and the unlucky teyanain tumbled across the room to crash into a wall that must have been over ten feet away. Expressions changed; knives appeared. The teyanain clearly weren't inclined to play any longer.

"*Deiq!*" Alyea screamed, fighting against her captor's grip again. "*Knives!*"

"He already knows that," a calm voice observed in her ear.

She twisted and stared back at the teyanain behind her. He regarded her dispassionately, then returned his attention to the embattled ha'ra'ha.

Deiq had changed his fighting style; had been changing it, she realized, before she even screamed the warning. Now he was defending, as the teyanain pressed in even closer. In what seemed moments, a thin line of blood appeared on his cheek as a long knife scored; as though that had been a signal, the teyanain all backed away swiftly. A heartbeat later, Deiq simply collapsed, his knees giving way as though the tendons had been slashed.

Alyea screamed again, unable to help herself. In the back of her mind, she'd believed Deiq could win free and get them all out of this disaster.

The teyanain swiftly clustered around the tall ha'ra'ha, lifting and carrying him from the room. Another group ferried Idisio's limp form away. Both Deiq and Idisio appeared to be breathing, but unconscious; so murder wasn't, directly, the intent.

As soon as the two ha'ra'hain had been taken from sight, her captors released their grips, and Lord Evkit moved to stand in front of her. His expression displayed no triumph or sneer. If anything, the little lord seemed grave and concerned.

"Now you are safe," he said.

Chapter Nineteen

Deiq opened his eyes, scrabbled upright and lunged forward before awareness even came clear—and slammed face-first into a hard stone wall.

"You fucking little *rotworm!*" he screamed, curling his fingers against the rock, searching for a crack, a flaw, any dent he could exploit to rip the wall apart.

The smooth surface defeated him. It felt oddly slimy, and his fingers slipped over what his eyes insisted was dry rock. Unable to gain any purchase, he stepped back and threw himself against the wall; his only reward was a blazing pain flaring through his shoulder and head.

Reason caught up at last, and stopped him from another useless charge. He sucked in a deep breath between his teeth and turned in a deliberately slow circle, studying the prison. Idisio lay in a heap in the middle of the floor; still breathing, if shallowly.

The slick yellow walls climbed like those of a well: rounded, tall, and impossible to scale. Far overhead a thick-barred metal grate blocked the only opening. Sunlight streamed in from above, but with an oddly diluted quality. Squinting up at the grate, Deiq finally saw a thin screen laid over the bars; he grinned without any real amusement. Another Aerthraim invention: it would let in light, but block a large proportion of the heat. That told him that this prison hadn't been built only for ha'ra'hain, who could easily regulate their body temperatures, but also for lesser enemies—like desert lords.

He took a closer look at the yellow stone as his rage faded, and sighed.

"Aenstone," he muttered under his breath. "Bloody hells. And stibik powder." He scuffed a foot against the floor, hopefully; but that too was aenstone, and cut as tightly as the rest. The only way he'd be calling out for help was by voice, and then only if someone stood directly overhead.

Their packs lay against a wall, apparently undisturbed, and nobody had searched their persons, either. One game ruled out, a thousand possibilities left.

He retrieved a full waterskin, took a sip, then crouched next to Idisio. "Wake up," he said. "Idisio. Wake up." He set the waterskin aside and shook the younger ha'ra'ha, reflecting rather sourly that here, at least, Idisio didn't surpass him.

Idisio coughed, rolled to one side and dry-retched, his whole body convulsing and his eyes rolling back in his head.

"Gods damn it!" Deiq said, alarmed. "Idisio! Sit up. You have to sit up. Look at me. Sit up! Idisio!"

The younger hitched over to his knees and kept gagging, but nothing came up. Deiq looked closer: stibik powder coated Idisio's nostrils and eyes. Of course: he hadn't known to stop breathing and shut his eyes; nobody had ever told him what to do during a stibik attack. Deiq hadn't even thought of it, because the godsdamned stuff wasn't even supposed to *exist* anymore.

Idisio's eyes were beginning to lose the whites, a black stain creeping across white and grey like spilled ink.

Gritting his teeth against the impulse to curse for the next two years, Deiq shoved Idisio roughly back into a kneeling sit and slapped him. Idisio rocked back with a soggy gasp, his eyes paling back to almost normal. He stared past Deiq without recognition.

"Idisio," Deiq snapped. "Look at me." He reached out and roughly jerked Idisio's chin up as his watery gaze wandered to one side. "Can you see me?"

"Nuh . . . colors. Shapes."

"Shit. Hold still." Deiq reached for the waterskin, hating what he had to do; but human tears wouldn't wash out the powder, and he had to get the nostrils clear too.

Idisio screamed, his back arching, as water sluiced through his eyes and up his nose; sneezed violently, and collapsed forward to hands and knees. Deiq shoved him over onto his back, planted a hand on Idisio's thin chest, and kept pouring until the waterskin was empty, ignoring the flailing attempts to push and kick him away.

"Blink," he ordered, his voice ragged with strain. "Don't wipe your eyes. Just blink. Again. Again."

Idisio's eyes, though reddened, were now a sharp white against black, and the tears streaming down his cheeks held no sparkle of stibik powder.

"Good." Deiq leaned back, lifting his hold, and let Idisio scramble clumsily to his feet.

Deiq stayed on his knees, looking up at the younger, ready for a retaliatory attack; but Idisio whirled away and slapped his hands against the walls, feeling his way along as though searching for some secret exit. Deiq watched for a time, amused, then hoisted himself out of the puddle in the middle of the floor and went to sit against the wall.

After making a complete circuit of the room, Idisio turned and glared at Deiq.

"What the *hells* is going on?" he demanded. "There's no godsdamned *door*!"

He glanced up at the grate overhead, then back to the walls as though considering trying to climb; finally shook his head and looked back to Deiq. The grey color began to return to his eyes. Deiq let out a quiet breath of relief.

Idisio's stare focused on Deiq's cheek. "You're bleeding—what *happened*?"

Deiq blinked, only then remembering the slicing sting of a teyanain knife down his cheek. He didn't bother reaching to touch the cut. It would heal soon enough if he didn't fuss with it.

He gave the only answer he could, in the circumstances: "What happened is that I was an idiot."

He hesitated a moment; but Idisio deserved to know the truth of their situation.

"And it's probably going to get us killed."

Chapter Twenty

Lord Evkit insisted on Alyea being settled in a room before explaining himself.

"You honored guest," he said with pleasant and unshakeable determination. "You rest, refresh, come eat. Then we talk."

Two teyanain dressed in sober shades of grey and brown accompanied her as guides and, she assumed, guards. While they displayed no visible weapons, the cut of their clothes allowed for fast, violent movement in any direction, and their precise, graceful movements spoke of extensive aqeyva training.

She was shown to a small, plain room with walls of alternating coarse grey and smooth tan blocks. The guides bowed out of the room without a word and shut the thin wooden door behind them as they withdrew. She hadn't noticed a lock; but sure as sand in the desert, she thought sourly, one or both would be standing out in the passage, waiting.

Escape was not only improbable, but useless. She had no idea where she was in the teyanain fortress, and where that lay in the Horn. With Deiq, maybe even with Idisio, she could have found her way through the rocky expanse outside these walls; alone, she knew she had no chance of survival.

She dropped the light pack on the bed and sat beside it; giving in to a moment of despair, she cradled her head in her hands. But there was no use agonizing over the mistakes that had brought them here; she only gave herself a few breaths for self-pity. With a sigh, she straightened and looked around. Small and plain, with a simple, northern-high bed and table, the room had a single, wide, east-facing window high overhead, which let in a surprising amount of morning sunlight. On the floor near the bed sat a large jug of wash water with a cloth neatly folded over the wide handle, and the chamber pot had been tucked discreetly under the bed. A stone cup, so small it could easily fit in one of Alyea's hands, sat on the table beside a silver jug that sweated chill drops down the sides.

She crossed to the table—a matter of two steps in the tiny room—and picked up the cup, marveling at its smooth translucence. Carved from some pale amber-orange stone, with swirls of milky white, it would have graced a king's table. Without a handle, it nestled in her palm rather like half of a delicately painted egg. She shook her head, set the cup down, and filled it with water.

Sitting back down on the bed, she finally allowed herself to think about Evkit's odd statement: *Now you are safe.* Assuming that the statement had been sane—which she wasn't at all sure of, given his attack on the two ha'ra'hain—and that he hadn't been simply trying to throw her off guard, what had made him think she was in danger?

She sipped the chill water, which tasted vaguely of oranges, frowning as she considered. He hadn't killed the two ha'ra'hain, hadn't harmed her or shown any malice at all. He hadn't shown any special animosity to Deiq or Idisio at Scratha Fortress, nor made any attempt to warn her of danger there. So had Scratha Fortress figured in his perception of her peril? Lord Scratha had tried to warn her about Deiq as well, so he couldn't have been involved . . . Perhaps someone else at Scratha Fortress?

Or—She straightened, lowering the cup to her lap as she was about to take another sip—some*thing*? Could it be that the teyanin lord was worried about the Scratha ha'rethe?

It seemed an incredible notion. Evkit was a desert lord himself, after all, so he must have gone through the blood trials. And as *the* lord of the teyanain, he should have been bound to the Horn, if Alyea understood the process correctly.

For the first time, she wondered how Evkit could travel so far from his presumably bound lands, when Scratha had said heads of desert Families couldn't leave their sworn ha'reye. A shiver rippled down her back. Maybe Evkit wasn't bound, after all, which implied the absence of a ha'rethe or ha'ra'ha strong enough to protect the area.

She rubbed at her face, trying to work through the logical implications of that. After a few moments, she shook her head and rose to set the cup back on the table. Her mind felt too filled with the rush of fear and worry to sort out anything right now. She'd just have to listen to whatever Evkit said with a skeptical ear and think about it hard before she agreed to anything.

Running her hands through her hair, she pushed it into reasonable order, then straightened out a rumpled sleeve. She glanced at her pack, thinking of the comb and fresh clothes inside; then remembered Chac's advice: *Don't toss and flutter like you're the prettiest in the room.* Tidying up too much might come across as vanity to these dour people; instinct warned her that she couldn't afford to lose any fragment of their respect.

She turned to the door, which yielded to a light pressure, swinging silently outward. A cold part of her mind noted that she'd never know if someone came in while she slept.

The two teyanain who had guided her to the room stood against the passageway wall, facing her door. They looked at her with the silent, dark-eyed impassivity she was coming to expect from the teyanain.

She drew a deep breath. "I believe," she said firmly, "Lord Evkit mentioned a meal?"

Chapter Twenty-one

"Why would Evkit want to kill us?" Idisio demanded.

Deiq let out a snort. "I'm not well-liked among the humans, Idisio," he said. "Tends to happen over time. Things one century thinks are perfectly fine get you painted as a monster in the next round. You'll run into it too, eventually."

He slid his hand along the stone of the floor, feeling the rough surface scrape against his palm. Contemplating whether he could dig through the floor—and whether that was even a smart idea—he almost missed Idisio's reply:

"And so *I'm* going to die because *you* pissed Lord Evkit off?"

Deiq blinked, focused on the moment again, and decided to shift the conversation to a less dangerous question. Losing his temper in here would be a very bad idea.

"Idisio, do you remember the ugren cuffs?"

"Yes. . . ." Idisio's face shifted into horrified understanding. "But they *wouldn't*! I mean, that would be . . . that would breach that . . . what's it called, the Agreement? Isn't that—I mean, enslaving us, or killing us, would be—wouldn't it?"

"Only if it were found out," Deiq said, and patted the floor lightly. "This is called aenstone. It blocks mind-speech." It did more than that; but he decided to keep it simple for the moment. "We can't call for help, and nobody can see us here. The teyanain can put round any story they like about where we went; they're exceptionally good liars."

Idisio's face went ashen again. "Oh, gods," he breathed.

"Oh, yes," Deiq said without humor, and shut his eyes, giving Idisio a chance to compose himself. "If you're going to pray," he added as an after-thought, remembering that Idisio probably did believe in some form of deity, "pray that Alyea stands up for us. Because she's the only one who can demand we be released, and Evkit declared her guest, which means he won't hurt *her*. And you can bet he's doing his best to convince her that ha'ra'hain are monsters who can't be trusted at your front or at your back."

"But *why?*"

"Because that's what humans *do*, Idisio. They hate anything stronger or different; they attack it and tear it down." Deiq didn't open his eyes as he spoke. "I've been watching it happen for hundreds of years."

"That's too easy an answer," Idisio protested.

"Then find your own. Now shut up. I want to take a nap." He didn't, but it was the simplest way to stop the younger from his endless questioning.

Idisio fell silent, sulking. After a while, he said, "It didn't count, you know. The marriage you told me about. You never really wanted it."

Deiq opened his eyes and stared at the younger, bewildered and more than a little annoyed. "Where in the hells did that come from?"

"If we're going to die," Idisio said, jaw set in stubborn lines, "I want you to know that I don't think you ever really tried with that girl. Woman. Whatever. You could have made it work."

"You weren't there," Deiq said tartly. "You don't know what I tried or didn't try."

"I know *you*," Idisio said. "You didn't really want to be married, so you didn't really try. It was a experiment for you. It didn't mean anything. And I'm betting that's why none of your other attempts ever worked. You didn't care enough."

"Are you trying to get *me* to kill you?" Deiq snapped, but the words held little force, and no real anger rose in him. Idisio's arrogance was too close to the self-righteous, smug attitude of his own younger days, although it was laid at a different slant.

"If I was wrong, you'd be laughing and calling me an idiot," Idisio said, not moving.

"You're *ignorant*, is what you are. She was human. They die by seventy, eighty, maybe ninety; I would have had at best twenty or thirty years with her before she began to fade. That's *nothing*."

"No," Idisio said. "That's twenty years of something honest."

Deiq shook his head, amused by the younger's stubborn hold on innocence. "You're going to drive yourself insane trying that approach, Idisio."

Idisio didn't say anything in response to that, and Deiq let the silence remain unbroken.

He thought about what Idisio had said, his sour amusement fading. Onsia had been a good woman: slight, compact, quick-moving. Quick-tempered, too, rather like Alyea; Deiq grinned, remembering the wooden bowl shattering beside his head. Onsia would have aimed at him, not the wall. . . .

In almost every other way, the two women couldn't have been more different. Alyea was still young, and stubbornly clung to her northern convictions of propriety. Onsia, after losing two husbands, hadn't cared what her neighbors thought; although had she taken up with a less wealthy, influential man, the gossip might well have turned uglier.

Well, done was done, and Onsia's grandchildren were long in their graves. No point thinking the matter over at this late remove. Idisio would learn how to see these things, if they managed to come out of this situation alive.

Deiq sighed, letting go of worry as a waste of energy, and surprised himself by falling into a light doze after all.

Chapter Twenty-two

The meal proved as simple and yet elegant as Alyea's room: delicately spiced flatbread and clear cool water, along with a bowl of pale beans and dark grains tossed in a light, floral oil. The wooden plates had been so carefully shaped and carved that they felt like gifts from the tree instead of mere surfaces to transport food. The cups resembled the one in her room, but of a darker, more speckled stone, carved translucently thin.

Alyea ate in silence, savoring each bite; she'd never had anything like it. She started to ask about the ingredients, and especially the intoxicatingly scented oil used to dress the beans, then caught herself just in time. Under southern rules of courtesy, Evkit held the higher status and so had to be the first to speak.

Evkit tucked into his own meal with a healthy appetite, ignoring her completely. It didn't feel hostile; more as though he wanted her to focus on her meal without distractions. The teyanain were turning out to be far different from what Deiq's grimly suspicious view of them—and the attack—had led her to expect. The artistry, delicate courtesy, craftsmanship, and obvious appreciation for beauty were at sharp odds with her previous image of people everyone else seemed to view with intense distrust.

She wiped the last traces of oil from her plate with the last piece of flatbread. Immediately, a servant whisked the plate away and offered her a small bowl of water and a napkin.

"Thank you," she murmured, cleaning her hands. The bowl and cloth disappeared with the same rapid grace as the plate.

Evkit leaned back in his chair and regarded her with a faint smile.

"So: belly full, mind calm, now we talk," he said.

Alyea raised her eyebrows and waited, folding her hands on the table in front of her, careful to keep her shoulders and back straight and her expression neutral.

Evkit laughed. "You do not trust me," he said. "I understand. I would be—would have—same distrust. Is healthy caution. So. You have question. Ask. No cost."

She nodded slowly, considering, then said, "How is it that you can leave the Horn?"

His face stilled as though he hadn't expected that question. A long moment of silence hung in the room, and the lines around his eyes tightened. His face shifted briefly into a hard expression, then smoothed back to blandness.

"Teyanain different," he said at last. "New question."

She tried another topic. "What was that white powder you threw at us?"

This reply came out prompt and unworried. "Is called stibik. Old, old creation, from ketarches. Only affects those with ha'reye blood. Puts them to sleep, make them weak."

"What is a ketarch?"

"Healers. Herb-lore. Medicine, all sorts. Aerthraim is best, developed stibik, developed many drugs and medicines. Much complicated politics involve ketarches; you might learn. Might not." He smiled at her, an unsettlingly cheerful expression that never reached his watchful black eyes.

She sat quietly, thinking that over. So the ketarches had developed a weapon against the ha'reye? And the teyanain had it to hand, and were ready to throw it as soon as Deiq and Idisio came through the portal. Which meant that they'd known at least one ha'ra'ha would be coming through after Lord Evkit . . . Either that, or the guards of the portal always held it to hand, and Evkit had told them, on his arrival, to use it.

Why would Evkit hold such distrust of the two ha'ra'hain? Why had the ketarches felt compelled to create such a weapon? And why did the teyanain have a supply laid by? If the Horn boasted a ha'rethe, surely it couldn't be happy about that. It didn't make any sense.

She looked up to find Evkit watching her closely, with the first hint of a smirk she'd seen since their arrival.

"Many questions," he said. "Many strange questions, yes? And the answers are no good."

He stood, motioning her to follow him. Not daring to hesitate, she rose from her seat, forcing her expression to remain bland although her heart hammered in her ears. *He's doing far too much smiling,* Deiq had said, and Alyea found herself thinking: *He's also being far too nice.*

As though sensing her thoughts, Evkit raised his hands, palms out, and grinned at her. "You guest, no harm," he said. "I show you something. I give you good answers, true answers. You trust. Come."

Her two guards trailed behind as she walked with Lord Evkit through a maze of passageways and up a winding flight of steps. Another passageway, another turn, a few low steps, and they faced a door decorated with an astonishingly delicate design picked out in gold leaf that seemed to flow over the dark background of the wood.

Evkit paused and looked at Alyea soberly. "You not like this. But you interfere, she die. You stay clear. This important you see, but you not touch, you not interfere. You trust. I tell truth. Promise me you not touch, not interfere."

She drew a breath, bit her lower lip, then nodded.

Evkit motioned to the guards. They took up positions on either side of the door as the teyanin lord opened it and waved Alyea through. She stepped cautiously through the entry, her heart hammering.

The room seemed perfectly ordinary, much like her own but wider. A large metal tub sat in the middle of the floor, filled with water. Two small, teyanin-dark women, their expressions drawn and worried, glanced up from their positions on stools beside the tub, and hastily stood when Lord Evkit entered. He asked them something in a fluid, rapid language Alyea had never heard before, and they shook their heads.

"No change," Evkit said, and sighed. He nodded towards the tub. "You go look, Lord Alyea. Remember, no touch, no interfere."

She wanted to bolt from the room. She forced herself to move, a step at a time, to the side of the deep metal bathing tub. Made her head tilt and her eyes stay open as she stared at the film of blood spread across the water's surface; it lent a thickly rotten, iron tang to the nearby air. Set her teeth in her tongue, hard, and kept her hands at her sides as she saw the body slowly writhing in the water: a small frame, an *old* woman with white hair and an expression of intense agony on her wrinkled face.

Alyea recognized the healer who had saved her life after the Qisani blood trial.

"Her name Teilo. She does not know time," Evkit said quietly from behind her. "She sees time as moments passing. She does not know days go by."

He touched Alyea's elbow with a light, fingertip pressure.

"Come, we go talk now."

Alyea backed away, unable to take her eyes away from the horrifying sight, until distance put the wall of the tub in the way; then she shut her eyes and turned away sharply, fighting nausea. Staggering to one side, she put out a hand to catch herself against the wall and leaned against the cool, reassuring support for some time, breathing hard.

"What the hells are you *doing* to her?"

"We do nothing," Evkit said. "Come, we go walk."

He took her elbow gently, his bony fingers cool and dry against her skin, and guided her from the room.

"She saved my life," Alyea muttered, letting him urge her back down stairs and through passageways and up stairs without really noticing her surroundings.

"I know," Evkit said. After some more walking, he pushed open another heavy door. "Come, sit down in air."

Alyea stepped out onto a small patio bordered with low stone walls and stood still, shocked back into awareness of the moment. Ahead was blue sky, impossibly bright and clean, not even a wisp of cloud visible. To the left and right rose jagged, ochre and sand-colored outcrops resembling a jumbled handful of broken children's blocks tossed in a loose pile. Moving forward to the edge of the patio, she found a steep drop below and a similar range of tumbled rock spread in a rough skirt to the glittering shore of the sea. Birds wheeled far below, their white and grey patterning barely visible at this distance. Ships, little more than dark specks, moved over the shimmering silver-blue water.

Evkit, at her side, said, "Western Deep Sea, that." He pointed north and west. "Look hard, you see Stone Islands."

Alyea's brain finally relayed how damn *high* she stood and how low the wall between her and a deadly steep drop. She blinked and stepped back.

"Good gods," she said shakily.

"Beautiful, yes," Evkit said, and steered her, unprotesting, to one of two simple white chairs.

Alyea sank into the seat and tried to control her breathing. Memory of that dizzying chasm just a few feet away trembled through her hands. She shut her eyes and bent to put her head between her knees, vomit coiling in the back of her throat.

"Only teyanain handle height so well," Evkit said, bizarrely cheerful, and pressed her to drink from a small flask.

The liquid went down smooth as water, then flared into a raw heat that made cactus peppers seem mild. She choked and coughed, her eyes watering.

Evkit laughed. "And only teyanain handle proper desert lightning so well," he noted, patting her on the back. "You not out-drink me, Lord Alyea. You never out-drink me, not in hundred lifetimes."

She sat back in her chair, wiping at her eyes, and glared at him. "You sure went down hard."

"Faked," he said, still smiling. "Not safe for me to get real drunk at ha'rethe home place."

"So you don't have a ha'rethe here. You're not bound to one like the others are."

His expression shifted a little, something less genial creeping into his smile.

"Not like others are, no," he agreed. "We different. We always different, from beginning."

Even the small sip of liquor she'd taken buzzed along her veins like nervous sparks. She blinked hard, feeling as though her thoughts flew faster than the birds circling far below. It seemed safest to return to the original topic: twice now he'd reacted badly to that prod. She doubted his thinning patience would stand for a third try.

"Deiq didn't believe you lost," she said. "He told me you'd never lost a drinking contest."

"Never," Evkit confirmed, amused again. "Teyanain grow up drinking heavier than what lowlanders ever see. You never put even young teyanain under table. No lowlander ever will. We *different*."

"But you didn't mind having everyone think I won."

He shook his head. "Nobody who knows teyanain believed that," he said simply.

She looked out into the blue expanse of sky, unsure what to say next. At last she asked, choosing her phrasing carefully, "What happened to the healer?"

"Name Teilo," he said. "She leave Jungle some time ago. She told not to. She disobey. She save your life. She told not to. She disobey again. Not smart, anger Jungle ha'reye."

Alyea frowned. "Why did she—wait. Why did the Jungle—hells." She shook her head. Too many questions jammed through her head, making coherence impossible.

Evkit watched her with a sympathetic expression.

"Questions go much further back than you think," he said. "Back before Split. Back before humanity start walking. And nobody but teyanain asking questions that far back. Desert lords especially not ask. They *careful* not ask. They already know they would not like answers. And they not like giving out answers, either. They would never tell you this much, Lord Alyea. Never answer so much questions, especially not far-back questions."

"Let's just look at the right-now questions," Alyea said sharply. "We can work backwards from there, but I want to know what's going on right now. What's happening to that woman?"

"I tell you, I tell you all," Evkit said expansively. "You will see, I tell you truth others would not. Healer not human. Name Teilo, but not human. Not now, not for many years. She old, Lord Alyea, many years old. Older than Deiq. And right now Teilo maybe dying for helping you. Not once, she help, but twice, maybe three time. First time not just for you, but for everyone in Bright Bay; she help bring down mad Ninnic and destroy mad elder ha'ra'ha that control mad Ninnic. But you benefit, yes? So she help you."

"Good gods," she breathed, shocked. "I had no idea. There was a—why didn't anyone *say*—good *gods*." She gave up trying to express her dismay.

Evkit snorted. "If someone had said to you, before you leave to become desert lord: monster under city causing king to act crazy, you would have said what?"

She shook her head and looked down at her hands.

"Yes. You see. Crazy-talk, demon-talk. Northerns not understand these things. Not ever."

"Yes," she said, barely vocalizing the word. "I see. So what—what happened next?"

"Teilo not supposed to be in Bright Bay at all. Humans spend so much time with ha'reye in Jungles as she spend, they change. They become other. Not-human. Ha'reye-kin, what we call true-ha'rai'nin. And Jungle ha'reye never tell their humans, their ha'rai'nain, what will happen to them one day. They not ever want changes happen away from home place. They know Teilo close to changing; they forbid her leave Jungles. She go anyway, to help humans battle mad ha'ra'ha. Jungle ha'reye send word all round: Teilo banished, outcast. Let be, let die in dry-change, land-change, no help given."

She stared at him, appalled.

"Jungles invest many years to bring ha'rai'nain ready for change," Lord Evkit said. "Teilo first to reach turning point, and they afraid of creating renegade ha'rai'nin. Change makes big power, big strength. Bigger than blood trials. Ha'reye want desert lords and changed ones stay close, stay under control. Too dangerous, let them walk around before right time. Desert lords always stay close after trials, until ha'reye see they safe, stable, not mad, crazy, dangerous; ha'rai'nain need even more so."

"But *I* didn't—" She stopped, remembering how close she'd come to dying.

Evkit regarded her without speaking for a moment, an eyebrow quirked.

Then he said, "No. You leave Qisani early. Very unusual, and part of right-now story. Listen; I tell truth you not know yet.

"Teilo do smart thing, not knowing it smart: she go into water when she think she is dying from battle. But she not dying, it is change coming; and she go into *Bright Bay* water. There many young ha'ra'hain in Great Sea waters near Bright Bay. She find one. It find her. It knows who she is, knows she is supposed to be let die. But it is young, and stupid."

Evkit paused, as if searching for the right words, then went on:

"It thinks it can control her after change, make her *its* ha'rai'nin, gain much status, much power." His expression became severe. More quietly, he added, "Now it is dead. She kill it during change, and is now pregnant with its child. Part of change is mating. And killing."

Alyea blinked at the teyanin lord, unable to reconcile the fragile, gentle presence that had healed her with the *creature* Evkit described.

"How do you *know* all this?" she demanded.

Lord Evkit's stare remained direct and dark. "You not trust Teilo," he said, apparently ignoring the question. "Not ever. She not human now, Lord Alyea; she *ha'rai'nin*. Very much different and very much dangerous."

He paused, watching her take that in, then went on.

"Then you go to Qisani, go through blood trial, and Qisani leader scream for help because you dying. And Jungle say to Qisani: 'Let die. Let be. Qisani ha'reye have child. Woman useless now.'"

Alyea sucked in air through a suddenly tight throat, swallowed hard, and stared at the impassive dark face, unable to believe what he had just said.

"They just wanted my *child*?" she demanded. An ache spiraled through her entire body for a moment, a dull sense of having been dreadfully, wrongfully tricked out of something precious.

He nodded, head bobbing emphatically. "Women not go through blood trials often," he said. "And Ishrai always last. And Qisani rare, rare, *rare* place for any Ishrai trials. *Dangerous* place. Damn dangerous. Women try be desert lords, all die when they go to Qisani. Every last one. Many men, too. You first woman to survive in many hundred years."

Her pulse thundered in her temples. Her hands shook again. She shut her eyes, hearing Acana's words in memory: *I wish I could say I believe you will survive this.* She'd taken it as bluff, an attempt to scare her off; apparently that part, at least, had been absolute truth.

They took my first child . . . maybe my only child.

"Did . . . did Deiq know that?" she whispered, unable to voice it any louder.

"I do not know," Lord Evkit said soberly. "But Teilo hear call for help, and hear Jungle refuse, and decide to go help you. So she come, she save your life. That second time she disobey Jungle, and now they know she alive, and changed, not dead. They *really* mad now."

Alyea leaned back in her chair and stared up at the sky, dazed.

"Ha'reye talk together, miles away," Lord Evkit said. "They not need be together in body to talk, Lord Alyea. They pass the word through the air, through the miles, relay, spread the word they want. Qisani almost next door for them to talk.

"So now Qisani ha'reye know Jungle mad at Teilo. Qisani ha'reye cannot go into Qisani after Teilo, but they shout and scream and threaten, because Jungle says: Get Teilo, kill both healer and woman she save, this Alyea human who Qisani was told to let die. But Qisani refuse to give you, give Teilo, to Qisani ha'reye. So now *Qisani* ha'reye mad at head of Qisani, *Jungle* ha'reye mad at head of Qisani. Very much not smart, this head of Qisani, to have helped you so much. Lots of people saying 'no' to ha'reye suddenly. This very much not smart. Qisani probably not exist much longer."

"Oh, gods," Alyea said, numb. Visions of the ruined city they'd just left filled her mind, and Acana's voice overlay everything again: *It would have been safer for all of us if you had failed the first part of the trial.* Another perceived bluff that had been deadly truth.

She'd had no idea what she was leaving behind when she walked south with Deiq. If she'd known . . . What could she have done? Probably nothing. Still, the thought that the silent, smiling ishraidain might be harmed—might already be dead, just for helping her become a desert lord—sickened her.

"Now Qisani in trouble," Evkit went on relentlessly. "So head of Qisani get you out as fast as can, and get Teilo out fast as can. Teilo come here, ask us for help, ask how to turn aside anger of Jungle, protect Qisani. But I am one she must talk to, and I am at Scratha Fortress for Conclave. And before I return, her child. . . ."

He paused, pursed his lips, as if searching for the right words again.

"This area, the Horn, our home place, not good ground for ha'reye or ha'ra'hain. And ha'ra'hain children *different*. They aware, they smart, earlier than human babies. So this child not happy. Child want out. Child want away. So child start ripping free, taking mother life to build its own. That what you see, in room back there. We try to keep child from killing healer. Not easy."

Despite her earlier resolution to keep a skeptical ear to what the teyanin lord told her, his words made too much sense to argue. Alyea found no lie in the tone or expression or phrasing; everything she could see or hear told her Evkit was presenting unvarnished, unattractive truth.

"We not know how much Deiq knows about all this," Evkit said. "We not know what Scratha ha'rethe tell Deiq to do once you out from Lord Scratha's sight. Deiq bound to obey, if full ha'rethe say *Kill her*; but he smart enough to do it in his own time and his own way, to avoid offending human allies. So we take him, and the young one, and put them aside for your safety until we find out. We one of very, very few can prison ha'ra'ha when needed. If Deiq mean harm, you go on your way alone, we keep them here as long as you like. And now you have the right-now questions answered."

"He *can't* mean to hurt me," she protested.

"Mm," he said, and watched her with a disconcerting, sharp dark stare.

She drew a deep breath and looked at the azure sky for a while in silence, until her racing heartbeat steadied and her thoughts began working again.

I won't hurt you, Deiq had said, with a strange intensity, more than once; and she wondered if he'd been trying to tell her that even if ordered, he would refuse to do so. It seemed the only possible explanation at this point.

"I don't believe he means me harm," she said at last.

"You bet life on it?"

"Yes. Deiq could have killed me a dozen times over already if that's what he was after."

"He not love you," Evkit said suddenly.

She shot him a hard glare.

"Truth," Evkit said. "He ha'ra'ha. If he say he love you, he either lying or insane."

He met her anger steadily, his expression sober.

"Maybe younger one, maybe he able to feel like that, maybe his blood diluted enough. But the older one, never." Evkit rose from his chair. "You sit; you think who you trust now. I leave teyanain to guide you. You honored guest. When you ready, come talk to me, go sleep, walk round. Guides will tell where you may go. Please, do not try run away from guides. They here to help, to serve, for safety. And please do not go to see Deiq. It is not good idea you talk to Deiq right now."

He paused, one hand on the door, and looked back at her with a sudden frown.

"You take Deiq, as desert lord? You—" He made a crudely explicit gesture with both hands.

Alyea felt hot color flooding her face.

"No," she said. "And I have no intention of doing so."

Lord Evkit smiled. "Good," he said with an unmistakably smug overtone, and left her on the patio to think.

Drugs of the Southlands

(excerpt)

There are three main drugs exported from the southlands to the northern king-dom: esthit, also known as dream-dust; aesa, also called dream-weed or simply weed; and dasta. Of course there are others, as varied and ingenious as the human race itself; but those main three, being of the greatest concern to your more con-servative factions, should be addressed.

Esthit is produced largely by Darden Family. It is actually a simple combina-tion of dried sap from a particular cactus mixed with a few other similarly com-mon ingredients, ground into a coarse powder. It is taken by applying a small amount to the back of the tongue and allowing it to dissolve. Some prefer to dis-solve it first in a spoonful or two of warmed liquor or coffee, but that naturally dilutes the effect.

Esthit dulls the senses and calms the mind, producing a pleasant, dreamy stupor and occasionally hallucinations. It actually serves a very prosaic function. New desert lords tend to have difficulty adjusting to the increased acuity of their senses, and esthit returns them, temporarily, to a more standard level, provid-ing much-needed relief. Unfortunately, Darden Family has altered the original formula to make much of what they produce highly addictive and much more dangerous.

Aesa, also extremely common, can even be found in areas of your own king-dom. It is nothing more than the dried leaves of a plant similar to true pipe-weed, but smoking aesa gives one a pleasantly euphoric feeling and, rarely, mild hallucinations.

The last and most serious of the major southland drug exports is known as dasta. This, too, comes from the dried sap of a cactus; and this, too, started out as a vital tool for the southern ketarches. Originally developed by the Aerthraim ketarches, dasta served to relax and anesthetize patients with severe wounds, and by relieving their anxiety, tremendously assisted their rate of healing. It also as-sisted desert lords with the performance of certain duties.

Unfortunately, F'Heing stole the secret formula and, as Darden did with es-thit, altered it to something far more dangerous and unethical: dasta became a powerful and addictive aphrodisiac that lowered all boundaries and disabled all possibility of resistance from the taker.

That alteration led directly to the formation of the so-called katha villages—the term itself is a corruption of proper grammar, but I will not sidetrack here to discuss linguistics—along both east and west coasts. While kathain are part of a very old tradition, their abuse has never been tolerated previous to the alteration of dasta. *Kathain serve as honored servants to important guests, and so much as raising one's voice to kathain is absolutely forbidden. Older kathain may offer sexual services if they so desire, but again, at the first hint of abuse the visitor is ejected without ceremony.*

The katha villages are something else entirely. They consist of a community built around one or perhaps two central brothels, many of which use children and generally involve a very rough trade. This corruption of an ancient and sacred custom is reprehensible, revolting, and incomprehensible; as is the apparent reluctance of the other desert Families to step in and end the horror. One may only conclude that while F'Heing provided the means, the interest had already been present, as sickening as that thought is for me to contemplate; and that the katha villages are, in fact, tacitly underwritten by every desert Family in one way or another. I do not include Scratha, the Aerthraim, or the teyanain in that condemnation, as I believe those three names alone have never had a hand in the promotion of the katha villages.

I am well aware that this section of my notes to you will raise extreme protest from the other Families and quite possibly even the loremasters. But my revulsion for what a once-proud tradition has turned into is far too strong, of late, to hold my tongue to polite speech. Let them prove my accusations unfounded. Let them move to shut down those horrible villages and prove themselves above such filth. Then, and only then, will I apologize for these strong words.

From the collection
Letters to a Northern King of Merit
penned by Lord Cafad Scratha during the reign of King Oruen

Chapter Twenty-three

Night brought with it an intense chill unaffected by the Aerthraim heat-grid overhead, and no meal save what they had in their packs: trail jerky and water. Idisio sat huddled, arms wrapped around knees and both their blankets drawn round him, shivering.

"You don't have to be cold," Deiq said for the fifth time, patiently. "Just know that you're warm. Raise your body temperature to suit your comfort."

"I've been *trying*," Idisio retorted, his night-blurred glare warmer than the rest of him. "It isn't *working*."

Deiq sighed and tried not to roll his eyes. Idisio, locked into his human habits, would at the least get seriously ill from the frigid Horn night if he didn't learn to adjust his internal temperature. He wished he could give Idisio the energy directly; but the only available source to draw from was himself, and that would likely destroy Idisio's mind long before it warmed his body.

"Come here," Deiq said, putting out a hand.

Idisio, reluctant, skinched over closer. Deiq curled a hand around the boy's blanket-shrouded, skinny bicep and tugged him right over until their shoulders were touching. Twisting, he grabbed with his other hand and bodily hauled the younger into his lap. Idisio stiffened and jerked forward, scrambling to get free.

"Damn it, *stop* that!" Deiq said, exasperated, as a sharp elbow jammed against his shoulder.

"I don't need to get warm *that* badly!" Idisio snapped, kicking free and rolling halfway across the floor.

"I'm offering body heat, Idisio! You're hardly *hai-katihe!*"

"A *what?*"

"It means—oh, never mind—" As he spoke, residual energy from the brief contact sparked memories not his:

Dirty stone wall at his back, a larger body pressing against his front . . . sand and dirt under his back . . . grit shifting under hands and knees . . . hoarse grunts, a slap to the back of the head, a curse. . . .

Deiq hissed, yanking himself out of Idisio's memories before they swamped him completely. The most dangerous flavor of rage rose in him, sharp and swift; he rose to his feet, feeling control slipping.

"They *dared* use you that way?"

"I was a street brat," Idisio retorted, climbing to his own feet. A shimmering glow began building around him, an aura nobody but another ha'ra'ha or ha'reye would see. "Pull your pants out of your ass!"

Deiq stared, rage choked under surprise, and grabbed the moment, with the smoothness of long practice, to redirect his emotions. He forced a burst of laughter. "*What?*"

"Nobody ever said that to you before?" Idisio snorted. "Means—"

"I understand what it means," Deiq said, the last of his anger safely gone. He sat back down, still grinning and deeply relieved that Idisio had distracted him at the critical moment. Two angry ha'ra'hain in a confined space was generally a lethal situation for at least one of them; and Idisio wasn't experienced enough to restrain his own temper. "I just hadn't heard that particular version before. Never mind."

He watched, interested, as the vague glow around Idisio faded and dissipated. Now, that was an emotion-effect he hadn't seen often, or in a damn long time. The younger ha'ra'ha was turning out even more unusual than he'd expected, and as soon as they were in a place where it was safe to talk, he'd be having a *long* discussion with Idisio—about several things.

"Yeah, well," Idisio said, and slid to sit against the wall across from Deiq. "Thanks but no thanks, you know? I'm warm now, anyway."

"Yes," Deiq murmured. "I expect you are."

"What's that supposed to mean?" Idisio's tone spiked from hard to hostile.

"Anger's a very warming emotion," Deiq said easily. "Good night."

Idisio glared for another few moments, clearly mistrustful. At last he muttered, " 'night," and rolled onto his side, stuffing a blanket under his head to serve as a pillow.

Deiq sat awake, looking up at the stars, listening to Idisio's quiet breathing and considering what the younger ha'ra'ha had endured. Ninnic's child should have sensed Idisio's presence, should have sensed kin-distress, that close at hand. But it hadn't; and even if it had, given Rosin's teachings, it might have actually found the violent treatment of a younger by tharr to be acceptable.

Bad enough that Idisio had been raised by tharr as a "street rat" and thief. If the ha'reye of the Jungles ever found out what Deiq had just seen, they would likely retaliate, as Ninnic's child should have. He had to keep Idisio from returning to the southlands. It was sheer luck that Scratha ha'rethe had been too lazy to pry after memories.

Deiq stared up at the night sky and wondered if there were more stars in the sky or dangerous secrets in his head. It felt like a depressingly close count, these days.

As the dark eased into grey, he heard something beyond the walls of their prison and rose, feeling rather like a asp-jacau ready to spring. Idisio snorted, coughed, and sat up, his gaze locking onto Deiq immediately; he scrambled to his feet just as a tall rectangle of stone nearby swung outward without a sound.

Lord Evkit stepped into the doorway, displaying his usual mocking half-grin. The little teyanin lord regarded them dispassionately, then made a quick, warning gesture as Deiq shifted his weight.

"Not smart, attack me," Evkit warned.

"Smart or dumb, I'll still take you to pieces," Deiq snarled, and started forward.

Evkit held up a hand, and Deiq stopped moving; every muscle locked into utter stillness, however hard he strained to take another step.

"Not smart," Lord Evkit repeated. "I come let you go. You attack me, I do not."

Deiq stopped fighting the invisible bonds, his eyes narrowing.

Lord Evkit dropped his hand, a faint smile on his lips. "Better."

"You're going to let us go," Deiq said, staring hard at the teyanin lord and setting aside the question of how Evkit had managed that trick for later consideration. Not even an athain should be able to stop a First Born in his tracks, although a clee probably could. "Why?"

"I only take you for Lord Alyea safety."

"*What?*" Deiq took another step forward, unable to believe the man's gall. Evkit raised a hand again, but Deiq had already made himself stop moving.

"Is truth," Evkit protested, showing the palms of both hands in the ages-old signal of utter sincerity. "I think maybe you hurt her. But Lord Alyea say she trust you. I think, maybe she wrong, but she is guest. It is her decision. So I agree, let you go. And so you go to Bright Bay now. You go, you leave Horn, you not come back this way soon." His eyes glittered, innocence evaporating. "And for my part, I say: you stay out of teyanain land for long time. You agree, you go. You argue, you stay here."

Deiq stood very still for a few breaths, deeply suspicious and trying to decide what game Evkit was playing this time. It wouldn't be nearly as simple as ensuring Alyea's safety. There were at least two other plots underlying this moment. Evkit never took one-dimensional actions; and he was using the fractured speech patterns that made lies nearly impossible to pick out, which confirmed the suspicion in Deiq's mind.

"Idisio, too?"

"Same," Lord Evkit nodded. "Both stay out teyanain lands. Long time. Many years. Hundred. Two hundred. Many. Until we say you may walk our land again. You come back without permission, you die. No argue, no exception."

"He makes his own decision," Deiq said, temporizing.

Lord Evkit shrugged and flicked a dark glance at the boy. "You agree?"

"*Yes*," Idisio said fervently.

"Decision made," Lord Evkit said, and looked back to Deiq. "You agree?"

Deiq shot Idisio a dark, unhappy glare. He'd hoped for at least a few moments of hesitation in which to think. At last he shrugged. Being banned from the Horn meant he'd have to travel south by boat, and that meant weeks of being tremendously ill. But he'd endured that before.

"Agreed. Where's Alyea?"

"Lord Alyea wait outside," Evkit said. "With packs, supplies, horse. All ready to go. Sun ready too, about to wake up eastlands. You walk with waking sun."

"How kind of you," Deiq said with heavy sarcasm.

"You come, follow guide," Evkit said, and turned away without so much as a head-tilt by way of courtesy.

The deliberately insulting movement—from someone who damn well knew better than to provoke a ha'ra'ha already under a severe strain—brought the rage boiling back up, set the red haze dancing at the corners of Deiq's vision. Deiq took a step forward, already knowing just how he'd shred the little rotworm into a thousand pieces—and Idisio grabbed his upper arm hard.

"*Don't*," Idisio hissed.

Deiq turned a dark glare on him; the younger ha'ra'ha flinched, his face paling, but didn't let go.

"I just want to get out of here, Deiq," Idisio said, his fingers digging in even harder. "Please!"

Deiq drew in a harsh breath, forcing the anger down and admitting to himself that Idisio was right. Unwilling to voice that aloud, he shook off Idisio's grip, snatched up his pack, and strode through the doorway without looking back.

Chapter Twenty-four

Alyea stood waiting, one hand on the neck of the most muscular pony she'd ever seen, as the trail guide silently loaded panniers and saddlebags with numerous heavy packages. Besides her own pack, the pony carried two dozen full waterskins, a bundle of fine teyanain hand-stitched cloths, jars of dried Horn rosemary and other spices, candies, and assorted other gifts, including a largish tin of well-aged thopuh tea and a set of six translucently thin cups carved from agate.

She still wasn't sure if she should have accepted it all; but without Deiq to give a nod or a warning, she'd had no reason to refuse. It all felt rather embarrassing. Lord Scratha hadn't given her anything at all on parting. Granted, his situation had been a bit more complicated; but Alyea was left wondering, now, whether the lack of gifts ought to be interpreted as a snub on Scratha's part: and if so, what she was expected to do about it.

By northern terms, Evkit's gifts were an overload of riches for no particular cause, and might well be perceived as whore-gifts rather than due courtesy. She resolved to ask Deiq what it meant under southern custom.

As though thinking of Deiq had been the final summons, a teyanin guide emerged from the nearby tunnel that led into the heart of the teyanain mountain complex. Deiq followed, Idisio on his heels, and Lord Evkit stepped out a few moments later, smirking.

Alyea looked at Evkit's smug expression and the glower on Deiq's face, her heart sinking. She could tell that Evkit hadn't offered any apology. Deiq was good and stirred up; he glared as though blaming her for the whole incident. She shot a sour glance at Evkit, who seemed entirely unbothered.

"You give packs, I put packs right places," the trail guide directed, holding out his hands. "You need balance, you not teyanain. You need free movement, pack throw balance off."

Deiq shrugged and tossed his at the guide's feet, provoking a dark scowl from the man. Idisio, more respectfully, stepped forward to hand his pack over.

Evkit stood silent, smiling, as the trail guide settled the final burdens on the pony. Then he said, "Go with the gods, Lord Alyea." He bowed, straightened, and looked at Deiq and Idisio. "Ha'inn: teth-kavit."

"Teth-kavit," Deiq said, sounding anything but sincere. Idisio followed suit, stumbling over what was clearly an unfamiliar phrase for him.

"Come," said the guide, and led the pony onto a narrow path that cut between two steep rock faces. Alyea offered Lord Evkit a deep, carefully sincere bow, then turned and followed.

It didn't take long to be grateful for not having to carry a pack. The rising sun left large pools of shadow at the bottom of the steep cliffs, but the still air heated fast. Alyea was soon drenched with sweat and sipping almost constantly at her waterskin. In short order, she'd finished the first and started on a second. Idisio was drinking as well, more sparingly, but wasn't sweating at all, as far as Alyea could tell. She envied him, and suspected it to be a ha'ra'hain trait, since Deiq wasn't displaying any discomfort, either.

Then again, Deiq appeared more interested in holding on to his sour mood than in deigning to acknowledge bodily needs. He walked with his dark glare scouring their surroundings, not offering a word to anyone.

At last the tight canyon widened to a sun-drenched plateau speckled with enormous stones, which had been carved by wind and weather into astonishingly bent, twisted, and stretched pillars of red, orange, brown, and even a strange, glittery black. Desert sage and rosemary bushes spread their desiccated-looking branches wide, their tops looming just shy of tree-height.

An enormous brown and black bird perched at the top of a particularly large sage bush let out a shrill, warbling cry and spread its wings, beating the air but not taking flight. The trail guide looked up, a smile crossing his dour face, and called out something in a language Alyea didn't know. Behind her, Deiq snorted and said, "As if the damn thing can understand you."

"Bird named Guardian," the teyanain said, turning his head and looking only at Alyea. "He nest here, many years now. Longer than bird should live. He guard the passage. You come through and you not teyanain, Guardian attack, drive you away."

Deiq snorted again. "Superstition."

The guide ignored him and turned back to leading the pony, apparently not expecting a response from Alyea. The bird settled down, tucking its wings tightly against itself but continuing to glare; Alyea felt the malicious yellow stare boring into her back for some time.

They walked for a time in silence. Deiq's smoldering temper hung like a sullen heat at her back. At last, Alyea decided talking couldn't make Deiq's mood any worse, and might improve it. She thought about how to begin, turning over different approaches as they plodded through increasingly sweltering air. The sun raised heat-mirages across the flat areas.

"Deiq," she said at last, quietly, not looking back or making any motion. He moved to walk beside her. "Did they hurt you?"

"*Now* you ask that?" His tone could have etched steel.

She shot him a sideways frown, already regretting her decision to talk to him.

"No," he said after a moment. "Thank you for securing our release."

"It seems to have been a misunderstanding of sorts," Alyea said, her gaze straight ahead; very aware of the teyanin walking in front of them and the likelihood of a dozen more hiding and watching and listening nearby.

Deiq grunted. "And snakes fly. Evkit knew exactly what he was doing. What did he say to you?"

"I'm not going to discuss that right now," she said, jerking her chin to indicate their guide.

He grunted again and fell silent, his mood apparently not eased in the least. She repressed a sigh and tried again.

"All those gifts," she said, motioning to the laden pony. "I don't know what to make of them."

He gave a more thoughtful grunt than before, then said, "You're a new desert lord. Scratha ought to have given you as much or more, but I'm guessing once he sorts himself out, he'll send the gifts directly to your family home in Bright Bay. And the other Families owe you the same courtesy. It's a way of making sure you have monies to survive on. You can sell the gifts off, or use them to broker an alliance with a merchant who will then funnel a portion of all profit to you. When a Family has multiple desert lords, the later ones get less; but as you're the first Peysimun lord, you'll garner quite a hoard."

"I thought the Families supported their lords," Alyea said, startled.

"A desert lord can require rather a lot of upkeep," Deiq said dryly, with a sideways glance of his own.

Alyea sucked in a sharp breath and let it out in a long hiss, then said, "You're talking about kathain again."

"Yes. You may not like it, but you'll need—"

"I won't discuss this." The image of the older woman on her knees before the younger kathain still made her stomach lurch. All the cant about honor and choice be damned, certain aspects of the southern culture were flat-out *insane*.

He shook his head, his expression darkening again, and she gave up trying to talk him out of his bleak mood for the moment.

"Oruen will owe you as much; you're living in his city, so he takes on the role of host Family, in a way," Deiq said after a long silence. "At the same time, he's going to have to treat you as an equal, and you're going to have to insist on it. It's tricky, and unprecedented. You'll probably need to involve a loremaster at some point, to sort out the proper protocols."

He walked without speaking for a time, frowning in concentration. She let him be, relieved that his dark mood was being redirected into something useful.

At last he said, "Your own family will have to treat you as their most important representative. You'll be given some time to adjust, but within a fairly short time—a year at best—you'll be expected to hold to southern custom and host visiting desert lords with full honors. Three days is the rule. More than that is your own decision, but you're required to offer shelter and protection for three days to anyone of status—mainly desert lords. They're the ones who travel the most."

"I'd think desert lords would be the ones to stay home," Alyea said, intrigued. "To protect their Fortresses."

"No. They're usually the ones sent out when anything important is involved," Deiq said, and fell silent again, as though reluctant to explain further.

When it became clear he'd finished speaking, Alyea said, "What's the protocol for ha'ra'hain?"

Deiq shot her a surprisingly hard stare, and she blinked, not understanding how she'd managed to annoy him again with such a logical question.

"How would you host a demon?" he retorted.

"What? You're not—"

"Just introduce me as a merchant," he said, "and Idisio as Scratha's representative. That's the simplest way. Those who need to know either already do, or they'll find out in due time."

"But—"

"I can't be bothered with stupid human protocols," he said, glaring ahead.

She drew a breath to say something cutting in response, then let it go in a small sigh and left him to brood in peace. She dropped back a few paces to walk beside Idisio. Deiq didn't seem to notice, and she suspected the gesture had been wasted on him. But when she glanced at Idisio, he smiled wanly and nodded, as though to reassure her that she'd done right.

"I don't really want any honors, myself," he said in a low voice. "Scratha's representative is more than enough for me right now."

"Many year ago," the guide said, his voice carrying in the still air although he didn't even turn his head as he spoke, "ha'ra'hain were treated as kings. Given every honor, best kathain, anything they wanted. Now, not so much, very little trust left. Northlands very bad that way."

"Yes," Deiq growled, "now it's even permitted to *capture* ha'ra'hain, isn't it? Without apology or consequence."

"You talk Lord Evkit," the guide said. "I not involved in that." He stopped and turned to face Deiq. The two stared at one another for a few moments; seeing the tension settling across Deiq's back and shoulders, Alyea bit her lip and glanced around.

"Deiq," she said. She could almost feel hidden teyanain readying deadly poison darts all around them.

The guide said, softly, "Teyanain *different*, ha'inn. Always. We *justice*. We not bound to your laws, when you in our lands. You bound to *ours*. You forget?"

Deiq stood rigid for a long, frozen moment, then jerked his head sharply, producing a popping noise as vertebrae reset.

"No," he said. "I just don't think that excuses unprovoked attack and kidnap."

"You talk Lord Evkit," the guide said with a shrug. "I not involved in that. I just trail guide." He inclined his head. "Ha'inn." He turned around and began leading the pony forward again.

To Alyea's relief, Deiq took up the pace without further comment; and if his mood remained black, at least it didn't descend into open violence.

Chapter Twenty-five

As the Horn gentled around them and evening drew closer, long shadows cooled the scorching heat and small animals began to appear: black lizards, red snakes, corn moths and jumping-jokers. Deiq watched them to take his mind off his simmering frustration, and made himself speak long enough to point them out to his companions. After all, he was supposed to be teaching them.

"That was the symbol for Tehay Family," he said, deliberately stopping to look at a large rock on which perched a fair-sized black lizard, its crimson throat pouch swelling rhythmically as it stared blankly at them.

Everyone else had to stop and look, of course. Deiq derived a certain amount of satisfaction from the sour, impatient grunt of their guide.

"Tehay no longer exist," the guide said.

Deiq ignored him. "The black lizard is a symbol of subtlety," he said. "It's very intuitive, very quick to solve problems, and not afraid to lose in order to win."

"Tehay lost and lost," the guide said, and laughed.

Deiq shook his head, motioned to the guide to continue moving, and started walking again himself. "Tehay was a good Family," he said. "They were tricked."

"I seem to remember Lord Eredion saying something about a gambling debt," Alyea commented, falling in beside him; at the same time, the guide said, "Not proven."

"F'Heing," Deiq answered both of them. "Tehay held most of the Fertile Mountains."

"I thought you said F'Heing invaded—"

He'd expected that protest. "They did," he said. "It's complicated, like everything in the southlands."

"Glad to be going north," Idisio muttered.

"It's just as complicated in the north," Deiq assured him. "You have a whole new set of rules to learn there. Alyea will be a useful teacher for that." He aimed a smile her way, and surprised himself by being sincere with it. She shrugged, her own expression brooding now, and he realized he'd tripped her over into thinking about what lay ahead.

Not what he'd wanted; but then, he didn't seem to know from moment to moment what he wanted any more. He hadn't even been serious in that attempt to rile the teyanain into an attack earlier in the day. While it would have been satisfying on a number of levels, the risk that Alyea would get hurt was too high; he'd left it at verbal sniping.

Mostly, he admitted to himself as shadows grew over the ground and the air turned bronze with sunset, he was angry that *she* wasn't angry. She'd shown no outrage over his imprisonment, hadn't offered any apology, hadn't rebuked Lord Evkit publicly. Hadn't even offered any expression of greeting or relief when Evkit brought his two prisoners out. Her behavior subtly put him into a lesser status; she seemed to have no idea what a gross insult her attitude delivered. She even acted as though she accepted the notion that Evkit had been concerned for her safety—and how Evkit had sold *that* story to her he very much wanted to know, sooner than later.

But he couldn't pry: her mind was shut and locked like a sturdy door. He hadn't been able to pick up a single stray thought from her all day. Compared to her earlier mental chattering, the new silence was disconcerting and—given that it came after time spent with Lord Evkit—seriously worrisome as well.

Some drugs blocked mind-speech as effectively as aenstone. Whether Evkit would have given them to Alyea, and how, and *why*, Deiq had no way of telling. Bringing up the question while on Horn soil seemed unwise at the least and more than likely dangerous, if Alyea reacted with outrage at the prospect of having been unwittingly dosed. He'd have to mention it to her once they reached Bright Bay. He should have warned her long ago against taking any food or drink from the teyanain.

From *anyone* she wasn't entirely sure of, for that matter. Idisio had the right idea on that. No doubt he'd had run-ins of his own that taught the hard lesson; Alyea, apparently, hadn't been so betrayed before. More than likely, she didn't understand it had happened even now.

If it had happened. Deiq snorted, annoyed with himself. The questions that had been haunting him all day weren't any closer to resolution now than they had been at dawn, and just because he wasn't on the land of an active ha'rethe didn't mean it was safe to brood. He was getting careless; not a good survival trait.

But then, some days he was tired of constantly fighting just to survive; and this was one such day. He'd been having more of them than usual lately.

A moment later the guide stopped and announced, "We here."

A narrow path led almost straight down through the tumbled rocks, a repeat of the morning's canyon, but at a scramble-steep angle instead of flat.

"I go, you go," the teyanain said, pointing to Alyea. "Then you, and you."

He indicated Idisio and Deiq in turn. "You least likely to fall, ha'ra'ha," he added, nodding to Deiq. "You in rear."

Deiq nodded, accepting that rear guard wasn't a slight in this instance, and followed the single file down the sloping path. He found himself looking forward to Bright Bay—more than usual, at least. It would be *simpler*. And maybe this time he'd be able to finish his latest project, a secret indulgence he hadn't told anyone about—and probably never would.

He knew what they would say. Whether ha'reye or human, they would inevitably have the same reaction, although for vastly different reasons: *Foolishness.*

But Meer would have understood. And that, for Deiq, was good enough.

Chapter Twenty-six

Alyea's skin was slick with sweat in spite of her loose, light clothing; her calves and shoulders ached from navigating steep slopes and narrow trails for most of the day. Lunch had been a handful of dried fruit and nuts, along with a thick chunk of flatbread. It might have been enough for the scrawny teyanain, but it hadn't lasted long in Alyea's stomach, which began grumbling complaints not long after. Deiq passed her some trail jerky from his pack without comment, and that had at least stopped her body from craving more, though her mouth still longed for something better. Trail jerky tasted uniformly horrible to her: oversalted, oily, and rank. She didn't understand how anyone could survive on it for more than one meal.

A breeze swirled up to meet them, a salty tinge overriding the usual hot dust and rock aromas. She felt her shoulders loosen with relief at that sign: the ocean wasn't far away. Below, carts trundled along; groups of travelers walked and rode by. Nobody looked up the slope to the small party standing in plain sight atop a ridge.

"You go road," the teyanin guide said, pointing down. "You on road, north, you leave teyanain land. You go south, you back on our land. Lord Evkit say you go north."

He scrambled up the rough rock to his left and perched on an outcropping, watching them with an expressionless dark stare.

"You go," he repeated, pointing once more.

"We go," Deiq muttered. "All right, all right, we're going."

The traffic on the main road seemed to simply swerve around them as they reached the bottom of the steep slope. Nobody looked up to see where they'd come from; most people snuck brief, frightened glances at the newcomers before shying as far away as possible.

To the south, a twisted, blackened tree with a stone altar at its base was just barely visible; Alyea remembered seeing it on her way south with Chac and Micru. Bright Bay was within an hour's walk; but she didn't recall seeing any paths leading west at this point.

Alyea turned and looked up: a broken tumble of boulders and ragged chunks of rocky scree lay across the area she was sure they had just walked down.

She found herself on the verge of making the sign against witchery; barked a bitter laugh aloud instead. Deiq and Idisio shot her duplicate inquiring looks. She shook her head in answer and said, "Let's go."

They walked without speaking, each lost in his or her own thoughts and weariness; at last, as the sun melted into the Great Western Ocean, the sandy beaches of Bright Bay came into view. Idisio let out a great, sobbing gasp of relief and looked ready to kiss the ground, then immediately blushed a bright crimson.

Deiq shot him a sour glare. Alyea smiled, more lighthearted than she'd been all day.

"Home at last," she said cheerfully.

"We have to talk before you go charging in there," Deiq said, stopping in his tracks and lowering his head bullishly. "You don't seem to understand how much has changed."

Her patience with his dour mood snapped. She pulled the pack pony to the side of the road, out of the way of other weary travelers headed into Bright Bay; the last group that would be allowed in, more than likely. Ahead, empty day-vendor stalls lined both sides of the road: further indication that the gates would be closing soon.

"Here's what we have to talk about, Deiq," she said in a low voice. "I've been doing a lot of thinking today, and I realized some important things. You have something to teach me, go ahead, but don't think that puts you in charge. I made that mistake with Chacerly; I won't do that twice. This is *my* city. I grew up here. I can handle myself here. I know the rules—from the inside."

His scowl deepened, as though that barb hurt; as it had been meant to. Idisio had gone very quiet, still, and colorless, visibly trying to avoid drawing notice to himself. A small, cold part of her mind noted, for future reference, the boy's uncanny ability to blend into the background, and calculated that it had been a major part of his survival to date.

She went on, "You were my guide in the south. Fine. *I'll* be your guide here."

"I'm not that damn ignorant!" he snapped.

"Really? How do you plan to explain a rich merchant being in charge of a noblewoman and new desert lord? That would put you *superior* to the king, by what you yourself explained. How's that going to work, Deiq?"

He glared, sullen and offended. "That's for in public—"

"There *is* no private," she returned. "Servants gossip, which is why I won't keep them. But you can't very well shift between being in charge in private and being subordinate in public, Deiq. You'll slip, or I will, or someone will overhear something at the wrong time. It's one way or the other. And whichever way you turn, if you hover at my elbow with that ugly glare on your face, you'll stir up more trouble than I want to think about."

Deiq stared at her, the blackness gone from his expression. He looked as though he were sharply reevaluating his opinion of her. Idisio, in the gathering twilight, was almost not-there in his utter stillness.

"Understood," Deiq said at last. "No more brooding. You're right. But we still need to—"

"Anything you want to talk about can wait until we clear Bright Bay," she said. "I want to get through and back on the road as fast as—"

"But that's part of what—"

The group passing by had thinned to a handful of stragglers. She shook her head.

"The southern city gates close at night, Deiq. We don't have *time* right now. We go in now, or we're stuck at an outside inn for the night." She turned and urged the pony back onto the road. "Talk as we go or leave it until later."

He grunted in distinct annoyance, but offered no argument. "I heard that Oruen was going to lift the curfew on the southern gates," he said instead.

"Talk to Oruen," she said, blackly amused by echoing their teyanain guide. "I wasn't involved in that."

He made a growling noise; she laughed, unable to help it. Whatever else happened, she was *home*. She could handle anything thrown at her now.

Anything at all.

Chapter Twenty-seven

Aerthraim lanterns had replaced the tall torches at the southern gates. The eerie, ultra-white flame hurt Deiq's eyes, and he kept his gaze away from them as much as possible. The guards, dressed in white, now displayed crimson and black sashes; given that Oruen understood the southern color scheme, that had to be intended as a warning.

The guards themselves were hard-faced men and women whose sharp gazes picked over the incoming crowd and settled on Deiq with awakening interest.

He kept his expression neutral and his hands visible as they approached the gate, but wasn't at all surprised when two of the guards moved to block his path.

"*S'e*," one of them said. "Your business in Bright Bay, if you please?"

"He's with me," Alyea said, every inch the arrogant northern; an effect rather spoiled by her travel-stained southern garb of loose leggings and pale, long-sleeved shirt, both made from the almost translucently thin, layered material peculiar to the deep south. In addition, her newly southern-dark skin made her look as though she'd never set foot in Bright Bay before.

The guards studied her with dubious caution.

"And you are, *s'a*?"

"Lady Alyea Peysimun," she said. "Returning from a mission as King's ambassador to Scratha Fortress. This is merchant Deiq, and Idisio is bearing messages from Scratha Fortress to King Oruen."

Deiq shot her a sideways glance, surprised she'd used the northern title rather than her true status; but then, the gate guards really didn't need to know about that. It would only complicate and delay matters. Still, he'd expected her to trumpet her title to the heavens. Every other new desert lord he'd known had bragged on it endlessly.

The guards hesitated; then one, who had been staring at Idisio, said, "I remember that one! Lord Scratha called justice-right on him. Said he was a pick-thief."

Frowns gathered on all the guard's faces, and they regarded the group with even more suspicion than before. Alyea's forehead wrinkled.

"Lord Scratha decided to take me on as a servant," Idisio said, voice and gaze steady; but Deiq saw the tension ridging his thin shoulders. "Would he have done that for a thief?"

"You might have run off," the guard who'd recognized him said skeptically.

"Have you ever *met* Lord Scratha?" Idisio said, winning a grin from one guard. "Trust me, running wasn't an option. And he has no tolerance for thieves at all; I wouldn't be standing here today if he'd truly caught me with his money in my hand."

Alyea's face cleared, and she said, "I'll speak for him, *s'es*. He's no thief."

Idisio's shoulders relaxed, and Deiq hid a smile; apparently Alyea hadn't yet learned to pick out spoken lies from truth. Then again, Idisio showed a real talent for deceit; if Deiq hadn't known the true story, he might have doubted his own instincts.

"Still," said the first guard, his frown unwavering. "I think we should send a runner for the captain, let him decide this one. Or have them wait at one of the outside inns until morning."

Deiq stifled a sigh; this was going nowhere fast. He said, lacing the words with a subtle push, "*S'es*, we're very tired. If you could please simply let us pass?"

The guards blinked, glanced around at one another, and slowly stepped aside; much more slowly than they should have, and with clear reluctance. Deiq tried not to frown, knowing that would break the effect, and wondered if a bribe would be required.

"Thank you, *s'es*," Idisio chimed in. "We appreciate your courtesy in letting us pass; Syrta bless your boots."

The words seemed completely innocent and contained no ha'ra'hain persuasion at all, but the frowns lifted into a much more normal indifference.

"Go on already, then," the leader said, and waved them through, already looking back to the southern road for any last stragglers approaching.

Deiq shot Idisio a hard sideways glance as they cleared the gates. "Syrta bless your *boots*?" he muttered.

"Not something you want to know about," Idisio said, looking straight ahead. "I've met more than one of those guards before, and they just needed reminded of that. Leave it there."

Deiq checked, his mind connecting implications rapidly, and half-turned. Idisio's hand latched onto his arm a moment later, fingers digging in hard.

"I said *leave it be*," Idisio snapped, and they locked glares.

Alyea hadn't stopped. Her voice floated back through the darkening air over the steady clop of hooves: "Can you have this argument later? I want to go home."

Idisio dug his fingers in a fraction more, with surprising strength, then let go and turned away to follow her. Deiq hesitated a moment, looking back towards the gates, which the guards were tugging closed for the night. They wouldn't even see him coming.

I was a street rat. Idisio's voice cut into his mind. *If I don't care, what in the hells are you fussing about? Forget it. Come on already, I want a bath.*

It's—Deiq didn't have a word that Idisio would understand. He needed one that would convey *dishonor, insult, outrage, offensive,* and *treachery* all at once. *Our children should never be used as kathain!*

I wasn't kathain, Idisio said tartly. *I was a whore. It was a living for a while. I decided I didn't like it, and put my attention to stealing instead. Which I'm rather better at, thank you. And I didn't know I was ha'ra'hain at the time, so quit frothing over it.*

Did any of those men ever hurt you?

No answer; and Idisio's mind went sharply opaque, which was answer enough.

Alyea had all but disappeared ahead. Only the few torches lining the road showed her, leading the pony at a steady pace, Idisio beside her.

Deiq took a last glance back at the gates, then let out a hard, irritated breath, shook his head, and jogged to catch up.

Chapter Twenty-eight

Their sunset arrival threw the Peysimun household into a frenzy of confusion. Within the first hour, Alyea wished she'd gone with instinct and booked rooms at one of the inns near the Gates, or even gone to her apartments at the Palace, instead of Peysimun Mansion.

Her mother stared at Deiq, and he at her, with instant and mutual antagonism during the initial introductions. After so much time surrounded by southerners, Alyea found Lady Peysimun's pale, plump skin and mouse-brown hair a strange sight; she had trouble believing they could possibly be related. The clothes didn't help; Lady Peysimun, as always, wore a severely styled, long-sleeved and floor-length dress. It reminded Alyea of Sela, only with more glittering jewelry at ears, neck and wrist. She wore a small firetail bird feather dipped in silver as a brooch; Alyea remembered coveting that brooch before leaving Bright Bay. Now it seemed a pointless and even gaudy decoration.

"S'e," Lady Peysimun said, ice in her voice; "S'a," Deiq returned, his face as bland as Alyea had ever seen it. Lady Peysimun granted Idisio a brief, assessing stare, taking in his drab, dusty trail clothes, then visibly categorized him as a servant. Alyea let the assumption rest for the moment, as one less battle to fight on the front steps.

"Deiq and Idisio are my guests," Alyea said, putting a chill in her voice equal to her mother's, "and will be staying for a time."

Lady Peysimun nodded stiffly and motioned to a maid waiting nearby. "Make a room ready for s'e Deiq and his servant," she ordered.

Deiq's mouth twitched in faint amusement; Idisio lifted one shoulder with a tiny, resigned sigh. Neither protested, so Alyea again let the matter rest. She'd correct her mother in private later on. For the moment, she was just grateful that Deiq raised no fuss over being roomed away from her.

"We've already had dinner, I'm afraid," Lady Peysimun said, her back stiff and her gaze aimed somewhere over Alyea's shoulder.

"I'm sure the kitchens can put together a cold tray," Alyea returned, secretly relieved. Her mother's preferred dinner tended towards the light and fluffy foods Alyea hated, and right now a servant's meal of black bread, cold meats, bean salad, and hard cheese sounded much more appetizing.

Her mother cast a hard stare at her. "I'm sure," she said, and motioned to another servant hovering anxiously nearby. "A tray for our visitors, please. Bring it to their room. I'm sure they'd prefer to retire for the evening. And do bring them a bathing tub and water. They look to need refreshment after their long journey."

The words, delivered with impeccable precision, managed to stop just short of insulting. The implication underneath was clear: *You're dirty, you smell, and you're not welcome here.*

Alyea resisted the urge to roll her eyes. "Mother," she said flatly. "Thank you for your courtesy to my guests." She turned her head and looked Deiq full in the face, seeing the lines of amusement at the corners of his eyes and mouth. "Please consider this household at your disposal," she told him.

Her mother made an aggrieved, protesting sound. Alyea looked back and met her mother's pale eyes with a hard stare of her own; after a moment, Lady Peysimun dropped her gaze.

In a much more subdued tone, Lady Peysimun said, "Welcome to my home, s'e Deiq."

"Thank you," Deiq said, tone solemn, eyes lit with a deep amusement. "I'm graced by your honor." Idisio muttered something similar, barely audible, and Lady Peysimun's expression regained some condescension as she glanced at him.

"Well," she said then, "Alyea, my dear. If you'll be *kind* enough to join me for evening tea while your guests settle down for the night, we can catch up on what you've been doing while you were gone." She pressed her lips together hard, then looked at Deiq and added, "Breakfast is an hour past dawn, s'e, if you'd grace us with your presence."

"I would be honored," Deiq said gravely, and after a deep bow, steered Idisio after the servant detailed to lead them to a guest room.

Lady Peysimun drew in a long breath, watching them go, then let it out in a hard sigh. "Let's go have some tea," she said, and taking Alyea by the elbow steered her in the other direction.

Alyea's mother poured tea with a shaking hand, the distress she hadn't shown in front of outsiders emerging at last. "You look so . . . so *gaunt*, child. And so . . . *dark*. I almost didn't recognize you!"

Alyea accepted the cup, sat back in the heavily padded chair, and looked around without answering right away, feeling as though she'd never seen this room before. The heavy white drapes, which allowed light but cut down on heat, had always seemed plain, almost ugly. Now she noticed the lace trimmings and pale beads sewn onto the cloth; appreciated the way the folds fell and the feathery shadow-patterns the outside trees and bushes, backlit by evening lanterns, cast against the screen of curtain.

The walls held numerous paintings and portraits: she'd never really looked at them. They'd always just . . . been there, throughout her childhood. Studying them now, she found an oddly patternless mix: light-hearted flower sketches and heavy busts of famous figures flanked portraits of stern-faced, elderly ancestors. Amid the chaos stood enormous indoor pots brimming with long-stemmed, wide-leaved plants.

A floral scent drifted by as a breeze stirred the curtains, and a faint patter of rain began.

Her mother shifted in her own chair, a worried expression fixed on her broad, pale face. Lack of outdoor activity and heredity had mixed to provide a far more "northern" appearance than Alyea herself possessed. Alyea's father, one of the first casualties of the Purge, had been the one holding the stronger southern bloodline, and that had passed to Alyea. No doubt after all the time in the south, she looked even more like her father than usual. Her mother had always tried to make Alyea stay indoors, claiming that dark skin was unattractive on women.

Alyea had long since figured out that it was more a case of her mother not wanting to be reminded of her dead husband. The less her daughter resembled the southern side of her heritage, the calmer Lady Peysimun became.

Well, that game is out the window, Alyea thought. Studying her mother, she wondered if Lady Peysimun even consciously considered the difference between their appearances, much less the physical luxury of their surroundings anymore; or if, like Alyea, she had begun taking luxury, status, and safety all for granted.

It hadn't been so long since their assumptions of safety had been badly shaken. During the last months of Ninnic's reign, fear had kept them all within the grounds, indoors more often than not. The stomp of guard boots passing along the street outside had drawn a tightness over every adult face and a breathless silence to the few occupied rooms. Nobody had been safe towards the end; certainly not the Peysimun household, after Alyea's public disgrace and Ethu's death.

And now, because of me, more people are going to die . . . might already be dead. Just like Ethu, the Qisani tried to help me, and they're paying for it. And once again, she couldn't do a damn thing about it.

Alyea looked down at her teacup reflexively, ready to blink back tears; but her eyes remained dry. Outside, the pattering rain increased to a steady drumming, and thunder rumbled briefly somewhere far away.

Her mother said, "We'll have a feast tomorrow night, to welcome you home. And . . . and to welcome your . . . your companions, of course. Although I must say you came home with some *strange* company."

Alyea lifted her cup to her lips, despair over the past lifting into amusement. Her mother had no idea. . . .

The tea tasted of mint and oranges; one of her mother's herbal blends, then, not a true tea. Alyea kept her face still against a grimace of distaste, thinking longingly of the tins of thopuh even now being loaded from the pack pony into the Peysimun storage rooms. She should have dug one out and given it to her mother as a homecoming gift; too late now.

"Deiq is a powerful merchant," she said. "And a friend. Idisio is . . . an emissary of sorts."

"I know who *s'e* Deiq is," her mother said, her mouth thinning in clear disapproval. "He's got a name, that one. Just how did you come to meet him?"

"Apparently, he's a friend of Lord Eredion Sessin," Alyea said. "Lord Eredion asked Deiq to guide me through the southlands, as a personal favor. And he's not quite as bad as his reputation would say."

Her mother raised her eyebrows in a skeptical expression. "Hmph. So he'll be leaving, now that you're home safely." She looked distinctly relieved at the prospect. "And this . . . this boy, Idisio? He looks northern. How did he come to be traveling with you?"

"He's more traveling with Deiq," Alyea said, hoping to avoid dangerous explanations, and saw her mother's eyes narrow sharply.

"I *see.*"

Alyea exhaled hard, annoyed at the obvious assumption. "No, mother, they're not lovers."

"If you say so." Before she could protest further, her mother switched topics. "And what have you been doing? We've been terribly worried. Couldn't you have sent word when you reached Scratha Fortress? I told Oruen if he'd sent you to any harm I'd never forgive him."

Alyea raised an eyebrow, startled at the familiarity. Her mother always insisted on proper formality when discussing any royalty higher than themselves. To leave out Oruen's title was severely out of character.

"Oh, well," her mother said, catching Alyea's surprise, "he did choose my daughter as an important emissary, after all." She smiled. "We've been invited to quite a few dinners at the palace since you left."

Alyea kept her expression neutral with an effort and sipped tea without comment. Of course. Her mother would have leapt on the implied status and grabbed hold with both hands. She restrained a sigh, wondering if she could gather Deiq and Idisio and simply slip out of Bright Bay in the middle of the night.

"But tell me of your journey," her mother pressed. "We didn't think you'd return so soon. Holding a desert fortress is a big job. Did you leave someone competent in charge?"

Alyea studied the strain in her mother's face and understood: the woman was afraid her daughter had failed, had run away from the task. Afraid the new, cherished status would disintegrate like sand blown by the wind.

"I left Lord Scratha in charge," Alyea said bluntly. "I believe he's competent."

Her mother's hands began to shake again. She looked tremendously distressed. "He returned? But—wasn't he banished, sent off to the Stone Islands? How in the world—?"

"I don't know," Alyea interrupted, "and it's really not my concern. He showed up, I bowed out and came home."

Her mother studied the cup in her hands, turning it slowly, her whole face puckered into a worried frown. "So what are you going to do now?"

Alyea leaned back in her chair, cradling the fragile teacup in both hands. Her stomach rumbled quietly, reminding her that she hadn't eaten dinner yet. After this obligatory conversation, she'd slip off to the kitchens for something more solid than tea and sliced fruit.

"I need an audience with Oruen," she said, deliberately leaving off any honorific. She felt *she'd* damn well earned that right.

"Of course," her mother said, not looking up. "I've already sent...." A dark flush spread across her pale skin. "I've already sent word," she finished.

"Inviting him to the feast tomorrow?"

Her mother's head moved in a bare nod.

Alyea rolled her eyes and said, "Yes, wouldn't that be something, to have the king himself attend a dinner in your home. I bet you've been trying to work that in since I left."

"You needn't sound so sour over it," her mother said, glancing up with a flash of temper. "How was I to know you'd give the fortress back to Lord Scratha?"

Alyea sat up, astonished. "Did anyone really think I'd fight the rightful lord over the holding?" she demanded. "Were you all that mad?"

Her mother shrugged. "We didn't think he'd return so soon," she said thinly, her color still high. "And as I understand it, once you'd settled in, a case could have been made that you had rightful possession under desert law."

Alyea played out Bright Bay politics in her mind. Yes, that would have made sense to them. To people that had never traveled past the Horn, never looked a teyanin lord in the face, never heard a ha'rethe speak, never seen the rock and sand that surrounded Scratha Fortress; never seen how complex desert politics could quickly become.

Her mother, especially, wouldn't understand any of that.

"It wouldn't have been that simple," Alyea said at last. "Even if he hadn't returned, it wouldn't have been that simple."

"I don't see why not," her mother bristled. "You had the king's backing, didn't you? He was getting ready to send people to support your holding, as soon as we heard that you'd taken proper possession of Scratha Fortress. We've all been waiting on word from you!"

Alyea stared at her mother, astonished all over again. "He was going to send *troops?*"

"Well, that was certainly suggested," her mother said, looking away. The inflection was unmistakable: smug pride at having been so smart.

"By you, of course." Alyea watched her mother preen a little, then said, much more harshly, "I hope Oruen wasn't *listening?*"

The smile left her mother's broad face, replaced by stiff resentment. "You needed protection from all those warring barbarian factions. Why was that such a bad idea?"

Alyea shook her head. "You have no idea," she said, despairing. "I can't even begin to explain."

"Well, never mind," her mother said sourly. "It's over and done with. You're home, and the matter's between Oruen and Scratha now. We'll have the welcoming feast tomorrow, and host your companions for one more night, if they *want* to stay—" Her tone suggested a strong hope otherwise. "And then they'll return to their lives and you'll return to your place here. Perhaps Oruen will find other assignments for you." She didn't sound very hopeful over that part.

"Um," Alyea said carefully, "it's not actually quite that simple."

"Of course it is," her mother said. "I won't allow you to complicate things past all reason this time, Alyea."

"This time?" Alyea sat forward, anger flushing through her. "*This time? What was the first time? When have I complicated things? When I was almost beaten to death? Is that what you're—"

Her mother's expression turned severe. "Don't you bark at me, Alyea Peysimun," she said sharply. "Not in my own household. At the end of the day, you're still an unmarried young woman and I'm still, as your mother, in charge of you. Don't you forget that!"

Alyea stared, speechless; caught between the urge to shriek with rage and collapse in laughter at the vast misunderstanding that lay between them. She'd hoped to rest first, but clearly she would have to tell her mother the full news tonight after all. How to present it, how to get through her mother's willful ignorance, utterly escaped her.

Her mother raised the cup to her lips and sipped delicately. "Dinner should be ready soon. You ought to go clean up and change into some *proper* clothing. That disgraceful outfit you're wearing is—"

"No," Alyea interrupted, deciding to tackle the issue the only way she could think of: directly. "Listen. All those items I brought home—they're gifts. From the teyanain."

"The *teyanain*?" Her mother sat up straight, looking distinctly alarmed. "That's a child's story, Alyea, what under the Four are you—"

"They're not a myth. They're real. And they rule the Horn. They gave me the gifts," Alyea plowed on, over her mother's noises of incomprehension, "because Peysimun Family now has their very own full desert lord."

Now her mother was the one staring, openmouthed and incredulous. "What are you talking about? We're not some southern barbarian family, we don't have—"

"Me. *I've* been invested as a full desert lord. By a Conclave. I'm now Lord Alyea Peysimun."

Tea splashed down the front of her mother's dress as the fragile cup bounced from ample belly to wide knee to the small table and shattered.

Alyea hid a smirk and tried to sound apologetic as she said, "Maybe I should have phrased that more gently?"

Chapter Twenty-nine

Deiq tossed his pack onto the lower, plainer servant's bed and pointed Idisio to the larger guest bed. "I don't sleep much," he said when Idisio began to protest. "Let's go hunt down some food."

Idisio set his pack slowly on the guest bed and looked around the room. "I never thought I'd be in such nice surroundings," he said, almost under his breath. "It feels very strange."

Deiq glanced around the room, unimpressed. Creamy white walls and curtains the color of bleached sand; plain, dark rugs; fluffy, wide pillows and fine green bed-sheets; a few small decorations and wall-hangings: nothing exciting, to his way of thinking. The small table, while sturdy, was built of the cheapest woods and with the simplest construction. There was no writing-desk, and only one wide-bottomed chair. The empty central space had just enough room for a tub, which the servants would no doubt be bringing in soon.

This was the sort of lodging offered to guests who were encouraged not to stay. Even Scratha, with his limited resources, had done better.

"Let's go get some food," he said again, and urged Idisio from the room.

He stopped a passing servant as they emerged and asked for directions to the kitchen; he could have figured it out on his own, but saw no point in highlighting his differences. It was one of many small subterfuges he'd grown accustomed to over time. Even a "mysterious quasi-noble" needed to act humanly confused at times.

Remembering Alyea's phrase made him smile; the young man he'd stopped to ask for directions stammered, ducked and beamed in response. Deiq hastily turned the smile into something more indifferent, and the servant blinked as though coming out of a haze. Face setting into sharp lines of distrust, he hurried away without looking back.

Deiq sighed. "I hate the north," he said under his breath.

"Because he didn't drop them for you?" Idisio said tartly.

Deiq shot the younger ha'ra'ha a disgusted glare. "No. I didn't want that. But I hate that he felt ashamed for wanting to."

"You have an opinion of yourself, don't you?"

Deiq shook his head, forcing himself into a dry amusement instead of anger. "Not really," he said. "Right now I'm of the opinion that I'm hungry, nothing more."

Hungry on more than one level; the servant's initial, startled submissiveness had reawakened a dull ache he'd been ignoring for some time. He set his teeth together hard and pushed the haunting need back into hiding the usual way: by remembering Meer, and yellow eyes in the darkness under Bright Bay, and a shattering scream from one moment that blended into the other.

Idisio snorted, blissfully unaware of Deiq's thoughts, and headed for the kitchens with the arrogant assurance of youth. Deiq followed, more slowly, again pushing anger into bleak amusement.

He reflected, not for the first time, that if he hadn't taught himself that trick hundreds of years ago, he would likely have torn through the entire human race, and most ha'ra'hain, for insults they didn't even know they delivered. But the human world had steadily evolved over the years, and he'd changed with it; something the slower-moving ha'reye would never understand, any more than Idisio would grasp the implications of his heritage until forced into a crisis.

Remembering how sanguine Idisio had been in the face of the clee-trance, Deiq hoped he wouldn't be the one to provoke that confrontation. The thought was selfish; he couldn't bring himself to care. He was feeling far too tired and old lately to be sure of the outcome of any serious fights.

"I need to visit the Tower," he muttered, and lengthened his stride to catch up with Idisio.

Chapter Thirty

As soon as the door to her mother's sitting room closed behind her, Alyea headed for the kitchens at a trot.

She noticed, as she went, that the servants all appeared to be new, and wondered what had prompted that change. Probably Lady Peysimun had replaced her "ordinary" servants with ones boasting a history of serving the important, as a way of accenting her higher status. It was the sort of little game she loved.

The kitchens, at least, hadn't changed, and neither had the cooks. Apparently good cooks were too important to risk changing out for mere status points. Alyea gave devout thanks for that decision as she stepped up behind Nem, who stood stirring a gigantic soup pot, and prodded his broad right shoulder.

Nem turned, a lumbering movement, and grinned down at her. "I heard you coming," he said, his voice so thick and slurred that the words were hardly understandable.

"Sure you did," Alyea laughed, and prodded him in the stomach. "I'm hungry!"

Nem watched her mouth closely as she spoke, his mild, pale eyes narrowed. His chestnut-colored hair had begun growing out of its short summer cut, and almost covered his lumpy ears; she could see streaks of silver beginning to appear among the brown.

"All right," he nodded, the words as mangled as before, and pointed to an archway across the room. "Go sit with your friends. I will bring you soup." He reached out and poked a long, thick finger into her right shoulder. "Welcome home," he added.

She grinned at him and went into the servants' dining hall. Deiq and Idisio looked up from bowls of soup as she entered. A platter of black bread scraps and ends sat on the table between them, and a platter of cut-up hard cheese and peasant sausage; she groaned, seeing that last item, and almost lunged to grab a piece.

Thumping down onto the bench beside Deiq, she bit into the greasy, spicy treat with enthusiasm. Her mother never let food like this appear on the main dining table, but to Alyea, it was more satisfying than six courses of gourmet foodstuffs.

Deiq watched her with his usual sardonic amusement. Idisio kept his attention on his soup, sullen again.

"Your cook is very good," Deiq said, picking up a piece of black bread. "And your baker."

"Peysimun doesn't have a house baker," Alyea said. "My mother insists on buying all her bread from the White Gull Bakery, near the palace. But she doesn't buy peasant breads; that comes from a bakery well outside the Gates; I think it's called Shelly's. The outside is covered with hundreds of shells, and—"

She stopped, suddenly realizing that she'd been about to launch into a discussion of Shelly's versus the White Gull, and how utterly useless such a conversation would be. She didn't even *want* to talk. It had been old habit prompting her into a light social discussion of no consequence.

Deiq finished his soup, mopping up the last liquids with another piece of bread, and said nothing. Idisio prodded listlessly at his soup, as though utterly exhausted. He looked a bit grey around the edges; she resisted an urge to tell him to go to bed. He was ha'ra'hain, and old enough to take care of himself. No sense in her mothering him.

Outside, the wind picked up to a fierce howl, and the rain thundered down in audible sheets.

"Glad we made it in before nightfall," Alyea tried next, and felt that fall flat too.

Nem came in with a large bowl of soup and set it down before her, then produced a large-bowled wooden spoon from an apron pocket and held it out to her. She took the spoon, turning it over, and grinned broadly, tracing her finger across his latest carving: a rose in full bloom. A daisy, a sunflower, and a gods'-glory flower decorated handle and bowl. With the rose on the back, the spoon was complete.

"What will the next one be?" she asked, careful to look up at him as she spoke.

Nem shrugged, his gaze going to Deiq for a long, thoughtful moment. "Maybe fish," he said. "Not sure."

"Shellfish," Deiq suggested.

"Maybe." Nem studied Idisio for a moment, then looked over the table. "Need anything?"

"No. Thank you."

Nem nodded, poked Alyea in the shoulder, and withdrew.

"He's not entirely deaf, but very close to it," Alyea said. "He was born that—"

"Yes," Deiq drawled. "Is there a reason you're suddenly feeling the urge to chatter?"

She felt her face heat, but before she could speak, Idisio cut in, waspishly: "Is there a reason *you're* suddenly feeling the urge to be an ass?"

The air went dangerously still. The hair on the back of Alyea's neck rose. Without knowing quite why, she slammed her hand down hard on the table, producing a startlingly loud *crack!*

"Knock it off," she said severely as they both jerked to stare at her. In that moment, she reminded herself of Azni, and had to repress a smile. "Go get some sleep, both of you. We'll talk in the morning."

Idisio stood without further prompting and stalked from the room. Deiq watched him go, a faint frown on his face, but made no move to follow.

"Something's eating him hard," he said. "I don't know what. That wasn't the first shot he took tonight, and I'm getting damn tired of it."

Alyea sighed and began eating soup. "Gods, I've missed good food," she said between mouthfuls. "Not that southern food is bad," she added hastily.

"What you grew up with always tastes best," Deiq said, and reached for a piece of hard cheese. "When I was young, I liked bread and cheese. I've never quite left that basic staple."

Alyea hesitated on the verge of confronting Deiq about just how old he was, and about his lie regarding Lord Eredion; then remembered that she had a more pressing question to ask at the moment.

"Lord Evkit told me something about the Qisani, and I need to know if it's true," she said, and watched his face settle into harder lines. "He said that Acana wasn't supposed to help me. That the healer wasn't supposed to save my life. Is *that* true?"

Deiq set the cheese down with delicate care, as though it were made of glass, and spread his hands wide and flat on the table. "You can't believe a tenth of what a teyanin tells you, and Evkit far less than that," he said. "But in this case—yes. It's true."

Her mind flinched away from thinking about what that meant. "He also said that Acana and the Qisani are in danger because they helped me. Is that true?"

"That's too simple a question and far too complicated an answer," Deiq said, his gaze flat and emotionless. "Living with a ha'rethe protector cuts two ways, Alyea. It always has, and it's a delicate dance at times. Remember Scratha Conclave? I stepped in because Cafad Scratha doesn't understand yet how to posture without getting real emotions involved, and Scratha ha'rethe would have followed the emotion without looking at the flawed logic behind it. Cafad Scratha almost got Evkit *killed* with his little tantrum. I had a *shit* of a time convincing Scratha ha'rethe to let me handle it."

She stared at him, appalled. "Did they know? The other lords?"

Deiq snorted. "Let's just say Cafad didn't win any friends at that Conclave." He blinked and looked up at the arched entrance to the room, frowning as though listening to something.

Just as she was drawing in breath to ask what he'd heard, her cousin Kameniar sauntered into the room.

"*Dear* cousin," the tall, broadly built young man said, leaning against the archway wall and sneering at her. "How *cozy* you look. Welcome home."

Alyea let out the breath in a long sigh, realizing that by northern custom, Deiq was sitting intimately close beside her, instead of properly across the table from her.

She decided to go with what was left of courtesy, and said, "Deiq, may I present my cousin, Kameniar. Kam, this is Deiq of Stass; he's been helping me learn southern customs—"

"Oh, of *course*," Kam said, smirking. "I've heard about how Deiq of Stass *helps* women."

Alyea bit the inside of her cheek and very carefully did not look at Deiq, knowing that her aggressive cousin was trying, for whatever bizarre reason, to start a fight.

"How is . . . um . . . Harra?" She had to struggle to remember the name of the girl he'd been seeing when she left.

His expression darkened. "Gone," he said. "Run off with some southern bastard. 'Scuse me," he added, nodding to Deiq. "Nothing personal."

"Of course," Deiq said mildly.

"I'm sorry to hear that." Alyea reached for another expected courtesy. It felt like a tremendous effort, and rather useless, but she tried anyway. "Er . . . your mother? How's she doing?"

"Complaining all the time," Kam said. He shook his head and crossed to sit at the table across from them. "She's become very difficult. I think it's age. She's getting up there, you know? Over sixty now. Her mind'll be going soon." He didn't seem particularly sad at the thought. "You do know *I'm* in line now to take over the family estates when she goes," he added, preening a bit. "Ashin ran off to be a wandering tinker or something. Such a disgrace, she disowned him, can't blame her. But I think the shame affected her mind, really. She's been *hard*-hearted lately."

Deiq's mouth twitched. He said nothing aloud, but Alyea could sense his deep amusement. And she saw his point now: Kam's chatter felt inane and pompous, a waste of time and voice, and a poor mask for a deeper issue. He was angling for something, and Alyea was fairly sure she knew what.

"I take it," Alyea said dryly, "you mean she won't pay your gambling debts any longer. Or your brothel tabs."

Kam reared back in his seat with an offended expression. "Now, cousin, that's hardly polite talk in front of *company*. What *have* you learned for manners while you were gone?"

"Which means I'm right," Alyea said. "And I haven't any money either, Kam, so you'll find no help here."

"No money? What do you call that great load of trade goods you walked in with?" he demanded, dropping his pious act. "D'you know what you've *got* there? I saw a bundle marked with—"

"They're mine," she said, "not yours, and I'm not giving you any of it to sell."

"Just what did you do to pick up all those pretty trinkets among the barbarians?" he sneered. "And walking back in with *him*! D'you think nobody sees what—"

Her temper rose sharply. After all she'd been though, *damned* if she'd let this overfed fool call her a whore! Before she quite knew what she was doing, she'd half-risen, leaned forward, and slapped him hard. Just before her hand hit his cheek, Deiq's hand clamped around her wrist, almost but not quite arresting the blow.

Kam went over sideways, tumbled over the bench, and crashed to the floor, flipping the bench over onto himself in the process.

Deiq pulled her hand back roughly. "Damn it," he said, "I *warned* you about that!"

She stared at her motionless cousin, appalled. A moment later the cook came in and gave Deiq a hard stare, obviously assuming he'd been the one who hit Kam.

Deiq shook his head, stood, and moved to help Nem lift the overturned bench. The two men knelt next to Kam. After a few moments of examination, Deiq said, "He's still alive. It doesn't look like you broke his jaw, and he didn't break anything during the tumble." He looked directly at the cook and added, with careful enunciation, "He needs to be carried to bed. He will hurt in the morning, but he is all right."

Nem nodded, squinting at Deiq thoughtfully, and turned a sharp stare to Alyea. She suspected that, close as his ear had been to Deiq's mouth, he'd made out most of what the ha'ra'ha had said, and now knew that Alyea had delivered the blow. She shrugged, resisting the urge to apologize, and went to summon servants to carry her unconscious cousin away.

Chapter Thirty-one

Deiq waited with Alyea while servants removed her cousin; said nothing, and kept his expression neutral. But he could feel the shock reverberating through her entire body, and when she abruptly turned to leave, he followed close behind.

Three steps later, she whirled and said fiercely, "Leave me alone!"

"No."

She glared, sullen and defiant, and walked away at a fast clip. He kept pace, and when she tried to slam the door to her suite between them, he stopped it with a hand, eased inside, and shut the door behind him.

"Damn it, go away!"

He shook his head. "Not while you're this upset."

"I could have killed him!" She put the back of one shaking hand to her mouth, her eyes filling with tears. "How the hells should I feel?"

The world would be a better place if you had killed the little ta-karne, he thought. He knew better than to say that aloud, though.

"Upset," he said dryly, and urged her into a chair.

Alyea's room was much larger and lusher than the guest room he and Idisio had been given, but showed remarkably little of Alyea's fighting personality. Instead, delicate lacy designs and pastel shades dominated, more Lady Peysimun's style than her daughter's. Deiq had a feeling Alyea didn't spend much time in this room or even within the mansion, which meant she had an apartment within the palace itself.

He'd have to see about moving them there tomorrow. Being here was throwing Alyea back into all the old patterns he'd been trying to break her of;

even now, her muddled surface thoughts centered on worry over her mother discovering Deiq in her rooms, unsupervised.

He sighed and sat on the arm of her chair, one hand on her shoulder, wishing he could give her a shot of stiff desert lightning to settle her raw nerves; but the household appeared sternly dedicated to light wines.

"Alyea," he said, "this is exactly why you need me by your side right now. You can't afford to lose your temper when I'm not around. It wasn't the physical slap that knocked your cousin out; I stopped most of that when I grabbed you. But you were mad, and your anger can hurt people now. You wanted to hit him, and so even though I stopped your hand, the blow carried through just from your willing it to do so."

She stared at him, bewildered. "Because I . . . wanted . . . ?"

"Yes. You have to start being very careful when you decide you want something. You can do a lot of damage without meaning to, even though there's no protector bound to this area." *Any more,* he added silently, and held his face still against a pained grimace. "That's why aqeyva is an essential discipline for desert lords. You have to practice, every day, until it really becomes a part of you. Until restraint isn't just about not punching someone, but about stopping the anger before it goes to dangerous levels. And that's why kathain are so—"

She stiffened and began to say something, a ferocious light in her eyes.

"*No,*" he said, overriding her; trying not to think about leaning forward and gathering in that intoxicating fierceness. "You listen to me this time. Kathain are important for desert lords because they're trained to see when their lord needs distraction. If you start losing your temper, you're liable to find your kathain rubbing your back or acting silly, just to change your mood. It's much more complicated than a tumble, and kathain are not merely whores."

She looked away, the line of her jaw set hard and stubborn. He studied her profile for a moment, then decided to go for shock, to see if he could finally break through her preconceptions.

"Alyea," he said evenly, "at the moment, because you won't listen to me on this, *I'm* having to act as your kathain. And I don't care for that much."

She jerked around at that, and found him leaning in close. He heard the rapid tripling of her heartbeat; her eyes dilated instantly. He could feel the strength, the rock-solid confidence that her whole being rested upon, and his hands fisted against the need to pull her in closer.

Oh, Meer . . . Oh, gods, no. Not again. Never again.

"I'm not going to hurt you," he said, both to her and to the memories in his head; his voice barely rose above a whisper. Their faces were almost close enough together to brush noses. "I'm here to *teach* you. To help you stand on your own as a full desert lord. But I can't do that if you don't listen when I explain these things to you."

She stared at him, transfixed. He saw the light glaze in her eyes and realized he'd fallen into a trancing-voice without meaning to. Cursing himself internally, he carefully changed his pitch and tone to bring her back out to normal consciousness.

"Your cousin is a fool, and he's very lucky I was there." He leaned back as he spoke, slowly increasing the distance between them. "And you are lucky I was there—and damn lucky that I hold to my promises." He hadn't meant to say that last part aloud; it carried a betraying measure of his raw frustration.

Gods, it had been a long time . . . In the back of his mind he heard Meer's dying scream, and the deeper hunger dulled to mere physical desire; much easier to master than that other, long unmet, need.

Foolishness . . . He needed to visit the Tower. Soon. To remind himself of why he'd made the vow.

She blinked once, twice, shook her head as though to clear it of a fog; then stared at him with awakening suspicion. He'd seen that expression hundreds of times before: the awareness that he could have done anything he wanted in that moment.

And there goes what was left of her trust, he thought as she stood up and backed away several jerky steps. He made no move to stop her; studied his fingernails with ostentatious indifference, trying not to let the dull ache coiling in his stomach show in his expression.

"I want you to leave," she said, cold and precise. "I will see you in the morning."

He aimed a cool smile at her and moved, instead, to sit in the chair she had just vacated.

"I'll stay here," he said, "and make sure you don't flatten the *sanahair*. Chamberpot servant," he added in answer to her uncomprehending expression. "It's a joke. Never mind. Go get some sleep."

"I don't . . . I won't. . . ." She stopped and shook her head. "You're going to give my mother fits."

"Won't be the first time I've upset someone," Deiq said dryly, and leaned back in the chair, closing his eyes. "And you should be worrying less over your mother's sense of modesty, and more over how you're going to explain to her that you'll be moving into the Palace tomorrow, don't want to attend that dinner she's planning, and *really* don't want Oruen at that dinner."

He heard her draw in a sharp breath. "How did you *know* all that?"

"Because I know you," he said, not moving. "And I understand your mother, and I understand Oruen. And because I know how to train a desert lord. This household won't work for you right now. You need to get away from this place before you completely fall apart."

Not that he was happy at the notion of being in relatively close quarters with Oruen; but that was a situation he could handle. Probably.

"Go get some sleep," he said again, and faked a yawn, stretching a little and kicking his legs out long as though settling down to sleep in the chair. The simple maneuver worked. She murmured something that sounded like a good-night and went into the bedroom, closing the door between them.

Once the sound of her moving about in the other room stilled, he rose and warded the door of the suite, then returned to the chair and allowed himself a light doze as a reward for surviving another day without killing anyone.

Etiquette of the South

(excerpt)

It never fails to astonish me how widely etiquette has diverged between our two cultures, given that all life began here in the southlands. I suspect the advent of the Northern Church has done more to redirect notions of polite behavior than any other single influence. For example, in the southlands, a woman is generally free to take whatever partners she cares to indulge herself with. There are, of course, individual variations depending on status and Family, but a woman simply spending time alone with a man is not cause for comment or concern. In the northlands, this small matter is often enough to brand her as a whore and lose her crucial respect; as I understand it, further north, where the Northern Church has a stronger hold yet, such a simple thing can actually cost the woman her life.

This may come into more relevance as the cultures mix together, as in my earlier-noted concerns regarding northerns moving south and southerners moving north; but even in your main city of Bright Bay, you will already be seeing the effects of greater traffic from the south on the culture of your populace.

I suspect your more conservative northern supporters will not be at all happy with the changing dynamic of society.

From the collection
Letters to a Northern King of Merit
penned by Lord Cafad Scratha during the reign of King Oruen

Chapter Thirty-two

Alyea woke in the grey light of dawn to the sound of her mother shouting. Not at all uncommon; the woman seemed born to fuss over anything that came to hand, and had delivered tirades at all hours of the day and night over undusted side tables and dishes with water spots.

Alyea had long ago learned to sleep through it without stirring. She blinked and rubbed at her eyes, wondering hazily why she'd woken this time; then the words came clear.

"*S'e* Deiq, I don't know what passes for etiquette in the barbarian lands, if you even *have* such a concept, but in *this* house an unmarried woman does *not* have a man in her rooms—"

"Ohgodsoh*shit*—" Alyea muttered, grabbing a light robe.

She opened the door to find her mother about to storm into the bedroom. Face to face, Lady Peysimun continued her rant: "Alyea, I am *shocked* that you would allow—"

A glance past her mother into the main room showed Alyea that Deiq had, at some point, turned the chair to have a clear view of her bedroom door. He was grinning, utterly unbothered by his host's anger; his cheerful insouciance reassured her, and she managed to regard her mother's flushed face without fear.

"Good morning, Mother," she said. "Is breakfast ready?"

Lady Peysimun stopped mid-word, her mouth remaining open for a moment, then said, "Are you even *listening* to me?"

"No," Alyea said. "I'm not. Excuse me." She very gently shut the door in her mother's face and locked it just before the handle rattled violently.

She was being a coward, leaving Deiq alone to face that fury; but she also suspected that he could probably handle it on his own.

Digging into the back of her clothes cupboard, she picked out a simple outfit she had long ago hidden to avoid Lady Peysimun throwing it away: long black trousers and a blue long-sleeved shirt, both of a light, loose cut that held up well under humid Bright Bay summer heat.

The outer door of her suite slammed. Alyea winced.

After dressing, she took the time to tie her hair back into a simple, triple-bound tail down her back, and added some minor pieces of jewelry she'd left behind on her last stay at Peysimun Mansion. At last, admitting that she was stalling, she opened the door and stepped into the outer room again.

Deiq still sat in the chair, his expression serene. He smiled a little, meeting her eyes, and said, "I think your mother would very much prefer me to not step under her roof ever again."

"She had that opinion as soon as she saw you," Alyea said.

"True. She doesn't think much of southerners, does she?" He rose to his feet. "Breakfast will have to be quick. We've been summoned to see the king."

"Already?" she said involuntarily, glancing at the vague rosy flush limning the curtains.

"Yes. That's why your mother came to your rooms in the first place." His expression darkened. "Apparently Idisio decided to go walkabout last night and landed in a hell of a mess that got him hauled up in front of the king. The messenger didn't have details, but I'm guessing, from the tone of the message, that delay probably isn't a good idea."

Even with dawn barely spread over the sky, a crowd of people craned and stretched to stare at Alyea as she walked up the steps of the palace with Deiq at her side, and she felt an apprehensive chill run down her back. Just how bad a mess had Idisio gotten himself into?

She glanced sideways at Deiq—and admitted to herself that they might all be staring at him, not her. He had dressed plainly as well, but the overall effect was startling: he'd chosen an emerald-green shirt and black pants and drawn his dark hair into the same triple-bound tail style as hers, with one thin braid left hanging past his right ear. A polished marble of green jade on a thin gold chain hung around his neck, a small ruby earring glittered in his left ear, and a thick gold ring with a blood-red stone graced his right index finger. A bracelet rested on each wrist; three strands of polished wood and bone beads, barbaric in contrast to his finer jewelry. He looked . . . impressive. Powerful. A little frightening.

During their time at Scratha Fortress, Alyea had managed to acquire some understanding of the strange bead-language of the southlands, but Deiq's bracelets resembled nothing she'd learned about. Green meant wealth, as did gold, of course; and red generally involved bloodshed or death to some degree. And the more strands or width to the bracelet, the more important the wearer.

The variations introduced by material still confused Alyea, but she knew the ruby earring meant something different than the red stone of the ring. Every meaning she'd learned, however, involved metals or gemstones, not wood and bone.

Probably just a favorite piece of decoration, nothing more, she told herself, and didn't believe it for a moment.

In the peculiar cool light of a clear dawn sky after a night of heavy rain, there was an odd translucence to Deiq's dark skin. She thought, once, when he turned his head a certain way, that she saw a faint glitter, like silver scales; a heartbeat later it was gone. She decided it had been a trick of the light and her own imagination, and put the moment out of her mind.

She didn't quite dare to ask why he'd chosen this morning, this situation, to be so clearly visible and remarkable.

People moved out of their way in a great, sinuous wave as they strode through crowded palace corridors to the audience hall. Following Deiq's lead, Alyea ignored the whispers and pointing, the wide-eyed stares, as if deaf and blind to them. Inwardly, she gaped at the sheer number of people gathered outside, in the halls, and no doubt in the audience hall already.

What the hells had Idisio done?

To Alyea's surprise, the audience hall doors were still shut, not swung wide as they would be for open court. Stiff-faced guards edged the doors open just far enough to admit them and waved them through, barely glancing at Deiq and Alyea as they passed. Their attention seemed fixed on the gathered crowd in the hallway, as if to ensure nobody else entered the audience hall unseen.

That sent a chill up Alyea's back. For the first time, she wondered if Idisio's antics were the only thing drawing people to the palace in such crowds. The sight of the group assembled before the throne—only two of whom she knew—and the taut expression on Oruen's face did nothing to reassure her.

"Lord Sessin," Alyea said as she strode forward. "Lord Oruen. Idisio."

She stopped just shy of the group and met their examination directly, her head high. Although the gathered man all wore "ordinary clothing" rather than Family colors, she had no doubt they were all desert lords—although two of them looked young and a touch nervous, so they were probably in training. In any case, she was one of them now; no need to cower like a child. Eredion's eyes crinkled with his usual ready smile, but it seemed distinctly strained this time.

Idisio nodded, his expression miserable. He looked as if he hadn't gotten any sleep at all; dark circles marked the skin beneath his eyes, and his hands showed a tendency to tremble. He stood with his hands tucked deep into the sleeves of a rough dun-colored servant's tunic too large for him, his skinny legs lost in equally large green trousers.

He looked like a street-rat just barely dry after a rainstorm: all waif-thin face with too-large grey eyes, shivering pathetically.

"Lord Alyea," he muttered. "Deiq. Glad you're here."

Deiq bent a glare on the young ha'ra'ha; Idisio shrugged in response, fragile pathos melting into a flash of hard, cynical indifference. Alyea hid a smile at the brief exchange and turned her attention to the man on the throne.

Though Oruen wore full royal regalia of embroidered robes, jewelry, and crown, she still saw the gangly, rough-dressed man beneath: the one who'd walked along the beach and thrown rocks into the water out of frustration with the madness of the city behind him. But he'd developed some new wrinkles since taking the throne, and more since her departure; at the moment, he looked to be carving every one of them deeper.

"Alyea," he said. "Good to have you home. Apparently things didn't . . . quite . . . turn out the way I expected." He glanced at Idisio, his forehead puckering a little more. "Several things."

Alyea decided to ignore the lack of title. This didn't quite feel the right time to press that issue. "May I present my escort, Deiq of Stass," she said, deciding that if Deiq wanted to claim his real status he could speak up for himself. "And you've already met Idisio, I see. He's . . . under the protection of Peysimun Family."

"And mine," Deiq said promptly.

Idisio made no protest at being designated dependant, so Alyea's guess that he wouldn't want to discuss his true heritage just at the moment had been right. She relaxed a bit.

Oruen nodded at Deiq, his frown shifting to an expression of strained politeness. "Welcome to my court once again, *s'e*." He didn't sound particularly sincere.

Eredion cleared his throat. "I think, as we're reasonably alone here, it's time to drop the nonsense, Lord Oruen. You know who—and what—Deiq is."

Oruen grimaced. "Yes. You're right. My apologies, *ha'inn*." The last words sounded forced, and he avoided looking directly at Deiq as he spoke.

Deiq inclined his head, a faint smile appearing on his face. "'Honored One.' I do like the sound of that."

Oruen's mouth tightened, but he said nothing.

"Enjoy it while it lasts," Lord Eredion said dryly. "And I believe you owe Idisio the same courtesy, actually."

Oruen's eyebrows rose. "Are you telling me a *ha'ra'ha* tried to pick Lord Scratha's pocket?"

A long silence ensued, in which Idisio's face turned a bright crimson and the other desert lords stared in open astonishment. Alyea bit her tongue against a bark of disbelief; she'd been told Idisio started out as Scratha's *servant*, and later discovered his true heritage. But Oruen naming him *thief* was different from a gate guard's suspicions, and nobody was arguing this time. She couldn't believe she'd actually spoken in Idisio's defense at the gates, putting her own reputation on the line—How could Deiq have allowed that? It only took a glance at the lack of surprise on his face to see that he'd known all along.

He lies . . . Chac had been right, all along.

And now Idisio had "gone walkabout and gotten himself in trouble", had he? He must have stolen from one of these men. Well, *she* certainly wouldn't intervene against his punishment. She'd been embarrassed enough already—

She caught Deiq's stern stare and felt her own face flush. After being annoyed with her mother for jumping to conclusions, she'd done the same thing herself at the first opportunity. She'd seen no sign of faithlessness in Idisio, but a single loose comment had been enough to break her trust in him. Just because he'd been a thief once didn't mean he still was; Lord Scratha certainly wouldn't have put up with such behavior, and she didn't *think* Deiq would either. She looked at the floor, ashamed of herself.

"I think," Eredion said at last, carefully, "that might need to be explained another time. As it's a less relevant matter just at the moment."

Oruen nodded and flicked a hand, but his dark stare stayed pinned on Idisio for some time.

Eredion cleared his throat, glancing at Deiq as though for support, then said with more confidence, "Introductions." He motioned to the five men standing beside him. "Lord Filin of Darden Family. Lord Geier of Eshan Family, and Lord Madioc of Tereph Family. These other two are in training to become desert lords: Wendic, training under Tereph Family, and Rendill, training under Eshan Family."

He bent a dark glare at the last two as he named them. They looked barely old enough to shave, and with the gangly arrogance of youth were now openly looking Alyea over.

"I'm honored, my lords," Alyea said, and hesitated, not sure of the proper address to use for the trainees.

Eredion made a dismissive gesture. "Let's not stand on formality too hard," he said. His mouth quirked. "I know my family is famed for propriety, but this really isn't the time."

Deiq grinned briefly, then sobered again. "So what is important enough to bring four full lords and two trainees all the way into Bright Bay?"

Alyea blinked, surprised that his first question hadn't been about Idisio; then realized that whatever had happened obviously involved a much bigger situation than she'd expected. Deiq, of course, had seen that instantly.

Eredion glanced at Alyea, then back to Deiq. "How much does she know?" he asked. "About what really happened with Ninnic?"

"I have no idea," Deiq said, his mouth thinning as though the question deeply aggravated him. "Ask her."

"You mean the mad ha'ra'ha who was controlling Ninnic," Alyea said, and watched, out of the corner of her eye, as Idisio jerked, clearly startled. "Yes. Lord Evkit told me about that."

Deiq scowled thunderously; Eredion didn't look pleased to hear that name himself. The trainees stopped ogling Alyea and stood up straight, their expressions now showing startled, wary respect. Oruen leaned forward, his eyes narrowing.

Before the king could speak, Eredion said, "Did Evkit tell you we had to kill it?"

"He didn't say *who* was involved," Alyea said carefully, keeping an eye on Idisio.

The boy looked terrified, and she could guess why. He'd only just found out he was a ha'ra'ha; now he'd been presented with the information that ha'ra'hain could go mad, and would then be destroyed by a group of grim-faced men like the ones around him—who already regarded him with intense distrust. It would make anyone nervous.

She added, pointedly, "I believe you had good reason, though."

Eredion followed her gaze and winced. "Idisio, you're in no danger from us," he said hastily. "This was an extremely exceptional situation."

"And you're not going mad," Deiq added. "Believe me, Idisio, I would know, probably long before you did."

Idisio didn't seem much relieved by the assurance, but his face regained some color.

"I was involved," Eredion confirmed, returning to the earlier question. "As was Lord Filin. The two trainees are replacing lords that were lost in the . . . conflict. And two others have gone their separate ways; Lords Geier and Madioc stepped in to replace them. We stayed to clean up the . . . aftereffects."

"Aftereffects," Alyea said flatly; found herself briefly amused by the realization that phrasing questions as statements was becoming a habit for her.

"Mm," Eredion said, uncertain, and glanced at Oruen. The king watched them with a distant expression, his attention mainly fixed on Alyea, as if he couldn't take his eyes off her.

She ignored him.

"Well," Eredion said, scratching his cheek, "it was rather a large . . . event. Situation. The . . . child. . . ." He glanced at Idisio apologetically, then went on, "It had been influencing things in Bright Bay for a long time. The city had gotten . . . used to it. Some people, some things had started to almost depend on its presence. We had to keep things from getting out of hand afterward. It's taken a lot of subtle persuasion in the right spots, at the right moments. And it wasn't exactly a job we could hand over to the Guard."

"No," Alyea said, musing. "I can see that." And she could. What Lord Eredion was hinting at had little to do with the physical and economic chaos of a regime change, but a deeper, more spiritual set of problems.

People had grown accustomed to hard lives, had begun to expect horror on a daily basis; had learned to devalue their neighbors as nothing more than a distraction to be thrown in the face of an advancing threat. And when the threat no longer existed, the behavior didn't just fade away overnight. The population as a whole needed—she groped for the right words—to be retrained. She wasn't entirely sure just how Eredion's fellow desert lords were going about the matter, but this didn't seem the time to ask for details.

The only other people who might have understood the problem were the priests, but their reaction to the crisis hadn't been at all helpful, as she recalled. Even without Alyea pressing the issue, Oruen likely would have banished the s'iopes, just out of exasperation with their idiotic behavior.

"I stayed fairly public, while the others have been moving around the city more quietly, addressing the worst problems." Eredion said. "I kept my ears open in court. Cleaned out the . . . debris . . . throughout the palace. And beneath it." His expression turned slightly ill for a moment. "It's not a particularly pleasant job, and it's far from finished even now. But I found something unexpected when I started clearing the underground areas. Some*one*, actually—"

"Oh, how *tactful*," Filin snorted, crossing his arms.

"I'll admit the term might be a bit shaky at the moment," Eredion said, not looking at Filin. "But it serves the moment. The child had kept someone alive down there in its lair. I still don't know how, or why, or who; the moment I opened the door it—she—attacked me. I wasn't expecting it." He scratched his cheek again, his mouth quirking in an expression of deep embarrassment, and glanced at Deiq and the king as though checking reactions. "I went down. Blacked out. And when I got up, she was gone."

"When was this?" Deiq demanded, intent. "How long ago?"

Oruen glanced at him, seeming irritated that Deiq had cut in, but made no open protest.

"Not long after Alyea left," Eredion said. "It took me that long just to reach that spot. There's a *maze* of tunnels and caverns under Bright Bay. I'd been clearing the tunnels for months when I found that room. I thought there was nobody left alive down there. I was tired and impatient, and careless. She got past me. And ever since, she's been haunting the streets of Bright Bay; looking for something, but nobody can figure out what. She seems drawn to the grave-yard at the edge of town, which is where we set a trap last night—and caught *him*." He jerked his chin at Idisio.

"There was a certain amount of confusion over *his* identity," Lord Filin said as though impatient to have his turn at everyone's attention, nodding at Idisio pompously. "While we were standing around arguing, the creature—"

"Woman," Eredion murmured.

Filin shook his head but otherwise ignored the comment. "—attacked us. Thank the gods Eredion had his wits ready and a handful of stibik in its face while the rest of us were scrambling. *These* idiots drew swords on it." He glared at the trainees; they studied the floor intently, looking abashed and a touch sullen. "But after the stibik hit it, the *creature* took off." He directed a hard stare at Eredion, as though challenging the Sessin lord to argue the term again; Eredion's lips thinned but he stayed quiet.

Deiq's expression turned dark. "That stuff shouldn't even *exist* anymore!" he snapped. "What the hells are you doing with it?"

"Saving our lives," Lord Filin said sharply. Deiq ignored him, staring only at Eredion.

Eredion wouldn't meet Deiq's glare. "The ketarches made their own deci-sion," he said, staring at the floor, much as the trainees were still doing. "And it was a weakened dose we used, not full strength—"

"That doesn't make it better!" Deiq retorted. "It's *banned*, damn it!"

"Talk to the ketarches about that," Eredion said, still not looking up.

"I'll damn well talk to the ones using it!"

"Knock it off! This isn't the time to argue," Lord Filin cut in, shifting his weight from one foot to the other and crossing his arms over his chest. "Worry at that bone later. It worked; it drove the creature off. And that means we're definitely dealing with another mad ha'ra'ha. Unless you want to argue *that*?"

Eredion sighed and rubbed at the bridge of his nose; whether annoyed by or resigning himself to Filin's continued attitude, Alyea couldn't tell. The con-tinuing clash over gender-specific terms was giving her a headache; she hoped they'd stick with *female* from this point out.

Deiq seemed to slump where he stood, the anger fading from his face. He rubbed both hands over his face. "No. You're right."

Idisio's eyes widened and his face lost color again. Alyea tried to catch his gaze to offer a reassuring smile, but the boy seemed lost in some inner worry.

"*Another* one?" Oruen said sharply, leaning forward. "How many mad ha'ra'hain are there, exactly, if I may ask? I was under the impression that Ninnic's child was an exceptionally unusual occurrence."

"*Ninnic's* child?" Alyea said, startled. At the same time, Deiq snapped, much louder: "It *was*."

Everyone turned to stare at Deiq. An awkward moment of silence ensued, in which Deiq's ugly expression only intensified. At last Deiq shrugged, his scowl easing, and added, "Rosin Weatherweaver had more to do with the madness of Ninnic's child than heredity."

"He's right," Eredion said. "Ninnic's child wouldn't have twisted so far without Rosin's help."

Oruen sat back in his chair, frowning, and looked unconvinced. "And yet, I have another mad ha'ra'ha in my city, less than a year after the first died."

Filin said, as though generously conceding a point, "Well, we're dealing with a crossbreed of *some* sort, or the stibik wouldn't have driven it off so fast. And after all that time imprisoned, it's likely barking mad, too. But it *might* have started out human-sane. It's not acting like Ninnic's child did."

Alyea took advantage of the following pause and said, again, "*Ninnic's* child?"

"Gets a bit complicated," Eredion said, avoiding Deiq's renewed glare. "There used to be a full ha'rethe under Bright Bay, you see, and . . . er . . . well." He pursed his lips, visibly unhappy. "It would take so long to explain, and I *know* you'll ask too many damn questions to let me get to the main point here. Can we just say—yes—Ninnic's child, and skip the rest for now?"

"As long as you *promise* to give me the rest of the story one day," Alyea said. "*Soon.*"

Eredion shrugged assent. "In any case," he went on hurriedly, "this one's acting more like a ha'ra'ha trying to hang onto what's left of its sanity. It's not hurting anyone, it's not feeding—anymore. . . ."

Alyea's eyes narrowed. "*Feeding?*"

Eredion glanced at her, then at Deiq's fierce glower, looking first startled and then uneasy. "Ah, I thought you. . . ."

Deiq's sour expression intensified even further. Alyea opened her mouth to ask what, exactly, Eredion had meant by *feeding*; that sounded too important to wait for a later explanation. A moment later, she felt a vague, velvet pressure build and dissipate behind her eyes, so quickly she scarcely noticed it; she rubbed her eyes with one hand and blinked hard. Without being sure why, she found herself staring at Deiq; he wore a suspiciously bland expression.

Eredion said hastily, "Well, never mind—Right now, the woman is searching for something. She seems attracted to graveyards at night, and children during the day. She rushes up to them, examines them, and then just *screams* this unearthly wail and rushes away again. Doesn't hurt them, but gods, there's an ocean of piss on the cobblestones in this city these days."

Deiq didn't laugh. Neither did anyone else.

Alyea struggled briefly with the feeling that she had forgotten something critically important; looked around her for clues and found a faintly puzzled expression on almost every face. Eredion avoided her gaze, and Deiq was frowning, apparently over what the Sessin lord had said.

"During the day?" Deiq asked. "Has anyone gotten a good look?"

"It's been taking the *form* of a woman in white," Lord Filin said, cutting a sideways glance at Eredion and pointedly not looking at Deiq. "She moves too fast, and people are too busy running away, for anything else. She hasn't appeared often in the daylight, but half the city's terrified to set foot out of doors. Oruen's being pressured to call the northern priests back to help."

"They couldn't do anything but make it worse," Deiq said.

"That's what we figured."

Deiq turned his stare on Idisio again, his expression deeply speculative.

"Idisio," he said slowly, "why *were* you out in the middle of the night? In the middle of a rainstorm, at that?"

"I just . . . I had to get some air. I felt so hot, and restless, and I wanted to walk the streets alone, the way I used to." Idisio frowned, as if hearing the absurdity of his own words. "I don't know," he said after another moment's consideration. "I felt . . . called. Drawn. Like something wanted me to come out of the house."

"You shouldn't have felt our bait-call," Eredion said. "Not that far away. What did it feel like?"

"Like someone was riffling through my mind. My memories. I couldn't seem to stop it."

"*That* definitely wasn't us," Eredion said, looking alarmed.

"No," Deiq said, almost under his breath. "That was the ha'ra'ha woman you're after." He stared at Idisio speculatively. "She seems to have taken an interest in you, Idisio. I wonder why."

Chapter Thirty-three

Deiq stood to one side of the gathering, letting the desert lords hash out their ideas for handling the situation and argue over *it* versus *she*. That particular subtlety of wording didn't matter to him; he'd managed to ignore Filin's clear intent to antagonize him. And he knew better than to offer himself up as hunter. They wouldn't trust him: and in this particular instance, he had to admit they would probably be right.

A mad ha'ra'ha was even more dangerous for its peers than for humans. And in this city, with the memories he could never quite escape, the encounter wouldn't go well at all.

Yellow eyes in the darkness: laughter and a feeling like jagged lace stripping through his veins. A mocking voice ghosted through his mind: Leaving so soon, little cousin? No, that simply won't do . . . And as the pain hit, he screamed, louder and longer than Meer had, because Meer had been only human, and able to die to escape.

He blinked, swallowing hard, and gave silent thanks that nobody was looking his way; deliberately turned his back, breathing evenly until emotion eased and the stress-patterns faded from his skin.

It had probably been a very serious mistake to return to Bright Bay, a worse one to step into the palace. And now he had to deal with a mad ha'ra'ha—again—and that took precedence over everything else.

"Deiq," someone said behind him.

He set a mild expression on his face and returned to the group. "Yes?"

"This, ahhhh, this tath-shinn—"

Deiq grinned, amused by the chosen compromise, and Eredion's face relaxed for just a moment in response, then tautened again.

"—seems interested in Idisio, right? So how about using him as a draw—"

"As *bait*," Idisio said, voice edged with a shrill tension. "For another damned trap."

Deiq pursed his lips, considering. Idisio had already survived an attack by the strange ha'ra'ha once without succumbing to instability. Whether that steadiness came from his heritage or his youthful ignorance, Deiq wasn't sure.

He only knew *he* couldn't do it. Not here.

"Not a bad idea," he said, prompting a betrayed glare from Idisio.

What about dignity and honor? Idisio shot at him.

Sometimes honor requires losing some dignity, Deiq answered, and firmly closed down further private communication with the younger ha'ra'ha before it could escalate into an argument.

It took another hour of discussion before a plan was formed. Idisio, still markedly unhappy, at last agreed that the danger to the city was worth risking a bit of his own skin over, and accepted—dubiously—the assurances that he wouldn't be alone, and that they wouldn't allow any harm to come to him.

"And you said she hasn't hurt anyone, right?" he said hopefully.

"No, no, you should be perfectly safe," Eredion assured him, and if his response seemed a bit too quick and his face a shade too tight, nobody remarked on it.

"And you won't have any of that stubby powder."

"No. We won't use any stibik, except on the catch-ropes. We don't want to risk hurting you."

Deiq saw Idisio's mispronunciation of the word as a fair indicator of just how badly rattled the young ha'ra'ha had become. As the meeting began to wrap up, Deiq murmured in Alyea's ear, "I think I'd best go have a talk with Idisio, to settle him down. He's liable to go to pieces before nightfall otherwise."

"You trust me out of your sight?" she muttered.

"You did say this was *your* city," he remarked sardonically, hearing more frustration escaping into the words than he'd intended.

She winced, but before she could say anything by way of apology, Oruen called for their attention again.

"Alyea," the king said, tone pleasant but eyes tight at the corners, "would you mind staying behind for a few moments? I've a few things I'd like to go over with you alone before I open my court to the public."

The word *alone* held the faintest stress. The king locked eyes with Deiq, and they exchanged a brief, bitter glare.

"Of course," Alyea said.

What does she know? Eredion asked. *And is it safe to leave her unsupervised right now?*

Damn little, Deiq admitted. *There hasn't been time or quiet for teaching. And she's not fully healed from her trials, or fully changed over. She's still closed to mindspeech, for one.*

He left silent that she was already able to deliver a hefty blow from rage; she liked Oruen well enough still for the risk to be minimal. At worst, she'd embarrass herself and scare the king, neither of which seemed like bad outcomes.

Eredion didn't look surprised: that implied he'd tried mindspeech himself, and had no better success. Good to know.

Do you want some estiqi?

Deiq shook his head. *No. I don't want to force it. She'll open when she's ready.*

Eredion nodded. He murmured polite farewells along with the other desert lords and trainees, and withdrew to prepare for the night ahead. With one last hard stare at Oruen, Deiq followed suit: his hand casually resting on Idisio's shoulder, his thumb pressing hard to keep Idisio moving at a pace that kept Deiq himself from turning around and going back to stand beside Alyea—or sidetracking to ask Eredion for the estiqi after all.

Chapter Thirty-four

"Lord Oruen," Alyea said carefully as the doors clunked shut behind her. She found herself acutely aware of the two King's Guards standing behind her, on the inside of those doors. During the conference with the desert lords, she'd practically forgotten their presence. But of course the king would never be truly alone, not even in his bedchamber.

She bit her lip and yanked her mind away from that train of thought.

Oruen regarded her with an openly bemused expression, his long fingers worrying at a piece of embroidery on his royal robes. Alyea smiled a little; the palace seamstresses were probably throwing fits over his clothes-wrecking nervous habits on a daily basis.

"What in all the seventeen hells do I do with you now?" he said.

Abruptly, her muddled thoughts clicked into a sharp, unemotional focus.

"I don't see that there's much you *can* do at the moment," she said. "Or ought to do. Lord Oruen."

He grimaced. "Alyea, drop that nonsense," he said impatiently. "You've known me—"

"And bedded you. Yes. But that's not relevant any more, Lord Oruen."

His thin eyebrows rose. He sat back on his throne and studied her with a new intensity. "You're actually serious about this."

"I've gone through the trials," she said. "All three of them. I've had to kill a man. Pieas Sessin, as it happened, but it was almost Chacerly. Gods know he deserved it, from what he told me." She watched the skin around Oruen's dark eyes tighten. "Chac owes his life to Lord Scratha," she added, and let him have a moment to appreciate the irony in that situation. "I owe *my* life to Deiq.

I've met with desert lords in Conclave, and been formally invested as a full desert lord; I've been to the teyanain fortress as an honored guest. I won't even *start* on some of the other things that happened. Yes. I'm serious."

He listened quietly, his forehead furrowing deeper as she spoke.

"I see," he said. "I thought the trials took years. I assumed the title was simply . . . an expedient courtesy."

She shook her head and turned, raising the back of her shirt to show him the mark of the first trial burned into the flesh of her lower back. At his grunt, she turned back to face him.

"Not just courtesy," she said.

"I see that." His face had become grave and drawn. "This is a rather large complication for me, Alyea."

"It hasn't simplified my life a whole lot, either."

"Hnnph." He snorted near-laughter, then sobered again. "What do you plan to do now?"

"I'm leaving as soon as this hunt is settled. Tomorrow morning, I hope. Deiq, Idisio, and I are headed north."

"*North?*" He leaned forward, staring at her with unabashed bewilderment and deep concern.

"North," she said firmly. "Idisio's taken on the job of King's Researcher that you initially gave to Scratha, since Lord Scratha is now bound to his fortress and can't leave the area."

Oruen sat back, scowling. "I knew he'd returned, and called a Conclave; but he can't leave the area? I can see there's quite a bit of news that hasn't been sent to me. I thought I had better sources than that."

"I hope you didn't count on Micru and Chac as those sources," she said. He flinched, and she grinned, feeling supremely smug at knowing more than he did for once. "They've both gone back to the desert Families that bought them long ago: Chac to Darden, Micru to Sessin."

He sat very still, his jaw muscles taut. "I wondered why I hadn't heard from them," he murmured, and rubbed a hand over his face, grimacing. "*Damn* it. I should have known that."

"They're both very good," Alyea said, allowing a moment's pity for a plot gone badly wrong. "I only found out by chance and a lucky guess or two."

One of the guards by the door coughed quietly. Oruen glanced past Alyea and held up a finger in a gesture for the man to wait a moment.

"I have to open the court now," Oruen said, looking at Alyea again, "but I'll arrange time this afternoon for you to sit and tell me about this new development with Scratha, and about your journey." He reached for a thin bell-rope beside the throne. "Maybe even share some tea, how's that sound?"

His tone annoyed her; he sounded indulgent, as though speaking to a pet or a child. Deciding it was time to establish their new respective places, she shook her head. "No, Lord Oruen."

His hand paused, fingers just touching the cord. He frowned at her. "What now?"

She took a breath and kept her voice steady. "Would you address Lord Eredion that way? Offer tea like a treat for a child? I'm not under your authority any longer." She wasn't, actually, at all sure of that; but it seemed to follow from what Deiq had said about the king now treating her as an equal.

He dropped his hand from the cord and regarded her with a cold expression she'd never seen directed at her before.

"What Family do you serve?" he asked in clipped tones.

"Peysimun."

"Peysimun isn't a desert family; it's a northern one, and under my authority."

"Not any longer," she said, unwavering. "It's an unusual situation, I'll admit. But I *am* a desert lord, and I've chosen to serve Peysimun Family, which makes us independent by default. I won't swear my family back over to you, Lord Oruen. And if you refuse to accept our independence, I'll move the Family holdings to the south. You'll lose us as allies, not to mention the tax revenue."

It was complete bluff, and she had no idea if she was right or even how to accomplish any such thing; but Oruen took it seriously. He scowled and said, "I'd have the right to declare against you—"

"You don't want to start an internal war right now, Lord Oruen!" she said sharply, her stomach tight with sudden panic. "The city's too unstable yet."

"I also don't want you to declare your own little kingdom within my borders!"

She said nothing for a moment, thinking that over, then said, "I've been told I'll be expected to host a number of visitors once things settle out. Regularly. Mainly desert lords, if I understand correctly. It would probably be nice to have one central location for visiting southerners of importance to go, one that knows how to host them with full courtesy and won't send you complaints about them disrupting business or frightening the locals."

He stared at her, his expression one of almost comical astonishment.

"The south," she said evenly, "turned out to be *very* different from what we're used to here, Lord Oruen. I'm in a perfect position to act as liaison between the worlds; but I have to stand as an independent Family to do it."

He nodded slowly. "I'll consider it."

She drew a breath, steadying herself, and said, "There's no other sane option."

"And in a matter of tendays you go from a flitterbug to being leader of a major political entity?" he demanded, suddenly angry again; she realized she should have retreated and left him to think it over, to accept it with a certain amount of grace instead of forcing his hand. "If you're relying on Deiq's support to pull this nonsense off, you'd best think twice. He's more dangerous an ally than a viper, and with fewer morals. With him by your side, you'll find yourself with more enemies than friends, Alyea; so walk carefully!"

She drew a deep breath, her temper beginning to rise in response to his; but he wasn't finished.

"The only *possible* reason I can see for you to take leave of your senses and take up with *him* is that he's worked his way into your—"

"Stop," she said harshly. "Just *stop*." Her hands shook. She fisted them tightly at her sides, more aware than ever of the guards behind her—and of Deiq's absence.

You have to be so very careful now . . . But why did everyone assume Deiq was keeping her that kind of company? It was beginning to aggravate her past bearing.

"It's an obvious assumption," Oruen pressed, unwilling to let it drop. "Do you even *know* his reputation? Or has he charmed you into thinking he loves you alone? He's apparently very good at that—"

"Oruen, please, *stop!* I don't want to hurt you!"

He blinked and sat forward, staring at her. "You don't want to—*what?*"

"My cousin Kam almost died last night when he made me angry," she said, forcing the words from a dry mouth. "He accused me of the same thing. And I . . . hit him. Deiq caught my hand just in time . . . but it still. . . ." She shook her head. "Deiq's interference stopped me from killing him. But Deiq isn't here right now, and I'm *afraid* of getting angry without him to hold me back."

She drew a deep, shaky breath and strained to slow her heartbeat from its furious hammering.

He sat back, all the way into the depths of his throne this time, and regarded her silently, his face puckered with worry. To his credit, he didn't look at his guards once, although she could sense that they'd moved much closer behind her.

"I've been told that a desert lord's anger can kill," Oruen murmured at last. "Without even a physical blow involved."

"Yes."

"It's really not an empty title, then."

"No."

Close behind her, one of the guards coughed. The small sound seemed disproportionately loud in the taut silence, but Oruen's gaze never left Alyea's face, and no hint of a smile crossed his face.

"This is making my guards very uncomfortable," he noted. "I'd like to continue this conversation later, however. Perhaps after tonight's celebration?"

"Celebration? I thought we were hunting—"

Oruen's tone lost some of its tautness as the talk moved back onto safer ground. "There are plenty of people handling the tath-shinn problem already. And your mother sent me an invitation to a 'small welcome-home dinner' at Peysimun Mansion. I suspect she's already invited two dozen other notables, and you *are* the guest of honor; you can't duck out of the dinner completely. She'd have your head on a platter, and rightly so."

"Oh, *gods*," Alyea said in real dismay, covering her mouth with one hand. "I'd forgotten about that—You're attending?"

"I had intended to, as a courtesy to you," he said. "Would you rather I didn't?"

"Yes, I'd rather," she said passionately. "My mother's already insufferable. Make some polite excuse, *please*. I'll have to go—you're right, I can't avoid that—but I'll return to my Palace apartment afterwards, and I'll come back to speak with you tomorrow. *Here*. Not at Peysimun Mansion."

"She'll be furious." He smiled, amused—and, she thought, a little relieved.

"*Good*."

Relative Life Spans

(excerpt)

One item of grave importance, on which you may not have been fully informed, Lord Oruen, is the matter of differing life spans; especially as relating to the desert Families. While commoners, north to south, have the same life expectancy, desert Families tend to be very different. Desert lords, in particular, live for upwards of a hundred years; their children tend to live rather longer than commoners. Over the years, this tendency has created a sturdy and long-lived group of people. There are desert lords alive today who remember meeting Initin the Red, not to mention the infamous Dusty Rose.

It also means that feuds between individuals or Families can go on for a very long time indeed, and take on infinitely subtle complexities. There is no possible way you could avoid tripping over them. It would take a lifetime of study to understand the first third of the underground battles throughout the southlands.

Your previous advisor on southland matters, Chacerly, thought himself wise but had no more knowledge than that. Additionally, his understanding was flawed by his personal biases and background as a Darden supporter. Much of what he taught you will likely only get you into deep trouble with southern ambassadors. I strongly suggest attempting to recruit a southern lore-master as an advisor, but that will require significant negotiation and a strong incentive based on offered benefits, not threats.

Such negotiations can easily take years. The southlands, given their longer life spans, see urgency very differently than northerns. I counsel patience and tolerance; and in the meanwhile, listening to what Deiq of Stass has to say might well benefit you, as his knowledge of southern custom is unequaled. Offending him would be a grave mistake, for a number of reasons.

From the collection
Letters to a Northern King of Merit
penned by Lord Cafad Scratha during the reign of King Oruen

Chapter Thirty-five

Deiq led Idisio outside, into one of the least-used palace gardens: one composed largely of deep-southern plants, which held little interest for the northern court as a rule. He'd brought or arranged for most of the plants himself over the years, in fact; not he expected anyone to remember that, these days. He'd built the garden a long time ago, and in typical desert fashion it flourished even when neglected.

Dawn had moved into a brilliant, glittering daylight. The heavy rain of the night before, and the lingering dew of early morning, brought out the best in the garden. Morning-trumpet vines, heavily laden with gigantic white blossoms, swirled up lattices and trellises in a fragrant confusion of color; stubby *totobo* cacti spread ruffled, vibrantly red blooms at their tops. Desert ginger splayed oval leaves up woody stalks, festooned with clusters of berry-like white flowers, reaching higher than Deiq's head.

Insects rose and fell in clouds among the wealth of newly-available pollen. Deiq gently deflected bugs from his path as he steered Idisio towards the central portion of the garden, a sand-and-rock meditation area he'd taken particular pride in designing.

The recent upheaval seemed to have left this entire garden untouched; he relaxed as he walked among the familiar plants, feeling more at ease than he'd been for some time.

Idisio said nothing as they walked, his thoughts visibly turned inward, barely seeming to notice their surroundings. When they reached the inner garden, he slumped onto a bench and put his face in his hands. Deiq remained standing, looking over the black, white, and grey rocks stacked in groupings of three, six, and nine with a sense of deep satisfaction. Some of the stacks had been moved or rearranged, but they remained in multiples of three, so it hadn't disrupted the harmony of the pattern. The open patch of black sand to the right and the white sand to the left both looked freshly raked; the stepping-stone path was brushed clear of leaves and debris. Someone was still maintaining the place, even now: that set a warmth into his chest and eased a worry he hadn't even known was there.

"I should have stayed on the streets," Idisio said, his voice muffled.

"You'd be dead by now," Deiq said without any sympathy. "Not knowing what was happening when the changes began, you'd have done something stupid, and been killed."

"I never *had* anything weird happen before I ran into Lord Scratha!"

"Really? And what weird thing happened then?"

Idisio didn't answer right away. He looked out over the inner garden, his sullen expression slowly lifting into a vague interest. "That's nice," he said. "It's . . . quiet."

"Thank you."

Idisio shot him a startled glance. "*You* did this?"

"Some time ago. Yes. What weird thing happened to you when you met Lord Scratha?"

Idisio stared out at the meditation area again; Deiq waited patiently. At last Idisio said, "There's this vision I kept having. I never had it before I met Lord Scratha; well, I don't know. I think now that I might have dreamed it sometimes, and not thought anything of it. But it never—Anyway. I kept seeing this boy. This red-haired boy, about my age, maybe a little older. And he was so . . . so *angry*. And so deeply, deeply hurt. And so . . . dangerous." He fell silent.

"And?" Deiq prompted.

"That's all," Idisio said, looking up at Deiq, his expression honestly bewildered. "I don't understand it. But it felt so terribly *important*, every time, as though this was a boy I knew, or should know, or would know. And I started to wonder. . . ." He looked out over the garden again, frowning as though trying to sort out the right words. "There was this sailor. On the way south from Sandlaen Port. A big, red-headed sailor, called Red. He was looking for his son. When we stopped in Agyaer I went with him as company on his search, but the boy was gone . . . and the boy's mother was dead."

Deiq waited patiently, understanding that this had troubled Idisio for some time and that the younger needed to talk it out before being reassured of its unimportance.

"And I thought, how strange, that he's looking for his son and I keep having these visions of a boy with red hair . . . I wondered if I'd met the boy before, but that seemed like too much coincidence to believe. We received word, later, that the boy had been found; somehow or another, Aerthraim Family had adopted him."

Deiq's breath caught in his chest as pieces connected in his head; he barely kept his expression neutral. Not unimportant at all; Idisio had no idea what a dangerous chain of coincidence he'd stepped into. Apparently oblivious to Deiq's reaction, Idisio continued:

"And I remember that I *did* meet a red-headed boy, back before Ninnic died, on the streets. He stayed with me a day or two . . . useless as a pickpocket, worse with locks. I told him to look up the Freewarrior's Guild, as he was big and strong already. And now I keep wondering . . . if that was the same boy. But that's ridiculous, right? It's not possible."

."Not likely, but not totally impossible," Deiq said, carefully bland. "Was that, maybe, just *before* Ninnic died?"

Idisio shot him a suspicious look. "Yeah."

Deiq looked up at a nearby featherleaf tree, watching the pale purple blossoms swinging in a light breeze, and sighed. Of all the times to have this conversation . . . Well, at least it hadn't come out at Scratha Fortress. There was that small mercy.

"Ha'ra'hain tend to gather coincidences to themselves," he said. "I've never understood it, but no matter how hard you try to stay out of the center of the picture, something always drags you back in."

"You're saying it *was* the same boy?" Fear and astonishment warred in Idisio's voice.

"I don't know," Deiq lied. "Remember the mad ha'ra'ha under Bright Bay that Eredion was just talking about? The one who was controlling Ninnic?"

"Yes," Idisio said in a suddenly muted voice; glancing down at him, Deiq saw a haunted fear in the boy's grey eyes.

Distracted by that reaction, Deiq paused to consider what had caused it. After sorting through several possibilities, he settled on the most likely and said, "You're lake-born, Idisio. You're not born of Ninnic's child, nor are you brother, son, or anything closer than distant cousin. Madness is not heavy in your genetics, and you're completely stable as far as I can tell. You're not going mad. All the changes you're going through, however strange they may feel, are *normal*."

Idisio let out a hard breath and flung an arm over his face to hide the tears welling in his eyes; a sobbing gasp escaped him. "How the hells do you *do* that?"

Deiq smiled and turned his back on Idisio, giving him time to recover. After a while, when he heard Idisio's breathing steady, he went on.

"It's very hard to kill an adult ha'ra'ha, and this one was . . . stronger than most. The ha'rethe parent was . . . unusual. Old. And powerful."

Yellow eyes and a scream that went on . . . and on . . . and on. . . .

He cleared his throat, pushing memory back into silence, and said, "It's even harder to sneak up on a ha'ra'ha, especially one that lives in a state of paranoid high alert. There were several attempts . . . mainly focused on Ninnic, if I understand correctly, because at first nobody really understood what was happening. But the Aerthraim figured it out first, and put together a plan to attack Ninnic's child instead. . . ."

Deiq swallowed hard, his words feeling like acid in his mouth, and thought again about the stibik powder the teyanain had thrown, and which Eredion had apparently laid in a supply of; remembered endless agony and writhing in darkness: and couldn't blame any of them.

He'd have done the same thing in their place; he *should* have done the same thing. But he'd been a coward: fled rather than face that pain again, leaving the humans to deal with the mad ha'rethe and, later, Ninnic's child, on their own.

"I thought the Aerthraim don't have desert lords. Well, besides Lord Azni," Idisio said, visibly puzzled.

"They don't. But ha'reye and ha'ra'hain can sense a desert lord's presence." He drew in and let out a long breath. "To get close, they needed . . . a distraction. And as I understand it, the boy had some small natural ability—unusual strength of will, or some such thing. I really never asked for details."

Given that the ending had been a dead ha'ra'ha—however valid the reasons for it—the less he knew about the event, the safer everyone would be. Especially if he failed in his promise and had to return to the Qisani.

"So what . . . The boy?" Idisio's voice shook into a rough gasp. "They used him as bait? Just like they're using me!"

"Not quite the same," Deiq said carefully. He hesitated, then made himself say it: "You're likely to survive."

"You're a bunch of bastards!"

Deiq rose and walked away, out into the middle of the sand pattern, and knelt, leaning forward just enough to touch his fingertips to the ground on either side of himself. He sat very still, breathing evenly, until his chest loosened and the urge to destroy something passed.

"The boy's sacrifice saved this entire city, Idisio," he said at last. "I'm sure you remember how bad things were back then."

"Did he even *know*?"

"Probably not," Deiq admitted. "It would have been too risky to tell him his true purpose. Ninnic's child would have pulled it from his mind and the whole point would have been lost."

"But you told *me*. Or have you?" Idisio's voice wavered with sudden suspicion. "Are you using me, too?"

"No," Deiq said. "You know everything about this situation."

Idisio rose abruptly and left the garden at a near-trot.

Deiq stayed still, focused on the particles of sand under his fingertips, and narrowed his focus further, shutting his eyes in fierce concentration, until he was able to count how many grains he was touching.

It took a long time.

Chapter Thirty-six

Alyea listened to the rain hammering down outside and felt a guilty sense of relief at having a valid excuse not to join the hunt for the tath-shinn. Bright Bay's rainy season could be brutal, especially when the back streets began to flood, and this weather seemed unusually determined to swamp the entire city straight into the Kingsea.

Wind howled, broke something loose, and slammed it against an outer wall with a great crash. Alyea winced; her mother jumped, face pale. High-pitched, chittering complaints came from the nearby aviary: her mother's collection of white finches always had noisy, *messy* nervous fits during bad weather. The guests wouldn't be shown that room tonight.

Alyea remembered overhearing the servants of her childhood drawing straws to see who was cursed with cleaning up the Peysimun bird rooms. She doubted the new, status-conscious set would be any happier over the duty.

"I'm beginning to wonder who's brave enough to come through this madness for a party," Alyea noted. "Or maybe I should say, who's mad enough to brave this party?"

Her mother shot her a sour glare, still clearly unhappy. She'd had an entire closet of fancy dresses laid out when Alyea returned from the Palace. Alyea had brought her own outfit, a simple one similar to what she'd worn to the morning's audience with Oruen. Only Alyea's iron determination not to lose her temper had kept her mother safe during the resulting fight.

"They'll come," her mother said thinly. "I told them all King Oruen had agreed to attend. You can explain why he didn't show up."

Alyea sighed, regretting the harsh words they'd exchanged over the course of the day, and tried to think of some way to make her mother understand. Nothing came to mind.

"How's Kam?" she asked instead.

"Awake," her mother said, frowning. She gave Alyea a suspicious look. "Says he feels like a giant hammer's been hitting him all over. Serves him right for drinking so much."

"At least he's alive," Alyea said. "Maybe he won't be so quick to insult me next time." It sounded childish even as she said it, and she winced, wishing she could call the words back.

"Alyea Peysimun," her mother said sharply, "Stop that nonsense right now! You've surely gotten some foolish ideas in your travels. And speaking of your travels, a letter came in I've been meaning to speak to you about. Something about you swearing us liable for a debt?"

Alyea stared blankly for a moment, then remembered. "Oh," she said. "Yes, I met a northern women whose son had been—"

"You do *not* have the authority to put a debt of this sort against our name!" her mother interrupted severely.

Alyea looked at the spots of color high on her mother's pale face and said, "I wish you'd had the chance to meet Halla, mother. I think you two would have gotten along well."

Her mother glared. "I won't hear of you assigning debts to our house," she said. "I've allowed it the once, but now you've been told, and you're *not* to do this again!"

Alyea decided to sidetrack the conversation. The previous topic was looking more attractive by the moment. "But we were talking about Kam," she said innocently. "What were you about to say?"

Her mother easily moved onto the new path. No doubt she'd come back around to complaining about the debt later, but for now she was willing to go with complaining about Kam.

"I was *going* to say that the southlands are filled with mystical nonsense," her mother declared. "You've been around them too long. Kam *fainted*, Alyea. He'd had too much to drink, and it muddled his blood. *You* didn't knock him unconcious! Taking blame on yourself is just—it's *ridiculous!*"

Alyea gave up for the moment. Clearly, her cousin had spun the story sideways, no doubt too embarrassed to admit a girl had laid him out with a slap. She was only surprised he hadn't laid the blame at Deiq's hand, but he wasn't entirely stupid; he must have realized Deiq was more trouble than he needed to take on.

"I think someone just came into the carriage-house," she said.

Clearly relieved at the diversion, her mother hurried off to check on the incoming guest. Alyea sank into a chair against the wall and stared at nothing, suddenly deeply depressed.

She couldn't blame her mother for not understanding. Before Oruen sent her to the desert, before she found out about the world behind what she thought was real, she wouldn't have believed it, either. Even now, it seemed incredible. Blame Ninnic's madness on some underground creature manipulating his actions? Credit the desert lords with strange and deadly powers? Impossible. Ludicrous. Insane.

She wished she could tell her mother that she'd probably been responsible for the deaths of over a dozen innocents at the Qisani, and ask for some sort of comfort or absolution; but her mother would never be able to understand that whole situation properly. Any forgiveness would be based on the fact that "heathens" had been involved.

She ran her fingers idly along the arm of her chair; realized she'd sat down in one of her mother's "show pieces": supposedly designed for Initin the Red, or his wife, or some such. Alyea suspected it was a cast-off, too ugly for anyone with sense to bear.

The chair boasted a strangely curved back, wide seat, and a cushion dyed a weird shade of brown-purple. The studs were set with semi-precious yellow topaz and gods-milk chalcedony. Alyea had never been allowed to sit in it; her mother reserved it for the most honored guests.

Alyea had to admit that, although incredibly ugly, it was a comfortable chair.

"Look who braved the rain!" her mother sang out, reentering the room with Lady Arnil.

Alyea stood hastily, but not before her mother delivered a withering glare as a prompt to get her out of the guest's chair.

"Lady Arnil," Alyea said, thoroughly startled that the delicate woman would have come out in this downpour. "You grace our home."

Lady Arnil nodded, peering at Alyea myopically.

"Alyea," she said in a thin voice, then glanced at her host. "Is there something hot to be had?" she demanded. "That weather outside is perfectly dreadful!"

"Of course," Alyea's mother said, motioning to a servant. "Will hot brandy do? Or perhaps some wind wine?"

"Brandy," the woman said, and shivered. She patted her carefully-arranged golden curls and looked around, squinting appraisingly. She seemed to have actually lost weight and color since last time they'd met.

She's ill, Alyea thought, astonished at the sudden perception. *Really ill. I think she's dying. It's not a good idea for her to be out in this weather at all.*

She tried to keep her expression calm as she said, "It's a long, wet journey in from your estates, Lady Arnil. Would you like to stay the night, and return in the morning?"

At her mother's sharp glance, Alyea realized that offer should have come from the host. She shrugged apologetically.

"What?" Arnil turned from her examination of the room, her pale face furrowed. "No, no, I'd never be able to sleep in a strange bed. But it's a kind offer." She accepted the mug of hot brandy a servant brought her with a brief, regal nod.

"My daughter's a kind person," Alyea's mother said, visibly relaxing.

"But not the brightest, eh?" Lady Arnil turned a bright-eyed glare on Alyea. As mother and daughter stood shocked at the discourtesy, she went on, "Championed that little slut of a servant I had, that Wian. Said she was a good girl. Claimed a desert noble tried to attack her. You may not have heard yet, Alyea, dear, but the girl's been proven a liar and slut since you left. I let her go when the scandal came out." She stroked the firetail bird feathers woven into her lacy scarf, her lips pursed in a thoroughly smug way.

"What scandal?" Alyea said, through lips numb with shock.

"She ran off with the man *you* said attacked her. Came back when he tired of her; thought she could just step right back into her job as if she'd never run off without notice." She patted her hair again, smirking.

Alyea bit her lower lip and admonished herself to stay calm. The woman was so fragile it would hardly take a feather to knock her over right now.

"I heard somewhat different," she said steadily. "I heard Pieas kidnapped her. From Pieas himself."

Arnil sniffed haughtily. "I'm sure you misunderstood. My dear great-nephew Kippin spoke most highly of Pieas's character, when I asked him," she declared. "And Wian herself didn't deny having run off, when we confronted her."

Given Lady Arnil's willful refusal to hear anything that she didn't want to hear, Alyea thought she had a fairly good idea of how *that* conversation had gone.

"Where is she now?"

"I don't know. Likely returned to her roots and walking the streets for a living. All I care about is that she's not disgracing my household again. So—is the king here yet?" She looked around, a bright, expectant smile spreading across her lined face.

Reminding herself that the woman was a guest, and severely ill, Alyea shut her eyes and breathed through her nose.

"Is that another guest I hear?" her mother warbled, voice shaky. "Alyea, dear, go see who it is, would you please, dear?"

Alyea shot her mother a deeply grateful look and fled.

Chapter Thirty-seven

Rain never particularly bothered Deiq, but the amount thundering down onto the rapidly flooding streets was astonishing. He stood under a deep overhang, forced from his initial post by the deluge; four steps up, and the first two were already submerged. The city drains would be busy tonight. . . .

He squinted through the waterfall cascading from the overhang and the near-waterfalls slamming down from the sky beyond that. The sheets of moving liquid blurred even his vision, and proved difficult to push aside, like curtains, for a clearer view; it almost felt as though the water fought back against his attempts to redirect it.

Deiq wished, bleakly, that he hadn't insisted on being involved after all. He could have been sitting next to Alyea in the warm and dry, listening to empty chatter and watching Lady Peysimun glare at him.

But damn it, this was a ha'ra'ha—it was *kin*, whatever its crimes; he tested gender pronouns for a moment, decided that using gender-neutral made the situation marginally easier to bear. Human-raised ha'ra'hain took on human-distinct genders, personalities and desires; became *individuals*. He couldn't afford the distraction; thinking of this one as gendered forced a human-rigid *friend/enemy/ally/opponent* decision that threatened his own unique, uneasy balance on the borderline between his two heritages.

There was a chance, just a chance, that if the madness was new, not inborn, he could draw it off, like skimming fat from a broth; he had to try, whatever it did to him in the process. And if it did attack Idisio, then he could let loose and kill it before the desert lords got hurt trying to stop it . . . He had to try.

Idisio was just visible, a hunched and miserable figure across the wide stretch of Datha Road, which circled the entire cemetery area. He'd taken shelter under a black basalt statue of an eagle atop a tree. The wings of the eagle, cut absurdly large, were caught in a half-cupped flare, as though the bird were about to land on the tree; that, and the intricate lattice of the stone branches beneath, blocked a large part of the wind and rain.

Since Idisio still hadn't mastered regulating his body temperature, his feet were very probably cold and soaked, though. The nearest unblocked drain was two streets over; apparently the repair crews hadn't made it to this section of town yet.

Although blocked drains might not be from an entirely mundane cause of accumulated rubble and garbage. Not in this city, and not in this area. Deiq thought back to the maps of the city, and to Eredion's account of which under-city tunnels he'd cleared so far, trying to match that up to what he knew of the drain system. At last he gave up, deciding the question was something to research in the palace library later. Most probably, judging by the number of Aerthraim lamps appearing throughout the city, the king was already in negotiations with the Aerthraim for repairs.

A heavy gust whipped past, then shifted abruptly, crashing straight into the shelter of the overhang. Cursing under his breath, Deiq waded down the steps to find a new watch-post.

The wind slammed into his face ever harder as he slogged through the flooded street; he squinted to protect his eyes and realized he was walking almost blind, all his attention thrown into getting through the weather to another safe spot.

Which meant that at the moment he wasn't in a safe spot. . . .

Instinct whipped him round, slower than he should have been; he caught a bare glimpse of a hooded form dodging away. An image of wide, febrile grey eyes bored into his mind, and echoes of old screams and darkness mingled with his own memories in smoky threads of resurrected agony.

—Yellow eyes in the darkness, and a voice: That's right, that's it, listen to that scream, isn't it nice?—

Deiq had never heard those words before. They came from her memory, not his; close as they were, her self-identification of female overrode his attempts to keep perception safely gender-neutral.

In the ringing echo of the scream working through her/his mind, he saw with sick certainty what was coming next. He felt her reaching for that one vulnerable spot, and couldn't move fast enough to stop her—

Pain racking through every nerve and pore, Deiq opened his mouth to howl out the agony; but a hard blow connected with the back of his head, and he fell forward into mercifully silent darkness.

Chapter Thirty-eight

"You *lost* him?" Alyea stared at Lord Eredion and Lord Filin. The latter had the grace to look ashamed of himself, while Eredion just shrugged sourly. On the low bed, Deiq moaned and stirred; outside, the wind howled and rattled the shutters against the thick glass windowpanes.

She shook her head, gave the two desert lords one last glare, and laid a light hand on Deiq's arm. He opened dark eyes and for a frightening moment stared at her without recognition.

"Alyea," he mumbled at last, his face clearing, and licked his lips. His stare shifted past her to the watching desert lords, and darkened as memory visibly returned. "What happened?"

"You got knocked out and Idisio's gone," Alyea said.

"Kidnapped or killed?"

"They don't know."

Lord Filin said, "We all had to move from our original posts. The wind came straight at us, and the rain was too thick to see through. We lost sight of him, and when Eredion went to check, he was gone. For all we knew, he'd wandered off to take a piss. But then . . . we found you." He shrugged, looking annoyed. "You're lucky we did. Face down in the damn street; you almost drowned in a handspan of water."

Deiq grimaced and closed his eyes as though pained by the ridiculousness of that.

"Should have warned you," he muttered. "Didn't think she would know that trick. My fault."

"Ha'ra'hain can affect the *weather*?" Alyea said, incredulous. The thundering roar of the deluge outside hadn't eased since nightfall. Getting to the pal-ace had been a nightmare of slogging through flooded streets, and she'd been deeply grateful she had apartments of her own in which to dry off and change clothes.

The king had allowed Deiq a smaller set of guest rooms for the emergency, and sent in his own healer. The plump man reportedly took one look at the heavily-bleeding gash on the back of Deiq's skull and turned grey with horror. He'd refused to attempt stitching the wound; had, in fact, given over bandag-es, healing lotions, and painkiller potions, then fled the room.

Alyea had arrived just as Eredion was fastening the final bandage in place, his face still thunderously dark and his temper high over the man's cowardice.

"Sometimes," Deiq admitted now, not opening his eyes. "Tricky. What the hells did that *ta-neka* hit me with?"

"Looked like a chunk of loose rock," Lord Eredion said.

"Feels like it."

Alyea looked at the bandages around Deiq's head, and the blood even now spotting through them, and felt her stomach turn. She reached for the small bottle of painkiller potion on the bedside table and measured three careful drops into a cup of water. "Here. The king's healer said this would help."

"I'm in the palace, then?" He squinted, displeased, and picked at his thin nightshirt irritably.

"Better than my mother's guest-room," Alyea said. Deiq grunted and looked as though he wanted to smile, but couldn't quite pull it off.

Eredion and Filin helped lift Deiq up to a half-sit. He moaned, clearly nau-seated by the motion, and gulped the water quickly before sliding back down to lie flat again. The thin shirt slid and scrunched; he grunted annoyance and rolled up to one elbow to rip the garment over his head. He tossed it to the floor and slumped back down, breathing hard but looking deeply relieved.

Alyea averted her eyes reflexively, and heard Eredion cough as though hid-ing laughter; but when she glared at him, his face was utterly serene.

"Not much we can do for now," Eredion said. "In this weather, there's no point in even looking. And you're not going anywhere for a day or two. Even with your hard skull, that was a rough blow."

"Don' need to tell me," Deiq muttered, eyes shut again. His bronze skin had turned an unhealthy shade of grey. "Go 'way. Lemme sleep. *Gods*, this hurts."

"You shouldn't sleep," Eredion said.

"Bloody well *should*."

Eredion hesitated, flashing Alyea an unreadable glance, then nodded. He and Filin withdrew from the guest suite without further protest.

"Looks like it's my turn to sit over you," Alyea said lightly, and stayed in the chair.

"Shouldn't. I'll be fine." He blinked hard, as though to clear a haze from his eyes.

"Oh, this gives me a perfect excuse to get away from that dreadful party. I was about to find a high window to jump out of. Never knew so many fools lived in Bright Bay."

Deiq's mouth twitched in the ghost of a smile.

"Get some rest," Alyea said. "I'll stay and make sure nobody else whacks you over the head in your sleep."

"Hnnhn," he grunted, and closed his eyes again. A few moments later, he whispered, "Thanks."

"You're welcome," Alyea said, and watched the rise and fall of his chest settle into the calm breathing of deep sleep.

Sometime later, Eredion came back, moving ghost-quiet; he moved a chair near hers and studied the sleeping ha'ra'ha with a strangely wary expression. "How is he?"

"Sleeping," she said economically, and rose to pour them each a cup of water. Sitting down again, she studied Eredion; his solid, mature presence felt more reassuring than she wanted to admit. He returned her gaze with dry amusement.

"Quite a few miles since the last time we spoke," he said, then grinned. "You're sunburnt as a heathen, you know."

"So my mother tells me."

"Mm." He sipped his water, glanced at Deiq, then back to Alyea. "You need to be very careful," he said. "Ha'ra'hain don't startle awake very well. You could get hurt. The healer was right not to touch him, much as I hate to admit it."

"He hasn't hurt me yet," she said. Eredion's eyes narrowed sharply, and she added, "No, damn it, I haven't gone to bed with him. Why is that *always* the first damn—"

Eredion laughed, sitting back in his chair. "Welcome to the life of a desert lord," he said, grinning. "I suspect you'll have some kinds of fun explaining the concept of kathain to your family. Especially your mother."

His dark eyes tracked Alyea's change of expression, and his eyebrows rose.

"*Oh*," he said, instantly understanding. "You haven't hit that part of the change yet, have you? That's why you haven't—" He stopped.

She looked away, teeth tight.

"Mmph." Eredion ran a thumb around the lip of his cup for some time. At last he said, "Never mind, then. We can talk about that later. Right now, just be careful around Deiq. A wounded ha'ra'ha doesn't always know what he's doing, and while he hasn't hurt you yet, that's no guarantee he won't lose track of where he is and who you are."

"I won't just leave him here for servants to tend."

"No. No, servants *would* get hurt. But for some reason . . . Deiq seems to really like you. And that makes you the safest person to be around him right now. He's less likely to have a defensive attack reaction to you. But it's still not *safe*, if you understand me. So just be careful, and don't startle him awake."

Eredion handed her his empty cup and stood with a rueful smile.

"And now, *I'm* overdue on my sleep. I'll come back once I've had a nap, and give you a break."

"I'll be fine."

He shook his head. "Best to break up the watch. You can't just sit by Deiq's bedside playing nurse for the next few days. Filin and I will swap off with you until he's back on his feet."

"What are you doing about finding Idisio?"

"There's nothing we can do tonight," he said. Outside, the wind rose in a long, mournful wail, then died back under the roar of rain. "In the morning, we'll start combing the city—in pairs, at the least."

Chapter Thirty-nine

Pain washed Deiq through time and memory with no anchor in the *now* or even any real idea when, exactly, the *now* should be:

"How did they not teach you any of this?" he demanded, furious and appalled, unable to give any comfort to the shattered young man cowering in front of him. *"How could you be put through the trials and not* understand? *You're a desert lord, damn it, you should have been told about the ha'ra'hain!"*

Time spilled, like wine from an overfull cup, and drenched him into another moment:

"Why aren't you explaining to the human supplicants what they're getting themselves into?" he demanded, fury still heating his entire body.

Sessin protector said: The lord of this place has taken on the responsibility of educating the supplicants. I merely accept their gifts and give mine in return.

"It didn't strike you as a little odd that the last one had no idea what was happening?"

The lord of this place told me my explanations upset the supplicants too much, and felt it better to handle the last one himself, Sessin protector replied.

"Well, he's not *handling it!"* Deiq said tartly. *"Damn it, it's your job to be sure they understand, cousin!"*

He'd been so angry . . . and so frightened. Supplicants *had* to be told. It *had* to be an informed and willing choice. If the humans took that away, it would make their desert lords little more than slaves . . . fodder . . . *sacrifices*.

Time rolled again:

"You do remember the Agreement, don't you, Lord Sessin?"

"Of course I do! What's this about?"

"Eredion didn't know about the ha'ra'hain. About me. I almost drove him out of his mind because he didn't understand what was happening."

"You took—" Lord Arit Sessin wheeled to put his back to Deiq, his hands clenching into fists. *"Damn it,"* he said at last, turning around again. *"You've* ruined *him!"*

"What?" Deiq came up out of his chair and had Lord Sessin crowded up against the far wall before the man had a chance to even draw a shocked breath. *"Ruined?"*

Lord Sessin, eyes wide, scarcely breathed as he stared into Deiq's glare.

"Is that what happened," said a dry voice at his side, and Deiq startled into a lunge. Pain wracked through his entire body, and he fell back against the pillows with a hoarse cry.

Vision doubled and tripled, and his head felt as though it would come apart with another breath. He shut his eyes and panted like an overheated asp-jacau, more vulnerable than he'd been in years and unable to care.

Maybe *this* time the humans would show sense and let him die, or kill him off, instead of healing him to go on, to inevitably hurt more of them.

"Sorry," the voice said, very quietly. "Here. Water. And painkiller."

Deiq forced his breathing to slow, to find an even rhythm. When he could finally unclench his hands, he accepted the offered cup and a steadying cradle of hands around his to keep it from spilling; sipped, eyes still closed; little by little, drained the cup, then released it back into the other's grip.

"Eredion," he said then.

"Yes."

Deiq opened his eyes. Triple condensed to double, then to a slightly blurry single focus. "You're an idiot."

"Yes. So are you. Shut your eyes again. They're losing the white."

Deiq shut his eyes and breathed deeply, bringing his tattered willpower to bear; felt the internal blurring clarify as human-normal locked back into place.

"You saw my *discussion* with Lord Arit," he said, resting in the now-quiet dark behind his eyelids; not wanting to see Eredion's expression.

"Yes. You don't have much in the way of shields right now." Eredion paused. "I'm sorry. I didn't mean to wake you like that."

Deiq grimaced, understanding now why that particular memory had surfaced; Eredion's presence had been sufficient. That meant if Alyea came near enough, she'd see his memories of her time at the Qisani; he was only safe from that as long as she stayed deaf to mindspeech. And if she hit the full change while he was this weak, he'd do more than reveal dangerous memories; he'd hurt her badly enough to make the agony of her blood trials look like child's play. Sleep had restored some of this strength, but only enough for human-level functioning. For more than that . . . *No. Not again. Never again.*

He made himself open his eyes and face Eredion. The Sessin lord regarded him with an expression of weary amusement.

"I didn't want to hurt you that day," Deiq said, the words raw acid in his throat. "I'm sorry."

"I know. Never mind." Eredion smiled ruefully. "If anything, I wish you hadn't gone after Lord Sessin about it. That did much more harm than good."

Deiq shut his eyes again, the memory of another, more recent and much more dreadful misjudgment pushing at the back of his mind; but damned if he'd let Eredion see that one. He swallowed hard and said, "Idisio."

"Nothing yet. Nasty storm going still."

"When?"

"Afternoon."

"Huh." Deiq rested for a while, grateful for Eredion's brief answers; each word felt like another slam against his skull. "Alyea?"

"Safe. I'm watching her." Eredion paused, and Deiq had the sense he was thinking about whether to say something; finally he just said, "Sleep."

"Thank you," Deiq whispered, and let darkness take him away again.

Chapter Forty

The palace kitchens, unlike the Peysimun kitchens, did not welcome nobles sitting in the corner room eating rough bread and cheese. But they were willing to carry trays to the rooms, which had always struck Alyea as a waste of effort.

Still, a palace had to run by different rules than a small noble household. Alyea had long ago adjusted her suite to make dining in a comfortable option, and at least the servants here hadn't changed. She always gave them a small coin each time they brought her a tray or performed any housekeeping tasks for her.

In return, they always knocked; and if she didn't answer, they left her alone without argument. It had settled into a comfortable arrangement over time, one she felt a certain trust in; so when the door opened and she heard someone enter her outer suite, her first reaction was annoyance that they'd broken the understanding.

But: "Alyea," Eredion said from the outer room. She hopped out of bed, grabbing up a robe and cursing under her breath.

"What do you want?" Emerging from her bedroom, she stopped to stare.

He'd brought a tray. Almost overflowing with bowls and plates containing hot soup, thick chunks of peasant bread, soft cheese, roughly cut carrots and peppers, it filled the small dining table in the outer room and wafted thick, rich aroma into the air.

"I'm hungry," Eredion said, pointing her to a chair, "and I don't see any reason to eat alone."

She hesitated, glancing down at the thin robe she'd wrapped round herself;

looked up to find Eredion's gaze on the robe too.

"One moment," she said a bit sharply, and his gaze jumped to her face without the least trace of embarrassment.

Retreating into her bedroom, she shut the door and stood still for a moment, wrestling with sudden fear. It was stupid to think that Eredion would try force with her, when he could easily get any woman in the palace into his bed at a moment's notice. All the same, she put on her most conservative long blue dress—with a high collar that went halfway up her neck and sleeves that cuffed at the wrist; she'd used it last to hide the bruises Pieas had left on her— before returning to the outer room of the suite.

Eredion didn't even look up as she came out of the bedroom, too busy scooping black bean soup into chunky white ceramic bowls. He dumped a dollop of soft cheese on top of each, and tore off two wide strips of thick crust from the loaf of peasant bread to serve as rough spoons.

She sat and accepted the bowl he passed her. They ate without speaking until the tray was cleared. Eredion ate the bulk of the meal; Alyea found herself astonished at how much food the man could put away.

"You'll do the same, soon enough," Eredion said, then glanced up at Alyea's sharp intake of breath. "What?"

"I thought only Deiq could read my thoughts. Only ha'ra'hain." Sweat prickled the back of her neck; she ignored the itchiness with a fierce effort.

He stared at her, eyes wide, for a few moments. "No," he said at last, his expression smoothing out to a blandness she was coming to recognize as meaning he'd decided not to tell her something. "You've a lot to learn yet."

"Apparently." She sat back, annoyed, and thought hard about the stifling heat in the room, and the garlic-onion sharpness of the soup she'd just eaten.

Eredion, now looking mildly amused, commented, "Better. But I wouldn't worry over it too much. You can't keep yourself locked up all the time. Part of being a desert lord is understanding that, and not getting too upset over another person's stray thoughts, or even taking them too seriously."

"Why don't I hear *your* thoughts?" Now her arms were beginning to sweat. She should have gone with a lighter dress. Choosing this one had been a pure panic reaction, and stupid.

"Part of the change," he shrugged. "It'll come to you sooner or later."

"About the time I get randy?" she said, then bit her tongue, wishing she hadn't brought that topic up.

He laughed. "Something like that," he admitted, then studied her dress with an amused expression, as though really focusing on it for the first time.

"Good gods," he said, "talk about overreacting. Do you have a knife hidden in a leg sheath, too?"

She felt her face flare into hot color; he leaned back in his chair and hooted with laughter.

"That bloody thing is far too heavy for this weather," he told her. "The robe would have been better. It's not as though I would have raped you, for the love of the gods! I have better control than *that*."

She ducked her head, unable to face his grin.

"Ah, Alyea," he said, in a tone that suddenly reminded her of Azaniari. "You have *so* damn much to learn."

"Then tell me!" she snapped, anger pushing aside embarrassment. "Deiq's no better than Chac, handing out little bits and pieces of information as it suits him. I can't learn anything that way!"

Eredion's mouth quirked, and he began putting dishes back onto the tray.

"Believe me, I know the feeling," he said. "But remember that you're something of an unusual case, Alyea. You're out in the world much sooner than you should be after your trials. And training a desert lord is a very delicate process, part of which is gauging what information to deliver when. Deiq's the one in charge of your training, not me. I'm not going to interfere and tell you something he doesn't think you're ready to hear yet."

She glared at him. "But he's not here," she said, "and you are."

"That means absolutely nothing with desert lords and ha'ra'hain," he said soberly, and she suddenly remembered Evkit's words: *Ha'reye talk together, miles away . . . They pass the word through the air, through the miles.*

Alyea blinked hard and bit her lip, trying not to show her abrupt chill of fear.

Eredion smiled, a dry expression much like Deiq's usual humorless grin, and stood, gathering up the tray.

"I'll set this outside," he said. "And then, as it's stopped raining for the moment, I think you and I can risk a bit of a walk. I want to show you something. Go change first—you'd smother in that damn grandmother's garb."

Late morning sunlight feathered through honeysuckle-draped lattice that stood higher than their heads. Clusters of purple featherleaf flowers nodded over the top edges. Beyond the overgrown fencing someone played a flute, more noise than music, like a child practicing.

Alyea stared, bewildered; she'd never seen this before, and said so.

"No," Eredion said, and urged her to keep walking along the fence. "It's new. A matter of months."

She glanced around, finally recognizing a building here, a tree there. "I know this place!" she said, astonished. "This was *ruins* last time I saw it." She squinted at the fence, then moved to put her eye against the lattice.

Eredion pulled her back gently. "No," he said. "Leave them their privacy, Alyea."

"Leave *who*—" She stopped, remembering: Oruen had granted a last, stubborn holdout group of priests a small area at the western edge of the city. *This* area. Her suspicions darkened instantly. "What are they doing in there?" she demanded, glaring at Eredion.

"Healing the damage Rosin did," he said. "Or trying to, at least."

She stared at the lattice separating her from the last Northern Church priests in the city with a deep distaste. "Why did you want to show me *this*?"

"To remind you," he said, nudging her into motion again, "about what's worth worrying about. *This* matters. Not who you sleep with."

She stopped walking and glared at him, remembering the look on his face when she'd first come out of the bedroom in a thin robe. "So this is your idea of an invitation?" she snapped, and felt stupid immediately; of course it wouldn't be that simple. But apologizing wouldn't do any good either, so she maintained her scowl and waited to see what he would say.

He shook his head, not reacting to the challenge at all, and gestured her to start walking.

They made a complete circuit of the enclosure, then Eredion stopped and said, "What did you notice, Alyea?"

She stared at him, then at the fence, baffled.

"What *isn't* there?"

She glanced along the length of what she could see, and cast her mind back over the walk. "A gate," she said. "They hid the gate."

Eredion nodded. "They know people out here hate them, enough to make being visible dangerous. So they put up a high fence, and covered it with ivy, and hid the gate to avoid people even thinking about what's inside. They just want to be left alone to repair, in their own small way, what a few damn fools did to this city."

"What are they doing?"

Eredion shook his head. "It's not my business to say. And they won't tell you if you ask, because you could get them all killed with a careless word." He glanced up as a cloud drifted overhead, dimming the sunlight. "We'd better get back. It's going to start raining again soon."

Still baffled over why Eredion had thought this important enough to walk halfway across the city to see, Alyea followed him back toward the palace.

The western part of Bright Bay had distinctly different architecture than the eastern: the majority of buildings here were set on thick, sturdy stone columns, leaving a tall floodway beneath. Roads lay as high as sidewalks, with a deep gutter on each side. The recent storms had washed away most of the dirt and sewage, and the worn cobbles were dark with moisture.

Many of the buildings had been badly damaged or destroyed, over the last fifty years, from a combination of severe storms and the Purge. Alyea rarely visited this side of town, finding it by far too depressing. Even now, as they walked, she could feel eyes watching them: the dispossessed thieves and beggars who had moved into the ruins around them, cobbling together rough shelters in which to wait out the worst of the afternoon storms.

Idisio had been one of them, not so long ago. Perhaps he hadn't gone off with the tath-shinn after all, but simply slipped the leash and run back to his roots—

Lady Arnil's whispery, smug voice came to mind: *likely returned to her roots and walking the streets. . . .*

Alyea swallowed hard against sudden self-loathing and looked up to find Eredion watching her in a series of quick sideways glances as they walked.

He said, quietly, "I believe Idisio lived on the eastern side of town. But I doubt he returned to that life. He can't go back to what he was, even if he wanted to." He looked at the jagged remains of once-proud buildings lining the street. "But some of these drifters might well have known him. They move around regularly to avoid the guards."

A shiver ran up Alyea's back, and suddenly she felt very exposed. She realized that to a street thief, she would seem a tempting target. Her plain clothes would be seen as a badge of wealth, her boots a prize to be sold for food. She glanced over her shoulder, uneasy; the street behind was empty of traffic, but a skinny, black-haired child hung, head and shoulders, out of an upper window two buildings back. He stared at her with a calculating expression for just a moment, then withdrew from sight.

"They won't bother us," Eredion said, stopping and turning to look back himself. "They know who I am. In fact, while we're here—" He gave a long, warbling whistle.

"Up here," someone said to their left. Alyea looked up to find a gangly man perched on a stone column not far away. He grinned, revealing a mouthful of broken and missing teeth, and banged his dangling heels cheerfully against the stone on which he sat.

"Hai, hoy, you brought a pretty one by this time," he added, studying Alyea with a keen interest. "She coming or going?"

"Lives here," Eredion said mildly, hooking a thumb over his shoulder. "Inside."

"Hai," the man said, squinting. "Got 'er. News, then?"

"Yes."

"Bitch of the west side's dying. Her squirt's dying to move in on that." The man broke off to cough, long and hard. He spat a brown gob to one side, politely aiming well clear of them. "Four more northerns swapped out this past tenday; Fern's, Tavi's, Belter's, and that damn leatherman I been wantin' to slice. Good riddance to *him*, anyway, but I'll miss Fern. Man had a sense of rightness to him."

Eredion's brows drew into a faint, worried frown. "Are the newcomers fours?"

"One. Rest are just ordinaries." He spat again, to his other side this time. "Wailer's gone, too. Not a hint of it."

Eredion hesitated, glancing sideways at Alyea, then said, "Any sight of Lifty?"

"Hah, hai!" The man rocked back, almost unbalancing off the column with the movement. He squinted at Alyea again, with an entirely different flavor of appraisal than before. "She's that in it, hai?"

"Fair bit," Eredion agreed, motioning Alyea to be quiet.

"Huh. Got 'er." The man winked at Alyea, then looked back to Eredion. "Nah. Nothing there, since he wound up in your uptown house. Figured you had him under thumb. He off again?"

"Slipped us," Eredion said. "Looks like the wailer has him."

"Huh." The man shook his head, scratching just under his left ear for a moment. "Nah. Nothing here. We'll watch it."

"Thank you," Eredion said gravely, and jerked his head at Alyea, signaling that it was time to move on. As they began walking again, a warbling trill of whistles broke out from several spots behind them. Eredion didn't glance back; Alyea took her cue from that and kept her attention carefully ahead.

"Who's the bitch of the west side?" Alyea asked when the noise died down.

"Lady Arnil," Eredion said. Alyea nodded, unsurprised. "She's been ill for a time. I don't imagine she'll make much longer." He rubbed his forehead with a knuckle, seeming lost in thought for a few moments. At last he went on,

"You're safe walking around town for now; they've marked you as under my protection. Might be a good idea for you to make some alliances of your own, though. Street agreements change like the weather."

"Oh, my mother's going to *love* that," Alyea said sourly, thinking that she'd never been afraid of walking through town before. Eredion's protection seemed entirely unnecessary, and more than a little condescending.

"Don't tell her," Eredion said, as though Alyea were being unexpectedly dense. "It's not as though you'll be hosting thieves in your *house*, for the love of the gods."

Alyea thought about protesting that she'd been trying for sarcasm; decided it would only make matters worse, and let it go.

The West Gate guards let them through with respectful nods to Eredion and a sly smile at Alyea. "Let be," Eredion said in her ear before she could deliver a sharp rebuke for their obvious assumptions. He tucked his hand into the crook of her elbow, tugging her along.

"But they think—"

"Doesn't matter," he said. "If all they see is a desert lord with his latest lady of favor, they won't remember *you*."

"Why would that matter?"

"Right now it doesn't," he said, releasing her arm. "But one day, it might. Why make your movements more public knowledge than they have to be?"

"Spoken like a man who doesn't have to worry over reputation," she retorted. "Being branded as loose can cause me all sorts of trouble, Lord Eredion."

Eredion shook his head, his mouth quirking into a half-smile, but didn't speak again until they were walking through the western gardens of the palace. Then he said, "I'll tell you the point of this walk, Lord Alyea, since you don't see it yet. If you want to put up walls, make sure you have something worth dying for behind that barrier, and a real enemy ready to kill you for it on the outside."

The clouds closed in as he spoke, and a fat patter of rain began to splotch the ground around them. Bees and wasps lifted in an outraged cloud from the flowering oregano and fennel rows nearby, swirling and zipping to their sheltering nests. Alyea watched them, only half her attention on Eredion's words. There seemed to be a pattern to the movements of the insect clouds, something just out of the reach of understanding.

When the last insect disappeared, she looked up and discovered Eredion also gone. The rain intensified to a steady, thick drizzle; she started to hurry inside, then stopped, caught by a strange impulse, and tilted her face to the sky.

Water streaked her face and neck, funneling through clothes and along her arms with liquid chill. She stood still for a long time, not thinking of anything in particular; just feeling the rain, and the wind, and her own body responding to the cooling temperatures.

The world around her wavered in and out of hyper-clear focus. She could pick out the petals on a flower a stone's throw away one moment, barely see her hand in front of her face the next. Smells clashed and rioted in her nose: mold, damp leaves, dirt, rust mingling with fennel, rosemary, and the climbing roses on an archway to her right. She heard the patter of rain as a thundering cacophony, then as a gentle patter; heard footsteps passing, heard the murmur of voices and the burbling of a young child somewhere nearby.

Lost in the astounding collection of perceptions, it took her a while to realize that one set of footsteps had stopped somewhere behind her, and not begun again.

Blinking water from her eyes, she turned around.

Nobody stood behind her, or anywhere nearby. The nearest archway into the palace proper was a goodly stone's throw away, and the raised flower beds left little room for concealment. She stood still, listening, and heard only the rattle of rain streaming through gutters high and low.

The magic faded sharply from the moment, and she found herself soaked and shivering, standing like a newborn fool in a heavy rainstorm. Cursing under her breath, she headed for the nearest archway.

Three sides of the palace—west, east, and south—were enclosed by long, wide galleries punctuated with multiple archways. Each archway, in turn, stood flanked by two enormous brickroot planters filled with small evergreen shrubs. Alyea stood just inside an archway and wrung her hair and clothes out as best she could, wondering if she were losing her mind. What had possessed her to stand out in the rain like that?

"The changes," someone said. She yelped and spun, dropping reflexively into a fighting crouch.

Lord Filin stood there, in clothes of grey and yellow that blended in with the walls around him. He laughed; Alyea, watching closely as she straightened, saw that the humor didn't reach his eyes.

"Good reactions," he said. His long, dark face went oddly still for a moment, then relaxed. He moved a step closer, his eyes intent on hers.

"Lord Filin," Alyea said, her mouth dry.

"Eredion asked me to keep an eye on you," Filin said. A faint smile tugged his lean face into sly lines. "You look to need a change of clothes."

She didn't move, her nerves taut as a drawn bowstring. He wasn't precisely lying, but he had more in mind than keeping her safe.

"I'll take care of myself," she said curtly. "Thank you, Lord Filin, but I'll find my own way back to my rooms."

He regarded her with smoky amusement. "You're coming into the changes," he said. "Not a good idea for you to be alone right now."

She realized that somewhere during that comment, he'd eased another step closer, and his eyes were tracking every small move she made.

"I'll *manage*," she said, narrowing her eyes. Damned if she'd back up from this weasel!

Filin grinned at her and came forward another step; then checked, his head tilting as though listening. His expression tightened, becoming ugly. He stared at Alyea for a moment, a black glitter in his eyes.

"Damn it," Filin muttered. He bared his teeth at Alyea, revealing two dark gaps in the row of small, even whiteness. No longer the least bit friendly, he turned and strode away without looking back.

She drew in a deep breath, blinking hard, and looked around. Seeing nobody, she abandoned dignity and bolted for the safety of her rooms.

Chapter Forty-one

Deiq was lucky to be alive. Knowing that brought him no joy. Neither did being alive. He listened to the rain still pouring down outside and felt a thirst no amount of water would ease, a hunger no food could fill.

In the darkness beside him, someone stirred.

"You're brooding again," Eredion said softly. "What's the matter?"

Deiq stared at the ceiling, allowing his eyes to shift over just enough to be able to make out the swirled patterns in the plaster, and didn't answer. His head hurt, but it had reduced to a mild agony instead of an overwhelming one; his entire body still ached as from a brutal beating, and he knew what had caused *that*, all too well.

He'd underestimated the tath-shinn. Badly. In more than one way. She could have killed him; and again, he found himself wishing she had, and wondering why she hadn't.

"Deiq," Eredion said, and sighed at the lack of response.

Deiq heard him stand and walk across the room. A few moments later, an oil lamp flared to yellow life and a rank smell drifted across Deiq's nose: this one used fish oil, not surprising in a port city. It could have been worse: his own farms tended to use vegetable oils, and some of them smelled hideous.

Eredion turned the wick down to a bare glow, set it on the bedside table, and sat back down.

"You may as well tell me," Eredion said. "I'll pester you until you do."

Deiq turned his head, not bothering to revert his eyes to human-normal, and stared at the Sessin lord with as much ferocity as he could summon. Eredion just smiled.

"I'm not afraid of you, Deiq," he said. "Not anymore. You can't do anything worse to me than what I've been through the past few years." He paused. "Death would probably be a blessing for both of us, wouldn't it? But it's never that easy."

Deiq shut his eyes; they slid back to human-normal without his even willing it, and instantly flooded with tears. He heard Eredion give a low grunt of surprise.

"Are you *crying*?"

"Fuck off." Deiq blinked hard, lifting a hand to wipe his eyes clear. "Damn dust."

"Of course." Eredion's voice resumed its usual sardonic tone. "So tell me what's got you so racked over already. I've already picked up bits of it; you think about Meer a lot, you know."

Deiq turned another glare on Eredion; the desert lord didn't flinch.

"It's been me and Alyea," Eredion said softly. "Filin is too shit-scared of being near you; he stood one watch, said you gave him the creeps, and refused to take another. He went out with the others to look for Idisio instead."

Deiq narrowed his eyes, catching something *off* about that explanation. Eredion ignored that look, too, and went on without pause.

"And Alyea's still deaf, isn't she? Hasn't hit the change. And we haven't let anyone else near you. So I'm the only one who's seen anything."

Deiq grimaced and turned his head away, feeling tight muscles creak. He'd have to spend some time stretching as soon as he had the physical strength to raise a hand for more than wiping his eyes clear.

"Deiq," Eredion said again, with a maddeningly soft, patient tone that warned this could go on for hours; and Deiq surrendered. This was probably the safest time and person, all things considered. He couldn't get out of bed to attack Eredion, and if Eredion chose to attack *him* . . . Well, as he'd just said, death could be a mercy.

"All right. Let me think how to say it."

After sorting through events in his head for a while, he began unrolling into Eredion's mind, with painstaking delicacy, a story that he'd never allowed another—human, ha'ra'hain, or ha'reye—to hear.

He knew as soon as he eased, unnoticed, past the guard post at the southern edge of the city that something was dreadfully wrong. A choking sense of horror filled the air here, muffling and stifling his perceptions.

Traffic in this part of town was light; few people came north these days. Most went south, under whatever guise or guile would get them past the hard-faced guards. Nobody bumped into Deiq as he stood still, unwilling to move further into the city until he understood what was going on. The guards cast him more than one suspicious glare; he ignored them as he searched for the source of the dread. The emotion felt like a thick, clinging fog, like a living thing determined to seep into his pores and every possible opening.

Like a living thing. . . .

"Oh, hells," he said aloud, *and took a hasty step back towards the safety of the border. Half a heartbeat later blackness surrounded him and a thin, resonant voice spoke in his mind:*

Welcome, nephew. Going somewhere? Now wouldn't that be rude, not to visit while you're here. *Huge eyes opened in the dark, golden and catlike and flat; Deiq only had time to think how odd that appearance was before fragile laughter shredded the air.* And speaking of while you're here. . . .

Jagged lace stripped through his veins as the ha'rethe began, without any pretense of tenderness, to feed. . . .

Deiq cut that memory off before it had a chance to echo pain into Eredion's mind and moved on to a later moment:

He woke to white, a coolness on his forehead, and the discovery that he couldn't so much as lift a hand. But he wasn't bound, just exhausted, and someone sat to his left. He turned his head and blinked at the thin man watching him.

"Good morning," the stranger said, smiling. He wore a baggy, strangely styled white tunic without ornamentation; Deiq saw no jewelry, tattoos, or other rank indicators. His dark hair, blue eyes, and relatively pale skin spoke of a northern heritage, probably from somewhere above the line of the Hackerwood.

Deiq worked up enough spit to swallow, easing the desert dryness in his throat, and said, "Who and where?" Even that brief sentence tore at his voice, turning it into a rasping husk.

The man bent and retrieved a plain clay jug and cup from the floor by the bed. He had wide, strong farmer's hands, but clean and neatly trimmed as a courtier's. Pouring water from the jug into the small cup, the man said nothing until he had set the jug back down, and then only: "Can you sit up on your own?"

Deiq worked his way to a semi-upright position. Leaning on one elbow, he accepted the cup and sipped it slowly, eyes closed. It felt like the first liquid to pass his cracked lips in years, and tasted faintly of almonds.

He could sense the memory of that sharp taste working through Eredion's mind, calling the moment into vivid immediacy and provoking echoes from the desert lord's own past: some of which Deiq did *not* want to get drawn into just now. He gently deflected the ghost-memories and kept Eredion's attention on the story at hand.

When the cup was empty, he held it out without opening his eyes, held it steady as the man refilled it, and drank it as slowly as the first. They repeated the silent exchange three more times before Deiq turned the cup upside down and handed it back to indicate he'd had enough.

"You're in Bright Bay," the man said then. "We found you wandering the streets in a daze. Well . . . I found you, actually. And as I didn't want . . . Well, I brought you back here. To our tower. To heal."

Deiq stared at the man, frowning, then looked around at white walls, white curtains over a narrow window, and a mosaic of small blue, green, red, and black beads hanging over the bed. The air smelled of lavender, sweet-clove incense, and old sweat, a nauseating combination to his sensitive nose. He shut his eyes and slid back down to lie flat, unable to stay upright another moment and too sick with realization to try.

"Church," he said through his teeth. Of all the places to wind up . . . the man's loose clothing wasn't a tunic, but a Northern Church robe.

"Yes," the man said. "The tower of the Northern Church. Infirmary section. I'm Meer, by the way, Meer of . . . well, I suppose of Bright Bay now, but I was born in Isata."

Deiq found the steady calm of Meer's voice restful and unthreatening. The voice that broke in a moment later, by contrast, was harsh and more than a little whiny:

"I heard voices! Is he awake, Meer, or are you talking to yourself again?"

Deiq kept his eyes shut and his face relaxed as though he were, in fact, still asleep. Meer apparently shared that instinctive decision.

"Still asleep," the thin man reported without the slightest quaver of deceit in his voice. "I'll tell you when he wakes, Rettin."

"We can't keep him here much longer," Rettin complained. "He's been out for days. I don't like him being up here, Meer. Now that there's a spot available, I want him moved—"

"Not yet, Rettin," Meer interrupted. "Give me another day. Please. If he's not awake by tomorrow night, we'll move him. I just feel so strongly that he's going to wake soon that I don't want to risk that yet."

The simple sincerity in Meer's voice impressed Deiq. This man was good at lying with a straight face.

"You and your hunches," Rettin grumbled, moving away.

Again Eredion's memories caught and turned over, like tiles loosened by a strong wind. He'd known Rettin: a petty, scheming, selfish man, who came to a perfectly appropriate end not long after that encounter. Deiq resisted curiosity and left that memory alone; he'd ask Eredion about what had happened another day. If he sidetracked now, he'd never find the courage to return to this story. The worst part wasn't far ahead—if he could just get through it.

When the door had shut behind the intrusion, Deiq opened his eyes again to find Meer watching him with a pensive expression.

"It's good you're awake," Meer said in a low voice, obviously more cautious about being overheard. "I couldn't have stopped him from moving you tomorrow night to the lower rooms. And those are . . . not healthy places to rest. You're only up here because all the . . . beds . . . are full downstairs. And now that there's an opening. . . . " He shut his eyes and swallowed hard. "Gods save us and forgive us our sins," he murmured.

Deiq propped himself back up on one elbow and regarded Meer with interest. A little sifting, more challenging than he'd expected, gave him a vague impression of those lower rooms; places where the priests questioned those suspected of plotting against Mezarak—and made half-hearted attempts to repair the wounds of those already questioned: enough to allow another round.

He definitely didn't want to go there. The search through Meer's mind, which should have been simple, had drained what strength resting had given him. He needed to sleep for several more days, and Rettin clearly wouldn't allow that. Weak as he currently felt, fighting back would be difficult, and the images in Meer's mind suggested they'd tie him down well enough to make it completely impossible.

The water had relaxed his throat; he could speak clearly again. "You're a priest yourself?"

"Priest-healer," Meer nodded.

"Herbalist?"

"No." Meer glanced away, seeming vaguely embarrassed. "Well, somewhat. I use herbs too. But I was given something of a gift by the gods; a healing gift, for those in need. It's a small gift, nothing of consequence, really. But it helps."

Deiq regarded him with considerably more respect. A true healer, then: a damn rare gift among humans. Outside Church control, they were called witches, abominations, and monsters; but even Wezel had been a hypocrite about permitting healers who worked under the banner of the Church.

"Are you the only healer in this tower?"

"No. The only one . . . not working the lower rooms. I've been refusing to do that." Meer looked down at his hands, twisted together in his lap, and sighed. "Well, that's not important. Right now I need to know who you are, friend, and what you're doing here. Before Rettin finds out you're awake. We didn't find any papers on you. No pass tokens. Nothing at all."

"They must have been stolen," Deiq said. "I came in through the southern gate . . . a while ago. And I suspect someone hit me over the head. It's all rather hazy." He met Meer's eyes and smiled a little, seeing the healer recognize the same bland sincerity Meer himself had used with Rettin.

Meer's generous mouth twitched. "I see," he said gravely. "Do you happen to recall your purpose in town, s'e? Who you were coming to see, perhaps?"

Deiq considered the relative safety of various answers, then said, "I own a business with interests in town. I was coming to speak with one of my factions here, to check the accounting books."

"Really?" Meer said, eyebrows lifting in polite skepticism. "Which business is that, s'e?"

"The southland Farms," Deiq said, and watched Meer's expression crash into astonishment.

"Oh, gods," Meer breathed, eyes wide. "You're Deiq of Stass?"

"Yes."

"Oh, Rettin would love to get his hands on you, s'e. And I doubt you'd like that much." He glanced at the door, chewing his lower lip anxiously. "I've got to get you out of here."

That hadn't been the reaction Deiq expected. Without the strength to try another fast sifting for information, he was reduced to voicing the question aloud: "Why?"

Meer seemed surprised at his patient's ignorance. "Because your farms, s'e, are seen as dangerous to the northern economy. The head of this tower, s'iope Itilin, has been getting very fierce about how Bright Bay shouldn't have to rely on southern imports. What's so funny?"

Deiq lay back, chest heaving with suppressed laughter, trying not to make too much noise. At last, catching his breath, he said, "I set up the farms so the southlands wouldn't have to depend on the north for food any longer."

Meer grinned nervously, his lips staying tight shut over his teeth. "And now they're doing so well the north likes food from your lands better than that grown in our own soil. I see. But Itilin, and others, are convinced that your farms were a deliberate attempt to steal away precious income and resources from Bright Bay and the coastal villages. There's been a fair amount of discussion over your farms, s'e, and some of it's ugly." He cleared his throat, looking uncomfortable. "Along the lines of taking some of them over in the name of the northern kingdom."

Eredion sighed a little at that, remembering his own attempts to steer opinion away from that option. Deiq saw the faint traces of violence edging through the desert lord's recall, and suspected Eredion had gotten his hands thoroughly dirty in service of keeping the peace. That was his job, after all; still, just for a moment, Deiq felt the pressure of a deep sadness that it had even been neccessary.

Deiq sobered. "That would mean war with the entire southlands," he said. "None of the desert Families would stand for that."

Meer shrugged, spreading his hands helplessly. "I'm only a priest-healer, s'e, and I only know what I overhear. And that tells me I need to get you out of this tower before they find out who you are—and without them seeing you leave. But you can't even walk yet, and I have no way to carry you out unseen."

Deiq drew a breath and shut his eyes for a moment, feeling the first stirring of awakening hunger. Once he fed, he'd have the strength to simply step out of this tower to a safer spot miles away, without any worry about the priests following or finding him.

"I know a way," he said, "but it's . . . not going to be easy."

Meer said nothing for a long moment, then, very quietly, "You're not human, are you?"

That popped Deiq's eyes open and brought him up on one elbow.

Meer stared at him, nervous but determined. "When I found you wandering, you spoke in a language I'd never heard. And your skin . . . looked almost like scales." He looked down at his hands and swallowed hard. "I thought I heard your voice in my head when I found you. Asking me for shelter. It was . . . frightening. I really thought you were a demon."

"But you still helped me," Deiq said with matching quiet, his chest tight with near-panic and astonishment. "Thank you, Meer."

"It's what I've been led to do all my life," the priest said. "When I was a child I tried to save baby badgers, wild cats, and even a snake once. When I grew up into proper training I felt drawn to help those nobody else would touch; the criminals, the shunned and scorned and evil. Somebody has to do it, I suppose, and it seems that somebody is me." He raised a drawn expression and met Deiq's gaze. "What do I have to do to get you to safety, s'e?"

Deiq couldn't speak for a long moment. "You're very brave, Meer," he said when his throat unstuck. "I don't want to hurt you. Is there someone in the tower that . . . maybe isn't so nice? Someone the world might be better off without?"

Meer looked down at his hands, frowning; traced lines with a finger on first one palm, then the other, before answering. "I won't deny someone else their chance at redemption," he said. "Even the most cruel and evil people in this world might choose a better path in the next moment. I can't see the future, and I won't end anyone's life over past actions. So if you have to take a life, take mine, s'e."

Deiq blinked, incredulous. "I don't want to kill you, Meer; but what I need will. And that would be a dreadful waste of a good man." His own honesty surprised him as much as Meer's willingness to sacrifice himself for a stranger.

"Are you evil, s'e?" Meer asked. "Are you a demon from the old tales?"

"No. I'm not a demon. And I don't think . . . that I'm evil." He paused; then the same insane honesty prodded him into adding, "But I know I've done evil things.

Without understanding them as such, as first, and then without being able to control them, later. But I'm trying, Meer. I'm trying to stop doing those things, and that's why I don't want to hurt you. The world needs men like you more than it needs me."

Meer rested a hand on Deiq's arm. Hunger surged at the contact, and Deiq began to breathe heavily, fighting against the cresting need.

"No, s'e," the priest said, his blue eyes eerily serene. "You are exactly what this world needs. You are one of those who I've been put on this earth to save. If my life helps you turn to the good, it's worth the sacrifice to me."

"You're mad," Deiq panted, staring at the priest, baffled by the man's calm acceptance of imminent death. He ought to have been howling for Deiq to die; should have been calling in his brethren to destroy the monster as it lay helpless before them. It would ensure Meer's place in heaven, as Deiq understood Church philosophy; why was the man just sitting there?

Meer smiled. "I've been told that I'm mad before," he admitted. "But I felt those words, as I spoke them, as though they came from my soul, not my lips. I think that's a sign from the gods that I'm doing the right thing. I'll die content, if the gods are with me." He sat on the edge of the bed. "There are others who believe as I do. If you would go find them, when you're done, and help them with their efforts to keep this city from the control of men who don't understand the value of life . . . I'd be grateful."

"I will," Deiq husked, then gave in and gripped Meer's arm, digging his fingers in hard.

Gently, he admonished himself, and fought to begin the draw with a faint feather-touch rather than a desperate grab. But even that light touch set Meer arching his back, his eyes bulging, crooked top teeth sinking into his lower lip in an futile effort to stop his scream.

Deiq tried to use the initial surge of energy to move them elsewhere, away from the pristine, dangerous calm of this room—and failed. Before he could try again, a red haze descended, and he fell helplessly into the moment's endless desire, washed along on a river of agonized human screaming.

And as he emerged from that small madness and began to take the step that would take him away from this place into safety, a golden haze washed over him—

—the white walls faded into rank darkness, and a smug voice said, *Oh, how nice. I didn't think you'd be ready again so soon. . . .*

Deiq opened his eyes to the now, relieved to find darkness surrounding him again. The lamp had gone out during the telling, and Eredion hadn't moved to relight it.

"Oh, gods," Eredion said blankly after a time. "Oh, Deiq. Good gods and spirits."

Deiq stared at the ceiling and didn't answer; Eredion sat by his side and said nothing more for the rest of the night.

Chapter Forty-two

Grateful for the rain, which made a perfect excuse for not returning to Peysimun Mansion, Alyea slept, ate, took her turns watching over Deiq, and rested, treasuring the quiet. It felt like a drink she'd been craving without knowing its name: time alone to *think*, or to simply stare at the walls, as she chose.

So much had happened since her encounter with Pieas in a back palace hallway had sent her racing to protect Wian; now Pieas was dead, Wian had disappeared, and the king was no longer likely to offer unquestioning support for anything Alyea brought before him.

So much had changed, and not just with her status. Before she left for the desert, this much time alone would have begun rasping against her nerves, and she would have gone hunting for a dance, a walking-partner, any distraction. Now, the peace of an aqeyva trance felt more and more welcome, and she sat on her striped mat often, letting her mind fill with quiet and empty of thoughts.

The dark grey day blended into darker nights, all filled with torrential downpours and howling winds; she and Eredion ate meals together now, in Deiq's suite. When Deiq was awake, he accepted a few sips of water and a few bites of food, but most of the time he slept, barely seeming to breathe. And he said little to nothing, his dark stare fixed on the ceiling, seemingly lost in his own brooding thoughts.

On the third morning after the attack, the weather broke; and Deiq got out of bed to join them at the small table for breakfast.

Eredion, without comment, rose and pulled the servant-summoner; waited by the door and sent the servant who responded after another tray of food.

"A large one," Alyea heard him say. "Twice what we asked for, at least."

Returning to the table, he stepped around behind Deiq and began unwinding the bandages. Alyea wrinkled her nose at the rising smell of old sweat, pus, blood, and dirt. Eredion grimaced a few times as well.

Deiq reached for an orange and simply bit into it whole, not bothering to peel it first, and ignored everything else. His eyes held a vague, hazed look; Alyea wasn't even sure he saw anything other than the food in his hand.

Alyea stood, unable to face eating with that stench in the air, and circled round to see what lay underneath the rotten bandages.

Eredion dropped the last of the bandages in a heap on the floor and stroked Deiq's matted hair aside with a deft, delicate touch. The motion revealed only a strip of faintly over-pink skin, bare of hair but otherwise unremarkable.

Alyea gasped, astounded; she'd expected an ugly scar at the least. Eredion sighed a little, then scooped up the filthy wrappings and took them to the door, again pulling the servant-summoner; handed them off and came back to the table.

"Deiq," he said, seating himself across from the ha'ra'ha.

Deiq made no response other than an unfocused glance, apparently more interested in reaching for another orange. Eredion shook his head and leaned back in his chair, motioning Alyea to sit down again.

"Let him be," Eredion advised.

"Have you done this before?" she demanded, sliding into her chair, unable to take her gaze from Deiq.

"Not with a ha'ra'ha," Eredion said, "but yes. I've tended some ugly wounds in the recent past." He cleared his throat. "Let him eat as much as he likes. I expect he'll go back to bed afterwards and sleep a while more. He might be coherent next time he wakes."

"Is he sleepwalking now?"

"Not exactly. I think he's just focused really tightly, and doesn't have anything to spare for conversation." He paused, watching Deiq finish the second orange and reach for breakfast bread. "I think leaving him completely alone might actually be best, at this point. Why don't you go tell the king he's awake? I'll stay until he goes back to sleep."

The king only held Open Audience three times a tenday: Syrtaday, Fireday, and Windsday. The audience about the tath-shinn had been on Syrtaday; three dawns past that put it at Waterday. Alyea worked her way through the maze of palace hallways, stairs, and rooms, knowing just where Oruen would be.

She found him, as expected, on a tiny, semi-enclosed patio, facing off against one of his advisors over a game of *chabi*. This morning's victim, an elderly man wearing the striped robe of a chamberlain's clerk, looked up with a distinct expression of relief when Alyea stepped through the doorway. He hastily stood to offer her his seat.

Oruen stood as well, and bowed, his expression wavering between solemn and mischievous. "Lord Alyea," he said. "Your presence does me honor."

Alyea bit her lip against a laugh. The advisor blinked, then dropped into a bow of his own, rather deeper than the king's.

"I think we can resume the game another day, Elsin," Oruen murmured. "Thank you for keeping me company this morning."

Elsin bobbed another deep bow and fled without argument.

Alyea let her grin surface and sat down, studying the board. He'd taken the northern side, and chosen black as his color; his *furun*, the king-coin, was two squares away from the northeast fortress, so it had been unlocked. Which fit what she remembered of Oruen's style: keeping options open, to be able to move the furun out of danger. Elsin's furun had also obviously been unlocked; it sat three squares away from the nearest fortress, open to capture.

"How many games have you played so far this morning?"

"This would have been the first with Elsin," Oruen said, seating himself across from her.

She could feel his gaze, and didn't look up; instead, she slid a white *shassen* two paces forward, from Water into the northeast sector. Elsin hadn't been doing so badly; she could see that his attempts to attack the opposing fortress had prompted Oruen to pull several pieces over as defense, but Elsin had left his own furun out and undefended in the process, and Oruen was about to close a trap around it.

"You would have won in four moves."

"Three," he said, and hopped a black *ayn* three diagonally and two forward: one wall of his planned trap. She wouldn't get her furun back into safety in time. "He didn't understand the game one bit. Almost nobody does."

She examined the layout, cocking her head to one side, thinking about the possibilities. No point trying to move her furun back to protected ground; which only left attacking as a distraction. She studied the northeast sector more closely—and smiled.

Her initial move had put white control into the northeast sector, which meant she could move the greys. Oruen had been so intent on his planned trap setup that he'd missed what that meant for his own defenses: she moved a grey shassen sideways and said, "Trapped."

Every exit route was covered by one of her white pieces or blocked by his own accumulation of defenses; with the grey cube out of the way, her white shassen, only three paces away, had a clear shot at the furun. All of his black pieces were too far away, chasing after her furun, to intervene. Technically, it was a stalemate; he could move a grey piece to block her, and she could promptly move it back out of the way. Custom dictated ceding the game to her at this point, though.

He stared at the board, then stared at her. "What the hells?"

She shrugged, more than a little surprised at herself; she'd always been dreadful at chabi. The rules were complex and confusing. She'd played with Oruen a few times for idle amusement and given up in favor of easier games.

It had become one of the few complaints his advisors and courtiers held against him: he kept trying to teach them how to play; insisted that at least one person sit with him, every single Waterday morning, to learn the southern strategy game. Alyea assumed Chac had taught him, but she'd never asked.

Today, though, the moves seemed oddly simple, the consequences clear; *kahar* for wind, *ayn* for water, *shassen* for goods, and *furun* for coins. It was a desert game: all the moves and strategies reflected the simple principles of survival in a dry, hostile environment. Each player chose black or white as a color; greys were servant pieces, movable by anyone with a presence in that sector. Player pieces could be captured; servant pieces couldn't. Capturing the opposing player's furun won the game, but it could only be captured outside a fortress; inside the fortress, the furun could be overcome if it was "ringed" — surrounded on five sides by grey pieces, with an opposing presence inside the sector.

Complicated, but so many chabi rules made real-world sense now: for example, servants went wherever their masters told them to, like those left behind after Conclave to help Scratha. And while those loaned-out servants currently obeyed Scratha, their loyalty would revert in an instant if their original masters stepped in to take them away; which could leave the lord of a fortress helpless in his own home.

Oruen began resetting the board. "Tea, coffee, breakfast," he said vaguely, waving a hand towards the sideboard.

Alyea shook her head. "No, thank you. I came to tell you Deiq is awake."

Oruen paused, the white furun in his hand, and looked at her for a long, quiet moment before returning his attention to setting the board. "I hear you've been sitting at his bedside."

"Along with Lord Eredion. Yes."

He placed the white furun on the northwest sector of the board, claiming white as his color, and sat back, giving her a challenging stare. "Your move."

She sighed, knowing he wouldn't let her get out of it, and took a few moments to study the board and think about her new understanding of the rules. At last she set her own black, coin-shaped furun on the board, claiming the southeast sector, then moved her shassen forward one step: goods advancing.

"Why?" he said, not looking up from the pieces. He moved a northeastern white ayn two paces south and three southeast; water spilling from one place to another.

"Because he's hurt. And your healer wasn't much use."

"But why is that *your* problem?"

She studied the board for a bit, thinking over where he was likely going with that ayn move; it gave him possession of the central Air block, which held two grey ayn. She finally mirrored it with her own, contesting his control and giving herself the option of moving the grey ayns.

He moved the grey shassen in his sector back three paces: probably angling to free his locked-in furun. Not the most efficient move; he should have gotten his white shassen out of the way first. He still wasn't taking her seriously.

She moved her grey south shassen into the southeast sector and bumped the next grey shassen over one square; then answered his question. "Why wouldn't it be?"

He moved the grey shassen west one square, as she'd expected, his mouth twitching as though he'd just realized his mistake. He didn't answer her question right away, his attention entirely on the game.

A few moves later, he had captured one of her kahar and she had captured one of his ayn. Setting the black kahar aside, he finally said, "Because he's bad news, Alyea. Every time he shows up, everything goes all to the hells. I wish I could ban him from the city outright, but he practically owns half of it."

She glanced up, startled. "Really?"

He snorted. "When you get through all the misdirections, yes. For one thing, he's behind the southland Farms, which means he's responsible for supplying almost half of the produce vendors in the open marketplace; Darden and F'Heing together supply the other half."

"What about the northern farmers?"

"Minimal. There's been a boring-bug influx, and it wiped out half the crop this year so far. And now this damned storm has destroyed any new local plantings, and will probably leave an epidemic of grey-leaf or root rot in its wake."

Alyea moved her westernmost shassen forward three paces. "You sound like a farmer."

"I sound like a king," he said sourly. "I had no idea how many godsdamned details are involved, or I would have run like all the hells were at my heels when Chac approached me."

He stared at the board for a while, then shook his head.

"I can't care about this right now," he said. "You'd probably win, anyway. You obviously understand the game now. How often did you play, while you were in the south?"

"Never," she said. She didn't think she would have won, actually, but didn't feel like finishing the game either. He aimed a skeptical glance at her. "No, really. I swear."

"I believe you," he sighed. "This has all become a gigantic mess. I still can't believe Chac was a traitor. And Micru! He was the best of my Hidden."

Alyea said nothing. She picked up a white ayn and turned it over in her hands, rubbing a thumb against the smooth whitestone cylinder, looking at the kaen-marks on one end; when that side was showing, it could move forward or backwards, instead of only one direction. It only went kaen-side up when it had crossed into the opposing player's territory: with her new understanding of the philosophy behind the game, she saw a reflection of that rule in her own life.

Her visit to the southlands had changed everything.

Looking up, she found Oruen watching her with a thoughtful expression.

"You've come back, not just with a title, but with a much sharper mind," he said. "I expected the first. Not the second."

She frowned, then conceded him points for honesty, and said, "You didn't expect anything like what I went through once I cleared Bright Bay borders, I think. I hope not."

He watched her without speaking, his gaze suddenly hooded.

"How much *did* you know about what Chac had planned?" she asked. "Did you know about the heir to Scratha, and his teyanain alliance?"

He blinked like an owl and stayed silent, not admitting anything aloud; which said everything.

"You almost got me *killed*," she said, setting the piece down on the stone board with a hard click.

"But instead you're a desert lord," he pointed out. "And you're more powerful than you ever dreamed of being."

She stood and turned her back on him, staring out through the arches to the small garden of rosemary and blue sage beyond. The rising sun caught glimmers of dew into tiny rainbows, and she felt overwhelmed by how much water surrounded her, how much northerns took for granted every day of their lives.

"Do you expect me to thank you?" she said, watching a fat black bee bumble its way across the flowers. Her lack of anger surprised her a little; she felt only a dreadful, resigned weariness. Whatever she'd expected, this was the reality, and always had been: maneuvering for the best result. It was all a game, with people as pieces.

"No," he said. "Do you expect *me* to thank you for your invaluable service?"

She snorted and turned, crossing her arms over her chest. "No."

His mouth pulled sideways in a dry almost-smile.

"I'm glad you're home safely," he said, and stood. "I'm sorry for using you."

He moved forward to stand in front of her, and put his hands on her shoulders. She stood very still, her mouth dry. When she'd left Bright Bay, the look now in his eyes would have meant everything to her; but all she could think of at the moment was Lord Filin edging steadily closer.

It's not true interest, she told herself. *Just another attempt to use me. One more chabi move.*

"No," she said, and backed up a step, pushing his hands away. "Excuse me, Lord Oruen."

"Alyea—"

"Excuse me." She turned and walked away, not hurrying; and couldn't decide if she felt relieved or annoyed that he made no move to stop her.

Chapter Forty-three

Once Alyea had left the room, Deiq dropped the pretense and sat back, shooting a hard stare at Eredion. "'Focused really tightly'?" he said scathingly. "Was that the *best* phrasing you could come up with?"

"On that short a notice, yes," Eredion said, reaching for a piece of bread. "What do you think I am, a bard? And do ha'ra'hain follow the human recovery model that the crankier you get, the better you're feeling?"

Deiq snorted, unamused, and worked a bit of orange peel out of his back teeth. He took a sip of water, swirling it to rinse the bitter taste from his mouth; but swallowing just spread the bitterness down his throat. He coughed and drank more until the taste was gone.

"You could have at least gotten her out of here before I had to eat two oranges whole," he noted, then caught Eredion's brief grin. "Ta-karne."

"You're the one came up with that," Eredion returned. "I was just enjoying the sight too much to stop you. What was so important about getting her out of here, anyway?"

"I want to talk to you." It had taken him three days to work up the courage to say that much; he felt resolve slipping away as he spoke.

Eredion finished the bread in his hand and grabbed another piece. "Go ahead," he said around a mouthful.

Deiq found he couldn't say it; not just yet. Instead he said, "I don't want Filin near her again." He'd seen that encounter, fresh in her mind: had reached, without apology, into Eredion's to confirm he'd been the one to warn Filin off. It raised his trust in the Sessin lord another notch, and left him desperately aware of how little Alyea still understood.

"I know. He's been kept busy elsewhere," Eredion said without surprise. "That's trivial. What's the real problem?"

Deiq sat quiet, at a loss for how to begin now that the opening he'd wanted was here. Birdsong warbled outside, and he could feel the air heating with the risen sun. The streets would soon be damp and steaming. Walking outside would leave everyone drenched in sweat—except for him, which would make him stand out to any close examination.

It would be the sort of day when he hated to go outside; not because of the weather, but because everyone else would be miserable, cranky, and unpleasant, which always set off his own temper.

But he had to go outside, because of Idisio, and because of his own stupidity. Which brought him back around to the question at hand: whether Eredion now saw him as an idiot or a monster.

He was afraid to find out; he had to know. At last he said, "Meer," and left it at that.

Eredion chewed his way through two more large bites of the bread before answering. "Done is done," he said then. "Look forward."

"That's cant."

Eredion shrugged, swallowed his mouthful, and looked directly at Deiq. "What do you want me to say, Deiq? That you're a monster, that you ought to die for your crimes? You're not human. I can't judge you by human standards. I'm not a teyanain, ha'rethe, or ha'ra'ha. I don't have the right under any law or agreement to hold you to account for anything you do. And I'm hardly pure myself. I've been responsible for my share of unfair deaths, these past few years."

"Which is my fault," Deiq said, barely audible.

Eredion stared. "How the hells do you figure that?"

"If I hadn't . . . fought with Lord Sessin, you'd still be sitting safe in Sessin Fortress."

"Safe and bored," Eredion said, licking his fingers and reaching for a napkin. "You're not a god, Deiq. You don't control *everything* that happens around you. I was banging heads with the old bastard before you ever grabbed me in the garden that day. I would have gotten on his last nerve sooner or later. And I've done some good here, at least, while my cousins and uncles cowered in safety. No. I'm just as content things worked out this way; at least I can be proud of *trying*. As can you."

He stood, dropping the napkin on the table.

"I do expect you'll need more sleep now," he said, looking down at Deiq. "And I know what else you need." His jaw set, his eyes narrowing just a fraction; enough to show his true feelings in the matter.

Which meant the true answer was *monster*.

Deiq shut his eyes. He felt lightheaded with self-loathing. "No," he said, a bare breath of protest, then, louder: "No. Thank you. But it's not that bad."

"It's my duty, ha'inn—"

"*Fuck* duty." Deiq pushed himself up from the table, steadied himself with his hands on the top. "Get out. I'm going back to sleep."

Eredion rolled his eyes and bowed in exaggerated deference. "As you say, ha'inn."

"Out!"

As Eredion left, the aches Deiq had been holding at bay came spiraling hungrily back; he moaned and staggered to the bedroom to collapse again.

Deiq had expected the day to be hot and muggy; but in the aftermath of the storm, a cold wind had moved in, dropping the temperature to an unseasonable chill. Alyea shivered and drew her cloak closer round her; the motion reminded Deiq that he *still* hadn't taken the time to teach her how to regulate her body temperature. Hells of a teacher he was turning out to be.

The sun, oddly pale and small, stood well past noon already, and they hadn't gone far from the western edge of the Seventeen Gates. Alyea's impatience worried against the back of his neck: the phrase *hobbling like an old man* drifted across her thoughts, and Eredion covered a laugh with a cough.

"I'm fine," Deiq said sharply, glaring at Alyea from the low stone wall on which he'd sat down to rest a few moments ago. "Your worrying is *really* aggravating me!"

"Your limping around like an ancient isn't doing much for my temper," she retorted.

Eredion laughed. "The way you squabble, you may as well get married."

They both glared at him, which only made his grin wider.

"He's not in the city any longer," Deiq said. "I'd feel—" A light wind swirled by, laden with the scent of rot and death; he lifted his head like an asp-jacau to a scent, inhaled sharply and blinked hard. "How close are we to Datha Road?"

"Two streets over," Eredion said after glancing around. He sniffed the air himself, his eyes narrowing, then looked at Deiq. "That's not Idisio."

Alyea sniffed, then shook her head a little, looking bewildered and sullen, as though suspecting them of playing some obscure joke.

"No." Deiq hauled himself to his feet. "It's worse." He paused, looking at Alyea. "You should go back to the palace," he said. "This is going to be unpleasant."

"No," Alyea said at the same time as Eredion.

Eredion looked at Deiq steadily, and said without words, *You're more dangerous than she is, ha'inn. If that's what it smells like, it's not safe for you to investigate this.*

I'll be fine, Deiq retorted. *I don't want her seeing this!*

Why are you babying her? The words were laden with deep frustration. *You're not doing her any favors, handling her training this way!*

"Damn it, stop that!" Alyea snapped, sparing Deiq the necessity of a reply. "Say it out loud or shut up!" So she'd figured out that much on her own; good.

Eredion's smile didn't reach his eyes. "I was telling Deiq that if anything, he should go back to the palace and let us handle this."

"Handle *what?*"

Deiq shook his head to both the question and Eredion's sardonic glare, and lumbered into motion.

"Come on, then," he said over his shoulder. As they stepped onto Greener Street, he paused and concentrated: the smell was stronger and more specific now, laden with vague images that the tath-shinn had left in her wake. "There's something . . . a cottage. Is there one nearby?"

You already know the answer to that, Eredion observed.

Shut up. Let me handle this. Alyea needed to feel as though she were doing something more than trailing at his tail.

Alyea glanced around, frowning. The buildings around them, while short and stubby, didn't qualify as cottages. After a moment, her face cleared. "The grave-keeper's. Yes. This way."

He followed Alyea's lead, moving more quickly now, apprehension pushing aside the aches. As they walked down the deserted Datha Road towards the grave-keeper's gate, clouds began to gather in the sky.

The grave-keeper's gate was more a symbolic than an actual barrier. The stubby stone pillars that made up the outer ring of the graveyard were spaced more widely here, enough for two carts to drive through. A well-oiled black metal chain hung across the gate opening, low enough to step over.

Within the oval expanse of the graveyard grounds stood three massive burning biers, three smaller ones, a small crypt containing the remains of King Ayrq, and, at the south-western end of the oval, the grave-keeper's cottage.

Deiq halted, regarding the small cottage ahead of them with a dark frown. "The grave-keeper. Does he have a family?"

You're stalling, Eredion observed.

Deiq didn't answer.

"Actually," Alyea said, oblivious, "I think it's a woman. She's been living here for as long as I can remember. Makes sure that the pyres stay lit until everything's gone, and. . . ."

Deiq turned and gave her a searing glare, abruptly unwilling to tolerate nonsensical chatter; she faltered into silence.

"I know what a grave-keeper does," he said. Stepping over the chain, he strode towards the small cottage, Eredion on his heels and Alyea right behind. "I know what they do in Bright Bay," he went on over his shoulder as he pushed through the low picket fence into the tidy front garden area. "I know what they do in the Horn." He paused in front of the cheery green door. "I know what they do in Water's End, and what funeral rites every desert Family uses."

Now who's "chattering"? Eredion commented, just as Alyea's aggrieved thought chimed in: *Now he's the one chattering!*

Ignoring them both, Deiq stared at the door, reluctant to move forward. The stench was thick, and definite: a bloody death, several days old already. Eredion had already begun to breathe more shallowly; Alyea seemed too overcome by sheer anxiety to be the least bit attentive. She reached around him and banged on the door with a flat palm. He gave her a severe glare.

"There's no need for that."

"What, you think we're too important to knock?"

It was a stupid comment, born of nerves, and he gave her the look it deserved.

"No," he said, and reached for the handle. "There's no need because she's dead."

Inside seemed as cozy and friendly as outside, but the air was thick with the buzz of flies and the viscous smell of death. Deiq leaned against the doorframe, gripping the handle hard, unable to continue: knowing what he would see, not wanting to face the reality of it. Not wanting his hopes of rescuing the tath-shinn from her madness to be utterly destroyed.

He could feel her presence, even days old, like an oily slick coating the inside of his nose; could feel the hunger she'd been forced into, over and over, until she barely knew who she was any longer. Felt his own nature respond to that desperation, and two desert lords within arm's-reach—*No. Damn it, no.*

His eyes shut, his breath grew ragged, and his knees began to buckle; Eredion moved to steady him, and Alyea, naturally, took that moment to slip by and head inside.

"Alyea, *no*," Eredion said sharply, too late; she pushed aside the flower-print curtain that separated the small bedroom area from the main room. A moment later she recoiled, hand to mouth, as the sight and smell of a truly ugly death hit her.

Get her out of there! Deiq ordered, with a hard push of command.

Eredion leapt forward, abandoning Deiq, and roughly pulled Alyea out of the cottage just before she vomited. Then, recovering from the compulsion, Eredion went grey with strain.

"*Godsdamnit,*" he muttered, glaring at Deiq. *Don't damn well do that to me!*

Deiq shook his head, unapologetic, and forced himself upright against the doorframe. The images in Alyea's mind confirmed his fears: blood everywhere, feces smeared halfway up the walls, and scattered bone fragments that displayed distinctive gnaw-marks.

She's lost. I can't reach her, if she's gone that far into the madness. I can only kill her. He couldn't tell if he'd sent that thought to Eredion or held it to himself.

Eredion said nothing; didn't even flicker a glance Deiq's way, which meant centuries of restraint had—probably—managed to keep the thought private after all. Then again, Eredion was good at keeping his own reactions hidden.

Unable to conceal his own revulsion, Deiq made himself stagger to the nearest stone bench, muttering imprecations in a long-dead language.

"What kind of creature—" On her knees, Alyea wiped her mouth with Eredion's handkerchief, then wadded it up and held it against her mouth for a few moments. "*Does* something like that?"

Deiq's nerves, keyed high enough to pick up the wingbeats of a passing bird, easily picked up on the pre-echo of Eredion's words: *The kind sitting right next to you.*

Deiq turned a fierce glare on Eredion and laid a binding across his tongue before the words had a chance to emerge. Eredion's mouth snapped shut and tightened just as Alyea looked up.

Eredion looked away and said, "Go back to the palace. I'll clean up here. It won't be the first time I've—"

Again, pre-echo alerted Deiq to the coming words: *cleaned up a ha'ra'ha's mess.* Just as promptly as before, he slammed the man's vocal cords still.

Eredion almost choked this time, caught between breath and swallow; Deiq released him in time to turn the gag into a hard cough.

"Damn it." Eredion blinked hard, his eyes damp, and refused to look at either of them. "Get out of here. Both of you. Go!"

Deiq lurched to his feet, drew a deep breath, and steadied. He looked down at Eredion and said, *Do you want me to stay and help?* It was the closest to an apology he would allow himself at the moment.

No. I handled worse, in the tunnels under the city. Eredion's tone was curt and unforgiving. *But you need to get away from here, so* go *already, and give her the godsdamned answers she needs!*

Eredion was right this time: Deiq tugged Alyea to her feet. Still grey around the edges, she offered no resistance as he steered her away from the cottage.

Alyea did deserve an answer to her question; deserved to know what had caused the splattered horror inside the grave-keeper's cottage. But not yet. Not while she was still shaking from the sight.

Not while *he* was still shaking.

He made it as far as the palace steps before his energy began to flag again; caught himself against a wall as his knees went weak, warding off Alyea's instinctive move of support with his other hand.

"No," he said roughly. "Don't. Not right now."

The hunger, raked high by injury and what he'd just seen, was compounded by years of deliberate deprivation, aggravated by knowing this was a new desert lord standing within reach, even though the change hadn't entirely hit yet. He shut his eyes and drew a deep breath through his nose, then shoved himself to his feet again and almost threw himself into motion.

Never again. Never.

The agony they went through wasn't worth it. Until and unless he found a way for it not to hurt so godsdamned much. . . .

"Deiq—"

"Shut up." He kept his attention on moving forward. Anything in his path he simply shoved aside. He heard a few startled, angry cries; then he sensed Alyea moving in front of him to clear the path.

He followed her gratefully, his vision almost gone under the haze; fighting back hunger with thoughts of Meer and what had once been a female grave-keeper. Whispers invaded his resolve: *Foolishness. Why do you fight what you are? Why? Why?* The whining complaint dissolved into a hoarse chorus of crow-caws; he blinked hard and kept moving.

Because I won't do that, won't be like that, he tried to say; realized he was talking to ghost-memories, not live voices, and stopped.

At last the door to his suite loomed up, and Alyea opened it. He staggered inside with a low moan.

"Get out," he ordered. "Out!"

"You're welcome," she said blackly, and slammed the door behind her.

Barely aware of moving, he found the bed coming up under him seconds later; collapsed onto it, burying his face into the blankets, gripping great handfuls of pillow: and shook for a very long time.

On The Matter of Ha'reye and Ha'ra'hain

(excerpt)

I mentioned, in an earlier letter, the extreme life span of desert lords and their offspring as compared to the general population. This is as nothing when compared to the ha'ra'hain, the mixed-blood descendants of ha'reye and humans. The progression of generations has likely never been explained to you, Lord Oruen, as the Loremaster Council has declared it information to be withheld from northern rulers. Again, I strongly suggest hiding this letter in the most secure possible place, if not burning it altogether once you finish reading.

The ha'reye have not been seen in hundreds if not thousands of years; if, indeed, they were ever actually, physically beheld by human eyes. There is doubt on that score.

Their first round of offspring, called First Born, were extremely unstable and had to be almost entirely destroyed. I believe, after extensive research, that the ha'ra'ha under Bright Bay, which tormented your city for so many years, was one such; the difference between the generations has much less to do with genetics than upbringing, from what I have been able to discover. The First Born were given far too much power, then left without the necessary assistance to reconcile their two disparate heritages. There is only one exception to this that I personally know of, and so there is only one surviving First Born in today's world; for which we should all, perhaps, be infinitely grateful.

After the First Born, ha'ra'hain were given less power and provided a more structured upbringing, and while they also displayed a tendency for cruelty and instability, they were much more reasonably disposed than the First Born. Ha'ra'hain born of human/ha'reye crosses after the First Born have come to be called "first generation". The children of first generation ha'ra'hain and humans—usually desert lords—came to be known as second generation, and like their predecessors prefer to live in damp underground environments or in deep water, and occasionally among their ha'reye and ha'ra'hain kin. It is extremely uncommon for any of the ha'reye-kin to live above ground for any amount of time, or to involve themselves in human affairs to any degree whatsoever; which, perhaps, explains how in a relatively short time all knowledge of them has shifted into the realm of myth and fable among northerners.

From the collection
Letters to a Northern King of Merit
penned by Lord Cafad Scratha during the reign of King Oruen

Chapter Forty-four

Deiq woke from uneasy dreams of regret to the sound of someone hammering on the outer door of the suite. He rolled from the bed and trotted, half-mazed, to answer. Eredion would have simply entered, and servants wouldn't knock with such urgency. The visitor had to be Alyea: and it was, taut-faced and shivering with something between panic and shock, a grubby note in one hand.

He stepped clear of the door, unwilling to touch her until he'd woken completely, and pointed her to one of the severely plain chairs around the small tea table. As she obeyed, he glanced into the hallway out of long-established reflex: a skinny servant in the grey and blue striped tunic of the chamberlain's staff was just ducking out of sight around a corner. Deiq repressed a sigh, not in the least surprised, and shut the door without comment.

At least the king hadn't tried setting his Hidden to watch the room itself. A ha'ra'ha's sleeping area was as close to sacred as the concept would translate for humans; and while Deiq had allowed a number of changes to how humans treated him over the years, *that* custom he insisted on keeping inviolable.

He rubbed his eyes clear and studied Alyea for a moment, focusing his attention to full alertness, then said, "What is it?"

She laid the note on the table and pushed at it a little, as though that would release the contents to his eyes.

"Idisio sent us a letter," she said.

He crossed the room at that, and sat down across from her, frowning at the stained piece of coarse paper. She prodded it again, then picked it up and offered it to him; he motioned her to put it back down again, a thin dread growing in his stomach. There was a smell to the paper, an aura of oily smoke at the edges: he didn't want to touch it.

"What does it say?"

She flipped it open and read words that had no relation to anything Idisio would have used, phrases the younger ha'ra'ha hadn't crafted on his own:

I have met my mother and left you. Her name is Ellemoa. I am going home and I do not want to be bothered. I want you to leave me alone, and leave my mother alone. I do not want you any more. I do not want your company, and we will hurt you if you follow us. Leave us alone. We are going home and you do not want to follow us. I do not belong to you any more. Go away and leave me alone.
-Idisio

Impatiently, she slapped the note down facing him, as though insisting that he look for himself. He studied the writing without moving, tracing with his eyes where the writing faltered, where it smudged; that told him as much as the words themselves.

Apparently the tath-shinn couldn't read or write. Deiq found that deeply peculiar.

He picked up the note with deep reluctance; even though he was prepared for it, the oily aura spread halfway up his hands in a heartbeat. He grimaced and dropped the note to the table, flicking his fingers hard to disperse the unpleasant energy. Alyea stared at him as though he'd gone mad; he ignored her, too busy fighting the rush of images to explain something he didn't have words for anyway.

Rot-filled darkness and ravening hunger . . . thin, cruel laughter; something soft and wet shredding under her teeth and fingers . . . and an unsteady female voice whispering to itself in the darkness: *My son. My son. My son. . . .*

Deiq dry-washed his hands, squeezing shut his own eyes and teeth, until the agonizing waves of hunger and madness faded; then drew a shaky breath, well aware how close that had been. The foul memories that overlaid the paper had very nearly tipped him into losing control himself. Gods, she was strong, and that had, without question, been a warning—or trap—left just for him. Apparently Ninnic's child had taught her more than how to play with the weather.

The bitter taste of real fear crossed the back of his tongue for a moment; long reflex prompted him to retreat behind an unemotional shield. No point in letting Alyea see him rattled.

"At least we know he's alive," he said. "And not in the city any longer. I'll tell Eredion to call off the search."

"I don't believe Idisio would write any such thing," Alyea said. She began to reach for the note again. Deiq flicked a finger against her wrist as though popping an intrusive asp-jacau nose. She jerked her hand back with an injured expression; he managed a small smile at that.

"Oh, he *wrote* it," Deiq said, and leaned back in his chair, pushing hair out of his face. Sometime in his sleep, he'd pulled out the ties and the braids, as usual; a habit he'd been fighting since his first steps in the human world.

Alyea's expression changed as she looked at him, and he realized she'd rarely seen his hair down. Mildly curious, he took advantage of the moment's distraction to slide his perception behind hers, just to see what she saw: loose, braid-waved dark hair softened the planes of his face and eased the impact of his stare; sleep-creased clothes did nothing to bring back his dignity. He looked entirely human: a little tired, a little cranky; vulnerable. *Approachable*.

He withdrew before she could sense the intrusion. Bemused, he sat quietly for a moment, thinking it through; then looked up at her. She held his gaze for a bare heartbeat, then dropped her stare to the letter between them, her hands fisting in her lap and tension winding through her shoulders again. He let the moment pass, resolving to try *vulnerable* next time he really needed to get her attention. Idisio would have had no trouble with her at all.

He looked back at the letter on the table, his amusement fading, and said, "I don't think he knew what he was writing. Look at how the note was addressed."

It had dropped face-down, revealing an unsteady scrawl across the backside: *To those lords as who travlered with Idisio.* He frowned at that, thinking it over; from the pattern, she'd written it herself, probably drawing the basic information on how from Idisio's mind. That told him she learned fast, adapted quickly; Idisio was in real trouble. He wasn't nearly experienced enough to handle this situation.

Deciding against saying any of that aloud, Deiq settled for observing, "He'd have used our names if he were in full control of his wits. But the tath-shinn was controlling him."

She regarded him skeptically. "How can you tell that?"

He sat back and looked up at her. Not answering the question directly, he said, "The tath-shinn is stronger than I expected, and much more dangerous."

"So it—*she*, if the letter is from the tath-shinn—"

"It is."

"So she's stronger than you are?"

He looked away, surprised to feel embarrassment spreading warmth across his face. "At the moment—yes."

The silence hung for a few breaths; at last, Alyea said, a little hoarsely, "Deiq, I think it's about time you told me what I ought to be expecting of you."

Not at all sure how she'd gone from one point to another, he frowned at her.

"I'm not a complete idiot," she went on when he said nothing. "This tath-shinn is a ha'ra'ha. The mad child under Bright Bay was a ha'ra'ha. You're—"

Ah. That was the connection.

"Yes," he interrupted, bemusement melting into annoyance. "I'm a ha'ra'ha. Obvious parallel. Good job seeing that."

He rose and paced the small sitting room to shake off his irritation, reminding himself that her ignorance was his own damn fault; he was supposed to be teaching her these things. She watched him without speaking. His legs began to wobble under him; he sank into the chair again, silently cursing himself for a fool. He ought to send her away, and that damned trap-letter with her, and get himself in hand before talking to her again.

"I don't think you're a monster," she said, the quiet words shattering his half-formed intent to order her from the room.

"Thanks for that much," he said bleakly. *Not that you know the half of it*, he added to himself.

She ignored his comment and went on, "But I do think you're not telling me the truth about yourself. About a lot of things. And I think it's time you did."

No sending her away after that challenge, even though she clearly didn't understand that was what she had issued. Deiq shook his head slowly and held up a hand, breathing evenly, his eyes half-shut, until he felt aggravation fade to simpler irritation.

"I haven't been *able* to tell you much," he said at last. "Alyea, most desert lords study years just to get to the trials. And then for years more to get what you've already learned. You're getting a lot of sensitive information without any supporting background context."

"That sounds like an excuse to me," she said.

He grinned without any humor. "True enough, from your perspective, I suppose." He shut his eyes, sighed, then sat forward carefully and looked at her straight on. "Ninnic hurt a lot of people," he said. "Are all humans like Ninnic?"

She hesitated, frowning, and stared at her hands. He let her be, watching thoughts flit across her expression like ghostly moths.

"I think," she said after a few moments, "I think we all have the potential to be."

He nodded and leaned back again. "Exactly. Same with ha'ra'hain, same with ha'reye. That's the easiest way I can put it."

"So what didn't you want Eredion to tell me, at the grave-keeper's cottage?"

He startled at that, and found himself confronted with an implacable black stare; he dropped his own gaze fast, before he could respond to her expression as a challenge. Damn it, she was not making this easy.

"What makes you think—"

"Deiq," she said sharply.

He sighed and rubbed the back of his neck with one hand, then gathered his hair back and began braiding it into one thick weave. The time for being vulnerable had definitely passed.

"It's not easy to explain, Alyea."

"Try."

He looped the completed braid over his left shoulder and sat back in his chair, lips thin.

"Ha'ra'hain are two races in one," he said. "You ever think about what that means? Human and ha'rethe. It's . . . something of an uneasy mixture at the best of times. The two races are very different. *Really* different."

He paused, considering words.

"It's like . . . like an asp-jacau cross-breeding with a sea turtle. The asp-jacau eats meat, the sea turtle eats kelp and small fish. They live in two different environments. They *think* differently. They *breed* differently." He made a helpless gesture with both hands. "They need different things. The asp-jacau would never understand why a sea-turtle likes kelp. The sea-turtle—"

"I get it," Alyea cut him off, impatient as a child. "The point?"

He grunted softly, annoyed; but the best explanation in the world did no good if she wasn't listening. He tried to condense the answer to something she'd hear clearly. "It's a delicate balance, keeping both sides straight," he said. "Sometimes . . . the balance tips. And you get . . . what you saw at the cottage."

"What exactly tipped the balance in this case?" she demanded. A murky anxiety passed across her expression for a moment, then cleared; Deiq suspected she'd been wondering if he'd ever lost control as badly as the tath-shinn.

He hoped she'd never ask that aloud, as he really didn't want to give her the answer.

He gave her the answer to what she *had* asked instead: "The tath-shinn was the prisoner of a seriously mad ha'ra'ha for years. She started to enjoy causing pain. I don't know that we'll ever manage to straighten her out. We may have to kill her, much as I hate the thought."

"After what she's done?" Alyea stared at him, appalled.

"She's *kin*," Deiq said, unable to stop the fierce pain from coming out in his voice. "It would be like you killing Kam; however much you might think he deserves it, he's still kin."

"Kam hasn't killed anyone by tearing them to bits! And I don't want to—"

What she didn't know about her cousin would fill a lake. "He hasn't torn anyone to bits," Deiq corrected, then held up a hand to forestall her indignant response. "Don't sidetrack right now. You wanted answers, so ask the damn questions while I'm still on my feet!"

He hadn't meant to say that. The wobble from his legs shivered up through his body, followed by a familiar flush of heat. He'd burned through the slight reserve he'd built up with sleep, and if he didn't get her out of here—

"You need to rest—"

He opened his mouth to say *Yes, I do, go away.* It emerged, instead, as: "Don't damn well tell me what I need to do!"

She stared at him, her mouth set in a thin line that reminded him of her mother's severe disapproval. Strangely, it helped: he was able to catch control of his emotional balance again.

"One more question," he said. "Then you get out."

Alyea hesitated, looking him over as though judging whether to retreat now. After a moment, she said, "Do you believe what he—what she wrote in the letter? That the tath-shinn is Idisio's mother?"

"It makes sense," he said. "Opens up lots of other questions. But yes. I believe it. I think that's why she can control him so easily. Blood bond. . . ."

The word *blood* proved to be a mistake: he saw, reflected from her memory like a mirror, the gruesome disaster of the gravekeeper's cottage. The loss of control. The destructive freedom that would come from not fighting what he was . . . He stopped talking, blocking the sight from his mind, and rested his head in his hands.

It's my own damn fault she has no notion what she's doing to me, he told himself, and drew a careful breath to steady his nerves. When he had control of his voice again, he finished the sentence he'd begun: "Being related makes it easier for her to control him. I'm done talking. Help me to bed."

Immediately he realized the mistake, but she was already rising.

"No," he said through his teeth, trying for command-voice and utterly missing; she wasn't listening to him any more than a horse who'd gotten a hold of the bit did. "Not you. Get Eredion." Another idiotic idea; but sleeping wouldn't be enough this time. He shut his eyes and swept other-vision across the area, searching for Eredion's distinctive rough-paper presence.

"I'm perfectly capable," she said, moving to his side.

"That's not—hells." He let her help him to his feet and leaned on her hard for the few steps to his bed. *Eredion,* he said, finally snagging against the desert lord's sturdiness. *Eredion. Please—I need you.*

Silence.

Please, Deiq begged. He didn't care any longer if the desert lord responded from simple duty. Alyea wasn't ready for this; her pulse was steady and her thoughts only on getting him medicine for what she saw as a developing fever.

The mattress came up under his hips; he sat still, blinking and dazed, listening to the silence with a growing sense of dread. Her arm brushed his shoulder as she reached past to arrange the pillows for him, and he saw himself through her eyes: ill. Exhausted. *Vulnerable.*

Oh, gods, Alyea, you have no damn idea . . . Her defenses had dropped on seeing him apparently weaken, and he could see the path to what he wanted, like a broad river shining in front of him. His hand closed around her wrist; she stopped pushing pillows around, frowning a little.

"You're throwing a fever," she said, freeing her hand from his grip and touching his forehead.

His hands latched onto her hips; he held her still and leaned his forehead against her stomach like a child seeking comfort. Her pulse beat against his fingers: he followed it, stroking, with an ethereally light touch, the flowing movement within her veins.

Alyea flinched, pulling back, and he felt a heavy cramp sear across her stomach as though it were his own; echoes from the agony of her blood trials.

She wasn't ready, damn it. And he didn't *care.* He flattened one hand against her stomach, drunk with conflicting needs.

"You need some medicine for that fever," she said, touching his hair even as she pulled away another half-step. The hand resting on her hip tightened despite himself, stopping her retreat.

"What he needs," Eredion said from behind them, harshly, "is for you to get out of here."

Alyea jerked round, startled; Deiq forced his fingers to loosen.

"Go," he croaked. "Alyea, *go.*"

"I'll take care of him," Eredion said, and held up a small vial. "I've got medicine for him to take, and Oruen wants to see you. He's in his casual room. Go on."

She hesitated; but Eredion's expression was uncompromising, and Deiq waved her off when she looked back at him.

"*Go,*" Deiq repeated, unable to offer better reassurance than another fierce hand-motion towards the door.

"Don't keep the king waiting," Eredion said. "His pride's a bit tender yet for that."

She lifted one shoulder in a faint shrug, cast one last misgiving stare at Deiq, and turned away without more protest.

Eredion shut the door behind her, threw the latch, and turned to frown at Deiq, assessing.

"You're a damn fool," he said after a moment, and went around the suite locking hidden doors: two of which Deiq had known about and one of which came as a surprise.

Deiq sat still, eyes half-shut, and waited, gathering his scattered senses more easily now: he was back on safe, familiar ground with Eredion. The desert lord finished securing the entries, then stopped arm's reach away, studying Deiq closely.

"How long has it been?" he asked. Deiq shut his eyes and shook his head dumbly. "Too long, obviously. Damn fool. I should have known when the tath-shinn laid you out like a baby."

Deiq blinked, frowning at the insult, and found his eyes crossing; he couldn't focus on outrage long enough to do anything about it.

"Why the hells have you been starving yourself?" Eredion demanded. "And with a new desert lord right to hand, you called *me*?"

"She's not ready," Deiq whispered, shutting his eyes again; ignoring the question he didn't want to answer. "I don't want to hurt her. I promised."

"And you don't mind hurting me?"

He made himself open his eyes all the way, and inhaled deeply; cinnamon and ashes, ink and leather and dust. Eredion had been going through old books recently. He looked up into the desert lord's frown and said, reasonably clear, "I'll try not to."

Eredion's frown melted into resignation. "Don't bother," he said, and broke the wax seal on the small bottle in his hand. "I've been through it enough to be used to it by now." But his hand shook, just a little, as he tossed back the spoonful of dark liquid.

Deiq stood up, moving with intense care; felt his eyes shifting out of human-normal as he put a hand on Eredion's broad shoulder. "No," he said, feeling Eredion's muscles bunch reflexively. Mirrored memory gave him back a sobbing youngster, crouched in a stream of moonlight: "No," he said again. "Not like that. Not this time."

"Does it *matter*?" Eredion snapped, shivering a little.

Deiq didn't bother answering. He could feel the dasta syrup streaking through Eredion's body, soothing the man's nerves and lowering defenses; and knowing that he had what he needed made it easy for Deiq to take his time, the way a human might pause to savor each bite of a long-delayed meal.

"Pass the salt, he's a little bland," Eredion muttered, voice already thickening.

Deiq blinked, a little surprised that his thoughts had carried so easily; then grinned, belatedly catching the humor. "I doubt that," he murmured, sliding his hand down Eredion's arm: tracing the veins with his fingertips. Eredion sucked in a breath, eyes hazing, and shivered.

"Don't bother," the desert lord said hoarsely. "I've been through . . . don't."

Deiq left his fingertips on the inside of Eredion's wrist, feeling the pulse thudding past, the energy swirling in thready colors through the man's body: collecting, dissolving, pooling, dissipating. Choking and stuttering over the invisible scars Ninnic's child had left; pooling and overflowing riotously where the tath-shinn had, more recently, left as yet unhealed marks.

"Ah, damn," Deiq whispered, his eyes dry: only human-normal vision allowed him to cry. "I wish I had some healing skill, Eredion. . . ."

"It's not so bad," Eredion said; a lie he clearly didn't expect to pass, and

Deiq didn't bother challenging aloud.

The dasta syrup hadn't even been necessary. A second-generation would barely have any trouble pushing past what was left of Eredion's defenses.

Deiq slid his hand back up Eredion's arm, deciding, in spite of the strain it would put on his own dangerously low strength, to take this even more gently than he'd intended. Eredion deserved that much consideration, after what he'd been through.

In the back of his mind, he saw Meer's face, just for a moment; felt the echo of a ravenous hunger, pushed past enduring.

Gently, he told himself, his breath catching hard. *Gently. For Meer's sake, if nothing else.*

The desert lord's knees began to buckle; Deiq hastily guided him to sprawl on the bed, then sat on the edge, watching Eredion's eyes haze and clear repeatedly. He'd taken a damn strong concentrate, from the looks of it: measure enough not only of his tolerance but his terror.

"Get . . . over . . . with," Eredion muttered, his eyes sliding shut.

Deiq shook his head without answering and sifted delicately through Eredion's exposed memories until he found what he was looking for; tugged it, feather-light, into the desert lord's perception of *now*.

Eredion jerked, his back arching and his breath dissolving into a ragged series of gasps. "Oh *gods*," he moaned, vision fixed on something from years ago, his body responding to memory as though it were happening in the moment.

Deiq expanded the memory/reaction with infinite care, like stretching fresh taffy just shy of the breaking point; catching flashes of *sweat* and *heat* and *slick* and *pressure* that made his own breath catch in his throat and his own promise of chastity seem like an asinine vow.

You never really tried, Idisio had said. *You could have done it. You never really cared enough to try.*

Well, so: he was damn well trying now. He felt sweat break out on his forehead as he struggled to keep Eredion balanced without losing himself in the memory of the man's first passion; found the grey border where pleasure turned to pain, and wove a path through that, a circuitous route that took ten times the effort a straight pull would have.

Eredion's gasps grew more strained; his body jerked, head thrown back. *Wait*, Deiq said, easing the command into the memory of the long-ago girl's own moans. *Not yet . . . not yet.*

The tendril-thin draw finally reached the right spot inside Eredion's *self*: Deiq had never found a better word for it. A furnace-heat flushed through Deiq's own body at the contact. Control slid, gone on the instant, and he pulled hard, barely remembering to kick loose the stop he'd put on the memory-moment at the same time.

Eredion screamed as boundaries blurred, mixing agony and ecstasy as one; then collapsed, panting. Deiq rolled onto his side, gathering Eredion in to rest, broad back to slightly narrower chest, against him; they lay still, breathing hard, until their stuttering heartbeats steadied to a more normal rhythm.

"You," Eredion said at last, voice still rough and shaky, "you are a complete fucking bastard, you know that?"

"Hhh." He didn't have enough breath yet to answer that; didn't entirely understand it, or care, just at the moment.

The desert lord drew a ragged breath, another, coughed; "Bastard," he said again, and elbowed free. Deiq made no attempt to stop him. He watched, heavy-lidded, as Eredion left the room without looking back; then dropped all interest in outside matters and let himself fall into a deep, untroubled sleep.

Chapter Forty-five

Hands shaking, Eredion drew the outer door of the suite shut behind him and stood in the hallway for a moment: he'd seen much more, during that far-too-intimate moment, than he'd wanted to. He fought to even out his breath, making himself think about the indignity of what Deiq had done, instead of the centuries of black pain he'd just brushed up against.

Before he entirely succeeded, one of Filin's trainees trotted around the corner, step slowing as he caught sight of Eredion.

"Lord Eredion!" He grinned, boyishly enthusiastic; sobered at the glare Eredion aimed his way. "Uhm, Lord Filin's looking for you."

Lord Filin, Eredion thought uncharitably, damn well could have come wandering round himself to track down a conversation, or spoken from across the palace to find Eredion. Sending the trainee was an unsubtle snub.

Just at the moment, Eredion was not in the mood for Darden-style power games; but he knew how to play them well enough, and mood never had anything to do with necessity.

"Stay here," he told the trainee, pointing to the door he'd just shut behind him. "Stand outside this door, and don't let anyone in. Deiq is sleeping, do you understand? He's not to be disturbed."

"Not even Alyea of Peysimun?" the trainee said, brash enough even to lower one eyelid in a half-wink.

"*Especially* not Alyea," Eredion said, drenching his tone with enough ice to stiffen the boy's spine and wipe the smirk off his barely-stubbled face. "Do you think you can *handle* this, or should I find an *ordinary* servant who will listen to orders?"

The boy jerked his head in a stiff nod, all amusement gone from his face, and set his back against the wall by the door.

"Good," Eredion said. "You stay here until *I* tell you to go. And you don't send anyone to come bothering after *me*, either."

That raised a protest: "But Lord Filin said—"

Eredion moved close enough to almost press his nose against the trainee's. "Boy," he said, "maybe nobody's bothered to explain how things work to you. But in this instance, in this place, I *outrank* Lord Filin. So you *sit* and you *stay* until I tell you otherwise!"

"Yes, Lord Eredion," the boy stuttered.

"Lord *Sessin*," Eredion snapped. The trainee gulped and nodded frantically.

"Lord Sessin," he said, "Lord Sessin. Right. I'll stay here. Right here. Lord Sessin."

Eredion grinned and stalked away. Let Filin deal with *that*. The boy would piss himself before moving for a bathroom break now. It was a petty business, bullying a trainee; but tremendously satisfying as an outlet for strained nerves.

And focusing on belligerence kept him from thinking about what Deiq had done. *Gods*, of all the memories to corrupt—Eredion shook his head and increased his pace, wanting to reach the distraction of Lord Filin more quickly.

Lord Filin hadn't been entirely crass: he was waiting outside Eredion's suite with studied indifference, arms folded, one foot kicked back and both shoulders leaning against the wall.

"Lord Eredion," he said, not moving as Eredion approached. "I was beginning to think Rendill had gotten lost. Even for an Eshan, he's a touch dim at times."

Eredion stopped just out of reach, pointedly not moving to open his door or to offer an invitation. "What do you want, Filin?"

Filin took his time answering, his dark stare traveling over Eredion from head to toe with sharp thoughtfulness. "I had hoped to assure myself of your impartiality," he said at last, "but I can see that's a lost cause already." His gaze dropped towards Eredion's knees, then came up again slowly, pausing at the fresh, awkwardly placed damp spot Eredion had no way of hiding. "Since you're obviously . . . *allied* with Deiq."

Eredion set his teeth together hard to stop his first, unwise answer from emerging. Damned if he'd tell Filin anything about Deiq's current vulnerability. "It's my duty," he said, instead, "to give what's asked, when asked, without question. Yours as well, by the way—not that *you've* been around much of late."

Filin's thin nostrils flared. "I've been hunting across the city after traces of the tath-shinn as *you* asked," he retorted. "Risking my own neck, thank you ever so much, and that of the trainees."

"Appreciated, and over with," Eredion said. "So I imagine you're here to say that you're leaving?"

Filin stared at him. "I'm here to say you're making a mess of everything," he said abruptly. "Deiq never should have been allowed back in the city, and you're making a damn bad mistake, allying yourself with him. And you're making a hash of the girl's training—Hells, she isn't even ready to be out in public yet! What the hells were you *thinking*?"

"Not my decision," Eredion said flatly. "Take that up with Deiq. He's the one in charge of her training."

"That's even worse," Filin said, pushing away from the wall to stand square, shoulders coming forward in a sour hunch. "He doesn't have the first damn idea what he's doing. All he sees is a new game. I'd thought you had more care for a new desert lord than to let him use her that way."

Eredion snorted. "You're just pissed because she didn't drop to her knees for you," he observed.

Filin's face darkened. "The way *you* did just now for Deiq? Must have been good—I think they heard you in Water's End!" A flutter of fingers by one temple indicated he wasn't talking about ordinary hearing.

Eredion felt his temper cresting; then, abruptly, the whole argument seemed absurd. Filin's stupid, ignorant posturing just didn't matter. He'd been brave enough to come to Bright Bay and help kill the mad ha'ra'ha at the end; but he hadn't been there for the worst of it, hadn't seen, except through others' memories, the depths into which Rosin had forced matters. He didn't really understand, any more than his fresh-faced trainees could.

"Alyea's training isn't my decision, nor my responsibility," Eredion said, knowing that trying to explain wouldn't do any good at all. "I have enough of both decisions and responsibilities on hand to last me years yet, Filin. You have your trainees, and they ought to be learning more south than north of the Horn; that's *your* business. Go take care of it."

Filin's black stare could have scorched sand. "You're on the wrong side," he said. "How can you not *see* that yet? After seeing what that creature *did*?"

"I'm not on any side," Eredion said. "I'm just doing the job given to me, Filin. Now go *away*. I have work to do."

Filin stared another moment, as though contemplating more argument; finally shrugged and turned away, striding down the hallway with sharp, rapid strides. *You're a damn fool,* he shot back just before rounding the corner out of sight.

Eredion sighed. "Don't need to tell me," he muttered. "But it's my. . . ." His voice caught in his throat. He couldn't finish the sentence aloud; he remembered Deiq's savage rebuttal: *Fuck duty!*

He'd seen what lay behind that rejection, during the shared vulnerability of the feeding: *jagged agony; blood spilling, pooling, streaking; muffled screams evoking a searing, centuries-old shame; a whining, incessant complaint: Why do you fight, why do you fight what you are, why do you fight yourself?*

Deiq had been trying to be gentle; no other ha'ra'ha, of any generation, would have made the effort. That alone made his occasional blind spots worth enduring. He really hadn't understood that humans saw the memory of their first time as sacred; that mixing a replay of that memory with a blast of agony would ruin it forever for Eredion. He'd been trying to be nice.

But Lord Filin wouldn't understand that, either. Not without seeing what Eredion had just seen.

Fuck duty . . . because this isn't about duty. Not now.

Eredion passed a shaking hand across his damp eyes and went into his suite; reached for the servant-summoner with only two desires in mind: a bath—and enough rotgut to drive Deiq's memories from his mind, at least for the night.

Chapter Forty-six

The palace only went quiet late at night; evening still echoed with the raucous laughter of courtiers and jesters, the shrill giggles of women whose companions had succeeded in getting them drunk enough to tumble later, the barking of restless asp-jacaus, the chatter of young men challenging each other to casual shows of strength and agility. Even taking the back hallways didn't erase the echoes, but at least Alyea didn't have to walk through most of it.

The guards let her into the king's casual room with a friendly nod. She returned the greeting absently, her mind still running over that strange moment when Eredion had chased her from the room.

"Lord Oruen," she said, then blinked, shocked back into awareness of her surroundings, as the door clicked shut behind her.

Oruen nodded and motioned her to a chair near his left hand. Alyea sank into the seat without protest, staring at the gaunt woman who knelt, sobbing quietly, before the king.

"I thought you'd like to be here," Oruen said over the dark-haired head that leaned almost in his lap, his gaze sober and his voice barely audible.

Alyea almost asked *For what?*; then the weeping woman lifted her head and the words died in her mouth. "Oh, gods," she said instead, leaning abruptly forward and holding out her arms. *"Wian!"*

Her former servant wiped a hand across her nose and sat back on her heels, refusing the embrace. Her once-lush dark hair hung dull and roughly cut short, revealing deep, recently-scabbed scratches and yellow-brown mottling across her face and throat. Her light, low-cut shirt did nothing to hide similar marks.

"Why'd you call *her* in?" Wian demanded, turning a furious glare on the king.

Alyea's jaw dropped at the hostile greeting, but Oruen didn't seem in the least surprised.

"Because she's the only person in this city," he said, "that would have ever championed you at the risk of her own life. I think she deserves some truth from you."

Wian ducked her head and wiped at her nose again, wincing as the motion pressed on a bruise.

"I didn't want her here," she muttered, and seemed about to start crying again.

Oruen regarded the girl with compassion but, it seemed to Alyea, little sympathy.

"Apparently, Lord Alyea," he said, "some of what this young woman told you about Pieas's attack on her was . . . not entirely accurate."

Alyea sighed. "I already know that. That got sorted out before I killed him."

Oruen shot her a hard stare but said nothing aloud.

Wian turned stark white under the bruises. "Oh, gods, you killed him? I really am dead," she whimpered. "They'll kill me now."

"Nobody's going to hold you to blame for that," Alyea said, puzzled. "I didn't kill him because of you, Wian. There were other things going on at the time."

"It doesn't matter," Wian said, shivering. She bit her knuckle, which already bore marks of similar recent gnawing, and rolled her eyes appealingly at the king.

"Pieas had some friends with tempers," Oruen told Alyea, his gaze remaining on Wian. "She's afraid of them, not us."

"He did say something about that," Alyea said slowly, trying to remember. "He said they were angry at him over . . . a disagreement."

She wasn't about to go into the matter of Pieas's promise to his sister; that tangled mess wasn't really relevant to anyone but Lord Scratha and Pieas's sister Nissa, at this point.

"He claimed," Alyea continued, "that the night he fled, they roughed Wian up and dumped her in his room to make him look bad, since he'd already been accused of attacking her once. That was part of why he ran, and took Wian with him. He claimed that he never hurt her along the way, but he had to tie her up because she was raving from some drug they'd given her."

Wian ducked her head and stared at the floor. "That's . . . true," she said, clearly abashed. "At least . . . I think it is. I don't remember much about that time. I only came clear . . . on the way back to Bright Bay. There was a man who . . . helped me understand things better."

"I don't understand why you're here, Wian," Alyea said, a little sharply. Oruen shot her a sardonic glance, as though understanding her thoughts perfectly.

Alyea found herself deeply annoyed by the girl's deceit. While she despised Lady Arnil's attitude, she'd actually been relieved at the thought of not having to face Wian again. Pieas's assertion of innocence in front of the gathered desert lords, and its acceptance as truth, placed Alyea, as Wian's previously staunch defendant, in an uncomfortable political position. She'd hoped to avoid a direct confrontation with the king over the way she'd involved him in the whole mess.

"I'm not going back to that life," Wian said, squeezing her eyes shut. "I won't. I can't. And so I thought . . . the king might. . . ." She opened her eyes and looked up at Oruen, then down at the floor.

"Wian came to me in open court," Oruen said mildly, "begging for sanctuary. I thought it best to take her aside before she said anything . . . unwise . . . in public hearing."

"Sanctuary from what?" Alyea demanded.

"When Pieas didn't come back, and no word came," Wian said, still staring at the floor, "and then you came back, as a powerful person, and in a rich merchant's company, they're saying. . . ." She snuck a glance at Alyea's face.

Oruen lifted an eyebrow, his mouth tugging to one side in a faint smile.

"True," Alyea said, ignoring Oruen's amusement, and motioned Wian to continue.

"They got angry. They told me they'd hold me to blame if anything happened to Pieas because of me. Because I should have done better at embarrassing him in the first place, instead of upsetting you into challenging him and winding up with him running away."

Alyea shook her head, bemused. "It wasn't your fault, Wian," she said helplessly.

"His friends apparently don't see it that way," Oruen noted. "And I doubt you would talk reason into men angry that they lost their prime source for illegal drugs and other black market items. Such as children for—and from—the southern katha villages. Those are the southeastern coastal child brothels, in case you're unfamiliar with the term, which I've been in negotiations to shut down since I took the throne."

His expression turned bleak.

"Wian has been able to supply an astonishing amount of information about Pieas's activities over the past few years. And a lot of it, I must say, sounds very much like *my* business, and I wonder why he wasn't brought back *here* for trial instead of being dispatched in the desert."

Alyea's stomach shrank into a small, swirly ball of queasiness.

I deserve death, Pieas had said, kneeling and staring up at her. *Several times over. And that's just for what I* remember *of the past few years . . .* She hadn't asked further after his crimes, so intent on getting through her final blood trial that the notion of bringing him back to face kingdom justice simply hadn't arisen in her mind.

And by that point it had been far too late for any such attempt; Sessin Family never would have stood for it; there were a dozen other reasons kingdom justice had never stood a chance. But she could have at least asked what else he'd done. . . .

"I didn't know," she muttered, biting her lower lip, and decided to redirect the conversation into less dangerous channels. "How in the hells do you know all this, Wian? I thought you'd never seen him before that day at the palace!"

"I was told to watch him," Wian said, listlessly wrapping the edge of her skirt around her fingers. "So I watched him. But I guess his friends noticed me, because they grabbed me one day and said I had to work for them now, or they'd kill me. And they set me to embarrass Pieas, so that he'd have to come back to them for help. It took me a long time to find an opportunity. It was my first try that you walked in on. I didn't expect you. I thought someone else was coming down the hall."

"Who told you to watch Pieas?" Alyea demanded.

Wian ducked her head further and mumbled something inaudible even to Alyea's sharp hearing. Oruen, his face grim, answered the question before Alyea could press the servant girl. With an air of extreme distaste, he said, "Rosin Weatherweaver."

Alyea stared at him, her breath suddenly short. "That *bastard*—?"

"Yes."

Alyea shut her eyes against the bloody memory of agony and a good man's death.

No tears . . .

She'd sworn, in the aftermath, that whoever betrayed them would suffer just as much. And had never considered Wian as a possibility before.

"Wian," she said, forcing her voice to a coldness she didn't feel, "are *you* the one who reported my aqeyva training sessions to the priests?"

Wian didn't look up or speak; a moment later, she stiffened and began to make a strange gagging sound.

Oruen said sharply, "Kindly don't kill her in my casual room, Lord Alyea."

The words jolted Alyea out of incandescent rage into a stark awareness of the larger situation—and the guards now standing just behind her. Wian slumped into a trembling huddle, sucking in noisy, rapid breaths; Oruen raised a hand and the guards retreated, much more slowly than they had advanced. She could feel their dark regard at her back, their readiness to attack if she turned on the king. It was time to get out of the room.

"Thank you, Lord Oruen," Alyea said through her teeth, and stood. "I'll leave you to your decision of what to do with . . . *her*. I think I need some air."

She stalked out, her hands fisted so tightly she thought the bones might crack from the strain.

Had any drunken fools, of either gender, crossed her path at the moment, Alyea would have slapped them into sobriety just to vent her temper. But the hallways were quieting now, the various parties moving into individual rooms and behind shut doors. All she saw was a lone, tired jester, who nodded at her and swigged from a hip flask, making no move to amuse her. She nodded back and passed him without speaking.

To her surprise, the door to Deiq's suite was not only locked, but guarded. One of the young trainees stood rather self-consciously before it.

"Sorry, Lord Alyea," he said awkwardly, bowing. "Lord Eredion's orders. He said not to let anyone in. Especially you." His relatively light skin darkened with quick embarrassment. "I shouldn't've said that part," he admitted. "He said to tell you Deiq needed rest and left alone for a while."

Alyea held her temper just barely in check and snapped, "Where's Eredion?"

"I don't—" He paused, assessed the glare in her eyes, and said, "His quarters are in the west wing. It's a blue door with gold leaf designs on it. But, Lord Alyea, you shouldn't bother him right now—"

Not listening to the remainder of his protest, she strode away. Deiq needed rest; that she wouldn't argue one bit. But she needed to let loose her temper, and Eredion would have been her next choice anyway. She had a feeling he wouldn't keel over quite as easily as an ordinary human would.

She hoped not, at any rate.

It took some time of hammering on the locked blue door before it opened. Eredion peered out, blinking sleepily. His hair was damp, as though he'd just come out of a bath. "Whayya want?"

She pushed past him into the room. "I need to talk to you," she said, then paused, taking in the sight of the thick clay jugs lined up on the floor. One had been tipped over, clearly indicating it was empty.

Eredion sighed and shut the door, absently locking it again. "I'm always the one they run to," he muttered. "Have a seat, Lord Alyea."

She hesitated, frowning at the liquor jugs, then glanced around the rest of the room. Eredion's outer suite was plain and masculine, with one large, well-worn overstuffed chair in the center of the room and four plainer chairs tucked up against the walls by way of seating. Not a couch in sight, but the windows were open, allowing an evening breeze to wander over the richly detailed rugs and the dark wood of the sideboard. The room smelled of sweat, dust, dirty laundry, and cheap liquor.

Alyea looked back at the jugs, then at Eredion, trying to gauge how much he'd already had to drink, and whether talking to him would do her any good at all.

"I'm not drunk yet," Eredion said, flopping down in the overstuffed chair. "I had a damn good start on it, though."

"I take it this isn't a good time," she said dryly. "Maybe I ought to come back."

"No," he said. "May as well stay and tell me what's blazing your temper. I felt you coming from halfway across the palace. Kinda hoped you were headed to boil the garden lake, but I suppose I should have known better. What's happened?"

His eyes and speech were perfectly clear, although she'd never expected to hear him speak so casually. Deciding to trust him, she pulled one of the chairs round to face him, sat down and told him about Wian's confession.

He grunted when she finished. "That's all?"

She stared at him. "The weapon master that trained me in aqeyva died because of that bastard Rosin Weatherweaver," she said. "I still have scars myself from that day."

Eredion sighed deeply and leaned forward to haul one of the clay jugs into his lap. Uncorking it, he said, "Lord Alyea—" He took a deep swig. Then, wiping his mouth, he continued, "Rosin Weatherweaver did a lot worse things in his life than whip a disobedient servant to death. Your scars are nothing. Hells—" He took another swallow of rotgut. "*I've* got worse scars than that, girl. And done worse myself."

Too astonished at his indifference to listen closely to the actual words, she protested, "But Wian betrayed me! I trusted her!"

He regarded her with a wry expression. "So?" he said. "She was trying to stay alive. Can you really blame her for that?"

"I would have protected her if she'd been honest with me!"

He laughed, and she deflated, hearing her own idiocy in the echo of the mirthless, bitter sound.

"Right," he said. "Very noble of you. And very useless." He drank deeply from the jug again.

"I know. I couldn't have done anything to protect her, not really," she said in a low voice. "But I swore back then that if I ever found the servant responsible for betraying me to the priests, that I'd see them whipped to death themselves."

"All right," Eredion said, utterly indifferent. "Go ahead. You're a desert lord now. You ask for something that trivial, Oruen'll fall all over himself keeping you happy."

She stared at him, horrified. *"Trivial?"*

"You still don't get it," he said, and set the empty jug on the floor. "This servant, what she did, whatever revenge you take on her for it—it's like a grain of sand on the beach. It doesn't mean a damn thing. Let her live, order her killed, it's all the same. It doesn't affect anything important. All it does is define what kind of person *you* are. If you can sleep at night after ordering her whipped to death, then go ahead. *I* certainly won't stop you. I don't give a shit."

He reached for the next jug.

"I killed Pieas," she said, not sure why she'd said it, except that she'd suddenly remembered the kinship. Eredion had been Pieas's uncle.

"I know." He uncapped the jug and rubbed the mouth of it thoughtfully as he stared at her. "Thanks. He was getting to be a pain in the ass."

"What?"

"You heard what the servant girl said about him," Eredion said roughly. "If you hadn't killed him, I was about ready to arrange a fatal accident for him myself."

"He was your *nephew*," she said, stunned. Deiq's comment about the tathshinn echoed through memory: *She's kin. Whatever her crimes, she's kin . . .*

"He was an ass," Eredion said, apparently not the least bit concerned over blood ties himself. "And he went way over the line a number of times. If he'd at least been intelligently discreet, I could have overlooked it. But he liked to indulge, and he liked to boast, and he wouldn't listen when I warned him he was drawing too much attention. He really thought it was a good thing that he had 'street contacts'; said they'd be valuable to me one day. I tried to tell him he had built up the wrong *kind* of contacts, and that they were more damaging than useful. He said I was a fool, and we never agreed on the matter."

He studied her for a moment in silence, still rubbing the jug lightly.

"You don't understand yet. But you will. Give it some time. You'll learn to look long-term. Nothing looks quite the same when you realize you'll outlive most of the people around you. And Pieas would have died of an overdose or some stupid thing soon enough anyway."

"He'd *stopped*," Alyea said, feeling an unexpected need to defend the dead

Sessin boy. "He'd promised his sister to clean himself up, so that she might have a chance with Scratha."

Eredion's hand stilled on the jug, his eyebrows quirking up.

"Did he? Well, it's good you killed him before he could lapse, then."

Alyea stood, unable to believe her ears. Somehow, the echo of Pieas's last words—*Best not give me a chance to ruin it, don't you think?*—made her even angrier than before.

"Oh, sit down, damn it," Eredion ordered, looking disgusted. "Don't you even think about storming out of here in high indignation. Pieas was another one of those grains of sand I mentioned earlier. A larger one, but not more than a pebble. Forget about him." He lifted the jug to his lips, then offered it to Alyea. She shook her head but sat back down slowly.

"You sound so . . . *cold*," she said.

"No. I've just had to get selective, over the years, on what things to care about."

He looked at her expression and sighed, then set the jug back down on the floor. Leaning forward, he clasped his hands together between his knees, elbows set on his thighs.

"Look," he said. "I know he was my nephew. I know that my sister is grieving over her son, and my niece Nissa is mourning her twin. Believe me, I understand the kin ties involved here. But I have to look at it differently than my sister does. I *have* to care more that you found a way to end an ongoing problem without bringing disgrace on my Family name. My sister's business is raising her children and running a household, and she does that, by and large, very well. My business is keeping Sessin Family in good standing with the southern community and with the northern king. And I do that, by and large, *very* damn well. Sometimes the two businesses conflict. It's that simple, Alyea. You'll have to face that choice yourself, sooner or later. It'll be harder on you, because your family has no idea how to handle a desert lord. That's going to get rough. But if you bend to favor them, you're going to wind up causing them more pain than if you'd just done your job. I should have killed Pieas long ago. It's my weakness that stopped me. I'm fond of my sister, and I held off, hoping to find some way to turn him around and save her the sorrow of his funeral. I won't make that mistake again, and half her grief right now is that she knows it—and knows she never should have asked me to spare him in the first place."

He drew a deep breath and let it out again, but didn't reach for the jug.

"And that long speech," he said, with a wry smile, "wore off the last chance I had of getting properly drunk tonight. There's not enough left for me to try again, and I've lost interest in any case."

"I'm sorry," Alyea said, and meant it. "I shouldn't have bothered you."

"It's as well you did," Eredion sighed. "Getting drunk never really solves anything, does it?"

Alyea smiled. "It's a good way to forget sometimes."

"Ah," Eredion said, shaking his head, "but I can't possibly drink enough for *that*; so what's the point, really?"

Chapter Forty-seven

Green peppers, red peppers, black beans, red squash, hard squash, cabba root; sage and rosemary and garlic and onions. Water. How much water? And sunlight. Have to put up the shade tents soon. Wind. What season is it? Have to watch the winds, have to stake and cage. Gods, what did I get myself into?

Deiq drifted through memory, lost in exhaustion, feeling cut loose in time and space. But no: he'd started the Farms years ago, before Alyea was born. They didn't need him any longer. The water canals and pipes were finished, the ground turned from wasteland to fertile soil; the farmers understood how to keep the land from returning to desert, and the Farms had long since become self-supporting, even successful. A small percentage of the profits funneled to a holding company in Stass, and from there to several other of Deiq's projects—including, most recently, funding a small collective at the edge of Bright Bay.

Not all the priests had been evil. Not all the priests had murdered, tortured, and destroyed life. Some had fought back, even at the expense of their own lives . . .

I won't deny someone else their chance at redemption, Meer said, his voice gaining resolution with each word. Deiq could almost see the walls of the sickroom lofting around them, cool and pale; could hear the faint movements of other humans moving about the Bright Bay Northern Church Tower. Far below their feet, someone screamed, a dying wail of torment drawn out by the skilled hands of Rosin Weatherweaver's questioners.

If my life helps you turn to the good, it's worth the sacrifice to me . . . There are others who believe as I do. If you would help them with their efforts . . . I'd be grateful.

Deiq moaned, half-conscious: *Where/when am I? The palace . . . the palace.*
Where he'd spoken to Oruen . . . when? Just moments ago, it seemed. . . .

He strode through the palace halls, filled with a simmering, shimmery anger that threatened to loose him into ripping apart everyone in his path; anger being marginally safer than guilt-stricken grief.

Time slid.

Oruen waved the guards off, and they picked up the fools who had tried to stop him as they retreated from the room. . . .

The argument blurred by: *You can't just empty the Tower and send all the priests away! Don't you understand they didn't all support Mezarak, much less Rosin and Ninnic?*

And Oruen's stubborn refusal to listen; an exchange of escalating insults, at which point Eredion stepped in and redirected the fight into saner conversation.

At least grant them space at the edge of town, those who wish to stay. There are those abandoned cottages . . . they can be repaired. I'll fund it. All of it. Wholly. In perpetuity. . . And give me the Tower. Don't rip it down; give it to me.

He still didn't entirely understand why he'd insisted on that point. Somehow, the destruction of the tower felt linked, in a hazy way, to invalidating the last scraps of meaning in the sacrifice Meer had made; he couldn't bear it.

In the end, with Eredion translating heat into reason, Oruen had agreed to it all. Deiq had set up a stipend for the priests and taken over their tower; and left with an unspoken understanding not ever to risk appearing in front of this king again.

He had no idea what the priests did with the granted land. He'd never wanted to know. Had avoided even thinking about the cottages, the priests, Meer . . . the pain, the betrayal, the madness and cowardice of flight.

But then Eredion had called in that long-ago debt of an agonized moonlit night for Alyea's sake, and everything had avalanched impossibly fast, dragging Deiq back into human politics, back in front of a king who would rather see him dead than tagging the heels of a former lover.

And isn't he going to be pissed when he realizes she'll be in my bed sooner or later. . . .

He found no laughter waiting behind the thought, only a bleak misery and self-loathing.

You fight what you are . . . Why? Why? Why?

He struggled to break out of haze into waking reality, into now, and discovered a presence nearby, too close for safety. Reflexively, he lashed out with both hands, grabbing hold of the potential threat. The physical contact released a cascade of feral hunger; he began to draw strength from the intruder without conscious intention.

A gasping, sobbing cough broke his focus and jarred him back to full awareness. He jerked back, shoving the human away with brutal haste, and snapped, *"Damn it,* what are you *thinking*?"

Eredion stayed loosely sprawled on the floor for a few labored breaths, then slowly climbed to his feet, face grey and strained. Sunlight pouring through the unshuttered windows caught out glimmers of silver in Eredion's dark hair; Deiq's breath caught hard.

"Your hair—"

"I'm trying to help," Eredion said. "And the grey hair isn't from you. Don't flatter yourself."

"I could have killed you!" Deiq pushed himself upright against the head-board of the bed. Fear—and the flush of energy he'd taken from Eredion with-out meaning to—shivered through his entire body.

"Not likely," Eredion said, settling into a chair. Color seeped back into his face; he drew a deep breath and let it out loudly. "You forget what I've already lived through. That was a tickle compared to what Ninnic's child liked to do."

Deiq shut his eyes and tilted his chin to his chest, fear draining away into nausea: vividly remembering the savage marks other ha'ra'hain had left on Eredion.

"I'm sorry," he said, resting in the colorful darkness behind his eyelids.

"I'm a desert lord," Eredion said, and sighed again.

"Did I snap a rib when I pushed you?"

"I don't think so." Eredion sucked in a breath, held it, and let it out slowly. "No. It's just bruised. I'll be fine . . . Don't you realize yet, Deiq, that I was the *only* desert lord that stayed in reach after Rosin Weatherweaver took over the Bright Bay Northern Church tower? Ninnic's child liked taking entire lives, but Rosin—and Ninnic, once Rosin got hold of him—liked watching people suffer. Over. And over. I was . . . perfect. I could even heal their victims sometimes."

Deiq leaned his head back against the headboard, unable to repress a dry, choked sob. *It wasn't supposed to be like this,* he thought. *How the hells did it come to this?*

No ha'rethe ever rejoiced in torture the way Rosin Weatherweaver had; but the ha'ra'hain, one and all, had turned out dreadfully susceptible to the mad-ness of domination and power. *And Idisio's probably learning all about it now from his mother . . .* Just one more reason to chase after him before she destroyed his innocence; just one more reason to stay the hells away from her.

"It's not your fault," Eredion said after a while. "Done is done, and it's over. I only came in to help. You were too afraid of hurting me earlier. I'm not so fragile these days."

Deiq opened his eyes and regarded Eredion soberly; thinking about Meer's last words, and how unworthy he'd proven of that priest's sacrifice. And think-ing, too, that there had been a different flavor to Eredion's submission this time; not as much *duty* and more of . . . something else less nameable. It might even have been a tinge of compassion. Of understanding.

Not that he deserved either.

"Thank you," Deiq said. "But please don't do that again. You've been through enough."

"That's my decision to make, ha'inn," Eredion said a bit sharply, and Deiq had to smile.

"And your help is my decision to accept," he noted. "So I'm refusing, with thanks. You've done enough. I'm . . . refreshed enough to manage for a while now. Let be."

Eredion nodded and stood, rubbing his bruised ribs gingerly. "Then I think you're strong enough for the next problem." His tone lost its soft edge, mov-ing into crisp normalcy; Deiq found that a relief. "The king wants to see you."

"About what?"

"What do you think?"

Deiq let out a deep sigh. "I'm trying not to, at the moment," he muttered. "But I'm thinking this isn't going to go well."

"That's why I'm not leaving you two alone for this talk."

"Hhh." Deiq exhaled hard and forced a grin. "All right. Help me up."

"Oh, hells no," Eredion said, shaking his head. "You stay right there, and do your best to look like you can't get out of bed just yet. He's coming here."

Deiq felt his grin widen. "He's that nervous?"

"Oh, hells yes."

"*Good.*"

Oruen wasn't a bad king, or a bad man, as humans went. But then, some humans, such as Eredion, tended to claim that Deiq "wasn't all that bad, as ha'ra'hain go". Intrinsic to that vast oversimplification was a large grey battle-field, ever ready to sprout the seeds of misunderstanding and unintentional insult into violence.

Deiq had long ago given up on the traditional courtesies he'd been taught to demand from humans; quite simply, he'd outlived the need. Most humans, thanks to fools like Lord Arit Sessin who *protected* their people from reality, didn't even know what a ha'ra'ha was, let alone how to be courteous to one. He expected nothing in the way of manners from Oruen, and said as much to Eredion while they waited.

"He means well," Eredion said. "He tries harder than Mezarak or Ninnic did, anyway."

Deiq snorted. "That's a handful of water in the middle of the ocean."

Eredion shrugged and offered no argument to that.

Oruen arrived in less time than some kings would have taken, and with only two guards.

"Wait outside, please," he murmured to his guards; they retreated to the outer room of the suite without protest. The king watched the bedroom door shut behind them, then removed his formal circlet and robes, setting them carefully on a chair near the door.

Deiq and Eredion watched in mutual bewilderment; stripped of the gold and gem-laced crown, without his embroidered and brocaded robes, Oruen stood before them in a simple grey and tan under-tunic and trousers, looking as ordinary as any commoner.

Taking a deep breath, the gangly man bowed, his head almost reaching his knees, then straightened and said, "*Ha'inn.* I am graced by your presence. The room is brightened by your honor—"

Deiq pushed himself a little further upright, intrigued.

"That's a damn old greeting ritual you're starting, Lord Oruen," he inter-rupted. "Where'd you learn about that one?"

Eredion snorted as though resisting laughter and observed, "Well, you've spoiled it now, Deiq. Couldn't you give him the grace of letting him finish it, at least?"

"No," Deiq said. "The bloody thing goes on for an hour before you get to any substance. Sit down, if you please, Lord Oruen. I'll take the ritual as read, shall I?"

Oruen smiled and settled into the chair he'd draped his clothes over, moving the thin circlet to his lap, where he toyed with it nervously.

"I'll admit to some relief at that decision myself," he said. "I wasn't looking forward to the next hour."

Deiq grinned to mask the sharpness of his gaze. Oruen's effort was admirable, but that only meant more trouble, not less.

"What brings you to see me today, Lord Oruen?"

Oruen raised a thin eyebrow. "You're injured," he said. "And someone warned me against setting watchers for this room while you occupy it. So I decided to pay a courtesy visit myself, to see how you're healing."

Deiq shot a sideways glance at Eredion, who returned it with a lack of expression that answered the unspoken question.

"Someone was smart, telling you that," Deiq said dryly. "As for the injury, I'm healing well."

"I'm relieved to hear that," Oruen said. "It's historic enough that you've been injured, let alone recuperating within palace walls. I'd rather not add more world-shaking events to the current tab."

"I try to avoid shaking the world whenever possible," Deiq returned amiably. "It makes the ground a difficult place to stand."

Oruen nodded and permitted himself a dry smile of his own. "I never did get the full story behind your presence at Alyea's side. May I inquire on that matter, ha'inn?"

Deiq studied the king, aware of Eredion shifting a subtle step closer, and decided that he was too tired to play games.

"I'm escorting Lord Alyea," he said. "I'm here to ensure her safety while she grows into her new life as a desert lord. And to make sure she doesn't accidentally kill anyone while she's learning."

Oruen flinched; then his eyes narrowed, and his tone moved closer to challenging. "And yet here you are, injured, unable to protect or advise her at all. And she seems not to be harmed, or to have harmed anyone, in your absence."

"I didn't have much choice where they carried me when the tath-shinn attacked me," Deiq said tartly. "But I'll be in her suite by the end of the day, resuming my obligations, now that I can stand and walk."

Oruen's gaze flicked to Eredion, returned to Deiq. "You can stand and walk? Then why are you still in bed?"

Eredion coughed, shot Deiq a black glare, and said, "That's my fault, Lord Oruen. I thought the discussion might go more smoothly if he stayed in a . . . vulnerable position relative to you. Given your history."

The king's stare turned dangerously hard. "A lie, Lord Eredion?"

"For the benefit of both of you, Lord Oruen. But he's hardly dancing around even now. His mobility and stamina are sharply limited. A short walk yesterday laid him out all over again. He needs more time."

Deiq shot Eredion a startled glance, suddenly understanding. *So the king would rather I get the hells out of his palace, is that it?* he asked.

Eredion lifted one shoulder in a shrug, not bothering to answer.

"Stay, then," Oruen said, the words emerging as though they turned sour on the way across his tongue. "But stay in your own apartment, if you please. I see no need to harm Alyea's reputation with your presence."

Deiq let out a bitter bark of laughter. "I think we're a bit past the point of *reputation*," he returned. "Haven't you ever heard the stories about new desert lords?"

Oruen jerked to his feet, almost snarling; Deiq rose at the same time, grinning like an asp-jacau. Both men took long steps forward; then Eredion moved between them, planting one hand firmly and unapologetically on the king's chest.

"I think that's enough of an audience for today, Lord Oruen," the desert lord said loudly. "Ha'inn Deiq is obviously growing tired and needs to rest."

Deiq could hear Oruen's teeth creak as the man glared past Eredion at him.

"That's *enough*, Lord Oruen," Eredion repeated, his hand tensing into the slightest push.

Oruen whirled, grabbed up his robes and circlet, and stormed from the room without bothering to put them on first. Deiq made a point of sitting down before the king had left the room. Petty, yes; but damned satisfying.

Eredion followed and latched the door behind the king, then returned to direct a hard glare at Deiq. "That was *rude*," he said sternly. "And unnecessary."

"It's *true*," Deiq shot back. "Just because that reaction hasn't actually been set off yet doesn't make it less a reality he's got to deal with at some point."

Eredion shook his head, disapproving. "You haven't won any friends today."

"Don't care." He tried to stand; thumped back down, his head swimming. The strength he'd drawn from Eredion seemed to have drained away already: a bad sign. He had to bring Alyea around to being ready soon, or face breaking his oaths again—if Eredion would even stand for it twice in such a short time. "Help me up."

"The hells you say! You can't even stand? Damn it, take more!"

Eredion's offer, and his step forward, came with a gratifying lack of hesitation; but faced with it, Deiq's stomach turned at the notion.

"*No.* And I'm *not* leaving her alone any longer. Not after that display. Damned if I'll let him twist her against me with his idiotic misunderstandings."

"But you need—"

"*No!* Shut up or I'll break your jaw to stop you talking."

Now Eredion's teeth creaked; after a moment, he shrugged and moved forward to help Deiq to his feet.

Chapter Forty-eight

Warm afternoon sunlight turned the walls in Alyea's suite of rooms golden. While her apartment didn't have an external patio, it did offer wide, latticed windows to one side, with shutters that could be thrown open. Couches and chairs were positioned to best take advantage of afternoon light.

It was a lovely, sleepy time of day, her favorite time to stretch out in a warm puddle of sunlight and doze contentedly. In the wake of recent tensions and rainy gloom, the respite felt even more precious and healing.

But her dreams held little peace. She dreamed of Acana, and the shadowed tunnels of the Qisani; felt the slick water swirling around her, and a searing heat: she woke in a cold sweat, trembling with remembered terror. Acana's words echoed in her mind: *I hoped you would fail . . . That would have been safer for all of us.*

But she hadn't. Hard practicality asked a hard question: What could she do about the Qisani right now? *Nothing* was the answer; Acana had made her choices fully aware of the consequences, and even if Alyea had some magical way to rescue the ishrait and her people, it was likely days too late at this point. Drowning herself in guilt wouldn't change that.

Her stomach cramped briefly, as though reminding her of the agony from her trials.

Alyea lay back down and stared at the ceiling for a time, watching the sun patterns shifting through the room; eventually, guilt and pain eased, and she slid back into an uneasy doze.

Not long afterward, she startled awake to find Deiq, leaning heavily on Eredion, coming through the doorway.

"He insisted," Eredion said as Alyea sprang to her feet, mouth open in reflexive protest.

"Staying nearby," Deiq husked, then folded onto the couch on which she'd been sleeping. Without really thinking about it, she stuffed pillows under his head as he went down. A bare moment later his eyes slid closed and his limbs loosened into sleep.

Alyea and Eredion stood looking down at the exhausted ha'ra'ha in shared bemusement.

"I thought the door was locked," Alyea said at last.

Eredion cast an amused glance at her and lifted one shoulder in a noncommittal shrug.

"What is he *doing* here?"

"Staying near you," Eredion said, tone as bland as the shrug had been.

She shook her head in frustration and let it go as an unchangeable situation, deciding instead to press another question. "What are we doing about finding Idisio?"

"Not much we can do," Eredion said. "I can't leave. Deiq can't walk half a mile yet, let alone chase down the Coast Road after him. And you can't leave Deiq's side, if I understand matters correctly." He paused, glancing at the sleeping ha'ra'ha. "I have sent messengers—birds—to contacts along the road, warning them to watch out; but there's not much they can safely do to stop two ha'ra'hain. All I can do is hope to keep people out of the way, and that Deiq recovers quickly enough to catch up before they reach the Hackerwood."

"There has to be *something*."

"No. There isn't. At the moment, doing what the tath-shinn wants and leaving them alone is the safest option."

She turned her back on him, her chest thick with sudden frustration.

"Alyea."

She reluctantly looked back at the Sessin lord; he regarded her for a moment, then said, "I'll remind you, although he's less dangerous than he was before—still, don't try to wake him by touching him. He might react badly, and you're not fast enough to stop him. Stay clear and call his name, or toss something light at him if you can't wake him any other way."

She nodded, understanding that, at least. Eredion bowed slightly and turned to let himself out. He paused near the doorway, looked back with an anxious expression for a moment, then shook his head and left without comment.

Alyea sighed, settled onto another couch and watched Deiq for a while. Even asleep, he looked dangerous; like a wildcat ready to leap awake at a moment's provocation.

If you build walls, Eredion had said, *make sure you have an enemy beyond.* Or something to that effect. She watched Deiq roll and twitch in his sleep, thinking about that statement; thinking about what made for an enemy worth warding against as opposed to *foolish resistance to offered help.*

Finally, she leaned back and let herself slip into another doze.

Evening grey drew a chill through the windows, along with a light patter of rain-spray. Alyea rose to light the lamps and draw heavy shutters and curtains closed. A different, more muted light filled the room, catching warmer shadows and glows from the few decorations she had picked out during the months she'd lived here.

She paused before a shelf display of several wooden carvings, touching each item lightly. Nem's flower-carved spoon was the latest addition to her collection, but it rested on a different shelf. This shelf was reserved for particular memories.

A startled-looking rabbit had begun this collection. Carved of some strange black hardwood, it came from a merchant seeking to gain Peysimun favor for his wares. He claimed it came from the Stone Islands, but she'd always had doubts. Not likely she'd ever find out the truth; he'd fallen in the last days of the Purge, and his amusing carvings now rested either in the vaults of the Palace or, more likely, had been distributed to Ninnic's sycophants as favors.

The next carving, a small turtle of ash wood, had been a gift from one of Alyea's nurses; the same one who taught her the story of Lord Krilla. That nurse disappeared soon afterwards, leaving behind only the carving as proof she'd existed.

Four other carvings rested on the shelf, each with a similar story: the original owner had fallen victim to the Purge. The last, a simple carving of a wren in flight, bore the shiny wear marks of much handling; she stared at it for a long time before picking it up. Cradling it gently in one hand, she stroked the smooth back and outstretched wings, as she'd done countless times. Absently, she turned to sit on her favorite couch and remember the man who'd died for her shortly after carving the small bird from a block of discarded maple wood.

She'd almost reached the couch when she remembered Deiq's presence; looked up, startled out of her thoughts, to find him awake, propped on one elbow, and watching her through alert if still heavy-lidded eyes.

He studied her for a moment without speaking, then held out his free hand, gesturing towards the carving in hers. Uncertain, she stepped forward and placed the wren in his large hand; he cupped it tenderly and bent his head to examine the bird.

After a moment he made a small, sighing noise and leaned to set it delicately on the ground in front of the couch, then looked up at her. She was astonished to see tears glistening in his eyes.

"Tell me about it," he said. His voice sounded rough with exhaustion and pain; she began to shake her head.

"It's not all that—"

"It is," he said, and with a grunt pushed himself to sit up more fully. "Please. Tell me what happened to the man who made this for you."

After another moment of hesitation, she shrugged and moved to sit at the end of his couch. He drew his feet out of her way and arranged the pillows behind his torso for support, then rested, watching her with still-damp eyes.

She sat silent for a few breaths, trying to decide how to start, then said, "You know Pieas raped me." Somehow the memory had lost its painful sting; perhaps because she'd gotten her revenge on him in the end. Deiq nodded, and she went on: "I didn't tell anyone. I was too afraid. But somehow . . . I don't know how, but somehow a weapon-master, a man named Ethu, either found out or figured it out. He'd never tell me. He just showed up, two days after it happened."

Memory rose as she spoke: her mother had been out visiting a neighboring noble estate, the house empty but for servants going quietly about their tasks. She'd been in Peysimun Mansion's back courtyard garden, curled up in her favorite patio chair, in a patch of sunlight, of course; staring at nothing and crying without sound. Lost in her private pain, she hadn't heard Ethu approach.

She later discovered he moved silently as a matter of habit; but her first reaction, when she realized a man stood nearby, was the irrational assumption that Pieas had tracked her down for another round of abuse. Determined not to go easily this time, she brandished the small knife she'd carried close to her heart for the past two days and leapt to plunge it into her hated attacker.

A moment later, the light gravel of the path and patio scraped and rasped against her skin, rattling down her bodice and into her skirt as she tumbled to the ground. Bruised and raw, she scrambled to her feet, discovered she'd lost the knife, and spun to face the man, raising her fists.

"You won't!" she cried, then stopped, realizing it wasn't Pieas after all.

Feeling utterly idiotic, she dropped her hands and brushed frantically at her dress and hair.

"Oh, gods, *s'e*, I'm sorry," she babbled. "Did I hurt you?"

The small, darkly colored man laughed and squinted at her, his face crinkling into well-worn lines of dry amusement. "I should be asking you that, I believe."

"No, no, I'm fine. I—my mother, Lady Peysimun, isn't here at the moment. I assume you're here to see her? She'll be back shortly; she's visiting—"

"No," he interrupted. "I'm here to see you."

From there the conversation had smoothed out somewhat, and by the time he left she'd agreed to secretly begin training in something he called *aqeyva*: "It's what I used to throw you so easily," he told her. "You'll find it valuable to prevent future attacks."

But Ethu never explained *how* he knew what had happened, and she'd eventually stopped pressing for answers.

Alyea finished relating that part of the story, then hesitated. "We were caught," she said at last. "Someone betrayed me; one of my maids. My mother and I were summoned to the Palace, and when we arrived . . . guards grabbed me and dragged me out into the whipping square."

She blinked hard and often as she told Deiq about the day Ethu died. In her mind she saw her own blood staining the ground, felt the slavering heat of the crowd, heard the whispering, whistling crack of the whip. The scars on her back itched fiercely as she spoke, and it took an effort to keep her hands still rather than trying to scratch the phantom pain away.

"And I . . . I begged for mercy," she ended. "I stood there alive, and watched him die because he had the courage to stand up to his beliefs and I didn't. All I have left is this wren. He carved it for me, and gave it to me just before . . . that day."

Deiq's gaze never wavered during her story, remaining intent and thoughtful.

"No," he said when she finished. "Ethu knew the risks, and knew well in advance what he would do when the day came. Just like Acana did. And they both wanted you to live, Alyea." He reached down, not removing his gaze from her face, and picked up the small wren carving again, handling it with gentle reverence. "Do you know what a wren means, in the southlands?"

She shook her head, her throat too thick for words.

"Resourcefulness," he told her. "Bold, crafty, smart and adaptable. It finds a way to survive no matter what the conditions. It hides its true nest close to the ground, but builds several more obvious fake nests to distract predators." He paused. "This wasn't just intended as a pretty carving," he added softly. "It was a message to you. A message to live, to survive, no matter what happened. And that's what Acana wanted, too: for you to live. They both chose their risks with open eyes, Alyea. You have no guilt to bear over that."

Alyea's breath choked in her throat, emerged in a low, feral moan as a wound she'd thought healed ripped open again inside her mind, mingled with the fresher pain of having left the Qisani in such mortal danger. She knelt on the cooling stone floor and wept without restraint, crouched in on herself, arms wrapped around her shoulders, rocking rhythmically back and forth.

"Oh, gods," she moaned. "Oh, Ethu, Acana, gods, gods. . . ."

She cried until it seemed impossible for more tears to emerge, then cried some more, until rough coughing spasms shook her body. Jarred out of her misery by the need to ease her throat, she finally swayed to her feet and located the water jug and a goblet. After filling and draining the goblet twice, she belatedly turned to offer a drink to Deiq. He accepted without comment, signaling for three refills before resting back against the pillows, nodding gratitude.

Alyea put the goblet and now-empty jug back on the small occasional table they'd come from, then moved to sit at the end of Deiq's couch again.

"Thank you," she said, unsticking strands of damp hair from her face and wiping her nose with one sleeve.

"You're welcome," he said gravely. "Can you handle two more facts?"

"I don't know," she admitted, then drew in a deep breath. "But tell me anyway."

"Ethu came from Sessin Family, and he was one of Pieas Sessin's teachers."

She stared at him, the breath frozen in her chest, then let it out in a barking cough. "*What?* How do you—how can you *possibly*—"

"I'm ha'ra'ha," he said, voice a near-whisper. "I see things, Alyea. I see into people. I can even see part of a person in an object, if there's enough emotion in them. Like that letter from Idisio. And for the second fact, this wren—" He stroked it with one finger, absently glancing at it as he went on. "It wasn't carved by Ethu. It was carved by Pieas, as an apology for that night. Ethu never told you, because he never felt you were ready to know."

"You can't know that!"

His gaze rested steadily on her face. "I do," he said. "I do know. I was there when Pieas confessed. I saw the truth in his words. Saw what was in his mind. Pieas honestly didn't know what he'd done that night. He was so wild on whatever new drug his so-called friends had fed him for fun that he didn't know his own name."

"Then how did Ethu know?" she demanded. The other question lurking in her mind, *Did you know about the wren this whole time and didn't tell me the truth of it*, hurt too much to even think on, let alone ask aloud.

"He knew *aqeyva*," Deiq reminded her patiently. "He wasn't a master at it, but he was good enough to hear the wind, sometimes, and he could read his students very well. And he'd been tutoring Pieas since childhood. He came to Bright Bay to track Pieas down, in fact, and drag him back to Sessin Fortress to avoid a political disaster. When he saw what had happened, he decided to stay and teach you instead, to compensate you for the pain his pupil had caused. He felt, I think—"

Deiq glanced down at the carving again, and his forehead furrowed as though he were listening for a moment. A sick suspicion settled in her stomach: was this staged? Was he dispensing information he'd held for weeks, and covering it with a show of mysticism?

"No," he said, glancing up at her. "I won't deny I've done that in the past, but this is as new to me as it is to you. Put aside your mistrust for a moment, and listen."

He looked down at the bird again, his eyes half-closing.

"I think Ethu felt that if he hadn't taught Pieas how to fight, Pieas wouldn't have grown so arrogant. Wouldn't have made such an ass of himself, or gotten involved with the rough crowd he ran with. So he wouldn't have wound up attacking you that night; and so, the incident was partially Ethu's responsibility. That's how he thought. That's how most southerners think."

She stared at him, open-mouthed, caught between indignation and horror. It did sound like Ethu's typical reasoning: *You take responsibility not just for what you did, but what you caused others to do*, he'd said more than once. *If you steal from a man, you owe not just the man you stole from, but the people who rely on him for their living.*

"Yes," Deiq said, nodding. "That's exactly it. Pieas could not have become the street tough he was without Ethu's training, so everyone Pieas wrongfully hurt was Ethu's responsibility."

"You can't possibly know all that," she said, her voice thin and brittle.

"But I do know all that," he said simply, and held out the bird carving.

Alyea took it with trembling hands and stared at it for a long time, unable to speak.

"Do you *swear* you're not making this up?" she demanded.

"I swear by the same oaths that bind you," he said. "By Fire, by Air, and by Water; by Datda, Comos, and Ishrai. I am telling you the truth."

"And I killed him," Alyea whispered, stroking one outstretched wing lightly. Her chest felt as though it might implode at any moment, and breathing seemed nearly impossible.

"You did right," Deiq said. "He died clean, and forgiven. It's what he wanted. He could have fought you, and won, even though you'd passed all the trials and he hadn't. You weren't ready to fight him, and he knew that. He *chose* to let you kill him for the sake of restoring his honor and removing the damage he'd caused to his family name."

Her eyes swam with tears. "It's not right," she whispered. "He should have chosen life."

Deiq said nothing, but something murky stirred in his gaze for a moment, then faded. They sat in silence as the sky outside slowly darkened into true night; and as the lanterns burned down, Alyea made no move to turn up the wicks.

Alyea awoke to dawn brightening the curtains and an unusual internal warmth. Pushing to get free of the heavy blanket, her hand slid through air. That puzzled her; she pushed again, blearily, and felt only her own hand scraping across her stomach and hip.

Annoyed enough to wake up the rest of the way, she sat up and discovered that she'd failed at pushing the blanket off because there was no blanket covering her; in fact, she wasn't wearing any clothes at all. They lay in a heap on the floor beside the couch.

Deiq sprawled, thoroughly asleep and equally naked, on another couch. Looking around, she realized that she lay on the couch he'd chosen upon his arrival, while he was on the one she'd dozed on afterward. She rubbed her eyes, trying not to stare at the sleek line of muscle rolling under dark almond-colored skin as he shifted in his sleep. It wasn't easy; he had a thoroughly eye-catching body.

Gods, I'm glad I stopped allowing servants and maids into my quarters, she thought as she reached for her clothes. *My reputation would be even more shredded than it already is if they walked in on this.*

She shook her head, annoyed with herself; she'd slept shoulder to shoulder with Deiq more than once in the past, so why should this matter? He'd never made a move to harm or seduce her, just as he'd promised; why was she thinking about reputation now, when she'd always disdained it before?

Because now, it matters, she thought ruefully. For the first time, she wished they were still in the desert, where having a man by her side without a chaperone attending had seemed unremarkable. Although even there, nakedness might have raised some eyebrows.

The silk and fine linen of her clothes normally felt like infinite feathers against her skin, but seemed harsh and heavy today. She shrugged uncomfortably and tried to ignore the feeling as she went in search of a light blanket.

Finding one, she returned with intentions of draping it over Deiq to restore some modicum of decency; but as she drew within reach, he stirred and opened his eyes, focusing on her with a startling, wild-animal rapidity that caught the breath in her chest for a moment.

Belatedly, she remembered Eredion's warning: *Don't touch him when he's asleep.* She backed up a step, almost dropping the blanket.

Deiq shut his eyes, face screwing up in a taut grimace, then relaxed and sighed. Sitting up, he held out his hand for the blanket and said, neutrally, "Good morning." He draped the blanket across his lap without comment.

"Good morning," Alyea said, a bit uncertainly. "Did you sleep well?"

He regarded her with a strange, sharp stare, then said, "You're beginning to feel the changes that come with becoming a desert lord. That's why you were so hot, and why your clothes still feel strange on your body. It's a common reaction. Ha'ra'hain and ha'reye have higher body temperatures than humans. We hate cold weather, by and large." He stood, winding the blanket around his slender hips. His gaze never left her face. "You'll get used to it. And I'll teach you how to control it. Excuse me."

Alyea sat back down on the couch, one hand over her mouth, as Deiq went into the water closet. "I don't think I'll ever get used to his just being able to *read* me like that," she muttered against her palm.

"Probably not," Deiq said from the other room. "Most humans never do get used to that. Or to how good my hearing is."

Alyea shut her eyes and bit her knuckle to keep from moaning.

Chapter Forty-nine

Resting on Alyea's sun-flooded couch, Deiq admitted to himself that he was a little awed by the quiet serenity in the room: it nearly matched the feel of an aqeyva master's quarters. The humming, orderly calm of frequent meditation filled the air, and Alyea's striped aqeyva mat bore signs of recent use, which accounted for the internal changes she was finally displaying.

Most new lords blocked themselves without realizing it, subconciously terrified by what was happening to them. Meditation was the most self-directed part of the training to remove that block; Deiq hadn't had time or safety to get into the other aspects just yet.

Given the multiple handicaps of her northern upbringing, her godsdamned fool of a mother, the rape, Oruen's manipulations, her youthful ignorance, the disaster of her blood trials, and her refusal to face the reality of needing to hire kathain, he knew better than to try working with her on certain areas of her new life. She had to surrender her damned precious independence, just for a little while, and come to him with her questions, worries, and needs.

And this was a good time for it. If the humans would just leave them alone, even for a day or two, he could rebuild the damage recent events had done to her trust in him, and could coax her in the right direction. He'd never had so many distractions when training a new desert lord before; he'd always been given as much uninterrupted time as he needed, without question.

What about Idisio? said a nasty little voice in the back of his mind, and guilt prickled. *Just because chasing him down is less pleasant than working with Alyea. . . .*

But the road of obligation had split, and a choice had to be made: he could put his limited energy into chasing after Idisio, or into filling his promise to train Alyea. Instinct said that he needed more time to heal before confronting the tath-shinn again, and that Alyea was the more important obligation at the moment.

More fun, the nagging, sour voice insisted; he shut it away from his consciousness and sat up at a knock on the door.

"More bloody interruptions," he muttered to himself, staggering unsteadily to his feet and taking the handful of deliberate steps needed to reach the door.

On the other couch, Alyea stirred and rolled over, propping herself up. Seeing him headed for the door, she dragged a light blanket over herself and flopped down again, her back to the door. He could feel her embarrassment glowing through the room; irritated by the triviality of her reaction, he almost ignored northern propriety and opened the door as he was: naked.

But that would just upset her more, and serve no useful purpose; so he grabbed his pants from a chair as he passed by, stepped into them without much delay, and opened the door.

He was immediately glad of his decision. The boy standing in the hall wasn't above ten years old, dressed in common-messenger grey and with the plump, innocent face of one born to at least a merchant-level of wealth. Northern customs, and Oruen's prejudices, being what they were, opening the door unclothed might well have seen Deiq firmly evicted from the palace.

"Message for Alyea Peysimun," the boy said, looking up at Deiq and blinking a little, as though astonished by Deiq's height.

"I'll take it," Deiq said. "She's sleeping."

"From Lady Peysimun," the boy said readily; Deiq wondered at the foolishness of a noblewoman employing a common messenger, rather than a sworn house servant. But Lady Peysimun hadn't impressed him with her intelligence. This probably served as her best attempt at being subtle.

"Go ahead."

"Alyea is asked to attend on her mother at the soonest possible moment," the boy said, face earnest with recollection. "At soonest. That was stressed. And not to bring . . . er, anyone." He looked up at Deiq's height again, and backed up a cautious pace. "It's to be a private conversation."

Deiq stared at the boy, who retreated another step, clearly disinclined to ask for a messenger-gift. "Understood," he said. "I'll relay the message. Thank you."

The boy bobbed a quick bow and trotted away, casting anxious glances over his shoulder from time to time. Deiq watched him go, bleakly amused, then shut and locked the door.

Returning to the couches, he found Alyea sitting up with a frown, blanket wrapped around herself. "A message from my mother? To come see her?"

"Yes." As she began to rise, he added, "But you can't go just yet."

"Why not?" She paused, feet on the floor, one hand holding the blanket closed around herself, and looked up at him with a mixture of annoyance and puzzlement.

"Because trotting off right now will give the impression that you're under her orders," he said, resisting the urge to sit down next to her. "You need to establish that you're answering her summons in your own time."

"What if it's urgent?"

"She sent a common messenger, not a house servant," he pointed out. "That's an insult, and stupid on top of it. The boy's going to gossip over the message before he even clears the palace steps; and seeing you rush out of here to obey will set every ear twitching."

She began to answer, then stopped, obviously thinking that over. "An hour?"

"Make it two," he said, and sat down beside her, noticing the slight flinch he'd expected. He'd have to work with what he had; two hours might be enough for a solid start.

"I should dress." She leaned to stand up; he put a hand on her shoulder, keeping her on the couch.

"Alyea," he said, "do you trust me?"

She sat still, looking at him sideways, and didn't answer.

"Did you trust Ethu?"

Her head dipped in a wary nod.

"Think of me," he said, pitching his voice with care, "as you thought of Ethu. I'm here to train you in ways to protect yourself from harm."

"I know," she said, her voice very quiet. "But I never felt as though Ethu might hurt me."

Under his hand, her shoulder felt warm and bony; the pulse shuddered against his fingers. He made himself relax his grip to a light touch.

"What do you want me to do?" he said, proud of his even tone. "Alyea, if I wanted to hurt you—"

"I know you don't *want* to," she said. In her surface thoughts rose the horror of the grave-keeper's apartment. He blocked his view of her mind sharply, even turning his head away from her; and realized he'd just proven her point.

He let out a frustrated breath and faced her again. "If I don't train you, *you'll* go mad," he retorted. "*You* will hurt someone without meaning to. I've been holding my balance a long damn time, Alyea; I'm not about to lose it over something as simple as training you. But we won't get anywhere if you don't trust me; if you're always arguing and questioning and refusing to listen. What would have Ethu done, presented with that attitude?"

"Thrashed me bloody," Alyea said, her mouth curving in a reluctant smile. "And then walked away, if it happened twice."

She looked down at her hands, laced together in her lap; and in the slight movement of her shoulder under his fingers, he read that she finally understood.

"All right," she said, barely audible. "What do you want me to do?"

He took his hand from her shoulder and said, "Stand up. Let go—" As she stood, he tugged the blanket from her hands; at her involuntary tension, he added, "Trust me, Alyea."

She drew and let out a long breath; he circled her slowly, watching the tiny twitches as she fought to stop herself from reaching for blanket, bolting after clothes, or even just moving her hands to cover herself from his gaze.

He kept his thoughts and expression practical and unemotional, not sensual, and waited until she finally grew bored with being nervous; her hips shifted to a slight angle as she settled more easily in her stance, weight moving to her right leg. She returned his stare with more confidence.

He smiled then, and said, "Hands out. Palms up. Eyes closed." He let her grow comfortable with not being able to see him for a while; when the tension left her shoulders and her fingers loosened, he went on: "Tell me when you can feel my hands, and where."

"Ethu did this," she said. "As part of the aqeyva—"

"It's basic," he told her. "Now be quiet, and focus."

He drew himself quiet; gathering all his energy tight and close, as he did when trying not to be noticed. No point making it easy on her. He began moving his left hand towards her right.

"Right hand," she said.

He blinked. *Damn!* he thought. *Now, that's interesting.*

"Good," he said aloud.

He took a step back and visualized touching her left hand; a heartbeat later, she said, "Left."

Deiq stood still and just stared at her, astonished. She was drawing the information from his intentions, not the flow of air and energy around them; she should be fully open, fully changed.

Alyea? he said, and met the same muffled incomprehension as before.

Unwilling to push her into that arena just yet—he might need the estiqi after all—he withdrew and said, "Open your eyes and relax."

She regarded him with a faint frown. "Did I do something wrong?"

"No," he said. "You don't need that part of the training. I'm moving on to the next." He moved closer and held out one of his hands. "Grip my wrist. Tight as you can. I want to see how your strength has developed." She delivered a respectably strong grip; he looked at her eyes and said, "Is that all you have? You won't hurt me."

She increased the pressure; just as he did begin to feel an ache, she let go, shaking her hand. "Losing feeling," she muttered. "Was that enough?"

"Yes." Strength and sensitivity; she'd already moved well into the change. Why hadn't the physical needs kicked in yet, and why wasn't she setting off his instinctive reactions to the change? Something was very odd here. He blinked lazily to hide a rising worry, and said, "Call for a servant. Any."

Without hesitation, she crossed to the servant-summoner and pulled. He'd forgotten about the ugly scars on her back. Now that she'd told him the story behind them, he could admit their existence, even use them as part of a lesson. When she returned to his side, moving easily and not at all concerned by being naked now, he motioned her to turn around and flattened a hand against her shoulder blade; slid it down to her lower back, not intending to provoke an erotic reaction but curious to see if that would be a result.

She stood still; the angle of her head and the way her hands closed into fists spoke of old anguish, not passion. He left his hand on her lower back and said, "These are the only scars you'll ever carry."

"The way your head wound healed," she said.

"Yes. No more scars. Unless you run into. . . ." He paused, damning himself for even beginning that sentence, knowing he had to finish it now. "There are still wounds that will be hard for you to heal," he said at last. "Cuts that will leave scars. But that's . . . not likely to happen."

He hated himself for offering such a weak explanation, but couldn't bring himself to speak the truth. Alyea stirred; her head dipped, down and to the left, not quite looking over her shoulder at him.

"If a ha'ra'ha or ha'reye hits me? Is that what you're saying?"

Deiq shut his eyes, his throat dry; felt her begin to turn, and pulled his hand away.

"Yes," he said, resisting the impulse to clarify: *If a ha'ra'ha hits you, it could scar; if a ha'rethe hits you, you'll be dead.* Her stare bored through him like concentrated sunlight. "But that's not likely to ever happen."

A knock on the door interrupted the moment. Relieved, he went to the door and waved in the servant who'd responded; a young woman, not much older than Alyea, with carroty hair and wide green eyes. Seeing her, Deiq was reminded of Idisio's story about the northern sailor and his missing son, and of his own remark: *Ha'ra'hain draw coincidences to themselves.*

He studied the girl closely, although he had no way of knowing whether she looked anything like the boy in Idisio's vision. She flushed, mistaking his interest, and backed up a step towards the door.

"It's all right, I'm not going to touch you," he said, putting calm in his voice; she relaxed instantly. "What's your name?"

"Lini." She glanced at Alyea, then around the room, clearly searching for clues as to the task for which they'd summoned her. She showed no reaction to Alyea's nakedness, obviously assuming Alyea to be another servant, but her gaze lingered briefly across Deiq's bare chest, and a faint flush crossed her pale skin.

"Lini. Thank you for coming here. This is Lord Alyea. I need to teach her something, and I need you to help me." He kept his voice easy, almost trancing; Alyea gave him a sharp look but made no protest. "I swear I won't hurt you, Lini. I won't even ask you to do anything wrong. Will you help me?"

She blinked, and met his gaze directly, and he knew he had her. He could feel the shape of her willpower, saw all the gaps and weaknesses clearly. Not a virgin, not a whore; she'd had her fun, but kept herself free of tangles. She wasn't above stealing a bit, to put aside for emergencies, but had the sense not to get greedy. With a solid base of strength and reason, she'd be a good starting challenge for Alyea to work with; but only if he didn't bend her to his will first.

But *gods*, she was perfect . . . absolutely ready . . . and human. She wouldn't survive. He drew a deep breath and looked away, fighting a sharp pang; reminding himself of Meer, of the grave-keeper, of the moment's need: train Alyea. That had to come first.

"Of course, my lord," Lini said readily. "What do you want me to do?"

Deiq blinked hard, centering himself back to teaching, and moved to speak in Lini's ear, in a low murmur carefully shielded from Alyea's hearing: "Lord Alyea is going to tell you to do some things. I want you to refuse to do those things. No matter how reasonable they seem. Can you do that for me?" She nodded, her expression innocently perplexed; he straightened and moved to stand behind Alyea, bent to murmur in *her* ear: "Tell her to go pick up the blanket you dropped on the floor. As you would normally address a servant, nothing more."

"I wouldn't normally ask such a—"

"Alyea."

She let out a small sigh, her head jerking a little, like a restless horse. "Lini. Please, go pick up the blanket on the floor over there, and bring it to me."

"No," Lini said, then glanced at Deiq as though checking for confirmation. He smiled and nodded; she relaxed again, but the bewildered crease above her pert nose remained.

"Now," he said in Alyea's ear, "*tell* her to go get the blanket. Don't let her say no."

"Lini," Alyea said more sharply, "Go get the blanket. Now!"

Lini's shoulders and hips shifted, and her right foot began to move; then she gulped and said, defiantly, "No!"

Deiq grinned at the servant, delighted. Lini was even stronger than he'd expected. "Again," he said in Alyea's ear. "This time, *expect* her to obey. No need to yell. Just *know* that she will do as you say. Just like when we were walking to Scratha Fortress, and you knew your body would do what you wanted."

Alyea hesitated, and he felt her unease, her resistance; waited, knowing it would either pass or not, and if the latter, he'd be sending Lini away and trying again another day. Most desert lords were trained to order servants around for years before the trials, taught to expect deference and obedience. Alyea had backed away from that attitude; and while that might win her friends among the lower classes—the *tharr*, as a ha'rethe would say—it would do her no good at all as a desert lord.

At last she swallowed hard and said, in an eerily cool voice, "Lini. Get the blanket. Bring it to me."

Deiq's grin widened as Lini instantly trotted across the room, retrieved the blanket, folded it into a neat bundle, and brought it to Alyea.

Alyea opened her mouth; hearing the pre-echo of the intended words, Deiq hastily reached over her shoulder and put his hand over her mouth.

"Thank you, Lini," he said. "You've done very well. Beautifully well." He caught the servant's gaze and let seductive warmth flood his voice. "The blanket needs to be washed. Thank you for coming to take it away to be washed."

Lini's memories of the last few moments dissolved under a gentle nudge; she flushed bright red, bowed, and scurried out the door.

Alyea shoved Deiq's hand away from her mouth and turned around; close as he stood, her body brushed against his. Still mildly hazed himself, he put his hands on Alyea's hips, a thoroughly human reaction coursing through him.

"That was *disgusting*," she snapped, and jerked back a step.

Deiq shut his eyes and winced, crashing back to the moment. "That's going to save your life one day," he said without looking at her. "You need to know that it's possible, and how to do it."

As he spoke, it became easier to resume the practical detachment. He opened his eyes and realized that she hadn't even noticed his moment of sharp interest. Her gaze rested on the door, her eyes narrow and tight with loathing.

"It's *wrong*," she said. "She didn't deserve that!"

"We did no harm," Deiq said, forcing his mild annoyance into patience. "She won't even remember it happened."

That earned him another black glare.

"Remember what I said about trusting me? About listening? This is like the question of kathain. You may not like it, but it's part of what you are now. It's part of your life. If you don't know how to influence people, you can't defend against being influenced yourself. And the ability to do this is just a tool, like a knife or hammer. It's not evil or good in itself; it's what you do with it what defines the meaning."

"Have you ever done that with me?" she demanded.

"Of course," he said, raising his eyebrows. "I put you to sleep at the Qisani, for one thing. And I tried to talk you out of going down the Horn with Chac."

"Anything *else*?"

Frustration tightened his stomach muscles. He let it turn his voice crisp. "I don't make a practice of persuading people to act against their wills, and desert lords are more difficult to influence than humans. That's all the answer I'll give you, because damned if you deserve anything more."

He turned his back then, deliberately, and walked away, scooping up his shirt as he went and trying to ignore the aches; this time, they weren't caused by any physical injury. He'd almost had her trusting him, and she'd backed off again. What the hells did he have to do to convince her to stop doubting him?

"I'm sorry," she said from behind him. "You're right. I just . . . got scared."

Deiq paused, thinking over her tone and checking for the emotions behind it; sensing honesty, he swung round with deliberate ease and said, "Understandable. And I got frustrated. Consider that your bloody thrashing. Next time I'll leave you to sort it all out on your own. Agreed?"

Her eyes narrowed. "You're lying," she said, her tone working high in surprise.

He took two quick steps forward. She held her ground without flinching, her stare intent and intense now. He could feel her settle internally into a newly solid confidence; it felt like an echoing *click* in his mind. A grin forced its way across his face.

"Yes," he said, delighted beyond reason, almost crowing.

"You won't leave. And you won't hurt me," she said, eyes widening. Her tone grew stronger as she went on, "You really hate the idea. *Really* hate it. I think . . . I think you'd hurt *yourself* before you let me come to harm."

"Yes," he said, and moved close, watching, with awakening hunger, for her reactions to flare; but she stared at him without any sign of desire.

"All right," she said. "I still don't agree with how casually you take all this, but I'll listen. I'm sorry I've been so difficult."

Icy chill doused his eager attention. She wasn't ready after all. "Don't apologize more than once," he said, rather wearily, and went to sit on a couch.

"What's the matter?"

"I'm tired. I still don't feel well. I'm not as recovered as I thought, apparently. Why don't you go see your mother; we'll pick up on lessons again when you get back."

He manufactured a smile, then realized she'd have to walk alone. Something about the notion bothered him tremendously, but he suspected that walking with her, constantly seeing hints of how damn *close* he'd been, would only increase his frustration past bearing.

"Bring a servant," he added. "Better yet, ask a palace guard to walk you there."

"I don't need—"

With the last of his patience, he said, "Just do it, Alyea. Humor me."

She hesitated, frowning, then shrugged and went into her bedroom to dress. The lack of protest, even though she obviously saw the lie in his excuse of illness, only confirmed his suspicion that she was still fighting a basic distrust. Going to see her mother wouldn't do much to ease her fears. He'd be working from the ground up all over again when she returned.

As the door closed behind her, he dropped his head into his hands and let out a gut-deep groan of frustration.

Chapter Fifty

Alyea walked easily—and alone—down the cobbled streets towards Peysi-mun Mansion, having decided that Deiq was being overprotective, as always. The mad king was dead; the mad creature controlling him had died; the mad-woman imprisoned by the creature had fled the city. Pieas was dead. As far as Alyea knew, nobody else in this city held any ill intent towards her, and on top of it all, she wouldn't be leaving the Seventeen Gates. No point at all in a servant or bodyguard, even for the sake of status.

The blow to the back of her head came as a complete surprise.

She woke with a ringing headache and a thoroughly foul temper, neither of which improved when she discovered she was tied hand and foot to a sturdy chair. Her arms were bound at an awkward angle that gave her no leverage; the knots held when she strained against them, and the chair wouldn't budge, either bolted to the floor or secured to something she couldn't see. After wast-ing another moment cursing, she looked around the room, tossing her head to shake loose hair out of her eyes.

At first glance, it looked small, cluttered, and dingy; not anywhere in the noble quarters, by the mess and smell. She wrinkled her nose at the sour odor of old wine and ale, mold, dirt, sweat, and garbage. A narrow window up high in the north wall let in a dim version of sunlight.

A tavern was her first guess, and one near the docks; the air held the faintest tinge of brine. She ran down the list of the taverns she'd seen while walking around in the past, considering possibilities, and finally narrowed it down to three of the most disreputable: the Brass Ring, the Grey Wind, or the Red Storm.

She set her mind to figuring out why anyone associated with those taverns would want to harm her. *Eredion* was her first thought, along with his street-contacts: had he been playing some obscure game all along? Was she tangled into some aspect of his personal and Family business *conflicting*?

It didn't seem likely, but it brought a more probable name to mind: *Pieas*. It felt *right*, felt true: the drug-smugglers Wian had spoken of must have found out about his death, and be planning to punish her for it. It had been stupid to discount them as potential enemies; stupid and prideful. Apparently her new status wasn't as much protection as she'd thought.

Another attempt to break free failed to do anything but work the rough rope painfully into her skin; she gave up, annoyed. So much for her new strength; it wasn't enough, apparently, to break through several loops of heavy rope.

But since they hadn't killed her yet, they would come to taunt her or abuse her sooner or later. And the longer they waited to do that, the less chance they had of surviving.

Remembering her sudden understanding of just how fiercely Deiq wanted to protect her from harm, Alyea spared a moment's pity for the fools who had kidnapped her. Deiq would go berserk when she didn't return. He'd tear the city apart looking for her, and tear *them* apart when he found her.

She relaxed into a half-trance that would help pass the time.

All she had to do was wait.

Chapter Fifty-one

With the exception of the four main guard towers, the palace boasted only a few balconies and patios set high above ground level, each with its own distinct character and history. Deiq's favorite, which had been designed as a display of Aerthraim outdoor toys and wonders, had been utterly destroyed during the Purge and turned into a shrine to the Four. Another, an aerie-garden, showcased an array of air-plants and light, jointed metal sculptures that twisted hypnotically in the wind; Deiq generally avoided that one. The peculiar sickly odor air-plants emitted always gave him a headache, and it was too easy to be drawn into watching the dancing sculptures and lose track of human time.

Deiq wandered from one balcony to another, Eredion at his side, looking over the changes since the last time he'd had this freedom; talking quietly over trivialities, and trying not to think about his growing unease. At last the Sessin lord said, diplomatically, that he actually did have rather a lot of business to attend to, and left Deiq to stand on the Blue Balcony alone.

Deiq paced the balcony, mood souring; returned to the railing to stare out over the city. He couldn't see Peysimun Mansion from here; that was on the other side of the palace. And human lives weren't all that interesting to watch from a height. They went about their days like ants crawling after food; wagons bringing this in and that out, whores tumbling clients and clients paying for the service, merchants and politicians and commoners negotiating a million tiny, unimportant details with every moment. And somehow, miraculously, it all added up to a working society; a civilization that had produced both astonishing beauty and appalling ugliness.

They call me *a monster. . . refuse to trust me . . . No ha'ra'hain has ever perpetu-*

ated such conscious, ongoing cruelty as Rosin Weatherweaver did for years.

At last he sighed and went back to Alyea's suite, hoping to find her there; the sun stood well past noon, and she should have returned. But the room stood empty, with no trace of recent occupancy; she was still at Peysimun Mansion. He closed his eyes and tried to search for her, but met only a fuzzy greyness. With her mind still closed, she was as untraceable as a tharr.

He sat down on the couch and stared at nothing for a long time. A strange restlessness rose in him, and he began to pace, watching sunlight fade towards night. At last he focused his attention with care and said, *Eredion?*

A slight delay; then, *Yes?*

Are you still busy?

I'm always going to be busy, Eredion replied, sounding tired and a little annoyed. *Never mind. It can wait. Where are you?*

A short time later, Eredion let himself into Alyea's suite. "Why are you sitting in the dark?"

Deiq shrugged without answering and sat down on the couch. Eredion picked an Aerthraim match from the box on the side table, then went around the apartment, lighting the table lamps and wall-sconces in the main room. A sulfurous smell lingered in the air for a moment, then faded under the reek of fish oil.

"Where's Alyea?" He returned the matches to their spot on the side table and moved to stand before Deiq.

"Went to see her mother," Deiq said, staring at his hands. "Hasn't come back."

Eredion drew a sharp breath. "And you're not worried about her safety?"

"I told her to have a guard escort her there and back. We would have heard if something had happened. So it has to be a choice. I almost had her trust. *Almost.* Godsdamnit!" He put his head in his hands.

Eredion said nothing for a moment, then gave a strange gagging noise. Deiq looked up, alarmed; realized that Eredion was *laughing.* Deiq surged to his feet. A breath later, Eredion lost his attempt to smother the noise and let it out in a long, hooting howl of mirth.

Deiq stood bewildered and stunned, staring at Eredion; not at all sure what to do with that reaction. He didn't even understand what the man was laughing *at.* Perhaps he'd finally gone insane under the strain of recent events.

Eredion wiped his eyes and sat down on the other couch, still chuckling.

"Deiq," he said, "for a thousand-year-old ha'ra'ha, you occasionally do a remarkable imitation of a fifteen-year-old human."

Deiq glared, feeling strangely sullen and embarrassed. "I don't understand."

"I know." Eredion gave one last coughing chuckle and looked up at him. "Her mother is a very persistent woman. I can imagine her dragging Alyea's visit out past all reason with any number of strategies. Why don't you simply go fetch her, for the love of the gods? Much later than this, and staying overnight will be the next strategy employed."

"But what if she doesn't *want*—"

A knock on the door cut him off, as did Eredion's exasperated glare. He shook his head and went to answer it, dread coiling in his stomach. As he'd half-expected, another common messenger stood in the hall; this time, a scruffy adolescent with mismatched eyes. He held out a folded message without comment; when Deiq took it, the boy gave a short bow and walked away.

Deiq stood watching the boy go for a moment, then shut the door and returned to sit on the couch, staring at the paper in his hand. On the front, it said: *For Merchanter Deiq of Stass only.*

Probably not from Alyea, then, despite the similarity of messengers; and nothing exceptional or even informative resonated from the paper itself. He broke the seal and unfolded the note.

Four the safe return of yur woman, be at the Green Bridge by midnigte tonigte.

He grunted, not sure whether to laugh himself, and held the paper out to Eredion.

The desert lord read it. "So much for the guard who went with her," he commented dryly.

"I'm guessing her mother never sent the message after all," Deiq said, leaning back on the couch. He felt strangely relieved. This was an easy situation to handle, a simple answer to give. "It was a lure to get Alyea out of the palace."

"What are you going to do?"

Deiq stared at a nearby oil lamp, amusement loosening his muscles. "About common bandits looking for a ransom? What would you do, Eredion, if you were kidnapped and held by ordinary idiots?"

"They wouldn't make it far," Eredion said dryly. "But Alyea doesn't seem to have grown into her own strength yet."

"She can do what needs doing," Deiq said. "I tested her on that just before she left. She may not want to, but she can turn her captors on their ears and make them dance. And she's strong enough, if they let her get loose, and fast enough that it would only take a moment's laxity. She'll be fine."

"Now, *that*," Eredion said, "sounds much more like a ha'ra'ha's attitude."

Chapter Fifty-two

As the light coming through the small window faded to black, Alyea began to feel just a little anxious. She sat in the dark, smelly room, her stomach rumbling, her bladder aching, and wondered why nobody had even come to taunt her, let alone rescue her.

Deciding that if she didn't at least get a chance at a chamber pot she would be sitting in thoroughly damp clothes, she drew in a breath and shouted, loudly as possible, "*Hey!* I have to *piss!*"

Undignified, but true, and hopefully it would get a response.

After far too long a silence, she heard the sound of something being dragged aside. Light limned the door in pale yellow; then the door opened, letting in a narrow wash of golden illumination. A short, dark-haired man looked in at her, his face sour. His dimly lit features reminded her, for a panicky moment, of the teyanain; then he moved his head further into the light and she saw his nose was far too stubby and his skin too pale to claim that lineage.

"What makes you think we give a shit?" he demanded.

"Because you'd have to clean up the floor and the chair. *Please.*"

"You're the one would be sitting in it," the man pointed out, then shrugged and tossed a metal chamber pot on the floor near her feet. "Suit yourself," he said over the rattling clatter of it settling square, and turned away.

"Hey!" Alyea said. "That doesn't do me much good if you leave me tied up."

The man looked back at her. She read the expression on his face and her heart sank; this was a man who loved little cruelties.

"Is that so," he said with feigned surprise. "Well, what do I get for letting you loose? You're not stupid enough to think of attacking me, are you?"

"Right now," Alyea said breathlessly, "all I can think about is that damn chamber pot. *Please!*"

"Oh, I like the sound of you begging," the man said. He came closer. "I'll have more of that."

"After I piss, I'll beg you for whatever you want," Alyea said. "Hurry up or you'll lose that leverage."

"What a bargain," he said, and stepped behind the chair. "I'm told you know some fighting, little girl. Don't try it on me. I've been winning fights for longer than you've been alive." The knots loosened. "And beyond that door are men who won't hesitate to treat you very badly if you make it that far."

Little girl? She almost laughed. Clearly, he didn't know she'd come home as a desert lord. That changed the situation considerably; but her bladder had to come first.

She lurched forward, falling to the floor as limbs stiff from hours of motionless sitting gave way under her. Scrabbling for the chamber pot with one hand and at her clothes with the other, she abandoned all dignity for a few moments, fiercely ignoring the man's presence.

A knife point pricked the side of her neck.

"Now you get up, nice and slow," the man said. "Don't bother with pulling your pants up. You can just step out of them and leave 'em on the floor. You won't be needing them for a while."

Alyea stood, kicked her pants aside, and remained still. The chill air raised prickles on her bare legs. "You don't want to try raping me," she said.

"I don't plan to *try*," the man said, and chuckled. "See, the message we sent didn't get any response. Nobody came to ransom you. So I'm guessing you're just a whore of convenience for your *friend*, merchant Deiq of Stass. I always figured noblewomen to be sluts underneath the fancy talk; *you'd* sure have to be, to slum it with a merchant and walk around in pants like a man."

Her heart seemed to freeze in her chest.

"We thought you'd be a useful way to get him to help us out," the man went on. "But he's not interested, which leaves you no good as leverage. Looks like you shoulda been better to him."

Deiq hadn't responded? Had left her to fend for herself? A simmering rage began to build in her chest. So much for *I won't let anyone hurt you!* He'd proven himself a faithless liar at the first real test. But she'd get free of this in a moment, and then she'd go throw him out of her apartments at the palace; she didn't need his help, if this was how he reacted to real threats.

He was a coward.

"Leverage for what?" she asked steadily.

"None of your business, sweetie," he said. "Now—I think you promised me some begging. I'd really like to hear th—" He leaned in a little closer as he spoke, the knife shifting just a touch to one side.

The last word died in a gurgle as Alyea swept out a hand, knocked the knife away, and slammed her other fist into his windpipe. Another blow, to a more critical spot this time, and the man sagged to the floor, blood drooling from his mouth, looking thoroughly astonished as he died.

"Looks like you lost that one, *sweetie*," Alyea muttered, yanked her pants back on, and headed for the door.

The room beyond held five startled men around a long table, all rising to their feet and drawing daggers as she came through the door. She stumbled to a stop and stared at them, her whole body loose in shock.

"*Kam?*" she said, unable to believe the sight of her pale, sneering cousin standing in the middle of the men in front of her. He'd always been something of an ass, but *this?* Had he known she was in the room beyond?

She couldn't think of anything, couldn't see anything, except his face; she took another few steps forward, vaguely aware she ought to be thinking about something more important to the moment.

A faint sound came from behind her, and she looked up sharply, suddenly remembering; realized she'd moved almost into the middle of the room, and far too close to the four men staring at her—

Four? Where was the—*oh, shit*—

Someone hit her from behind, and everything went black again.

She woke tied to the chair again, just as securely as before, but this time she wasn't alone. A lantern on a crate cast light enough to see three men sitting in the room with her, talking in low voices. They looked up as she stirred, their expressions grim.

The body of the man she'd killed was gone. A dark blotch marked the floor where he'd lain, and a foul smell hung in the air. She was astonished they could stand it; her nose seemed thick with the scent, and she fought against gagging.

"You can sit in your own shit next time, bitch," said a thickset blond with a series of nasty scars down one cheek.

She stared at them, worry turning to a nibbling fear; a bleak violence in their expressions spoke of a serious capacity for nastiness. *The men behind that door won't hesitate to treat you very badly*, the first man had said; he'd been right. She began to wonder if killing the first man had done more harm than good for her chances of surviving this. They might not even care that she was a desert lord now; she suspected that information would just spur them to greater lengths to prove themselves against her.

"What do you want?" she demanded.

"Right now," the scarred blond said, "you writhing in agony would be real good to me. Pity the boss wants you in one piece."

He held her gaze, his own stare flat and dead. A shiver ran up her spine.

"Hey, I was just trying to stay alive," she said, determined not to show her growing fear. "Can you blame me?"

"For killing Seavorn?" the scarred man said. "Yeah. I can blame you real good for that. No hesitation at all." He stood and crossed to stand in front of her. "You made things real bad for yourself, bitch."

"Don't you want to try for that ransom again?" she said, desperate now.

"No," he said. "We know the merchant got the message. He ignored it. Another try won't change that, and nobody else who cares about your slutty ass has the resources to do what we want. You're just a toy for us now, looks like."

"My family—"

"Doesn't go past the Horn," the scarred man said. "We don't want *money*, bitch."

She shut her eyes, understanding at last.

"You want the drugs Pieas used to give you," she said in bleak despair.

"Smart," he said, and hit her across the face, hard.

Her head snapped to one side so hard she saw stars and felt an uneasy strain in her neck muscles; he'd almost broken her neck with the blow.

"Smart little bitch." He hit her again, from the other side; this time, her eyes open, she saw it coming and managed to roll with it a little. "*Stupid* little bitch."

"Hey, easy," one of the other men said. "Boss wants her alive, remember?"

The blond made no response to that. He stared at her, hands fisted at his side.

"You killed him, I hear. You killed Pieas. Is that right?"

She licked a split lip and glared up at him. "Yeah. I did."

"Must have been in his bed," the man said. "You sure ain't good enough a fighter to beat him."

"Good enough to kill Seavorn," she retorted, and received another heavy blow in response.

"He shoulda let you piss yourself," the scarred man said. "I would have. Don't think you're better than me, bitch. You're not. And you mouth off again, I'll explain that without words. You won't like the language I use, though."

Staring at the chill wildness in his blue eyes, she finally understood why Wian had been so afraid. These men were deadly.

And far too well-spoken, for all the swearing, to be simple street thugs or dock rats. She licked her lips again, feeling the lower lip beginning to swell painfully, and said meekly, "I'm sorry."

"That's better," he said. "You're getting the idea. Faster than that stupid little maid of yours did. Took me *days* to make her understand."

Alyea shut her eyes against a surge of nauseated sympathy for the poor girl. *They said I had to work for them now,* Wian had said, a strangely dead look to her eyes; and Alyea had never thought to ask how they'd secured her obedience. Now she knew.

She'd held out for *days*? And, Alyea suddenly recalled, Wian's prior master had been Rosin Weatherweaver . . . No wonder. What must Rosin have done to Wian, to make beatings by these men bearable for days?

And Alyea had offered no compassion at all. Neither had Oruen, really. All they'd been able to see was the betrayal, not what might have caused it.

Gods.

She was just trying to stay alive, Eredion had said, more accurately than she'd understood at the time. *Can you really blame her?*

Not anymore, Alyea thought as blood trickled from her split lip down her chin. *I'm a desert lord, and I'm ready to piss myself every time I look at this man. . . . Hold on. I'm a desert lord.*

She remembered, belatedly, what Deiq had said: *One of these days, that trick will save your life.* She hadn't believed him; but less than a day later it was being proven true. And against these men, she felt no compunction at all about twisting minds to her will.

"What's so funny?" the scarred man demanded.

She caught his eye and held it, in the flickering light. "Kill them," she said, very quietly, very calmly, and with absolute certainty that he would obey. Her stomach rolled in protest as if trying to turn inside out.

He was strong-willed; she was stronger. His name, *Cabe*, came to her: and with that last key, she had him.

"Cabe," she said. "Kill them."

Cabe turned, a knife in his hand; a fast step put him up against the nearest of his companions, and the sharp blade slid sideways, deceptively graceful, over an unprotected throat a heartbeat later.

"Cabe! What—shit, you're *witched*!"

The remaining man raised his own knife, not fast enough: Cabe's blade drove up into his ribs, and two bodies sprawled, twitching, on the filthy stone floor.

"Cut my bonds and let me go free."

As she stood, shaking cut ropes aside, Cabe stared at her, pale and shaken under the blood speckled over his face; then a smoldering anger began to burn in his eyes.

"You're a *witch*," he said, pointing the knife at her, then dropped the weapon as if it burned him. "Nobody told us you were a witch. That stupid little shit Kam never *told* us that."

"I don't think he heard the news," she said, but the scarred man's comment reminded her that she'd have to deal with Kam after this. She wasn't looking forward to that confrontation. She considered telling Cabe that she wasn't a witch, she was a desert lord; but that seemed too dramatic at this point.

She let him die thinking she was a witch. It didn't make any real difference.

Chapter Fifty-three

Deiq stood silently, his hands resting on the railing of the balcony, staring over the darkened city. Eredion stood beside him, equally quiet, patiently waiting; the two men understood each other well enough that no words were needed.

They had stood like this for hours now. Courtiers seeking a private spot for gossip and intimacy came and went, most of them rather soon after their first glimpse of the two men. Servants announced the dinner hour and left without a reply.

"*S'e?*" a light voice said behind them. A thin, dark-haired girl, her face heavily bruised, stood in the torchlit archway.

"I'm looking for La—Lord Alyea. Do you know where she is? I was told you might know."

Eredion made a quick restraining motion, stilling the retort in Deiq's mouth. He studied the girl with visible curiosity and said, "You'd be Wian, wouldn't you? Her former servant."

The girl looked startled and not at all pleased with being recognized so easily.

"Yes, *s'e*," she said at last, then put a hand over her mouth. "I'm sorry—my lord."

"She spoke to me about you," Eredion said. "She was rather upset by discovering you'd been the one to get her damn near whipped to death."

Remembering the feel of those vicious scars under his hand, Deiq growled under his breath and took a step forward. Eredion put out a hand, touching Deiq's arm with his fingertips.

It's not your place, the desert lord said. *Alyea has the right, not you.*

Deiq swallowed back a building rage, admitting to himself that Eredion was right, and stayed where he was; but bent a hard glare on the girl all the same.

She made a faint choking noise, her color fading, and dropped her gaze. "I know. I was wrong. I want to apologize to her, and warn her. It's important, my lords; I really need to see her tonight."

"Warn her of what?" Eredion said, frowning.

The girl hesitated, looking uncertain and flustered.

"She's already told me of your involvement with my nephew," Eredion said roughly. "Is that what the warning's about? Something to do with the asinine mess he left behind?"

Wian covered her mouth with her hands, wincing back a step, then straightened.

"Yes, my lord," she said with surprising poise. Deiq regarded her with more respect; she had courage. "I'm afraid . . . I heard rumors, this evening. I think . . . I think that the people Pieas used to spend time with are intending to hurt her. If she spoke to you about me, then you know . . . I spent some time with them myself."

She blinked and glanced away for a moment, shivering a little. Deiq narrowed his eyes, his respect fading rapidly; the words were true enough, but her emotions ran cold contrast to the *desperate* act.

"They're very angry right now. It's why I ran away and begged sanctuary from the king. They would have killed me. And the rumors I heard—I think, since I'm gone, they're going to try to hurt La—Lord Alyea."

Watching her face closely, Deiq saw the faintest flicker of cunning: the slip over the title had been deliberate, aimed at garnering more sympathy.

She went on, wide-eyed pathos drenching every word: "They're very cruel, my lords. They wouldn't care that she's important."

"She's also dangerous," Deiq said sharply, out of patience with her stupid games. "If they try laying a hand on her, she's liable to rip it off. So be more concerned for your former friends than for her!"

Wian backed up a step, her hands fisted at her sides now. "I'd be *glad* if she killed them," she said with sudden, genuine passion. "I'd *dance* on their graves. But, my lord, these men are dangerous, too. Please don't dismiss the threat!"

Deiq felt a growl building in the back of his throat again. If not for this *tharr*, Alyea never would have been put in any danger in the first place; the whipping had been the beginning of a chain of events that had put Alyea where she stood today. And if Pieas's friends put so much as a *scratch* on Alyea—

"We'll relay your concern when we see her," Eredion said sharply. "Good night, Wian!"

Wian bobbed a curtsey and left, seeming rather smaller than before, as though anguish and guilt had drawn her into a tighter package.

Eredion snapped a finger against Deiq's shoulder. "Stop it," he ordered. "It's not your damned business to get upset over this, Deiq. It's Alyea's prerogative to kill the girl, or dish out revenge."

Deiq turned away and stared out over the city again, rattling his fingers on the railing and trying to cool his temper. Eredion stood beside him, still and silent and suddenly thoughtful.

"I've been a *fool*," Eredion said at last.

"Nothing new there," Deiq observed pettily.

Eredion didn't rise to the bait. "I just remembered a report I read a while ago—I set Micru to following Pieas a few times."

Deiq shot him a sideways glance, his mouth pursing in reluctant amusement. "Dangerous," he commented.

"Not really," Eredion said. "Micru is damn good at his job."

"I meant using Micru like that, right under Oruen's nose."

"Oh, hells, Micru managed to get through Ninnic and Mezarak without being discovered as a plant; even Rosin never figured it out. Oruen only knows now because Alyea spilled it."

"That was stupid."

"Yes. Never mind—listen. Pieas was a lackey for the people Wian just mentioned. He brought things through the Horn for them. Drugs, mostly. Including dasta. I kept an eye on the people he ran with; they are a dangerous bunch. At least one of them knows the old lore, and understands how to deal with desert lords."

Deiq stood still for a moment, absorbing that, then said, under his breath, "And she hasn't come back yet."

"If they're the ones sent that note, thinking you nothing but a merchant, and Alyea nothing more than a stupid young noblewoman sharing your bed—looking to twist you into taking Pieas's place—and then realized what they really have in their hands—"

"*Fuck*," Deiq said, and sprinted after the servant girl, Eredion close on his heels.

Chapter Fifty-four

Alyea blinked, groggy, and tried to remember what had gone wrong. Walking out of that room, leaving three dead men behind, confident that she could handle the two remaining men, especially her cousin—

Only there hadn't been two, and Kam hadn't even been in the room. There had been a lot more than two: more than ten. She hadn't had time to count, because in the ensuing scuffle, someone had managed to get around behind her; at least she hadn't been hit this time. Instead, her attacker dropped a black hood over her head, the cloth heavily perfumed with a sweet-sick odor that swayed her knees out from under her before she knew what was happening.

And now she was awake again, but not tied up this time. She was stretched out on a fairly comfortable bed, and naked. She sat up, wondering if she'd been rescued after all while unconscious. Movement required a tremendous effort; she had to fight against a strange lassitude.

Cheerful blue curtains with a white diamond pattern fluttered in the night breeze coming through an open window. She'd seen those curtains, or that pattern, somewhere before; but the memory wouldn't come clear. Her mind felt hazed, thoughts slogging through a thick mire.

A lantern on a bedside table provided light enough to see that a man sat in a small chair across the room, watching her. She took in his dark hair, tanned skin, sturdy build; noted he wore good quality linen clothing in dark colors: then focused on his sharp-featured face.

The expression there said quite clearly that she hadn't been rescued at all. Fear gave way to a fierce anger; she rolled to her feet—and collapsed to the floor. He didn't move.

"You're not going to be moving so well for a while, darling," he said, voice clipped and harsh. "Side effect of the sleepy we used on you. It mucks up your muscles a bit." He paused. "If you like the floor, I'll leave you there," he added. "You rather I help you back up to bed? You'll wind up there soon enough anyway, you know."

She told him to do something anatomically impossible.

He just grinned at her. "No, I don't think so," he said. "Although I'll keep that in mind as an idea for you. It's quite an intriguing concept. But me? No. Far too many broken bones involved. And unlike you, I won't heal them overnight."

She fought to stand, and managed to lurch to her knees, grabbing the edge of the bed for support.

"Now, here's the situation, darling," the man said. "There's something I want. I believe you already understand that. You killed my best carrier, which puts a certain obligation on you to replace him in some fashion. I'd hoped to use you to turn Deiq of Stass into our service; you're the first woman we've heard of him taking up with for any length of time in quite a few years. And he'd be even more useful than Pieas was. But he seems to regard you as expendable, and I don't believe you have any other useful contacts we could bend into the *position* we require."

His smile made her stomach turn.

"Won't," she croaked.

"Oh, darling, I haven't even finished explaining the situation yet," he said, shaking his head. "I think you'll reconsider, when I have. You see, the original plan changed when I found out that you're a desert lord. I know quite a lot about desert lords. Especially about their weaknesses. And how fast they heal. I can hand out quite a lot more pain to you than I could an ordinary human, and for a much longer time."

She tried to stand; couldn't move a muscle. "*Won't*," she said. "Just kill me."

"Oh, no, no," the man said. "No, that's silly. And no fun at all."

"Go *fuck* yourself."

He sighed theatrically. "Perhaps you need to understand with more clarity," he said, then raised his voice. "Tevin!"

The door opened; a broad-shouldered, grey-haired man with a heavily pocked face came in, carrying a large wooden chest. He set it on the floor near the bed, then looked down at Alyea with a smirk that chilled her blood.

"You ready for me?" he asked.

"Almost," the man in the chair said. "Be patient for another few moments, please. Start planning out what you're going to do, while I finish explaining."

Alyea's blood went from chill to ice at the look that crossed Tevin's face. *I'm a desert lord*, she reminded herself frantically. *I can control my muscles. I can stand up. I can order my body to do what I want it to do. . . .*

She managed to get one foot under her, but couldn't move the other; sat in a weird, slumping half-kneel, glaring at her captors. The two men watched her with a kind of shared fascination.

"Oh, darling, I'm enjoying this, I really am," the man in the chair said. "You're remarkable. Now, I hope you're as smart as you are courageous. Listen closely, dear. Tevin is going to hurt you. Quite a lot, I'm afraid. He doesn't always know what he's doing, once he gets excited. But all you have to do, to stop the pain, is to say, 'help me'. That's all. And I'll pull him off you, and send him away, and we'll have a little talk about how you can help *me*. Very, very simple. All you do is say 'help me'. All you do is ask me to stop him. I'll even let you refuse to help me a few times afterward, to give you a nice break and let you heal a bit. But he's going to be more and more difficult to stop, and at some point he'll stop listening even to me. And at that point I really don't know if you'll survive for long."

He tilted his head and stared at her with an expression she'd seen before; the detached amusement that had glittered in Rosin Weatherweaver's gaze. It threatened to loosen her bladder. She felt tears rising in her eyes.

He said, "I know you think you're unbreakable, darling; you've probably been told that a desert lord can't be taken down by an ordinary person. But it *is* possible to break a desert lord in a remarkably short time, if you know what you're doing. And I do. Please believe me. I do."

His voice stayed mild, but the clipped words and harsh accent reminded her of a crow's derisive caw.

"Hold her, Tevin."

She tried to punch out at the big man as he approached, willed herself to kick, to spring, to claw, *anything*. But her body simply refused to listen; muscles remained limp and unresponsive. Tevin gathered her up from the floor and turned her around to face the man in the chair. He pinned her arms behind her, although it seemed hardly necessary; she couldn't even stand without his support. She could barely hold up her head and look forward without her eyes crossing.

Tevin smelled of rosemary, garlic, and tomatoes; that had probably been his most recent meal. Alyea's stomach rumbled loudly in response; she hovered between laughing at the incongruity of the moment and shrieking in unbridled terror.

The man in the chair stood and drew a small vial of dark liquid from a belt pouch. "You're going to drink this," he told her as he walked forward. "You can open your mouth and swallow, or Tevin can pry your jaw open. He might break it, though, he doesn't always know his own strength." He paused in front of her, waiting. "Open or force open? Your decision. I understand a broken jaw is tremendously painful. And it will make asking for help difficult."

She drew a breath and caught his eye. He smiled at her, completely unaffected; she couldn't even feel his mind.

"Oh, no, darling," he said pleasantly. "I did say I was prepared, didn't I? There's a trick or two you don't know about yet, involving drugs that help defend against a desert lord's little whimsies. I'm loaded to the lips, dear, so you won't get me that way. And so is Tevin, so don't waste your time with him, either. Nobody else is going to come into this room until we're through with you, and by then you won't be in any shape to try imposing your will on a sick rat. Now open your mouth. Last time I'll ask nicely."

After a last useless struggle to force her body into any kind of defiance and achieving only a feeble twitch, she allowed her clenched jaw muscles to relax. Her mouth sagged open.

"And swallow properly, of course," the man said, uncapping the vial. "You don't want to spit this back in my face, you really don't." He tipped the dark liquid into her mouth.

Alyea half-considered spraying him with it anyway; but what other options did she really have? She swallowed the whole mouthful without protest. It tasted like rancid, thickly honeyed mint tea.

He smiled and touched the side of her face lightly, like a parent comforting a child.

"What you just swallowed," he told her, "is called dasta tea, or dashaic. It's a very concentrated syrup, which is usually diluted back out before we sell it up the coast; but for you, darling, I thought it best to leave it pure. Put her on the bed, Tevin. Time to get started."

She landed on the bed clumsily, an unexpected warmth rushing through her body. The weakness in her muscles faded, replaced by a startling flush of strength. She rolled and sat up, glaring at them.

"Lovely," the smaller man said, watching her closely. "It's working faster than I expected."

"I'm going to *kill*—" She paused, blinking.

There were suddenly two of him. No, three. And sweat trickled down her face and body as though the room had spun into a Bright Bay high summer.

"Uh. Gods." She couldn't move. Her muscles had gone flaccid again.

"Lovely," the smaller man said. "See, dear, the thing with dasta is that it's normally just used as an aphrodisiac; but it's rather more than that, if you know how to apply it. In the pure dose, as in what I just fed you, it lowers all your defenses. It makes you hypersensitive to every little touch, every pinprick. You can't escape into your own mind now, because you won't be able to block anything external from your consciousness."

"I've been raped before," she said, grimly hanging on to clarity against a wave of dizziness. "You don't scare me."

"Oh, no, no," the man said, appearing surprised. "You're misunderstanding, dear. *That* isn't the point at all, although it will doubtless be part of Tevin's routine at some point. Oh—I see. I forgot to mention the relevant bit, which is that Tevin's previous employer was Rosin Weatherweaver. And Tevin worked in the cellars of the Church Tower, ferreting out traitors and enemies of the king."

The nausea in her stomach congealed to a freezing, empty horror.

"Ah," the man said. "*Now* I think you understand." He smiled. "Did you want to say anything, before we get started?"

With the last of her courage, she spat towards him; it fell far short, and he didn't even flinch.

"Very well," he said. "Go ahead, Tevin."

The big man flipped open the box, revealing quite a lot of shiny, sharp metal items and thick leather straps; Alyea let out a low whimper, unable to help herself.

"Anytime you like, just say the word, darling," the other man said, sounding bored. "This can stop any time at all. I'll have a *lovely* meal waiting for you, too. All you have to do is ask."

Alyea threw everything she had into trying to kick out at Tevin. The attempt only shifted her leg a fraction; and Tevin's smile only widened.

Chapter Fifty-five

The first place Wian led them to, a noisome tavern near the docks named The Grey Wind, was empty. *Completely* empty, doors locked, abandoned; Deiq smashed the door aside with a single kick and went in anyway.

Three paces into the taproom he could smell her. And blood. And human death.

He followed the scent trail like an asp-jacau on a hunt, bashing aside doors with a complete lack of regard for irreparable damages, through hallways and down a set of hidden stairs to a cellar that *reeked*. Four dead bodies had been piled carelessly near the foot of the stairs, a rough tarp thrown over them the only concession to human dignity.

Deiq lifted the tarp away and looked at their faces, making sure Alyea wasn't there; the stench overwhelmed his ability to tell without sight. All men.

"Alyea killed them," Eredion murmured, coming up beside him, his own face grey in the dim light filtering into the room from the street-level windows high above their heads.

Deiq dropped the tarp without responding and prowled into the other rooms of the cellar, studying blotches on the floor and listening to the past-echoes of violence still raging through the air. Against the background of recent death and the horrific smell in the dank room, he had to concentrate harder than usual to hear anything useful.

"Yes," he said finally, returning to the central room, where Eredion waited. "She killed one, then three, then . . . I think there was a third fight. I think she killed a few more, there. But in the end, they took her down again and moved her. And there's something. . . ." He tilted his head, eyes almost shut, trying to place the elusive aroma.

Eredion inhaled through his nose, and scowled. "Damn. No question left on who has her now, or what kind of trouble she's in; I know that smell. It was one of Rosin's favorite tricks when dealing with desert lords: stibik oil mixed with ether. It would have dropped her like a rock. And she'll be helpless when she wakes up."

Deiq let out a low growl and spun on the desert lord. "How do so many damn people suddenly have access to something that the ketarches were *ordered* to destroy?"

Eredion licked his lips and backed up a cautious step, then three more. "You'd have to ask the ketarches," he said. "I was only told they found it wise to keep a limited supply active."

Deiq snarled again and stomped up the steps without answering. Wian, hovering just outside the tavern with a sick look on her face, ventured a question as he emerged; he shot her a glare that silenced her instantly and snapped, "Where next? *Hurry*, damn it!"

Trembling, she took them to two more places, both also deserted; they contained no trace of Alyea's presence, stibik, or dasta. Wian didn't know any other places Pieas's friends might have taken her. She sobbed on the ground in a heap, utterly miserable.

Deiq leaned against the outer wall of the third place, staring up at the sun, which was descending through the sky. A corrosive, bleak despair gnawed through his veins. He'd failed his responsibility again. He should have stayed with her; but he'd let emotion get in the way, as weak as any human could have been.

And then, when the ransom note came, he hadn't even considered that anyone truly dangerous might have laid hands on her. He'd thought it best for her to learn her own strength without his interference. He'd thought it would be a good lesson, gods help him.

He'd been a *fool*.

The people passing by steered a wide circle around the three standing outside the broken door to a disreputable home. Deiq ignored the suspicious stares he was receiving.

"What's going on here?" a voice with authority behind it demanded.

Deiq looked up into the hard stares of a King's Guard patrol, all with their clubs held ready as they took in the smashed remnants of the door. Oruen had cleared out the sadists who had almost taken over the Guard under previous rulers; the shift to more honorable recruits had made it both safer for the city and more dangerous for true criminals to operate. These guards had to have an answer, and a good one, and fast; but Deiq didn't feel up to offering courtesy, let alone clarity, right now.

Eredion roused himself from his weary slouch and stepped forward. Deiq let him handle the situation, closed his eyes, and took a moment to search for Alyea's mind, even knowing it was useless.

"Her cousin," Wian said suddenly, sitting up and staring wildly at the men around her, as if she'd only just noticed the patrol arguing with Eredion. "Kam. He'd know. He's one of them."

Agonized hope flaring, Deiq reached down and pulled the girl roughly to her feet. "Where is he? Where would he be right now?"

"Wait a moment—" the patrol leader objected. "What's this about?"

Deiq glanced at him, then focused more intently. The patrol leader was one of the men who had been at the southern gates on their way in from the Horn. Memory supplied a faint blush crossing the man's face in response to Idisio's strange code-phrase, and that he'd let them pass after hearing it. Deiq's temper rose swiftly, broke past restraint.

"You tharr bastard—"

Eredion hollered, "Deiq, *wait!*"

Three of the guards made the mistake of trying to lay hands on Deiq; they quickly went sprawling into each other and across the ground. The leader of the patrol froze like a frightened rabbit as Deiq lunged at him.

Eredion's voice came from somewhere behind a red haze: "Deiq, *don't—*"

"Bless *this*, you *tharr ta-karne ii-shaa—*"

Bones snapped; the patrol leader howled.

"Deiq, godsdamnit, stop!"

The patrol leader landed atop his men, both arms broken in multiple places; his screaming, sobbing curses drowning out all other nearby sounds.

"Come *on*," Deiq snarled, slapping Eredion's shoulder hard enough to rock the visibly appalled Sessin lord back a step.

"Damn it, you godsdamned *idiot*, you can't just—hey, *wait—damn it—*"

The shouts and curses faded into the distance as Deiq sprinted to catch up with Wian, who'd taken advantage of the distraction to get a head start; and he heard Eredion galloping, still cursing, to catch up.

But two blocks later, Eredion skidded to a halt, shouting, "No! Not that way! I know where they are! Gods, I'm an idiot—this way!"

Wian was still visible ahead; for a human, she possessed a remarkable turn of speed. Deiq went after Eredion without hesitation.

"Where?" he said once he caught up to Eredion.

"Something Pieas said once just came back to me," Eredion panted, already winded from their sprint. "He was close to Kam, and to Kippin. And he said something about meeting at Kippin's aunt's house. But Kippin doesn't *have* an aunt; his father was an only child."

"You study northern family trees now?"

"When a Sessin is involved with a northern maniac, yes," Eredion snapped, and directed them over to a side street and back out to a larger one. "Kippin's *father* had an aunt. Lady Arnil. Her estate is on the far western edge of town, and I just heard a day or two ago that she'd died. Kippin's the only family survivor at this point; it would have gone to him. It's the logical place for him to take Alyea; too far away from anything else for anything unusual to be noticed."

Deiq slapped the desert lord's shoulder, a fierce grin stretching his lips. "What are we walking for?" he said, and heard Eredion groan.

Chapter Fifty-six

Many people died very quickly after Eredion and Deiq ripped through Lady Arnil's front doors. Eredion had never seen a ha'ra'ha truly let loose before; he hoped never to see it again. Under the extreme stress, Deiq's lineage came through more clearly than Eredion would have believed possible.

A fine pattern of silvery scales, glowing as though lit from within, caught and refracted the torchlight. His eyes turned a disturbingly solid dark shade, no white visible at all; and when he roared during a charge, more than one opponent simply wet himself and knelt tamely down to die.

Eredion soon decided it was wisest to stay back and let Deiq clear the way; the ha'ra'ha seemed beyond the ability to distinguish friend from foe. Every so often, Eredion paused, with absolutely no remorse, to finish off someone still twitching.

He could *hear* Alyea screaming, on a level beyond words; he was fairly sure her voice had given out some time ago. He knew Deiq could hear it too, far more clearly; the non-sound seemed to be driving the ha'ra'ha completely berserk.

Eredion ducked as another limp body hurtled past to crash into the far wall. He didn't bother telling Deiq to watch his aim. The rebuke would have fallen on deaf ears.

The slaughter didn't take very long at all. While Kippin had clearly wasted no time setting up his great-aunt's mansion as his new base, only about two dozen men and women had so far moved in, and of those only the men fought. The women, clearly, had been used for other purposes; they mostly cringed, hid under tables and behind couches, and screamed a lot.

One woman, her dark eyes flashing with brilliant fury, grabbed a knife from one of the fallen men and began stabbing the corpse with it, over and over. Silently. Her eyes remained dry and bright with hatred.

Eredion left her alone.

They found Alyea in a ground-floor room that faced west. The setting sun gilded the walls and a restless breeze wandered through the open window. The blood in this room all came from Alyea; she lolled, witless, as though hastily thrown on the bed and abandoned.

Eredion looked around the room to spare himself the sight and found nothing more pleasant in view; heavy leather straps, slick with blood, lay in an untidy heap on the floor. Whip-thin chains of iron, with handles fastened to one end; a hood; short, braided leather whips; and long, thin knives.

All damp with fresh blood.

Eredion shut his tearing eyes, wishing the sight didn't feel so damned familiar; but as he had told Deiq, Rosin had enjoyed hurting people—often—and on more than one occasion had forced Eredion to attend a "questioning".

But this was worse. From the look of it, these men had crammed into a day what Rosin had drawn out over ten; clearly Alyea had fought, over and over, even when she had no wits left to understand what was happening. And they'd just as clearly moved from trying to break her spirit into enjoying the torture itself.

I knew I should have killed Kippin a long damn time ago. And I should have killed Pieas myself. This is my damn fault. Mine.

The nauseating aromas of stibik, dasta tea, urine, feces, and sex brought a heavy lurch to his stomach. He couldn't imagine what agony Deiq's more sensitive nose must be in.

Deiq spared the room a brief, bleak glare, then scooped Alyea's limp body from the bloodstained bed.

Eredion didn't say anything as he followed the ha'ra'ha outside; he was busy thinking how to explain all this to the guards he knew would be fast approaching at this point.

In the end, they brought Alyea back to Peysimun Mansion. If she died, it would be best at her family home, not the palace; and if she lived, she'd need family around her during her recovery.

Her mother went into shrill hysterics at the arrival of the two blood-soaked men carrying her battered child; dissolved even further into wild shrieking when she was told, very flatly, that Deiq *would* be staying with Alyea, and caring for her himself.

Wian, who'd gotten all the way to the Peysimun estate before realizing the men weren't following her any longer, steered the crazed woman away with surprising strength.

Eredion stayed, acting as intermediary, buffer, explainer, and a relatively sane voice amid the chaos. After several hours, he persuaded Deiq to bathe and eat; spoke with Alyea's mother long enough to settle her down somewhat;

persuaded the guards to wait for a resolution, swearing on his own Family honor that none of them would flee the city; and sent word to the king absolutely forbidding him from coming anywhere near Alyea until she'd either died or recovered.

Right now, Oruen and Deiq in the same room would spark off mortal combat. Eredion didn't particularly want to hunt up another candidate for the throne on such short notice.

Lady Peysimun calmed once Eredion convinced Deiq to allow her to sit with him by Alyea's bedside. It was a mark of the ha'ra'ha's intense distress that Eredion even had to explain why that was important.

"She's Alyea's *mother*, Deiq," he said with strained patience. "This is her house. *Please*. Be reasonable. She has the right."

Deiq shrugged, shot the woman a dark, suspicious glare, and ignored her after that. Alyea's mother returned the favor, speaking only to Eredion, acting as if the ha'ra'ha simply didn't exist. Eredion suspected Deiq was mucking with the woman's perceptions, but let the uneasy compromise rest without comment.

Much later in the evening, after settling the most pressing issues, Eredion managed a light doze, too worn out to stay alert another moment. He'd only slept a short time when a messenger came to announce a wild-eyed mercenary on a lathered horse at the Seventeen Gates, demanding access.

"Says he's got a message for Lord Alyea and Deiq," the messenger said, his face and tone skeptical. "From someone called Idisio."

Eredion roused himself fully and with a few sharp words sent the boy off at a run. After brushing his hair back into order and grasping control of his tattered emotions, he went out to the front steps of the Mansion and waited. It didn't take long for an exhausted horse to clatter up to the gates and into the courtyard.

The messenger, riding behind the ragged, filthy mercenary, slid to the ground with the wiry bounce of youth and took the reins, pointing up the steps towards Eredion; the mercenary dismounted more slowly and stumbled forward. There was something familiar about the young man, but Eredion couldn't quite place his face; he let it go as unimportant to the moment.

"My lord," the mercenary said, "Lif—Idisio sent me."

Eredion's breath caught in his chest. *Lifty* had been Idisio's street name; what did it mean that it was the first name to this mercenary's lips? He squinted, trying to figure out why the boy looked so damned familiar.

"Idisio," the mercenary repeated, then blinked as though trying to remember what he'd been about to say. "He's in Sandsplit. With his mother."

Eredion felt a dizzying calm come over him, and had no idea how to respond to the news. All he could think was *At least Idisio's still alive.*

The young man's hair was red; something about that should be important, but he couldn't figure out why. *Gods, I'm tired. . . .*

The mercenary's words came more easily now, tumbling out like the water splashing in the fountain behind him. "His mother, she's . . . Idisio needs help, my lord. I think she ripped someone apart in Obein. Two people. I don't think he knows about it. And I don't think he believes she could hurt him, but I do."

He stopped babbling, pulled himself upright, and swayed like a drunk.

"She's going to hurt him," he said starkly. "I know she is. He said he needs help. He says to hurry. I couldn't help. I stopped her when she came at me but I wouldn't be able to do it again, and he wouldn't let me stay in any case—"

His words blurred; he stopped talking, his eyes unfocused.

This mercenary had stopped the tath-shinn from attacking him? Eredion regarded the young man with growing respect—and unease. He wanted a long talk, once they both got some proper rest. He knew this boy from somewhere, damnit, but his weary brain simply wouldn't connect the pieces.

"Thank you," Eredion said, careful to hide his startled interest. "Come in and rest."

"He needs *help*," the mercenary repeated, squinting up at Eredion with an aggrieved expression.

"I understand. We've got something of a crisis here ourselves, *s'e*. Come rest. You're about to fall over."

"But—" A moment later, the mercenary's legs simply gave way, and he sprawled, unconscious, on the cobbles of the courtyard.

Envying the boy his loss of stamina, Eredion directed servants to carry the mercenary to a spare guest room, then walked out to a small garden courtyard and sat staring up at the stars for a while, too exhausted to make plans. Names trickled through his mind, only vaguely connected to faces and events: Idisio and his mother. Alyea and Deiq. Scratha. The teyanain. The Horn. The ha'reye . . . and the ha'ra'hain.

The desert held too many damn convoluted plots. Too many secrets. Too many lives had been put at stake, too many dreams and ambitions.

But that was reality: never neat, always messy. You did what you could with what you had, and you didn't waste time whining over what ought to be.

He sighed and went to find a servant to run some messages.

Chapter Fifty-seven

Alyea lay motionless, her breathing so shallow as to be invisible. Deiq kept his fingertips against one of the few merely bruised spots on her ribcage, desperately tracking the tiny shifts of her breathing. On the other side of the bed, her mother knelt, praying in a low drone that had started out shaky and stammering, but long since smoothed out and turned to background noise in Deiq's ears.

The low light of a table-lamp was the only illumination in the room, and shadows stretched long and wide, as though to gather in everything they could. His eyes prickled and burned; he made himself blink, made himself look away from the still, pale form on the bed. Alyea's mother, lost in her prayers, swayed towards one side; caught herself with an outstretched hand, and stared at her daughter with an expression of utter despair.

"It's my fault," she said, seeming to have forgotten Deiq's presence entirely. "It's all my fault. I should never have. . . ."

As though something had startled her, she glanced up and saw Deiq watching her. A flood of color rose to her pale face, and she jerked to her feet.

"What are *you* doing here?" she demanded, her tone low and filled with venom.

"The same thing you are, Lady Peysimun," he said; in a moment of compassion, he laced his words with what persuasion he had left. "Get some rest. I'll send for you if anything changes."

She glared, then sagged where she stood, her gaze turning vague with exhaustion. "It's my fault," she repeated in a low mumble, and left the room without looking back.

He made himself blink a few more times, to keep his eyes from drying out, then went back to watching Alyea.

Her injuries were healing, but slowly—too slowly. The tharr bastards had taken her to the edge and damn near pushed her over, and he didn't know how to call her back. He'd never learned how to give energy, only how to take it; healing humans wasn't something a ha'ra'ha was ever expected to do, especially not a First Born.

Tentatively, he tried to thread a reverse draw out through his fingertips. It felt strange, and rather painful, as though his fingers had been set on fire. And once again he met that thick grey fog of refusal. He began to back off, then decided to try just a little harder; he had to know if it wasn't possible. He had to *try.*

Bright agony flared through his hands and up his arms; the grey streaked, abruptly, with red, and Alyea let out a wrenching scream, her back arching in protest. He pulled back instantly, and bent over her, trying to soothe her pain with helpless, agonized, ineffective hand movements; panic thudded through his entire body as he tried to figure out how to calm her.

She fell back, limp, into the same catatonic state as before. Moments later, Lady Peysimun burst through the door, screeching, and threw herself at him in a flurry of clawing blows.

"Get away from her! Get *away*! You *monster*! What are you *doing* to her?"

Deiq flung up his hands and backed into a corner, overwhelmed and desperately trying not to retaliate. One blow would send the woman through a wall, and Alyea would never forgive him for that. He fended her off, panting; it seemed an eternity before Eredion ran into the room and pulled the crazed woman away from him.

"I was trying to help," Deiq said, catching his breath; her ranting imprecations overshadowed anything else he might try to say.

Eredion glared, his arms wrapped around the struggling woman to hold her back from another attack. The darkness of exhaustion turned his face haggard as he snapped, "Go! For the love of the gods, Deiq—I'll sort this—right now, just *go*. Sit in the garden outside. I'll come talk to you later. Please."

Deiq cast a frantic glance at Alyea, at the hellish shadows reaching towards the bed; drew in a sharp breath and said, with forced calm, "Yes. You're right. Of course." He passed them without meeting their eyes; paused just before stepping out into the hallway and added, not looking back, *Tell her it's not her fault at all. It's mine.*

Stop being so bloody juvenile! Eredion shot back immediately. *That's not helping anything!*

Just tell her, Deiq said, and left.

Chapter Fifty-eight

Alyea swam through depths of orange and blue, red streaking down around her in a light patter of musical tones. There was a high mountain, and a patio, and she stared out into the blue, blue sky; watched the bright orange of a breathtaking sunset, and flung herself over the edge of the cliff to catch the sun before it went away forever.

And fell . . . and fell . . . and fell. The sun fell away faster, however hard she swam, and soon she flew through darkness, watching tiny red droplets dance in asymmetrical patterns where stars should be. Orange lined her vision, a bright haze, and she rolled sideways into the heart of the sun; surrendered to its immense heat and burned to ashes instantly.

She scattered into millions of tiny black flakes, fluttering off in all directions; felt her heart break because the sun could never love her.

The red droplets streaked into sudden, harsh order, slapped the ashes of her self into form and substance, then rammed through her body like a million razor-edged spears. She screamed, pain breaking into the relatively pleasant haze. Someone else screamed, and the two sounds braided, broke apart, and echoed through canyons; skipped across ridges.

Guardian, the teyanin crow, sat on a branch that led nowhere and clacked its beak at her, its yellow eyes filled with amusement. "You're lost," it remarked. "Lost! Lost! Lost!"

"Where do I go to find what I've lost?" she asked, kneeling before it. Guardian clacked its hard black beak again, as though laughing at her.

"Lost!" it screamed. "Lost!"

She grabbed a rock that came to hand just then, and threw, hard and true.

Guardian disappeared in a wild explosion of feathers and screeching. The feathers blew straight towards her as though on a sudden gust of wind; she put up a hand to protect herself, but they coated her, skin and hair and nostrils and mouth and ears, smothering her inside and out with bristly rankness.

She screamed, choking on musky feathers, and felt a hand on her wrist; heard a voice calling a name. *Alyea. Alyea. This way. Alyea. Over here. Alyea.*

She didn't want to be Alyea. She wanted to be someone else. Somewhere else. Following that voice, admitting to that name, would bring her back to pain past enduring. Would mean that she'd failed, in the end; because she couldn't go through any more. She'd do whatever they asked. Anything . . . anything.

No, the voice said. *You won. It's over. You're safe. Alyea, you're safe. You won. Alyea. Alyea.*

"Lost!" screeched Guardian, but far away, and fading with each iteration.

She hovered in grey fog, torn; she could still follow Guardian's mocking voice, chase him down and kill him again. That would go on forever, and there would be no real pain involved; only the fierce joy of the hunt, of the kill.

Alyea. Alyea. Alyea.

She knew that voice; and with that knowledge came silence from Guardian, and a lessening of the grey fog.

"Alyea," another, different voice said; this one was wracked with agonized relief.

She knew *that* voice too, and abrupt hatred blew the last of the grey haze away, turning it into crystal-bright rage, while everything else turned utterly black.

Chapter Fifty-nine

Deiq stood across the room from Alyea's bed, watching Eredion work to call her back. The desert lord knelt beside the bed, fingertips laid against Alyea's shoulder and hip, his eyes closed. Sweat beaded his forehead; he muttered her name almost continually under his breath.

Lady Peysimun had been put to sleep with a combination of desert lord persuasion and a simpler matter of drugs slipped into her drink; she wouldn't be interfering for some time yet. And Eredion had absolutely forbidden Deiq's involvement, at any level.

So Deiq stayed still, looking at his surroundings to distract himself from pushing into whatever Eredion was doing. Dawn limned the windows; the curtains had been drawn wide and shutters thrown back to allow cool air into the room. Not enough there to hold his interest; his gaze tracked back to Alyea after only moments.

The few cuts not concealed by the array of bandages wrapped around Alyea's body scabbed with slow, webbing stealth; cracked and bled, and closed again. Bruises shifted across a variety of colors, faded, brightened, highlighting gaunt hollows under her high cheekbones. Eredion paused to sip from a mug of water and cast a bleak glance at Deiq. "She doesn't want to come back," he said. "I'm having a hard time convincing her it's going to be worth it."

"I could—"

"No, you can't. Let me handle this. I've done it before. And at least *this* time, I'm proud of what I'm doing." Eredion took another sip of water, shut his eyes, and resumed the low droning chant of Alyea's name. Deiq settled into a chair, drumming his fingers against his legs; caught a sideways glare from Eredion, and forced himself to go quiet and still.

The air began to warm as the sun rose from dawn to early morning; Alyea gave a sobbing gasp, her dark eyes half-open but still hazed and unseeing.

Eredion sat back, grey relief breaking across his face. Unable to help himself, Deiq started up from his chair and said, "Alyea!"

Instantly, a staggering wave of rage crashed through the room. Deiq stumbled back, fetching up against the wall. Eredion ducked out of the way as Alyea's arms flailed out in erratic blows; then she rolled from the bed and to her feet, nothing sane in her eyes or mind.

Her hand closed around the bedside table-lamp; Deiq barely ducked aside in time. It shattered where his head had just been, adding the sharp greasy tang of oil to the already-rank room.

She looked down at herself and snarled; clawed at the bandages, shredding them like paper, and stood naked, blood oozing from underneath multiple, fragile new scabs. Eredion moved to a crouch, working his way around the side of the bed. She spun, grabbed an empty glass vase, and pitched it unerringly at Eredion's head. He only escaped by flattening himself on the floor, and the vase whirled past to shatter against the wall.

Someone screamed from the doorway, a shrill yip of astonishment: "She's awake!"

Deiq glanced over just as Wian ran into the room, calling Alyea's name; the girl's reward was to have the ceramic bowl they'd been using for sponge-water pitched at her head. Water sprayed everywhere, and Wian wasn't fast enough to duck in time. She went down with a yelp, and the bowl careened off, bursting apart into fragments when it hit the stone floor.

"Damn it, Alyea, stop!" Deiq hollered as she turned to face him again.

Her face was strange and grey, all angles and coldness. She stared without really seeing him, and reached for something else to throw.

"Eredion—" He ducked as the bedpan, mercifully empty, went past his ear. "Can't you *do* something?"

"Lady!" Wian cried, one hand to her head. Blood matted her hair.

"Shut up, you idiot!" Deiq snapped. "Eredion!"

"*Don't you touch me!*" Alyea shrieked, and picked up the night stand.

Medicines and salves slid off and crashed to the floor, creating an entirely new stench in the room. Deiq leapt to stand closer to the open windows, his eyes watering. Eredion ducked in another direction, and Alyea stood still, night stand held aloft, as though unable to track their movements well enough to aim properly.

"She's too fragile," Eredion panted. "There's nothing to grab hold of. She's raving from dasta, and gods know what else—"

A soft noise from the doorway caught Deiq's attention. He looked up to find a horrified-looking young man with bright red hair and blue eyes staring, appalled, at Alyea.

"Get out of here, you idiot!" Eredion thundered.

Wian spun, holding out both hands to the stranger, and shouted, "No! Tank! Come help her! The way you helped me, come help her! Please!"

"Are you out of your gods-blessed *mind*?" Eredion roared.

Furious and horrified, Deiq moved to physically throw both the boy and the servant from the room; but Tank's stare locked onto Alyea with a bizarre intensity, and then Alyea dropped the night stand and turned, her own haze clearing as she looked straight at Tank—

—and Deiq felt an inexplicable *click*, and a *shifting*—

"Shit!" Eredion said, in tones of deep, incredulous awe. "Deiq, wait—wait, she's stopped, she's *stopped*, she's not trying to kill him—or us—"

"What in the hells?"

"I don't know—but wait—"

Tank staggered a few steps forward, as though drawn against his will. Alyea watched him, unmoving, her face more alive and alert than Deiq had ever seen it: like an asp-jacau ready to attack.

"Godsdamnit, he's only a human, she's going to tear him apart," Deiq said.

"No, she's not, she's not going to hurt him, there's something else going on, wait—"

A moment later, Tank went to his knees, threw back his head, and screamed with nearly ear-shattering volume. Deiq put his hands over his ears, wincing.

"That's not hurting him?"

Eredion just shook his head and urgently motioned Deiq to stay where he was. "I recognize him now," he said as the scream wound down into a series of hoarse gasps. "I was even more tired than I thought, last night, not to recognize him. That's the Aerthraim boy."

Deiq backed up a hasty step. "The one who—" *You let him in* here, *you godsdamned idiot?* he thought but didn't say, too rattled to organize mind-speech.

"Yes. Now shut up—"

The Aerthraim boy staggered to his feet and lunged forward, catching Alyea in a tight embrace. She buried her face in his neck and burst into deep, gut-wrenching sobs. He stroked her hair and back unceasingly, his own head leaned into her shoulder; Deiq realized with a sense of icy shock that he couldn't feel any emotions from the two. They'd retreated into a silent, shared world, blocking off every outside influence; there was literally no way to reach either of them short of physical violence.

He exchanged a helpless glance with Eredion, not at all sure what to do next.

The boy reached into his belt pouch and pulled out something that looked like a twisted, dry stick of black trail jerky; murmuring reassurances, he worked it into Alyea's mouth. She chewed, obedient as a cow, but her eyes reddened and began to water almost immediately.

"I know," Deiq heard the boy murmur. "Tastes awful . . . keep chewing . . . good. Spit out what's left—" A blob of stringy mush landed on the floor, and Alyea sagged, her intensity draining away.

The boy caught Alyea up, cradling her against his chest as though she weighed nothing and he could carry the world without noticing.

Not looking at anyone—not seeming to even realize anyone else stood watching—he brought her to the bed, laid her down gently, and tried to step back. She shot out a hand, clutching at him frantically. He perched awkwardly on the edge of the bed; she continued to tug at him. After a moment he kicked off his boots, then stretched out, wrapping his arms around her.

Alyea gave a shuddering sigh and relaxed all over, her eyes rolling back then sliding closed. A rough shiver passed through the boy's body; his eyes shut, and he followed her into a profoundly exhausted slumber.

Deiq watched them sleep, unable to believe what he'd just seen. Eredion, similarly stunned, slowly righted an overturned chair and sat, favoring his right leg.

"I *knew* he could help," Wian said from her place on the floor, looking supremely pleased with herself, then flinched under the dark glare both men turned on her.

"How?" Eredion demanded. "When we couldn't settle her down, what made you think he had a chance?"

"I met him before, is how I know," she retorted. "He's one of the men brought me back to Bright Bay. He's got a gift. A healing gift."

"A *healing* gift?" Eredion said incredulously; glanced at Deiq, and visibly held himself back from further comment.

Are you sure this is the same boy? Deiq asked.

Oh, yes, Eredion answered. *But I never heard of him being trained as a healer!*

Wian, unaware of the side conversation, went on: "I knew Tank could reach her, because he'd already helped me without any idea what he was doing. I knew if he saw her, he'd have to help her. It's how he is. He couldn't have walked away."

"If you'd been wrong," Eredion said bleakly, his gaze going to the bed again.

"But I wasn't."

"She could have killed him, Wian, and what that would have done to her mind . . . You have no idea what risk you took. You should have warned him first. You should have warned *us*. Gods, my heart almost stopped."

She shrugged and climbed to her feet; then winced, putting her hand to her still-bleeding head. Deiq noticed that the pain seemed to bother her less than the feeling of blood trickling down her neck, and filed the observation for future consideration.

"I'll go tell Lady Peysimun her daughter's doing better," she said, and left the room without looking back.

Eredion and Deiq looked at each other. In the silence, the redhead snored quietly.

"Why him?" Deiq asked, feeling a deep ache press into his chest. "Why *him*?"

The desert lord sighed and pinched the bridge of his nose.

"I think," he said slowly, "because he's been through it too. Born in a katha village, as I understand it, and raised there for years. Didn't you hear about him?"

"I knew a human boy was involved in the battle with Ninnic's child," Deiq said, "but I never understood why they chose that approach. I thought he was just a sacrifice—a distraction, perhaps with enough innate ability to keep him interesting to Ninnic's child for a time; and I thought he'd died in the battle."

Eredion flicked Deiq a sardonic glance.

"No," he said. "His proper name is Tanavin Aerthraim, and he's as fully trained and able as I am, if somewhat less aware of the potential of his abilities.

And since he's still fully human, ha'reye and ha'ra'hain can't really see him, if I understand the theory correctly. You call ordinary humans *tharr*, right? 'The invisible ones.'"

Deiq shut his eyes and opened other-vision. He couldn't see the boy at all, beyond a vague blurriness. Beside him, Alyea's presence wavered with an odd translucence, hazed by such close contact.

"Yes," he said, barely audible. He swallowed hard, appalled. The humans had taken a ha'reye blind spot and turned it to their own ends with deadly efficiency. Not at all surprising that the plan came from the Aerthraim: the only Family without desert lords; the only Family without a protector. The only ones not afraid of retaliation for this gross offense against the Agreement.

Oh, gods, if the Jungles ever find out that humans made this leap. . . .

He reverted to human-normal vision and blinked at Eredion. "Did he actually get close enough to kill it?"

Before today, he'd deliberately avoided conversations or questions about that time. Best not to know things that could invite retaliation by his elders. But now he found himself filled with a morbid, horrified curiosity; and it was, after all, too late to be afraid now. Eredion's damned trust had put him beyond any chance of redemption among his own kin.

"Close enough, yes; as for killing it, not quite." Eredion began to pick up the larger shards of debris around the room. Deiq just stood still and watched, too shaken to seriously consider helping. "Things didn't exactly . . . go as planned. Tanavin took off on his own, and ran more or less straight into the right place at the wrong time. We arrived rather later, to find that he'd hit hard and run like all hells. But he did more damage with that one blow than myself and five other full desert lords managed, combined."

He piled the shards near the bedroom door and turned to regard the sleeping pair again, his expression grave.

"If it's any consolation," he added, "I really doubt he'll want to get between you two. He's not ready to settle down yet, and he's developed an intense hatred of politics."

Deiq stiffened. "That's not—"

Eredion turned his head and met Deiq's eyes.

"I know what it's not," the desert lord said. "And I know what it is. You forget, Deiq—the sharing goes both ways."

"Mmph," Deiq said after a moment, and looked away. "I didn't think you'd see . . . that deep." Most desert lords were too busy screaming and fighting to get away, or fighting themselves to stay put, to look at anything else.

"If I saw that," Eredion said, "so will she. When the time comes."

"Yes."

"I'll speak to her for you, when she recovers," Eredion said quietly. "I don't think you have the words to explain it."

"Thanks," Deiq said in a muted voice, and looked back at Alyea.

A moment's cautious examination told him she was, steadily and gently, drawing the energy she needed to heal from the Aerthraim boy; or perhaps, even more incredibly, the boy was feeding her.

Deiq had never seen a human or a desert lord do such a thing. It frightened and elated him at the same time; if this was possible, maybe—

He roughly squashed the hope. *Human mutation,* he told himself, *nothing I can ever duplicate. It's too late for me. I already proved that. I can't give her anything at all. I can only take.*

A shivering ache spiraled through his body, as though the hunger had just been waiting for a thought to activate it. He struggled to ignore it; he wouldn't put Eredion, or any other desert lord, through that agony again.

Never again. Never. Never. Never.

Tanavin snored again, his arms tightening around Alyea, and Deiq fought the urge to rip the red-haired boy away from her and fling him through a wall. It wouldn't be safe; Tanavin very nearly matched a ha'ra'ha for willpower.

Deiq grunted softly, remembering that Tanavin already *had* gone against a first-generation ha'ra'ha—and won. At full strength, Deiq knew, he could have done the same; but right now. . . .

"I don't think I want to tangle with this one," he said aloud. "What's he doing here, anyway?"

Eredion rubbed his eyes. "He came in late last night with a message from Idisio."

He briefly related their conversation. Deiq listened, frowning and anxious, then said, "What are you doing about it?"

Eredion shook his head. "Not much I can do, really. Filin and the others all left for the southlands yesterday morning, and they wouldn't have traveled past Bright Bay in any case. If Azaniari was home, I'd send her without hesitation, but you said she's staying on with Scratha to help him restore the fortress. There's nobody else nearby I would trust to send after a mad ha'ra'ha; *I* can't leave, and you . . . won't. So I don't know what help we can send him, unless you know something I don't."

"No," Deiq said, and sat back in his chair with a deep sigh. "I can't think of anything. I just hope she doesn't hurt him."

"I remember," Eredion said tentatively, "that you've been known to travel . . . quite a way . . . in short order. In the past."

Deiq shook his head, looking down at his hands. "Not any longer," he said. "There's a high price involved these days, for any real distance. I won't do it."

"Feeding," Eredion guessed.

Deiq didn't answer. Sensing Eredion looking at him, he glanced up and met the desert lord's questioning gaze; saw the double intent of that comment.

"No, Eredion. I don't want to hurt you again." He was far too restless and distracted, this time, to mask the draw as he'd done before; and didn't want to look a second time at what Ninnic's child and the tath-shinn had done to Eredion's defenses. Feeding from Eredion, at this point, was to become an accomplice to that cruelty.

"The longer you wait," Eredion said tartly, "the more it *will* hurt. There's not really a way around it."

"There ought to be," he said, letting his long-standing frustration color his voice.

"But right now, there isn't," Eredion said. "And if Tanavin wakes up angry, he'll flatten you, in your current state, even more easily than the tath-shinn did. You *have* to let me help you. Alyea *needs* you upright and sane."

"Damn it, *no!*"

Eredion's mouth quirked in a bitter smile. "I never thought I'd see the day," he said, "when I pleaded with you to hurt me."

The attempt at humor only added to Deiq's frustration. "It shouldn't *be* like this. Something's wrong."

Eredion hesitated. "If there is," he said with audible care, "the teyanain are the only ones who might know about it. And the ketarches—but they don't seem to be as helpful as they used to, these days."

Deiq grunted, thinking about the story behind *that*; not something he wanted to get into with Eredion, now or any other time. Although it went a long way to explaining why they'd held a supply of stibik handy, now he thought about it.

"No, all the same," he said, not meeting Eredion's gaze. "And stop asking, or I'll put you through a wall."

Eredion stood. "Fine," he said crisply. "Then let's go for a walk. They'll be asleep for hours yet, if I read it right. Sitting here and staring at them will only aggravate you more. I'll leave instructions not to disturb them."

"No," Deiq said, his gaze returning to the bed. The utter relaxation, the trust, in Alyea's limp body as she lay against a complete stranger made his eyes blur strangely for a moment; not tears, not even other-vision: more of a strained unfocus. He blinked hard and looked away again. "No, I'm not going to leave her side just yet. I'll be fine."

"Deiq—"

"Go tell the king Alyea will apparently be fine." Deiq didn't look at Eredion as he spoke; unexpected bitterness thickened his throat. "If he wants . . . to visit . . . I'll step aside." He blinked again, and swallowed darker words.

A long silence ensued, in which Deiq could feel Eredion's emotions shifting through worry and exasperation. At last the Sessin lord said, "I won't be long."

"Take as long as you need," Deiq said. He couldn't look at the bed, couldn't face Eredion's expression. He stared at the floor, at the curtains, battling a strong desire to pace the room.

"Stubborn," Eredion said dryly. "Is there going to be more blood in here when I come back?"

Deiq didn't answer. After a few moments, Eredion snorted and left without further protest. Deiq listened to the Sessin lord's departure until the sounds of booted feet ticking against stone floor faded into the small sounds of servants and nobles moving around their various businesses.

On the west side of the mansion, someone was singing; a servant, from the sound of it, washing clothes or going about some other mundane task. Deiq distracted himself by trying to figure out what day it was, and finally, hazily guessed at Fireday; centuries ago, in at least one now-obscure southern village, it had been bad luck to wash clothes—a water-based activity—on a fire-dedicated day. It might be Lordsday, though, in which case an entirely different village would have said. . . .

He blinked, realizing he just didn't care about historical trivia at the moment, and went back to watching Alyea slowly, visibly, heal from the inside out—in the arms of a boy no older than herself, who'd already damn near killed one powerful ha'ra'ha.

He stayed in the chair, and watched, and waited—very quietly.

Chapter Sixty

The stifling humidity of late summer had reclaimed the air. By the time Eredion walked a block, he could feel perspiration beading across his body. Even two years ago he would have simply adjusted his body temperature and moved through the streets with perfect ease; but that sort of thing was becoming more challenging by the day.

He walked and sweated, conserving his energy for the coming audience with Oruen.

Theoretically, each of the Mansions within the Seventeen Gates had equal access to the palace. There were supposed to be seventeen entrances, each set in a direct-line path. Over the years, many of the entrances had been blocked up or built over, as politics and whim shifted the architecture. Ninnic—which, really, meant *Rosin*—had insisted on blocking up almost every entrance to reduce the danger of invasion from without.

As with any such attempt, it had ultimately failed; the enemies had been inside the whole time. Even as Eredion brooded on that, a tall, broad-hipped woman in palace servant colors stopped in the middle of the street, staring at him. Her black eyes narrowed into a glare, and she ostentatiously slanted her path into a wide circle to avoid coming anywhere near him. Eredion blinked and nodded, keeping his expression bland; feeling her hatred even at the distance she'd chosen.

He didn't blame her one bit.

Eredion turned east, deciding to take the formal entrance rather than the servant's western access. It made no difference to the end result; this being Lordsday, Oruen would be in his centrally located "casual room", no doubt negotiating and discussing southern matters. But going through the servant entrance always depressed Eredion. He'd seen too many servants torn apart for base amusement, and couldn't stand to meet the eyes of the survivors. Like the servant he'd just passed in the street, they glared with unabashed accusation every time he passed through "their" areas; in their eyes an unvoiced, ever-present barrage of questions: *Why didn't you save her? Why didn't you save him? What gave you the right to pick one to save over another? It should have been my lover, my friend, my son, daughter, sister, brother. . . .*

But every time he had saved someone slated for the basement of the Church Tower or marked as a potential victim of guards, king, or advisor— every single time, Rosin had known, and had taken great delight in punishing Eredion—not physically, because physical wounds would heal far too easily. But some other innocent, some *worse* crisis, would be dragged out in front of Eredion, by way of torture . . . and Rosin had known Eredion would still do it again, and had probably known before each rescue, and allowed it, just for the greater joy of tormenting a desert lord.

Eredion hadn't trusted a woman in his bed since his last partner was the target of one such retaliation, just after he'd smuggled a family of four out of the city. He'd only found her final resting place recently, far under the city. She'd had somewhat of a revenge on him then, little though a faceful of rot seemed when weighed against being tossed into the cellars for a mad ha'ra'hain to torture.

He had long ago stopped trusting anyone. Even as the political atmosphere relaxed under Oruen's regime, he found it almost impossible to reverse that habit. Ironically, Deiq probably stood as the closest thing Eredion had claimed to be a friend in years.

The majority of the servants didn't understand any of that. All they had seen, back then, was Eredion's blank stare as their loved ones were dragged before the torturers; all they understood today was that Eredion hadn't stepped forward to help *them.*

Lost in memories of screams and far too much blood, he missed the shuffling skip of feet coming up behind him until a light voice said, "My lord?"

Eredion jerked round, instinct finding no danger, intellect at full alert when he saw the young, battered girl standing behind him.

"Wian," he said, and left it flat, without any questioning inflection at all. She shrank back, her expression wary as she picked up on the implicit warning.

"I thought . . . could I walk with you, lord?" she said, watching his face closely. "I have business in the palace, and I'm . . . I'm afraid to walk alone, lord."

He regarded her with a certain bleak amusement. "That would work on anyone else," he said. "But remember, Wian: now I know who trained you."

Her face, already flushed from the heat and her short run, deepened a shade. "Lord Eredion, I know I haven't always been a good person. But isn't it permitted to try to change? And I *am* telling the truth: I'm afraid to walk alone in the streets. Kippin got away from you! He'd love to get his hands on me again."

"But you don't have business in the palace." Eredion suspected that Oruen wouldn't want to see her right now, on any business at all; without a personal invitation, she wasn't likely to get past the outer ring of officials and flunkies that kept the public from wandering through the palace halls like broody sheep.

She looked away, lowering her chin to her chest, for just a moment; answer enough.

"You want to get into the palace, on my tail," Eredion said, studying her tiny, involuntary reactions to his words, "and even back into the king's presence. To seduce him?"

Wian jerked her gaze back up to his face, mouth pulling into a bitter line. "You think me that much of a whore?" she demanded.

"I think you that much of an opportunist," he said dryly.

"That's higher than I need to reach," she snapped. "And I'm not who he wants in his bed anyway—" She stopped, one hand clapping over her mouth, and made a small whimpering noise.

Eredion sighed, unsurprised. Servants gossiped worse than small children, and that had been bound to come up sooner or later. And the "slip" had likely been entirely intentional, to check his own reaction. Wian was proving to be a very good liar indeed.

"Find your own way into the palace, Wian," he said. "Not at my side. I won't be your pass."

Her back straightened, distress fading into a more honest glare. She turned and stalked away without another word or backwards glance.

Eredion stood watching her go for a few moments, absently admiring her figure and the way anger swayed her shoulders and hips; then shook his head, realizing that reaction had probably been exactly what she intended to provoke.

He'd have to be very careful to be sure that she wasn't allowed, unsupervised, anywhere near Oruen. Not that the man was a fool, but he wouldn't stand a chance against that level of skill.

The guards at the grey door shook their heads as he approached.

"No interruptions," one said. "Sorry. There's a waiting room—"

"I know where it is," he said. "How long?"

They shrugged, expressions bland; he shrugged in return and took himself down the hall to wait.

One of the plainest rooms in the palace, and the smallest, the king's waiting room offered four large, comfortable chairs, a wide couch, two small tables, and—a recent addition—a stack of southern and northern puzzle-games for visitors to amuse themselves with. A wide window let in air; a white screen over the window blocked most of the rising heat but allowed in light. Nothing could be done about the humidity, which had stalked Eredion through the streets and hallways. He was uncomfortably aware of the large damp patches on his shirt and the stink of his own skin.

He thought about retreating to his suite and ordering a bath, or going to the other side of the palace and visiting the sunken baths: one of the few Aerthraim marvels to survive the Purge. A clever diversion of the great river that swirled past Bright Bay to the east, the baths were constantly refreshed, a current of incoming water propelling dirty water out through a filtered drain.

Eredion had never been sure whether Rosin had left the baths in place for their usefulness or simply because taking them out would have meant ripping up half the palace floors in the process; more likely the latter. For all his manipulative guile, Rosin had been remarkably short on patience for extended projects—especially if they inconvenienced him in any way.

Finally deciding that he couldn't risk missing an opening in which to talk to the king, Eredion stayed put. He'd pick up some spare clothes from his suite before returning to Peysimun Mansion—and hope that Lady Peysimun would be gracious enough to permit him a tub bath instead of throwing him out, now that Alyea was relatively awake.

Although what the woman would say if she walked in to find her daughter stark naked and wrapped up in a close embrace with what she could only see as a common mercenary—and Deiq standing watch without protest . . . Eredion shut his eyes and covered them with a hand, realizing he really should have stayed.

And he would have stayed—except that Deiq had told him to go. Finally, too late, he recognized what Deiq had done: reinforced the suggestion with such a subtle push that it hadn't registered at the time.

"Gods *damn* it," he said aloud, exasperated. No wonder he hadn't caught it; Deiq didn't normally bother with *subtle*. But he didn't feel any less stupid. "That bloody ta-karne!"

A slight cough from the doorway brought his attention back up. One of the guards stood there, eyes crinkled with restrained amusement but expression politely grave.

"He's ready to see you now, Lord Eredion," the guard said, bowed, and retreated to his post once more.

"Thank you," Eredion sighed, and hoisted himself to his feet. Glancing back, he saw the dark sweat stain he'd left on the chair and grimaced in distaste.

It was something of a relief, when Eredion stepped into the king's casual room, to see that Oruen looked no less sweaty and uncomfortable. He'd even abandoned the official robes and sat in a simple pair of light desert trousers and shirt, barefoot, his hair drawn up into a topknot. Eredion smiled, recognizing the dual purpose: this casual presentation would put southerners more at ease than visiting with a formally-attired northern king.

Oruen rose and bowed as Eredion entered, smiling in apparently genuine welcome. "Lord Eredion," he said. "Honor to you this Lordsday." He went down on one knee, briefly and a bit awkwardly, then stood again, his eyes narrowing as he checked Eredion's face for reaction.

Eredion blinked, taken aback, then grinned. "Oh, you *have* been digging through the old books, haven't you?" he said. "I haven't heard that one since the days of Lord Arit."

Oruen spread his hands, shrugging. "In the absence of Chacerly and Micru," he said, "that's my only source of information on proper custom. I'm rather surprised at all they didn't tell me, actually. I should have started reading for myself a long time ago."

"I'd be more cautious of trying to follow the old books," Eredion said, deciding to angle the conversation away from Micru as quickly as possible. He didn't want to let the king ask the questions that had to be on his mind regarding that topic. "You'd do better to find a loremaster for your court, if you want to know the right way to do things."

"How do I go about hiring one?" Oruen motioned Eredion to a seat and sank into his own chair, frowning.

Eredion sat down on the least expensive-looking chair. "You don't *hire* loremasters, Lord Oruen. You negotiate for one. You offer inducements and promises, and a place for them to gather undisturbed; because loremasters work alone much of the time, but when they gather, it's like a flock of starlings in your yard: they arrive in dozens and settle in for a while."

"And leave a mess on their way through?" Oruen supplied wryly.

Eredion laughed, startled at the image. "Not really," he said. "Not in a physical sense. But they are awfully demanding, and touchy, and gatherings can sometimes be a bit difficult to host."

"You're not presenting a good argument for me to bring one into my court."

"No. I suppose not."

Eredion sat back in his chair, reflecting that Oruen likely wouldn't trust any individual advisors suggested to him at this point; the man wasn't a complete fool. He had to have figured out that anyone standing by his side to offer advice on the southlands wouldn't be an impartial source. A loremaster contingent in Bright Bay, while a complication for some issues, would solve several others.

"Still," he said at last, "loremasters are valuable, if you truly want to understand how to deal with the southlands. I think that would be a better use of your time and resources than searching through outdated books on southern etiquette—I'm surprised any even survived the Purge, come to that."

"A few were hidden well enough to escape discovery." Oruen tilted his head as though thinking about that, then added, "Or perhaps were left as irrelevant and ultimately misleading."

Eredion smiled. "You're learning, Lord Oruen."

"Don't patronize me," Oruen said without heat. "How's Alyea?"

"Healing," Eredion said. "She's going to live."

Oruen's utter stillness lasted for several breaths. He blinked several times, staring at nothing in particular. At last he cleared his throat, focused on Eredion again, and said, "Good. And Deiq is still with her?"

"Yes."

"I want to see him." The thread of emotion underlying that statement promised an ugly discussion. "I want him to come *here* and present himself to *me* this time." The king's lips thinned, the skin around his eyes tightening.

Eredion's stomach turned over. "Lord Oruen—"

"And I expect *you* to stay with Alyea while he's attending on me," Oruen went on, ignoring Eredion's attempt to speak. "I don't believe I need your interference this time, Lord Eredion."

"This is a very bad idea, Lord Oruen," Eredion said steadily, resisting the impulse to screech at the man. "There's nothing good can come of any conversation between you two right now. Please—you've allowed me to be your voice of reason so far; listen to me again. Don't summon him like a servant. Not right now. You're both too upset."

"Phrase it to him however you like," Oruen said. "But send him to me, and make it *clear* he does *not* have the option to refuse the summons."

Eredion drew a deep breath, organizing words. Before he could say anything aloud, Oruen stood, his expression far colder than the air around them.

"Honor to you, Lord Eredion," the king said pointedly.

Eredion stood slowly, weighing the risk of pushing the issue against the danger of obeying; and made one last attempt: "Lord Oruen, *please.*"

The king regarded him with an implacably flat expression and said nothing.

Eredion jammed his teeth together against the scathing observations about Oruen's mental capacity that he wanted to make. He settled for offering a stiff bow and stalked from the room without waiting for the return honor.

Chapter Sixty-one

Easing into a light meditative trance helped Deiq's frustration and brought a detached clarity to his thoughts. Facts unrolled in his mind, a slow, steady procession of logic: Alyea had fought him from the first. Had turned against him at every opportunity. Showed none of the reactions that should be present by now, and had gotten herself badly injured through her refusal to listen to him.

Through my own damn idiocy, the bleak part of his mind insisted. *I made a hash of this.*

He focused on his breath and blanked his thoughts until detachment took over again, washing away the queasy self-loathing. Alyea was as much to blame as he himself; if she'd allowed him to train her properly—hells, if she'd just listened on the matter of the kathain. . . .

Recognizing a slide back into emotional thinking, he shook his head and went back to just breathing for a time. Eventually, the outer suite door opened and Eredion's distinctive energies approached. Deiq eased himself slowly from the trance and looked up, blinking to make sure his eyes were still set in human-normal patterns.

Eredion appeared to have just come from a hasty tub-bath. He'd changed his clothes, and his black hair was slicked back into a single long, damp braid.

"Hot out there," he said, settling into a chair. He glanced at the sleepers for a long, thoughtful moment.

Deiq studied Eredion's face, residual clarity bringing into focus tiny wrinkles around mouth and eyes, the taut line of the man's shoulders, the tilt of the head. Eredion wasn't looking at Alyea; he was avoiding looking at Deiq.

He gave it a few moments, then said, flat and cold, "What happened?"

Eredion sighed and sat back in his chair, looking directly at Deiq. "Oruen wants to see you. I don't think it's a good idea, but he's insisting."

"Huh." Deiq sorted through what hadn't been said, and the various small implications of what had; then nodded slowly. "I'll go. Don't leave them alone."

"I won't. He's in his casual room. Deiq—" Eredion hesitated, as though wanting to say more; settled for a grimace and head-shake.

Deiq stood, offered a sour grin, and said, "Don't worry. I won't."

As he went through the door, the echo of Eredion's hard, worried exhalation hung in the air.

Bright Bay had begun as a cluster of mud-walled huts, a stinking display of the worst human architectural and engineering logic. The Aerthraim corrected the stink with their ingenious drainage system, which kept all but the poorest areas of the city from flooding under every storm; the architecture had been more random.

The logical thing to do, in extreme heat, was to build an enclosed city with thick walls to keep heat out and large, low windows to let breezes in; as the Fortresses, by and large, had done. Bright Bay initially tried to copy that model, but had to struggle against flooding, which the Fortresses rarely encountered. In addition, over the centuries, different kaens had decided to make their differences from the southlands clear; and finally, the rise of the Northern Church had pushed building designs into an entirely new direction.

As Deiq walked around to the servants' entrance, he idly catalogued the spots where the original, thick walls were still visible, and where additions to the palace had changed to thinner, less logical styles. The servants' side held to the old; centuries of tough ivy carpeted many sections of wall and pathway, resolute against the smothering heat and unaffected by foot traffic. The sprawling, lumpy roots and tendrils rolled lightly under Deiq's weight; he smiled a little, remembering when this section of path had been clear of any ivy. Ripping it out now would likely destroy the brick underneath; in the relatively short span of Ninnic's reign, the ivy had been allowed to take over, any gardening around the servants' areas severely neglected.

He took the servants' hall entrance, not inclined to walk through kitchen, laundry, or stillroom; moved through the least-used corridors, avoiding guards and servants alike. The heat wavered higher and lower as he went through sections with thin and thick walls. Towards the center of the palace, the walls were much thinner and the heat climbed sharply.

The people who hurried past, not really seeing him, had faces shiny with sweat and dark patches on their clothes. Deiq shook his head, amused by human idiocy. If they had any sense, they'd have Aerthraim engineers in to redesign the entire palace; but humans never had displayed much in the way of sense.

He paused just before entering the hallway that led to Oruen's casual room, thinking of the several hidden passageways that would take him in without any announcement or alert. Amusing as that would be, however, Deiq could almost see Eredion's anxious expression at the very thought: it would set Oruen on edge, and this wasn't the time for games. He snorted and went around the corner.

He allowed the guards to announce him into Oruen's presence with proper courtesy this time, and even offered a formal bow—then sat down before the king could. Oruen grimaced at that discourtesy but made no open protest.

"Lord Oruen," Deiq said, again not waiting for the king to take the lead, and laced his fingers together in his lap. "You asked to see me?"

Oruen stared down at him, his expression stony. "You assured me," he said, "that you were here to protect Alyea. And yet she seems to have done more to take care of you, in the past days, and has seen remarkable little in the way of safety from your presence."

He paused, watching Deiq's expression. Deiq stayed still, his teeth set lightly in his tongue, and said nothing. It was a normal human reaction, after all, to seek a target other than the true fault; especially when emotion was involved.

"She was only attacked to get leverage on *you*," the king added, his eyes narrowing.

"By men who thought me nothing but a merchant, and Alyea nothing but my whore," Deiq pointed out. The king's eyes went nearly to slits. Deiq went on, unhurriedly: "She would have been able to get free on her own if Kippin hadn't been involved, and I had no reasonable way of knowing about that complication, Lord Oruen. Once I did find out, I moved to take care of the situation."

"You broke both of a guard captain's arms, injured several other guards, wrecked three city properties, and almost got Alyea *killed*."

Deiq set his teeth together and drew in a long breath through his nose, then said, "And your point, Lord Oruen?"

"Your immunity only goes so far," the king snapped.

"No," Deiq said. "My immunity has *no* limits, Lord Oruen. I suggest you not test that fact."

Oruen glared. Deiq returned a deliberately bland stare.

"I want you out of this city," Oruen said. "Now. Tonight. And I don't want to see you within the borders again."

"I'll spare you the embarrassment," Deiq said, not moving, "and forget you just said that. Care to try again?"

Oruen's lips pressed together into a hard, thin line for a moment; then he said, "I'm going to see Alyea. And *you* will not be present. Is that somewhat more *acceptable*?"

Deiq blinked slowly, considering, then said, "She's still asleep. I don't know when she'll wake up, Lord Oruen."

"When she *does*."

"Of course." Deiq stood, aiming a bleak grin at the king. "Is there anything else, Lord Oruen?"

Oruen didn't move; his glare could have etched glass. "Get out."

Deiq bowed. "Honor to you this Lordsday," he said with cultured irony, and left without looking back.

After returning to Peysimun Mansion, Deiq sent Eredion off to tend to whatever matters he found necessary—largely, keeping Lady Peysimun from coming into the room, at this point—and resumed his vigil.

Soon afterwards, Tanavin, still fast asleep, gave a low moan. His arms tightened around Alyea and one hand slid from safe to dangerous territory, prompting a low, murmuring sigh from Alyea. Without hesitation, Deiq let out a sharp cough.

The boy twitched, grunted with entirely different emphasis, and rolled away from Alyea, his eyes still sleep-hazed. He scanned the floor as though looking for a chamberpot; then his gaze, clearing, came across Deiq. Color flooded, then drained from, his face—and other areas—in rapid succession.

"Bathroom's that way," Deiq said with as much restraint as he could summon. The boy scrambled out of bed and across the room.

Deiq evened his breathing and reached for detachment. If unleashing his temper against the king would have been disastrous, provoking this young mercenary into a fight would have ten times worse consequences.

Now that Tanavin was awake and the room quiet, Deiq could feel the boy's strength, willpower, and determination. The combination produced an odd tickling against the back of his skull that threatened to loose his leashed instincts. The mad ha'ra'ha, without any sense of imminent danger, had probably leapt on the boy with the dim perception that here was an unusually interesting toy.

Hit hard and ran like all the hells. . . .

Deiq set his teeth hard and shoved hunger back into hiding; looked at Alyea, still fast asleep, and decided to pass on all the questions he wanted to ask Tanavin. Far better to simply get the boy out of the area as quickly as possible—for everyone's sake—then erase any memories Alyea might retain of the boy's presence.

It didn't take long, once the boy returned from his ablutions, to subtly steer him out the door with the strong sense that returning would be a bad mistake. He did allow Tanavin—or Tank, as he insisted on being called—to leave behind a few of the strange pieces of jerky he'd used to ease Alyea's pain. Tanavin called them *chich*, and claimed Aerthraim Family had developed them as a way of handling dasta withdrawal fits.

What that implied about Aerthraim activities of late apparently didn't even occur to the boy, and Deiq didn't point it out. Getting him away from Alyea was more important to Deiq than getting involved in a political discussion.

Once the room was clear of the boy's dangerously intoxicating energies, Deiq let out all his air in a long exhalalation, clearing his mind with ruthless determination. Alyea was still fragile; he needed all his focus to clean those precious few moments out of her memories. Damned if he'd let her remember that boy and ask awkward questions about where Tanavin had gone.

Hit hard and ran. . . .

No, Tanavin or Tank or whatever he wanted to call himself at this point was best out of her life forever. And Deiq had plenty of practice with smoothing over awkward spots in human memory; even desert lords weren't really all that difficult.

The challenge, as he knelt beside the bed, came from holding back against the desire to slide a light touch sideways into her deep pool of willpower; he ached to draw, just a tiny bit, from that tempting shimmer. She was so damn *strong*, even after what they'd put her through—and so was Tanavin. Deiq could feel the boy's strength swirling, a rougher, darker color, through hers; like two strands of taffy, wound together in beguiling harmony.

He blinked, focusing, and realized that as tightly threaded together as those strands were, he'd never wipe her mind completely clean. He'd have to untangle too much, and it would wake her at the least and set her off into another rage at worst. Instead, he wove loops around the bookend moments, closing off access to the memories between. It wasn't a perfect fix, and wouldn't last forever; but it should serve to get Alyea through into full health and on a proper learning path again before she started asking dangerous questions.

It did serve to confirm his decision to send the boy away. He'd never have gotten rid of Tanavin if she'd woken before the boy left. Left alone, and without memory to back them up, the ties would eventually unravel and fall away, returning her attention where it belonged: to her teacher.

Not that I've been doing a grand job of teaching, he admitted sourly. *Tanavin might have been better for her after all.*

He'd rarely second-guessed his decisions before, but worry over whether he'd done right nagged at him over the following hours and days. A vast restlessness drove him away from watching over Alyea and sent him walking the streets at all hours of day and night, indifferent to temperature and weather.

Nobody bothered him; even the whores and pickpockets steered clear after a single glance, and no market vendors aimed their pitches to his ears. Deiq knew Eredion was watching him as closely as they both watched Alyea, and as worriedly; he couldn't bring himself to care, didn't have any reassurances to offer.

Alyea just . . . slept; breathing evenly, occasionally tossing with nightmare or rousing in brief panic before slipping under again. He could see her body healing, in tiny increments; what would be left of her mind when she awoke was another question. Had Tanavin been what she needed? Was his own presence superfluous?

At last, uncertainty burning like hot wires laid along every nerve in his body, he went looking for the boy.

The main building of the Copper Kettle, which catered to merchants wealthy enough to travel with horses, guards, and assorted flavors of wagon, sat low to the ground and sprawled over almost a quarter acre of land. A large, well-guarded barn sat at an angle to the inn building, and neatly trimmed hedges, flowerbeds, thick-trunked magnolia and southern white pine trees gave the place an air of genteel nobility.

Deiq stood under one of the magnolias, staring at the inn building, breathing in the thick fragrance of a nearby night-blooming rose and the spent petals of the magnolia that crushed underfoot. Poor mercenaries didn't stay at places like this; but Tanavin's trail, barely faded after two days, led here.

Deciding against direct confrontation, Deiq headed for the barn instead. It was divided into sections: one for horses, one for vehicles, and one for resident grooms and caretakers. He slipped into the stable section, easing past the guards without much effort, and moved slowly along the rows of stalls, sorting through lingering emotional resonances. Halfway through the second row, he felt the queasy, shifting sensation that told him he had found what he'd been looking for.

The stalls at the Copper Kettle were double-chambered; one outer section to hold travelers' tack, the inner stall for the animal. Deiq stepped into the outer section, closing the gate behind him. The horse, a big, black beast with noble lines, lifted its head for a moment, nostrils flaring, then subsided to sleep again without so much as a snort.

Deiq ran a finger lightly over the bridle without removing it from its peg, smiling in wry amusement at what *that* told him; Idisio and Scratha would recognize this horse immediately, but the king would likely never see it in his stables again. *Ha'ra'hain draw coincidences to themselves*, he remembered telling Idisio: here he stood, looking at the horse that had taken Idisio on the first leg of his journey away from Bright Bay, and it had been Tanavin who rode it back into Bright Bay.

He wondered if he'd ever know the full story behind that strange loop-around; but that wasn't important just at the moment. He drew a deep breath and splayed both hands over the seat of the saddle.

Fragments of Tanavin's memories flickered through his mind, near-past and childhood blurring together in a linked stream:

Damn you, Dasin, how could you . . . A glimpse of tousled black hair, a bruised face downcast in deceptive vulnerability . . . Recalling other, younger faces, with heavier marks of abuse and no deceit in their helplessness . . . Tan, don't die . . . we need you, Tan, please . . . A thick metal ring, glowing with fire-heat, and the smell of burning flesh tangled into a searing pain . . . and a killing rage—Dasin, how could you, after having gone through it yourself?

Deiq jerked his hands away and stepped back, throat tight and eyes prickling. He had what he'd come for, and more.

Gods, what humans do to one another. . . .

Tanavin wasn't the best teacher for Alyea. He had far too much to heal from and learn himself, and had only the most marginal notions of his own abilities, despite what he'd already achieved.

But one important recent memory came though clear as daylight: Tanavin had seen Idisio, and the tath-shinn, in Sandsplit Village. Tanavin had even knocked the tath-shinn out, with a blow to the back of the head as hard as the one she'd delivered to Deiq.

He found no satisfaction in that small justice. Tanavin's memory of Idisio's wide, haunted grey stare bored into Deiq's mind.

Tell them I need help, Idisio said. *And to hurry.*

Deiq stared into the darkness, thinking about that. The younger wasn't tainted yet. His eyes, in Tanavin's memory, still held the delicate innocence Deiq had been so loath to break, himself. It wasn't too late yet. . . .

He thought about kin ties, and about his vows; about Idisio's desperation and Alyea's nearly comatose sleep. Eredion would offer up his last breath if Deiq asked it, from duty; but Sandsplit lay too far away: even that wouldn't be enough. To manage any real speed, he'd have to stop multiple times along the way and take innocent lives—*human* lives, as no desert lords were likely to be anywhere along the Coast Road.

"I can't do both," he whispered at last. Tanavin's horse twitched and snorted in its sleep, as if mocking him for his weakness. "I can't, Idisio. I'm sorry. What I'd have to do to get to you in time—I can't."

Long ago, he'd encountered a seer unafraid of telling a ha'ra'ha's fortune, and the man's words had stuck with him ever since: *On the road to redemption, you'll kill at least one of your own kin and deny your elders a life they've claimed.*

Alyea's life was obviously the latter; was Idisio the former? Was his refusal to take multiple lives going to serve as a death warrant for Idisio?

I won't know until it's too late, he thought. *But I can't do it. I won't.*

Deiq let out a long sigh, then left the stall, and the stables, without looking back.

Chapter Sixty-two

Eredion sat, half-drowsing, in a chair beside the bed, slouched over to keep one hand on Alyea's shoulder; physical contact seemed to allow her to rest easier. The chair was too high, and uncomfortable: he wanted to ask for another one, but suspected Lady Peysimun's strained nerves wouldn't tolerate much more in the way of demands from her unwanted guests. He knew she'd tell him to get out altogether if she dared; and that threshold was fast approaching.

He felt more than half-inclined to go if given such an invitation; the room, with its frills and fashionable trappings, depressed him, and keeping vigil at the side of a sickbed had never appealed to him. But with Deiq roaming around in such erratic temper, and Lady Peysimun storming around in her current sour mood, there was nobody else he trusted to take over the job; so he sat, and stayed, as he'd once ordered a trainee to do: and waited for something to change.

A timid knock at the outer suite door brought him to heavy-lidded alertness; he glanced at Alyea, assessing, and decided to risk leaving her side for a moment. If she began to stir, he could be back in a few fast strides to reassure her back to sleep.

He ran his hands through his hair absently as he went to the door; stifled a yawn behind one hand as he opened it, and almost choked.

Wian blinked up at him, her expression sober and serious. "Lord Eredion," she said, just above a whisper. "I brought you a better chair. You looked uncomfortable in that one."

Beside her stood a wide-seated chair in tones of drab and purple; the frame was studded with yellow and white stones. It had to be the ugliest piece of furniture he'd ever seen.

"It's more comfortable than it looks," Wian said, seeing his expression. She folded her hands together and put her shoulders back a bit. "It's also an apology, Lord Eredion. For trying to get into the palace on your tail." She held her chin up and met his gaze directly. "It's hard to change years of habit."

He let out a long breath. "Yes," he said. "It is. Thank you for the chair."

She nodded; then an impish smile flitted across her generous mouth. "Don't let Lady Peysimun know I brought it to you."

"I'd rather not let her know anything at all," he said before tact could cut in to stop him; exhaustion always loosened his tongue.

Wian bobbed her head once in a sharply understanding nod. "I'll keep her away."

Eredion nodded in return and picked up the chair. As he retreated into the room with it, Wian reached out a thin hand on which mottled bruises still predominated and gently pulled the door closed for him, leaving herself in the hallway; he heard the soft patter of her bare feet as she trotted away.

Alyea began to stir just as he settled the new chair into place; he sat down hastily and laid his hand on her shoulder. She quieted, her breath smoothing out and deepening. He relaxed back into the chair, realizing that it stood lower than the old one, and the weirdly curved back fitted into his lower back perfectly. Wian was right: the chair was ugly as all the hells, but comfortable.

He tucked a small cushion behind his head and slipped into the first serious doze he'd managed all day.

Alyea slept for three days after Tanavin's departure, not even waking to use the bathroom or eat. Being alone in the room roused her to a half-awake, panicky stupor; Deiq's voice or touch started her tossing and moaning in her sleep, as did her mother's presence.

Eredion hadn't gone without proper sleep for so long in years; at last, he discovered that if he actually lay down on the bed, as Tanavin had done, she stayed quiet and he was able to fall into a restful level of light sleep.

Wian held to her promise: she proved able to invent apparently endless tasks, questions, and minor crises to keep the stiff-necked Lady Peysimun distracted.

To placate Lady Peysimun's sense of modesty—and to keep from being thrown out of Peysimun Mansion altogether— he tried not to be caught sleeping beside Alyea when the aggrieved woman came to visit. Wrapping Alyea in a warm nightgown as extra security proved useless; she managed to slither out of any garments within the hour, so Eredion settled for having a light blanket to hand and tossing it over her as soon as he heard the outer door opening.

By the third day, he was growing accustomed to the routine of waking to use the bathroom, returning to reassure Alyea, then reaching out mentally to check on Deiq before stretching out to sleep once more. There seemed little else to do; her wounds were healing, if a bit slowly by desert lord standards. He couldn't very well receive visitors or handle business while sitting at a sickbed; Wian brought him meals twice a day, slipping in to quietly set a tray on the table in the outer room and withdrawing without a single word.

She did seem to be trying; not that he trusted her, but he did admit to a certain empathy with her efforts to become a better person.

Eredion was holding Alyea in a loose embrace, half-drowsing and thinking about all the ways he'd been fighting to overcome his own past mistakes, when she finally stirred and said, groggily, "Whahhh?"

He propped himself up on an elbow as she rolled to face him.

"Good morning," he said, smiling. "Or perhaps good evening. I've lost track."

She rubbed her eyes and stared at him as though deeply puzzled.

"*Gods*, I have to *piss*," she said abruptly, swung to her feet, and bolted from the room, moving with surprising speed and grace for someone who'd been in bed for three days.

Eredion sat up, grinning, reflecting on the incentive power of a full bladder.

"Wonder if the ketarches could harness that somehow," he murmured to himself.

While he waited for her to return, he stuck his head out into the front room and sent Wian, who'd stayed near—whenever Deiq wasn't around—for a tray of food. A *big* tray of food. Then he dragged the small dining table and two chairs into her bedroom, to spare her the extra few steps and grant her a bit more feeling of security while she ate; the decorations might not reflect her personality, but any sleeping room assumed a sense of sanctuary after a few days of constant occupation. The less strain she felt at the moment, the better.

Alyea came back, moving much more slowly than before; detoured around the table without seeming to notice it, and flopped onto the bed with a deep, pained sigh.

"I don't think a piss has ever felt so damn good," she said, staring up at the ceiling.

"Tray of food on the way," Eredion said, sitting on the edge of the bed and smiling down at her. "How do you feel?"

"Hungry. Ravenous. And *sore*—what happ—" She stopped, shut her eyes, memory visibly returning at last. "Oh," she said very quietly.

Eredion put a gentle hand on her knee and rocked it lightly.

"Easy," he said. "It's over. You're safe. You're back home."

She looked up at him with a bleak, dark stare. "They said he wasn't coming. He didn't care enough to ransom me. I thought he would come for me."

Eredion rubbed a hand over his face and grimaced, seeing yet another aspect of the hell she'd endured.

"Not that simple," he said. "He made a bad mistake in judgment. He thought the people who'd taken you were just . . . people. Just humans looking for money from a rich man. It wouldn't be the first time someone's tried that on him. And you're a desert lord. You could handle yourself. He didn't see a need to rescue you. He thought you'd be walking back in the door any moment after tearing your captors apart."

"I started to," she said, and shut her eyes again. "It took me too long."

Eredion didn't say anything, just kept his hand on her knee and waited, breathing steadily against the pain he could feel raging through her. Not bad enough to give her one of the chich sticks that Tanavin had left behind; too intense for her to hear anything he said just then.

At last, when her agony eased, he said, "I'm sorry, Alyea. It's my fault you went through all that; if I'd taken care of Pieas long ago, or connected important information sooner, you'd never have even seen Kippin's face."

"Was that his name?" she said, voice oddly blurred. "He never introduced himself. He just told . . . Tevin . . . what to do." She paused, breathing hard. "Is he dead?"

"No," Eredion said. Sparing her from the truth wouldn't do any good. "He bolted before we got to your room. So did your cousin Kameniar. I don't know what Tevin looked like, so I don't know if we got him or not."

She gave him a brief but too graphic description; he bit his lower lip for a moment, steadying his voice before speaking again.

"No," he said. "I don't recall seeing anyone like that." *Among the dead*, he added to himself. "He must have jumped through the window with Kippin."

"The window. . . ." she said, and sat up, frowning. "Something familiar about the curtains. Where did they take me?"

"Kippin's father had an aunt that lived on the edge of town. Lady Arnil. She died a few days ago, and Kippin inherited the estate."

Alyea threw back her head and barked bitter laughter.

"Ironic," she said. "I sent Wian to Lady Arnil years ago to keep her safe from Ninnic. And now it turns out Wian betrayed me, and the place I sent her for safety was probably the most dangerous spot in Bright Bay I could have chosen. Gods, I'm an idiot."

Eredion didn't say anything, disinclined to lie. She *had* been stupid, dangerously so, and still didn't know the full extent of what she'd carelessly flung herself into. But this wasn't the time to go into all that, and she wasn't ready to understand most of it yet, anyway.

Wian came in from the sitting room, a laden tray in her arms. She set it down on the table without a word and began to withdraw, her gaze fixed on the floor.

"Wian," Alyea said, "wait."

The servant girl paused and snuck a fearful glance at Alyea. Eredion, watching, restrained a sigh. Wian was so used to deception that he doubted she knew how to give an honest reaction. He didn't interfere. Either Alyea could see through the act or she couldn't; either way, this particular matter wasn't any of his concern.

Alyea regarded the apparently nervous girl for a moment without saying anything, then pursed her lips briefly and said, "I'm sorry. I judged you more harshly than I should have, Wian. I didn't understand . . . the choices you've made." She paused. "Lady Arnil's dead, I'm told. Where are you going to go?"

Wian blinked, looking honestly surprised. "I thought . . . your mother's been very kind," she stammered. "I hoped to stay on here after you recovered."

Eredion kept his mouth firmly shut on his opinion of *that* idea, but Alyea's expression mirrored his thought. "I think I'd rather put a fox into a henhouse," she said. "You can't be foolish enough to think I'd let you come back *here*."

Wian's face turned a deep crimson. "So much for your apology!"

"I meant that whole-heartedly," Alyea said without taking offense. "That's an entirely separate issue. No. I won't have you working inside these walls again. I'll be happy to find you something more suitable, something that *will* be safer this time."

"I don't need your *pity*. I'll manage just fine on my own." Wian tossed her head and stormed from the room.

Alyea made no effort to call the angry servant back.

"I'll make sure she has enough money to go wherever she wants," she said, almost to herself, as the door to the hall slammed shut. She stood and crossed to the table, looking over the food with visibly awakening hunger. "Are you going to have any of this?"

At Eredion's amused head-shake, she dropped into one of the chairs and began eating, as he'd expected, with enormous appetite. He stayed where he was and watched her, reflecting that Alyea had just shown surprising political maturity. He knew Wian would never understand the rudeness, or the reasons behind it; the servant girl clearly believed she'd done the right thing all the way along the line.

Wian had acted from the perfectly valid need to stay alive. But that drive, unmitigated by moral restraint, had led her to some treacherous decisions. Once broken, never fully mended, as an old desert saying ran; Wian would always, under pressure, bend to the strongest hand. Kippin had that strength in full measure, and knew her weaknesses—and he was still on the loose, quite likely plotting revenge. Leaving Wian in the Peysimun household would be like hanging out an open invitation, as Alyea had said, for the fox to raid the henhouse.

Eredion shut his eyes, remembering, with a stab of deep pain, that Alyea—the same girl he'd once used as a pawn to shame his own nephew—had kept fighting though the same brutality that had broken Wian. If they'd found Alyea even a half day later, he wouldn't be thinking about her tactlessness, but preparing for her funeral.

Tray cleared, Alyea sat back, let out a thoroughly unladylike belch, and said, "Why were you in bed with me?"

"To keep you calm," Eredion said, not in the least disconcerted by her abrupt return to questioning him. He stood and crossed to sit in the chair across from her.

It was typical of new desert lords to switch topics rapidly, as they adjusted to the increasing speed of their thoughts. He found it a reassuring sign that some necessary internal changes were finally beginning to kick in.

Eredion smiled at her intent expression, keeping his muscles relaxed and his own expression calm. "You seemed to rest better when someone was with you. You didn't react well to your mother or Deiq, so I've been sitting at your side. Now and again I needed to get some sleep myself."

"Deiq," she said, her stare never wavering. He had a feeling she hadn't heard anything past that name. "I think we're due a talk, he and I."

Eredion was deeply relieved to see Alyea's fighting spirit rise, unbroken, to the surface once more. That meant more to him than the state of her body; if Kippin had succeeded in breaking her spirit, she'd have been worse than useless as a desert lord.

He sharply cut off that chain of thought before it went to its inevitable conclusion. No need to go there, as she obviously hadn't broken.

"Yes," he agreed, "you are. But the king wants to talk to you, and your mother wants to see you. And then I need to explain a few things to you, before you talk to Deiq."

"You first. Then Oruen. *Then* my mother."

He considered, studying her closely, trying to decide if she'd stabilized enough to have a long conversation with anyone. She still seemed a little pale around the edges, and her hands tended to tremble, but the determination in her eyes showed enough strength for at least a brief talk.

At least she seemed not to remember the incident with Tanavin. That was a relief. He hadn't looked forward to that explanation at all. Eredion also found himself deeply relieved that Deiq had taken to disappearing from the mansion for hours at a time. His hovering right now would make the issues even more volatile.

"You ought to reverse that," he said mildly. "Your mother, the king, then me."

"No. You first. Talk."

"All right. But if I say you need to rest, you're going to listen to me. We can pick up the talk later. Agreed?"

She made an impatient gesture. "I'm *fine*."

"Promise or I don't talk."

She snorted. "Fine. I promise."

He nodded, then looked down at his hands, trying to think how to begin. He considered numerous approaches, abandoned them all one by one; as he'd been doing since he'd volunteered, days ago, to take Deiq's place for this particular talk. Faced with a blank slate holding no ideas at all, he sighed and said, "I wouldn't call it love. Don't ever make that mistake."

Glancing up, he saw he had her full attention. Not surprising, with that opening. He smiled wryly and went on:

"There's always been something of a . . . translation difficulty between humans and ha'reye. They don't have any words to match our concept of love, which has led humans to believe that ha'reye don't possess any tender emotions. That's not quite true. Ha'reye are probably some of the most passionately emotional creatures you'll ever meet—but they channel their emotions into specific goals. By their view, humans waste their emotional energies all over the place, like water leaking through a sieve. Ha'ra'hain have just as much passion, but they constantly battle their human urge to waste against their ha'rethe urge to conserve. It's not surprising how many of the First Born went mad, before we learned how to help them through that conflict."

Alyea nodded, her eyes bright, as though finally understanding a number of things all at once.

"Add in," Eredion said, "that a ha'ra'ha usually lives for hundreds of years, and you've got a real translation problem when it comes to setting the human concept of love against a ha'ra'ha or ha'rethe's needs and desires. You just can't *love* something that can't understand you, can't match your strength in any way, and is doomed to die in a relatively few years. It's like loving a fish in a tabletop bowl. All it does is break your heart a dozen times a year."

"But desert lords. . . ." Alyea said, tone questioning.

He nodded. "Desert lords are the closest match ha'ra'hain can hope to find outside their own kind," he agreed. "We live much longer, we're strong enough to at least hold our own most of the time, and we're enough a part of their world to have a hazy understanding of their lives. But most of the surviving ha'ra'hain, over the years, have opted to stay closer to their ha'reye roots, and tend to live either underground or in the water, or, if possible, both. Deiq's one of maybe five true ha'ra'hain walking the human world right now, and I include Idisio and his mother in that number. And Deiq is the only First Born doing it."

He paused, thinking back over what he'd just said.

"Has anyone ever explained the differences between the ha'ra'hain to you, Alyea?"

She shook her head mutely.

"First Born," Eredion said, "were the original offspring of the Agreement."

Her face lost color rapidly, and he almost stopped there, afraid she needed to rest before hearing more. But then she said, in a thin voice, "So Deiq is . . . *really* old."

"Ah. Yes." Eredion cleared his throat. "I thought . . . didn't you already understand that?"

"I asked him once how old he was. He wouldn't answer. I thought perhaps a hundred years or so." Alyea swallowed hard, color slowly returning to her face. "And Lord Evkit said . . . something about the Split. But he doesn't *look* any older than thirty! It's so hard to think of him as . . . as older."

"Deiq was already well into adulthood during the Split," Eredion said dryly. "I can see how that would be a shock. I'm sorry, I thought you understood."

She sat staring at nothing for a time, then shook her head and motioned sharply for him to continue.

"Well, there are the First Born, and then there are the first-generation; those are still direct crosses between ha'reye and human, but came out much more stable. I don't know why. In fact, what I'm telling you isn't something one desert lord in twenty even knows, so if you want deeper answers than this you'll do better to ask Deiq." He paused again, watching the small shifts in her face and eyes, then went on. "There are also second-generation ha'ra'hain; those are the ha'ra'hain to human crossbreeds."

"So Idisio's children will be second-generation?"

Eredion started to answer, then stopped to think more carefully. "I don't know," he admitted. "I don't know enough about his heritage to answer that. If his mother is first-generation ha'ra'ha and his father was human, then Idisio himself is second generation, and his children will likely be as human as makes no difference. The traits just don't carry further than that. But we don't know enough about his parentage yet."

"And . . . Deiq?" Alyea said, her voice almost a whisper.

Eredion drew in a long breath, then released it, and said, "I don't know anything about the children of First Born, Alyea, although I'm sure there must be some. But Deiq is unique. Every other First Born . . . went completely insane. They had to be destroyed."

Alyea put a shaking hand over her mouth and stared at him in open horror.

Eredion let the silence rest for a moment, then said, evenly, "At times I have my own doubts about Deiq. But he doesn't kill unless he has to, and he doesn't enjoy killing when forced to it—"

He tried not to think about Deiq's charge into Lady Arnil's house.

"Ninnic's child is a good example what the First Born were like, if the stories I've heard are anywhere near true. And Deiq's nothing like that. Nothing at all like that."

Eredion wondered, privately, if he were trying to convince her or trying to convince himself. With a sigh, he stopped talking, giving her time to think and himself a chance to choose his next words carefully. She was looking decidedly pale again; almost time to put her back to bed.

And hope that change didn't kick in just at the wrong moment. Given how damned long it had been since Eredion himself had trusted someone enough to take them into his bed, and how overpowering a new desert lord could be when the need hit, *no* wouldn't really be an option. Deiq might not enjoy killing, but Eredion doubted the ha'ra'ha would work too hard at controlling his rage if he walked in on *that*.

He shut his eyes and swallowed hard, blocking that image, and train of thought, as swiftly as he could. This was not the time to fantasize, not with Alyea's perceptions edging steadily towards the highest they'd ever be and Deiq's nerves on a raw edge. He had to be very, very careful.

"So I won't say he loves you," Eredion went on when he had his thoughts under control. "That would lead you to some bad assumptions. But he cares, passionately, what happens to you, and about your safety and happiness. Sometimes it won't look like it: he thought he was doing right by denying the ransom demand. We both thought it was nothing but a few bandits out after a rich merchant's money. You could have handled that easily."

She shut her eyes and swayed a little. "I should have," she said in a blurred voice.

"Mm. Time for you to go back to sleep. No, you promised. Come on." Eredion stood and guided her back to the bed. "We'll talk more later. I promise. *After* you talk to Oruen, because he'll have me torn apart otherwise."

She mumbled something, already incoherent and likely not hearing his words at all. He sat beside her and cautiously stroked her hair until she fell into a deep sleep.

Chapter Sixty-three

Exhaustion racked through Alyea, leaving her more incapacitated than pain ever had. Just the small effort of dressing—with, embarrassingly, a servant's help—left her sitting on the edge of the bed, feeling like a limp noodle. Eating a bowl of cold fruit soup and a thick piece of peasant bread gave her enough strength to reach the couch in her outer suite, where she rested in a grey haze, listening to rain patter down in random bursts outside. A welcome cool breeze sifted through the room, dispelling the evil odors of convalescence, stirring vases of dayflowers and bundles of rosemary into releasing their fragrances.

Alyea held up her right arm, studying the smooth skin with an odd feeling of detachment. Only a faint tracing of red lines remained to show the damages, but she remembered: Tevin had set the edge of the knife just *there*, under the elbow, and had traced a sideways cut to *there*, just above the wrist—working the thin blade into the cut, and little by little *peeling*—

She shut her eyes, dropping her arm back to her side, and shook with remembered horror.

"Alyea," Eredion said, and his large hand closed around hers as he knelt beside the couch.

She jerked and let out a sharp yip, pulling her hand away; he let her, then patiently recaptured her wrist. This time she forced herself to relax and allow the contact. His hands felt warm and dry, and a strong pulse thudded in his thumbs.

"Alyea," he said again, searching her eyes as though to check for sanity. His face held a grey tinge. After a moment, he let out a hard sigh and sat back, releasing his grip; her hand prickled with a brief chill. "Gods. Hasn't anyone taught you the first damn thing about shielding yet?"

She stared at him, uncomprehending, then understood. "I wasn't—thinking about being overheard," she said thinly.

"Obviously." He ran a hand over his eyes. "Not that I blame you; that was . . . extreme. But you have to learn to remember . . . even the worst things . . . *quietly*. Or every damn sensitive in the area will see it. And Deiq will—" He stopped short and swallowed back the rest of that sentence, his gaze shifting to one side. His mouth set in a hard line.

"What will—"

"Never mind," Eredion said, tone curt. "This isn't the time. The king's waiting to see you."

He held out a hand. She took it, let him help her up to a proper sitting position. Eredion pushed pillows behind and beside her for support, poured her a cup of hot tea, then left the room, his taut, grim expression unwavering throughout.

Alyea sipped tea and tried to steady her breathing and emotions, feeling as though she'd just awoken from a heart-stopping nightmare and still hung in that aftermath of disoriented uncertainty. Nothing could be the same; her life would divide, in her own mind, as pre- and post-Tevin. She'd thought, previously, that she knew how depraved humanity could be; thought the whipping she'd endured the worst torture she could ever imagine, and the pain of the blood trials the highest end of the scale.

Now she understood those things had been mere annoyances compared to what was really possible—especially for a desert lord who could heal . . . so fast. . . .

She blinked hard and sipped tea, sharply restricting her thoughts to the moment. A grumbling, subterranean unease continued in the back of her mind, chewing over the simple, incredible fact of her survival.

A rattling knock on the door sounded. A moment later, Eredion stepped in and said with brief, cold formality, "Lord Alyea. May I present Lord Georn Oruen." He bowed and stepped out again. Oruen came in, shutting the door behind him.

Alyea felt a chill race down her spine. Oruen had opted to appear in full royal regalia, from blue and grey robes to the heavy formal-court crown. His expression held no trace of humility or friendship; his gaze was distant and aimed somewhere past her. He stopped, four long steps into the room, presented a formal bow deep enough to require a steadying hand on the crown, then seated himself in a well-upholstered chair facing her.

"Lord Alyea," he said, his dark stare settling on her at last. "How does the day find you?"

She fought the urge to respond with familiarity and said, matching the cold in his tone, "Well enough, Lord Oruen. I tire easily still, but that's about it."

"That comes as a relief," he said. "Some reports had me believing you on death's doorstep."

She said nothing, delivering a severe stare instead.

His gaze moved to the thin red lines still visible along her arms, then back to her face. "I am advised, by some," he said, "that I should not involve myself in prosecuting or searching for your kidnappers. That, as you yourself asked that Peysimun Family be made independent, this is, in fact, a desert Family matter."

Alyea's breath caught in her chest. "A valid point," she said, forcing her tone to remain level.

"Other . . . advisors . . . have suggested," Oruen continued, "that the actual crime occurred on Kingdom soil, by the kidnap being on the streets and the . . . damage . . . being performed at Lady Arnil's estate; and thus the matter lies under *my* jurisdiction."

"I wonder who *that* advisor was," Alyea muttered, glancing towards the door.

Oruen was the one who said nothing this time, his gaze dark and sharp.

Alyea studied his fiercely intent expression for a few moments, then said, "So you've just spent an hour listening to my mother and Lord Eredion go at you on the matter from opposing sides, is that it?"

Oruen's mouth moved towards a smile. "Something like that," he admitted. He removed the heavy crown and set it on his lap. "What do *you* want me to do?"

She leaned back against the cushions, seeing the larger question: to reaffirm Peysimun independence, or put herself under the king's authority once more.

"I believe," she said at last, "it's best to allow Peysimun Family to handle this matter ourselves, Lord Oruen."

He nodded as though he'd expected that answer. "I think you'll find some internal resistance to that decision," he said dryly.

"I expect so. I'll handle it. Thank you."

He pursed his lips, his gaze moving again to her arm, then said, "Your mother isn't going to take being set aside as Head of Family lightly, Alyea. Under northern rule, she has status of her own; you're taking that away from her."

"With all respect, I'm not discussing this with you, Lord Oruen."

He stared at her, half-smile fading to a frown, and said, "Can we *possibly* take this out of the formal for a moment or two?"

"Fine. I'm not talking about my mother with you, Georn."

The dry smile returned. "Understood. A more personal matter, then. What happened to you made me realize—I've been a fool." He glanced down and away, the smile gone; his throat worked for a moment. "Alyea, I'm sorry. I only saw political angles—that's how Chac taught me. Without him around, I'm seeing—some things differently."

Alyea said nothing, watching every small twitch of his hands and face with a new alertness.

"Chac was the one who advised me to set you aside; there were alliances that could only be made if I was . . . unattached."

Alyea raised an eyebrow, bleakly amused over where this was obviously headed, and decided to spare them both the embarrassment.

"Georn," she said, "A year ago I would have already been on my knees thanking you. Now I can't help thinking how much more advantageous an alliance I would be than any of the noble daughters who've been courting your attention, and how you'd have Peysimun Family back under your control if I married you."

He shrugged, not in the least offended or surprised. "True. But it's not politics alone that has me here today, Alyea."

She shook her head. "Georn—has anyone told you yet that I'm not likely to have any children?"

His skin went an odd grey shade. "Because of that bastard—"

"No," Alyea interrupted hastily. "It happened during the blood trials."

Oruen's mouth thinned, a flush replacing the shock. "So it's my fault? Is that why you won't—" He stopped, his gaze dropping to his fisted hands.

Alyea regarded him without any sympathy. "Done is done," she said after a few moments. "I made my own mistakes on that road. But I'm not interested in alliance through marriage, Georn; we went to bed together once, that's all, and not even because you loved me. I was there, and I was willing, and you'd just seen something awful; there wasn't anyone else you trusted not to stab you in the back that day. I was . . . I was your kathain."

He shot her a startled, sick glance. She laughed, genuinely if blackly amused.

"Don't make more of it than it was," she said. "Now, if you'll excuse me, I'm feeling tired and would like to rest. Good day, Lord Oruen."

He stood, slowly, staring as though unable to take his eyes from her face. "It's Deiq, isn't it?" he said. "That's what's changed you. His influence."

Alyea leaned her head back and shut her eyes, weariness threatening to swamp her thoughts into incoherence. "No, Lord Oruen," she said. "Not Deiq. I think it's actually something called growing up."

Silence hung in the room. After a few breaths, it was broken by soft, shuffling footsteps, and then by the door quietly closing.

Chapter Sixty-four

The rain made the walk back to Peysimun Mansion quietly pleasant; it matched Deiq's sober mood. He'd spent the day among some of the ghosts from his past, doing what he could to make amends, and thinking about all the mistakes he'd made along the way; remembering, too, more of the seer's words:

Your past holds many deaths that call for an accounting . . . I don't see whether you'll reach the road to the right or the left side of your soul, but you have a long way to walk yet, whatever efforts you make to shorten the path.

At which point a vision of Alyea's battered body came to mind, and he threw himself into his work with renewed attention to push it away.

I almost got her killed. She almost got herself killed.

He couldn't decide which view was more right. In the end, though, his feelings didn't really matter. Alyea would have to pick a side to land on, and he'd have to accept rejection if she placed the blame only on his failure to protect her.

He paused at the gates of Peysimun Mansion, studying the ornate coach in the carriage-way to the right side of the house. Four guards in royal livery stood around the coach, alert even in this drizzly grey weather. No doubt more were stationed indoors.

So Oruen had chosen to make this a formal visit, rather than a quiet slip in through the servants' entrance. More than likely Lady Peysimun's influence was at work there. Or perhaps Oruen had recognized, finally, that this was more than some former lover he was dealing with; in which case, Deiq suspected the man came armed with a proposal of marriage.

He smiled without any humor and eased over to lean against the inside wall near the gates. The guards stared straight at him and looked away without a twitch.

A suddenly intense squall funneled rain down his collar and slicked his hair. He stood motionless, breathing long and even, his gaze on nothing in particular. After a time, his restless thoughts soothed under the grey patter of rain on damp cobbles. He barely noticed when the carriage rattled past him on its way out of the gates.

Sunlight on his face pulled him from the meditative daze. The rain clouds scudded away to the east under a quickening breeze that kept the air cool. He blinked, realizing the king had left; found himself strangely reluctant to go indoors and find out what Alyea's answer had been. He decided to sit in the gardens, instead. Watching bees and butterflies darting round with vigorous intensity to collect freshly washed pollen always amused him. It was even more entertaining than watching paint dry.

Chapter Sixty-five

The door banged open, startling Alyea from a pleasant grey drowsiness. She pushed herself upright to find her mother bearing down on her, face flushed with emotion.

"Oh, gods," Alyea subvocalized, putting both hands up in a warding gesture. "Mother, *stop!*"

Lady Peysimun rocked to a halt, her expression astonished. The color washed out of her broad face, then returned sharply; her hands clenched in the folds of her elaborate, floor-length dress. She'd definitely dressed to impress the king: beadwork swirled in intricate patterns across the sleeves and waist, and the material itself was largely Stone Island white silk, which had to have drained Peysimun coffers significantly. The finery made Alyea feel awkward and slightly grubby, dressed as she was in loose shirt and looser trousers; she'd lost even more weight during recent days.

Her mother took another step forward, astonishment fading towards a scowl.

"I'm still sore all over," Alyea said hastily; not exactly a lie, and she felt a strange aversion to having her mother touch her at the moment. "And I'm afraid of ruining your dress. Please, sit down." She pushed pillows out of the way and sat up, drawing her legs closer in, then pointed to the other half of the couch. "Please? I'll take the hug as a good thought instead."

Her mother stared, her eyes going wide for just a moment, then said, "You thought I was going to *hug* you?"

Alyea's breath stopped in her chest. She forced it to restart, swallowed hard, and said dryly, "A natural reaction to seeing me awake for the first time since my kidnapping, I'd have thought." Not that her mother had ever been particularly affectionate; she sighed, recognizing the same smothered hope in herself that had once been provoked by any smile from Oruen.

"You're *fine*," Lady Peysimun said, and took the chair Oruen had occupied. Her lips spread into a taut grimace as she folded her hands together in her lap. "Despite initial appearances, you seem to have recovered from your little adventure just fine."

Alyea stared, her mouth slightly open. "Adv—? I almost *died*."

"If you'd been anywhere near death," her mother said primly, "you wouldn't be sitting up and talking a matter of days later. I imagine we all misunderstood."

"Good gods," Alyea said. "Did Lady Arnil turn into a *reeven* and possess you when she died?"

"Don't be absurd. Now, there are matters we need to discuss."

"Did you ever meet a woman called Sela?"

Lady Peysimun flicked her fingers impatiently. "Stop that."

Alyea hoisted herself more upright, studying the fine lines around her mother's eyes and mouth. "Do you *really* think it was all . . . fake blood, or someone else's blood, or minor wounds?" she asked. "Do you really think the broken bones were imaginary, or a misunderstanding?"

"I think it's *impossible* that you were as hurt as you appeared to be," Lady Peysimun snapped, her fisted knuckles white, "and are now perfectly fine. So the injuries *must* have been false."

"I think," Alyea said steadily, "I need to tell you the whole story. From the time I left Bright Bay. And I think we'll need another pot of strong tea. Or maybe two."

Over the course of three pots of tea, Alyea told a more complete story of her travels than she'd offered before; and her mother, expression unwaveringly grim, listened without comment and few questions.

Alyea ended with a heavily edited version of her recent encounter with Kippin and her discovery of Kam's involvement in a very ugly group, then sat silent, studying her teacup and waiting for her mother to speak.

It took a long time.

"This is intolerable," her mother said at last, her voice thin. "You've completely upset every single aspect of our lives."

Alyea looked up, frowning at that reaction, and caught sight of a damp shimmer in her mother's eyes. "It hasn't been fun for me either," she said dryly.

"No. I suppose it hasn't." Her mother dropped her own gaze to her teacup, turning it in slow circles. "So I have to tolerate this . . . this Deiq? In my own house? Or is it your house now? Eredion has been trying to explain what your becoming a desert lord means for us, but I don't understand any of it. Everything he said sounded quite mad."

"It's still your house," Alyea said. "Think of me as . . . as an advocate for the entire family now. And Deiq . . . yes. He'll be staying for a while. I . . . I need him."

"Considering the fuss he put up about staying with you, he's not shown his face in this room since you woke up," her mother said tartly.

"He knows I'm safe with Lord Eredion around. He'll be back soon enough."

"I don't know." Her mother shifted restlessly, tilting her empty teacup back and forth in her hands without looking up. "I don't know that I like any of this."

Alyea sat quietly, not sure how to respond. Weariness began to drag at her eyelids.

"This is *impossible!*" her mother exclaimed, setting the cup down and standing abruptly. She paced away, turned, and came back, face flushed with nervous tension. "Consorting with barbarians and monsters—it's not *right*. Can't you just . . . just *resign*?"

Alyea couldn't help it; she leaned back and let out a long hoot of laughter.

"No," she said once she caught control of herself. "I wish I could. But the changes are permanent. And they're not barbar—"

"Yes, I can see you actually believe all these, these, *hallucinations* . . . that some strange creature got you *pregnant* and then took the child before the soul had even entered its body, that another one *spoke* to you and asked you to travel to Arason, of all places; and this Deiq, what you tell me about him—it's ridiculous. It's nonsense. He's a *merchant*, Alyea. Merchants don't turn out to be . . . no. If this fantastical flimflam is your new life, I want no part of it. It's all lies. All nonsense. None of it can possibly be real. They *drugged* you, Alyea, you've been hallucinating all this time. You need to go on a fast and pray to cleanse yourself—"

Alyea stood, slowly, and said, "Mother? Look at me. I'm standing. I'm alive. You thought I'd die when they brought me in, didn't you? But I'm fine, in less time than it would take to mend a sprained wrist. How do you explain that?"

"We must have been mistaken," her mother said, but she looked away and her face drained of color at the question.

"No. You weren't. Let me tell you what I *remember* of what Tevin did to me." Alyea drew a deep breath and began talking. Before she'd finished detailing the first hour of her final captivity, her mother let out a rough sob, whirled, and ran from the room.

Alyea sank back onto the couch and muttered, "I *definitely* should have tried a gentler approach that time."

Chapter Sixty-six

Deiq sat on a bench in the Peysimun gardens, watching blue-speckled king butterflies loft from flower to flower, his thoughts darting like the insects taking advantage of the drying air.

Once again, he faced choices drawn from stupid mistakes: trapped against the hard reality that he didn't belong in the human world, couldn't play by their rules and abide by their ways. He'd been forced to walk away from Onsia and her irrational demands; Alyea, just as rigidly biased in some ways, would never be able to accept Deiq's essential difference.

Especially not now. Not after what her own kind had done to her. He'd seen human victims recovering from brutal torture in the past; it took them years to regain even basic stability. Alyea hadn't trusted him even before the ordeal, and he didn't have years to wait for her mind to heal. He'd missed his chance with her. He should have pushed harder, set aside emotional weakness, told her to ignore the false message. He'd had the *right*, damn it, as her teacher. He should have ordered everyone to clear out and leave them alone, instead of letting an inexperienced child dictate events based on shallow, stupid human politics.

But he hadn't, because he'd been lazy. And now the only paths out led through variations on pain he didn't want to contemplate.

He could feel the hunger gnawing at him again. If Alyea did slide into the full change next time he saw her, it would drag him past restraint; he'd hurt her badly, without time to explain.

Someone moved nearby: Eredion approaching. Deiq hesitated, then stayed still, allowing the Sessin lord to find him.

"Deiq," Eredion said with audible relief a moment later, and sat on the bench without waiting for invitation, tugging the laces on his formal shirt open. The emerald green and sand-tan of Sessin Family colors brought out the sallow exhaustion in the man's face. "Gods, I'm glad you're here. That woman is fucking insane." He rubbed a hand over his eyes and hacked a bootheel restlessly against the pebbly ground. "I'm glad I found you first, actually. It's not a good idea for either of us to go in there right now. Alyea really set her off."

"How?"

"I'm not sure. All I can make out from her screeching is something about you being a monster and me being a traitor, and both of us being responsible for Alyea turning against her."

"All of which," Deiq observed, "is, actually, true."

Eredion shot him a hard sideways glare. "Thanks." He kicked at the gravel again, then, with a hard sigh, bent to pull off his boots.

"You expected sympathy?"

"No. I suppose not. Ahh. . . ." He set the boots aside, stripped off his knee-stockings, and buried his large feet under the pebbles. "Damn, I hate wearing those things these days. Especially in hot weather."

They sat quietly, watching the butterflies, for a time.

"Did you . . . talk to her yet?" Deiq asked at last, not looking at the Sessin lord; trying not to think about the fact that Eredion hadn't protested Deiq's own implicit self-designation of *monster*. It added another layer of silent misery and frustration; he found himself wanting to say *Even now, you see me that way? Even you?*

If even Eredion couldn't let go of seeing Deiq as a monster at core, there really wasn't anything better to hope for from Alyea—after all, he'd almost gotten her killed.

Eredion shook his head. "Started to. Didn't get far. She had to rest, and then the king showed up—and then her mother insisted on going to talk to her. And now she's exhausted again, and sleeping like a rock. I'm hoping she sleeps through the entire of her mother's temper tantrum."

"Has she asked to—see me?" The words slipped free before he could stop them.

Eredion gave him a long, hard stare. "She wants to talk to you," he said after a moment. "I told her I needed to finish explaining some things first."

Deiq exhaled slowly. "So she doesn't know about . . . feeding."

"Not yet. That's the next part." Eredion paused, then added, "I'm starting to see signs that the final changes are kicking in. You ought to stay close, instead of wandering around. It won't be long now."

Deiq's stomach lurched with dread; he changed the topic. "Have we heard anything more from Idisio?"

"Nothing." Eredion hesitated, as though considering whether to allow the diversion, then asked, "Are you thinking of going to find him?"

"No. By this point, he's either dead or on her side. Let the Forest deal with them. Or Arason."

"You don't give him much credit."

"He's inexperienced, and barely adult." Deiq fixed his gaze on a nearby gods'-glory flower, methodically tracing the blue and cream striations on the blossom, the variations of green down the vine and leaves. *It's not my fault. It's not. I didn't have any way to stop it. The price was too damn high.* But that sounded too much like self-pity to voice aloud. He kept his tone hard. "She survived Ninnic's child. He doesn't stand a chance against her."

Eredion let the silence settle for a moment, then said, in a low and carefully neutral tone: "And neither do you, at your current strength."

Deiq blinked hard and stood. *If I'd been at full strength* was a road too painful to go down at the moment, and would leave someone writhing in entirely too much agony at the end.

He couldn't face Alyea, not after how he'd failed her; knowing he would fail her yet again, and hurt her. He couldn't go back to his kin, couldn't stay among humans. There were too many temptations, and sooner or later he'd give in . . . no. *Never again.*

"Where are you going?"

"To walk with other monsters," Deiq said. "And to learn about prayer."

Chapter Sixty-seven

Alyea sipped a cup of delicate mint tea, appreciating the early-morning quiet, and waited for Eredion to speak. He sat across from her at the small breakfast table, studiously attending to his own cup of tea, his head tilting now and again as though to shake thoughts into a better focus.

In contrast to his finery of the day before, he wore a dun and brown outfit made of fine linen; it hung loose from his shoulders and hips, as though he'd lost weight himself, and his dark hair had a dull, dry look to it.

"Your mother," Eredion said finally, "did her damnedest to throw me out last night."

"And failed, apparently."

"She couldn't tell me the order came direct from you, and you're the one in charge here these days. She didn't care for that truth much."

Alyea sighed, pinching the bridge of her nose; hearing echoes of just how bad that fight had been in the dryness of his voice. She resisted the urge to apologize for her mother's attitude. That would only show weakness, and even with Eredion as close to a friend as she dared have at the moment, she knew better than to think he would allow friendship to get in the way of politics. *My job is protecting Sessin Family interests*, he'd said once: a clear warning not to ever really trust his intentions.

She saw a glint in his eye that told her he'd followed that thought; decided not to pursue the point. Instead she said, "Where's Deiq? Did she manage to throw *him* out?"

Alyea half-hoped the answer would be *yes*. She was still more than a little aggravated with Deiq's egotistical arrogance, his manipulative methods. She could have died from his damn *lesson*.

"He left before she could throw him out and hasn't been back since. I'm not entirely sure where he is." He looked uncomfortable for a moment, as though the admission pained him.

"Can't you—" She touched her temple, uncertain whether she had it right; he shook his head.

"He won't answer me, and I can't get a fix on where he is if he won't talk."

"So he ran off to brood; so much for protecting me."

Eredion looked up at her sharply, his dark eyebrows contracting into a scowl. "Don't be an idiot, girl. And don't pick a fight with me as a way of readying to confront your mother, either."

Alyea set her teacup down hard and glared. Eredion returned it with equal intensity. After a moment, she dropped her gaze and grimaced, inclining her head in silent apology.

"Better," he said. "Deiq's not here right now because he's afraid of you, Alyea."

She looked up fast, truly shocked. "Afraid of *me? Afraid?* Are we talking about the same person?"

He nodded, unsmiling.

"Afraid," Alyea muttered, and sipped tea, thinking about that.

The chabi game with Oruen came to mind; she decided to shift the conversation on a tangent, as if it were an *ayn* she might slide diagonally across a chabi board. Perhaps she could even turn the discomfort around onto Eredion and gain an advantage in this already-strange conversation. Afraid? Deiq wasn't afraid of anything.

"Do you know, he told me once that you're his father."

To her surprise, Eredion laughed.

"That's . . . something of a joke between us," he said a bit ruefully. "Obviously, it's not true."

"Why did he lie?"

Eredion sobered. "It's a convenient lie with deep roots," he said. "All I can say is that when he told you that, he didn't trust you. Beyond that you have to talk to him for an explanation."

"Would he tell me the truth now?"

Eredion shrugged, looking uncomfortable. "I don't know," he admitted. "I don't really know how much he trusts you. Probably less than he trusts me, and that's not far at all."

She set her cup down on the table with a sharp click. "But you say he cares? That doesn't make any damn sense, Eredion! When you love someone you trust them! You don't *lie* to them! And you're not *afraid* of them!"

He snorted. "You've still got a very narrow definition of love," he noted. "But in any case, I did warn you not to call his feelings for you 'love'. Don't put human morals and standards onto his actions. He is what he is. He's lied so often over the years I doubt even he knows the truth behind half his words any longer. And he'll lie to you in a heartbeat if he thinks it's best—for him, for you, for a larger cause. But he'll always have a reason for the lie. Usually a damn good reason."

"That's not much comfort," she said dryly. "So far I've heard nothing that endears him to me, Eredion."

The Sessin lord's mouth quirked. "I know. Deceitful, manipulative, ruthless, and dangerously charming doesn't really add up to a nice picture, does it? But the same words could be used to describe Oruen. Or Scratha. Or me, for that matter. If you want simple honesty, Alyea, go find yourself a farmer at the edge of some tiny northern village. But don't look at that farmer too closely, or you might be dismayed by what's under his homespun."

She refilled her cup, not looking at him, and thought about what he'd said. Her anger began to wither a little; had Deiq really believed she'd be fine, left alone with ordinary bandits? She tried to see it from Deiq's point of view, and couldn't quite manage.

"A human," Eredion said after a while, "would lie for his own greed. A swindler out for money, a man sweeping a woman into bed. Small things. Small lies. Small lives. Deiq doesn't care about personal power. He goes through life searching for something to believe in for a few years, something to funnel his tremendous energies into for as long as possible. His Farms are a good example: he developed a passion to make sure the southlands didn't depend on the northern kingdom for food. Once they were established, he backed out and let humans take over. He only keeps his name on the Farms in order to protect the Farms from political shifts."

"What's his passion now?" Alyea asked, propping her chin on one hand and tilting the teacup slowly back and forth in the other.

"At the moment," Eredion said, "I believe he's about to embark on another mad quest to change the world. If he survives long enough."

"Survives?" Alyea sat up straight, alarmed.

Eredion sighed and rubbed at one cheek. "Yes. Survives. Which brings me to what I need to finish explaining. I don't know how to say any of this gently, so bear with me, please. And remember, too, that most of what I know comes from a number of very frank talks with Deiq. I doubt anyone beyond Heads of Family know some of what I'm about to tell you, and I think he's told me secrets even most of *them* don't know. So please don't repeat this information carelessly."

He waited for her nod, then drew a steadying breath, shut his eyes and said rapidly, as though the words actually hurt him, "Ha'reye and ha'ra'hain *aren't human*. They need more than just physical food; not every day, but on a fairly regular basis. Desert lords were created, in part, to fill that need. For ha'reye and ha'ra'hain to feed from."

"What?" Her cup slipped from her hand and splashed tea across the table.

Eredion opened his eyes and regarded her gravely, undisturbed by the liquid dripping into his lap. "Not a pretty picture at all, is it?" he said. "But that's what it comes down to. I've heard a hundred flowery explanations and lovely words about *sharing* and *helping* that miss the point completely. I won't hand you any of that nonsense. Something about a human's willpower, a human's spirit, inner strength, life, whatever you want to call it—Deiq's never been able to really explain it to me—offers a piece of essential nourishment for ha'reye, and by extension, for ha'ra'hain." He paused. "A bit humbling, isn't it, to realize that in exchange for all your new strength and clarity and power you've become nothing more than . . . than a cow waiting to be milked."

She stared at him, utterly appalled, unable to speak.

"I used to think it a noble sacrifice," he said. "When I understood what it really meant, I was horrified. But over the years I've come to something of a balance between the two extremes."

He sighed and rubbed the bridge of his nose with a knuckle.

"I suspect," he said, "your thoughts at the moment are something like: Why didn't anyone tell me before I became a desert lord? How could anyone willingly submit to something so horrible? Why doesn't someone stop it? Am I right?"

She nodded mutely, unable to speak her revulsion aloud.

"The answer is pretty much the same for all those questions," he said. "It keeps those who follow it on top of the stack. It's all about power, Alyea; human ambition, human greed, human desires. The desert Families wouldn't even have viable homes if not for the ha'reye and ha'ra'hain meddling with underground rivers and pushing water up into the Fortress wells. The desert lords wouldn't have crowds simply melt away in front of them, everywhere they go; and if you haven't had that happen to you yet, just wait. It's a horribly exhilarating feeling, and damned seductive.

"You weren't told; *nobody* is, anymore. I didn't know." His face wrinkled as though with painful memory. "Remember, there aren't many true ha'ra'hain walking the surface. Other than the initial encounter during the trial of Ishrai, most desert lords these days go through their lives without ever seeing another ha'ra'ha or ha'rethe other than the one their Fortress hosts, which is probably the one who went through the trials with them.

"And with so much mixed blood in each fortress, the resident ha'rethe or ha'ra'ha can just . . . skim a bit here and there. Nobody even notices. I guarantee it was happening during Scratha Conclave, but you wouldn't even have felt a tickle."

Alyea shut her eyes and put a hand over her mouth, feeling deeply ill.

"Deiq hates it," Eredion said. "He *loathes* it. I've met ha'ra'hain who think nothing of it, who take the milk, so to speak, without any compassion for the cow. Deiq would rather starve himself than take without permission, even though desert lords, by implication, have already given that consent. He insists on personal permission from each and all; but since most desert lords don't even know the truth about this, getting permission usually means explaining first, and he hates the explanation almost as much as the need. If he'd been at full strength, the tath-shinn's blow would have been like a mosquito bite to him. He would have sensed her coming half a mile away.

"He's starving, Alyea. He's been refusing to feed for a long damn time; I'm guessing for over fifty years. I've helped him a little bit over the last few days, but he won't take enough because he doesn't like inflicting pain, and it *hurts* if only one target is used. Even a small draw would kill an ordinary human."

The silence seemed like a living thing writhing in her chest.

"So what. . . ." she said at last, thickly, "What am I supposed to do? Let him. . . ." She stopped, nausea rising in her throat, and breathed hard through her nose until it subsided. "It's obscene."

Eredion sighed. "It is what it is," he said. "One of the changes desert lords normally go through is an increased libido. Yes—I see someone did talk to you about that. Well, that's tied in to this. As . . . compensation, you might say. Or incentive. Or coercion. Whatever you want to call it, it tends to . . . flare up when a ha'ra'ha is nearby. Especially a hungry or wounded one. And it masks—at least somewhat—the pain from the draw." He paused, regarding her with a worried frown. "Only you don't seem to be responding properly."

She felt her face flare into hot color at a sudden memory: Deiq, his hands on her hips, looking up with what she'd taken for a fever-sparkle in his eyes. Then Eredion had shown up without announcement and chased her out—

"*Oh,*" she said, comprehension slamming like a brick into her stomach. "You—"

Eredion winced but kept eye contact.

"Yes. I stepped in that day because he asked me to. Because he didn't want to hurt you. And I already knew . . . what he needed. He's been trying to protect you from that. He wants to find a way to stop it from hurting so much."

He paused with a grimace, as though remembering the pain; Alyea felt a hot stab of astonished guilt. Eredion had put himself in harm's way—for her? And Deiq had asked him to?

"That's what I mean," Eredion went on, "when I say he cares. No other ha'ra'hain would even think of asking first, or of shorting themselves to save a human—or desert lord—pain. And until Deiq understands why you're not leaping to offer what he needs, he won't touch you. Because without that . . . that driven response, he'd probably hurt you more than normal. And he finds *normal* too high a price already."

He drew a deep breath, let it out in a long sigh, and stood.

"That's the end of that long speech, and all the explanations I have for you right now," he told her. "I'll leave you to think it over. And—" He hesitated, then cleared his throat. "If you want to talk to Deiq later, I think—he did drop a hint. I think you might find him on the west side of town. At the Northern Church Tower."

Alyea shut her eyes and dropped her head into her hands. Of all the places in the world she did not want to enter, that was top on the list. Deiq had to know that.

Eredion made a noncommittal sound, then cleared his throat again and said, "I also have to warn you: your mother's not taking this whole situation well at all, so be ready for her to come in, frothing at the mouth, soon after I leave. I'm going back to my suite at the palace; I don't think you need me here any longer."

He let himself out quietly, not looking back.

Alyea stared at the tiny puddles and drops of tea on the tabletop, her mind alternately spinning furiously and drifting blankly among the abstract patterns of moisture. At last the sound of the outer door to her suite opening shook her from her thoughts; she looked up to find her mother, white-faced and grim, regarding her from the doorway.

"I think we need to talk about just *who* is in charge in this household," her mother said.

"Yes," Alyea said, "I think we do, too." She stood up. "But not right now. I have a more important conversation waiting first."

"More important than *me?*" Her mother moved at an angle to block the doorway, her tone and expression outraged.

Alyea drew in a hard breath, stared into her mother's eyes, and said, with flat certainty, "You will move out of my way, and let me leave. When I return, we will talk about the reality that I am in charge, and what that means for you. Right now, I am leaving."

Lady Peysimun took two steps sideways, her face bone-white and her eyes wide with real fear. Alyea passed her without pause, and slammed the door behind.

Chapter Sixty-eight

The Northern Church had long ago built a tall tower, wanting to look out over the whole of the city in what others had later named arrogance. Deiq rather liked the tower. The view over the city and the ocean could be stunning on a clear day; and when the rain and sea-mists came in, the tower felt isolated and alone, cast loose in a grey land of emptiness. Today was the former, and he watched the rebuilding of the western docks, which Rosin had long ago ordered destroyed—ostensibly due to smuggling activity. But like everything else in the world, there were many more layers to *that* story.

Distance turned the workers into scurrying ants swarming over structures much larger than themselves. Deiq smiled, seeing a metaphor there as well: of humans hurrying to conquer issues far too large for them to properly comprehend, building structures that would be swept away again under the first real storm.

Oruen had been typically human in his reactions: charging into the new day with a determination to erase the old, refusing to see anything beyond the short-term pain the priests had caused. Even Oruen's understanding of the *why*, the manipulations that lay behind the cruelties, hadn't eased his anger with the men; he'd emptied the Northern Church Tower with an edict that sent a wave of discontented priests back to their northern brethren.

Deiq had tried to point out the foolishness of sending men touched by the edges of a deep madness out of easy watching range, especially ones carrying a fierce sense of misunderstood pique along with them. Oruen hadn't listened, even before the disastrous audience that put the Tower in Deiq's hands. The king had never trusted Deiq, certainly not enough to listen. Like all humans who found out what Deiq really was, Oruen saw only Deiq's mistakes; focused on the biased stories; listened to fear instead of looking at what really stood before him.

Meer had been one of the very few over the years to see Deiq with clear eyes—accepting and forgiving Deiq's nature in hopes that his own faith would help Deiq change from monster to—what? To a saint of some sort? Deiq snorted sourly. It was too late to try for that, and he was tired of fighting himself for no good result.

Eredion would never get past remembering the pain Deiq had caused him. Alyea would never trust Deiq's judgment again, after what she'd gone through. Her first reaction to his voice had been a blinding rage, and she hadn't exactly insisted on seeing him after that. She wouldn't come find him, not after Eredion explained about feeding. Desert lords were still human, and he knew how human reactions worked by now.

She would find excuses: she would busy herself with handling her mother, and attending to the king, and Eredion would take up her teaching. Nobody would bother to look for Deiq until it was far too late, and even then, wouldn't look here.

Deiq had been caught for too long between the worlds of ha'rethe and human, both sides regarding him with distrust and fear. The abandoned priest's tower felt, symbolically, like *his* spot, a place filled with the restless ghosts of men pushed into situations they'd never expected. He felt oddly welcome here, in the emptiness; he could still feel Meer's prayers humming through the air, sent with the honest intent of healing and love. He focused his memory-vision and listened, sorting out his favorite echo:

To the gods who shelter us
From the gods who feed us
Through the gods who raise us
With the gods who praise us
We move through the dark, through the pain,
We move though, we move on,
We overcome and heal
We turn, we reach
We give to those who come behind.

He sighed. Usually the song reassured him; today, it only deepened his bleak mood. So many of the priests had fought to stop Rosin Weatherweaver in his endless plots. Some of the most sadistic priests had been killed by their own fellows. But the humans didn't want to know about that. Deiq's few attempts to point it out, to explain, had been met with such fury that he'd abandoned the argument.

Humans always needed someone to blame. The Northern Church had only been the most recent target. Deiq could sense the cycle steadily drawing around to needing another enemy; change always brought problems, and problems needed enemies.

He knew, from centuries of experience, how things would go: Oruen would find some way to effectively ban him from the city in order to have a clear path toward seducing Alyea. Eredion, consciously or not, would find ways of dragging Deiq into the middle of some trouble or other, because now he knew the guilt spots to press. Lady Peysimun would certainly campaign against Deiq with all her shallow strength, even without understanding what she was dealing with, because Deiq was less suitable a match than the king.

Going south again meant getting drawn into a different madness; hearing the ghost-whispers of the deaths he'd caused everywhere, the whining hum of his kin, insistent whenever he came within range: *Why do you fight what you are? Why? Why? Come back to us, come back, leave the tharr.* They probably wouldn't kill him; not even after what he'd done. But they'd see, sooner or later, the secrets he'd been so foolishly trusted with over the years; and then there would be no humanity left to worry about.

Weariness racked through him, every bone, every muscle, every bit of his brain and hair and nails, as he considered the final piece behind his decision.

Tevin's brutality, and Tanavin's memories, had reminded him of a stark truth: humans could commit cruelties that the worst of the mad ha'ra'hain had never even imagined. He couldn't face seeing that again, couldn't face knowing another victim was suffering through that sort of torture; and sure as humans bred like flies, it was happening somewhere, to someone, right now. Living in the midst of that potential while fighting his own darkness had become too much.

Far too much.

He sat quietly, contemplating the odor of drying paint as it steadily faded from the air. The hunger he'd been denying gnawed hard and deep, but somehow weaker than before.

His thoughts wandered over the last time he'd felt that twisted strain: remembering the people who had trusted his word and had died as a result. That mistake had cost him so much over the years; but at the same time, it had recently resulted in the key he needed to solve one final puzzle. The teyanain, of all people, had provided half the solution; and Kippin the other.

A small and tremendously expensive vial of stibik oil mixed with esthit stood on the table in front of him.

Drinking it wouldn't kill him.

But it would block the ability to regenerate through sleep. It would block the blood-rage. It would effectively paralyze him, and he'd be forced further into the hunger until it began to rip energy from his own cells for sustenance.

That would kill him. Agonizingly.

He really didn't care.

This seemed a good place to die. With the last task he'd really cared about complete at last, everything else could just . . . take care of itself. They didn't need him any longer.

They never actually had.

He hummed softly, listening to the music held in the walls, and let the weakness grow just a little more, distantly amused by the feeling.

Chapter Sixty-nine

Alyea stood looking up at the tower, still unable to believe Deiq was *here*, of all places. She almost turned and walked away, furious at his gall, his cruelty. How typical of him, to choose as sanctuary the one remaining spot in all of Bright Bay that held the most horror for her.

The tower was set high on thick pillars, like most of the western buildings. A round core section in the center protected stairs leading to the basements beneath, where Rosin's torturers had worked on their victims. Where Tevin had worked. . . .

She shuddered, the phantom smell of rosemary and garlic suddenly strong in her nose; shut her eyes, breathing hard against a surge of nausea. She couldn't go into the Tower—gods! How could he have come here?

Shadows filled the flood-space between basement and first floor; the darkness seemed to writhe, like the ghost-screams of the tormented rising in smoky distortions from below.

This isn't a damn game, Deiq, she thought, her lips tight, and stared at the ornate door with utter loathing. She'd never been in the tower, or even come this close before. The stench of evil that seemed to hang over it, her now-intimate knowledge of what Tevin had enjoyed doing to his helpless victims, repelled her.

To steady the trembling in her knees, she thought about Oruen ripping down the original Great Hall, burning and salting the ground to ease the agonized spirits whose blood had soaked into the tiles before the former throne. He'd banished the priests from the city, emptied the tower, refused to grant any audiences with the dispossessed priests regardless of pleading.

But he'd utterly refused to tear down their tower. It turned into one of the few raging fights they'd had after he took the throne. She'd seen it as symbolic of Ninnic's evil, and something the common people would be relieved to have gone from the landscape of their lives.

He'd simply, without explanation, refused. Eventually she'd given up and, like most of the city, stopped looking at it. Stopped noticing it. Blocked it from her perceptions completely, like a giant blank spot.

And this was where Deiq had retreated? She knew he was up there. She could feel him, could even feel his passage across the city as though she'd acquired an asp-jacau's tracking ability.

"Gods *damn* you," she muttered, not sure if she meant her mother, for making a difficult situation worse; or Deiq, for choosing this place to run away to; or even herself, for following him here. *But damned if I'll let fear run my life*, she thought. *I won't let that bastard win so easily.*

She went up the steps and pushed roughly through the unlocked door.

As the door swung shut behind her, latching with a faintly ominous click, she stared around in utter astonishment. She'd expected grey, dark, noisome walls; instead, brightly painted murals against a cheery white background took her breath away.

To her left, a field of tall flowers, painted with the detailed attention of a master's hand, stretched unbroken to a doorway several feet ahead. On the right, an equally careful skill had laid out a green field that faded to a range of mountains, hazy in the far distance. The windows overhead let in sun at just the right angle to allow the illusion life; she almost smelled the grass and felt the wind tossing her hair.

She walked forward slowly, studying the artwork, unable to believe that the same people who had tortured so many could have created anything so beautiful. In no hurry now to climb the stairs and find Deiq, she prowled through room after astounding room of simplicity and clean colors. Not all the walls bore murals, but everywhere lay the unmistakable marks of people who had used their surroundings to bring as much laughter, color, and joy to their daily lives as possible.

And she'd begged Oruen to rip down this tower . . . never knowing what lay inside the hated walls. All of her grousing thoughts on the way here suddenly seemed trivial, juvenile, and stupid; parts of a wall that had never really needed to be built in the first place.

She didn't quite dare go to the basement, though. Seeing that laid out in such beauty would be obscene. She could—barely—accept the notion that the priests in the main tower had been capable of focusing on purity at some point; she remembered the brown-robed priest at her whipping who had intervened to stop Rosin from killing her outright. And then there was that group of priests at the edge of the city—not far away from here, really—who Eredion had said worked to repair the damages of their fellows.

Not all the priests had been evil, apparently: finally accepting that notion rocked her long-held hatred and brought tears to her eyes.

She lifted a thoughtful stare to the ceiling, to where Deiq waited far above. She could feel him there, naturally at the highest point of the tower, looking out over the city. Even the ceiling was carefully painted; it felt like looking up into a bright, sunny sky. The clouds almost moved, they were so well crafted.

She reached out to touch a spot on the nearest wall. Her fingers came away tinged with damp greyness: fresh paint.

Alyea stared at the paint for a long time before wiping it off on her trousers, her mind reeling as she fitted this new surprise into place. As though prompted by her sight, the scent of fresh paint filled her nose for a moment, then faded.

This changed . . . everything.

She remembered Deiq holding the wren, and his words: *I see into people. I can even see part of a person in an object, if there's enough emotion in them. . . .*

He chose *this* place to retreat to. Now the thought held an entirely different emphasis. And he chose to paint it with such precise beauty.

Why?

She found the stairs and began to climb.

Chapter Seventy

Deiq sighed in mild annoyance that she'd followed him after all, but waited patiently as Alyea wandered the downstairs rooms, understanding the fascination the murals would hold for her; she would think the priests responsible for the decoration of the tower. He wouldn't disillusion her; in a way, it was true.

All he'd really done was to draw the prayers humming through the air, after all. Every time he'd entered Bright Bay since Ninnic's death, he'd taken a few precious days to expand on the previous murals; it was the only thing that made his visits bearable. He'd completed the last one just this morning.

Now this tower, this place which so many people hated as a symbol of a hell endured on earth, could gain new life with her support. He could feel the passion, the awe, waking in Alyea as she looked through room after room. She would bring more people here. She wouldn't be able to help herself. And they would see, and maybe understand, just a little bit, a side of the story they'd never heard before.

By the time she climbed the stairs and stood behind him, her initial anger had smoothed into a subdued, wondering peace.

"It's beautiful," she said, and moved, after a moment of no reply, to stand beside him at the wide window.

They looked out over the sun-drenched city together. He could sense she'd been shocked into a new awareness by the murals, and really *saw* it, the way he did, for a moment: the vast, glittering ocean, the expanse of small, rambling homes and buildings, the tiny, tiny lives moving, swarming, creating the city as they went about their daily businesses, like ants building their giant hill one grain of sand at a time.

She drew in a sharp breath and leaned against him. He put an arm around her without really thinking about it and relaxed into a long moment of unaccustomed peace. Awareness caught him at last; he stiffened and withdrew from the contact, sharply rebuking himself for the weakness. Another moment and he'd have reached for her; and once that started, he'd be unable to stop.

Never again, he told himself, and put himself several paces away, each step an agonized effort.

She stood still, looking at him with eyes that saw far more than he'd expected, and said, "It's all right, Deiq. I understand what you need, and I know you'll be as gentle as you can."

He sucked in a breath, his determination wavering, and almost went to his knees with the effort of not moving. He'd been so relieved by her initial anger; it would have been easy to fan it further, to send her away in a strengthening fury.

Calm acceptance had never crossed his mind as a possibility; but then, she was the first human to see the murals. He hadn't anticipated his artwork having such a strong effect.

"I *won't,*" he said through his teeth, and tried to think of a way to make her angry enough to go away.

She turned her hand over, showing him a grey stain on her fingers, and he felt a sick chill: she knew. He hadn't wanted that. It would have been so much better for people to think the priests left the murals.

"They're beautiful," she said quietly.

He looked at the floor, unable to answer for a long moment, then said, "Thank you. But I won't hurt you. Please . . . please just go away."

"I think," she said, not moving, "it's probably not going to hurt as much as what Tevin did to me. I don't think it will hurt as much as the blood trial of Ishrai did. And I think it won't hurt nearly as much as the pain you're already feeling because you're too godsdamned stubborn to take care of yourself. So take what you need."

He did go to his knees then, as the only way to stop instinct from driving him forward.

"*No,*" he said again; regretting, deeply, that he'd chosen this place after all. He didn't want to taint the purity he'd built with the screaming pain she'd go through if he gave in. He didn't want that sound added to the songs in the air. He'd never be able to come back here.

And after feeding as deeply as he would if he let her any closer, he'd have no real choice but to live. He wouldn't want to die any longer; the surge of energy would be too intense, too strong. He'd spin through another hundred years of increasing agony before growing depressed enough to attempt this again.

He couldn't go through that again. Wouldn't.

"No," he said again as she came forward. Dimly, he realized that she seemed to hold absolutely no fear of him. He tried to remember if he'd ever encountered that before; only images of trembling, white-faced desert lords too terrified to resist his need rose to mind.

Nobody had ever *offered,* not like this, not so openly and fearlessly. Even

Eredion had forced himself to help, drugged himself into submission to endure something he hated giving almost as deeply as Deiq hated taking.

He couldn't make himself reach for the stibik oil. The table seemed miles away, the effort too much for even ha'ra'hain muscle and bone to endure.

She stood in front of him, well within arm's reach, and took his face lightly between her hands. He threw his head back, trying to pull away; a howl built in his throat. If it let loose, he'd be lost; he moaned, desperately commanding his disobedient body to flee.

"*No,*" he said again; almost screamed the refusal.

She smiled down at him with a paralyzing peace in her eyes.

"It's all right," she said, and traced a feather-light touch down his cheeks with her fingers.

The howl broke free.

She went down with him, hard, into a deep moment of endless need.

Chapter Seventy-one

Eredion left Alyea staring at water patterns on the tabletop and went to his suite in the palace to wait. Either she'd stand up to her responsibility and force a confrontation with Deiq, or she'd run away; if she chose the latter, Deiq would be knocking on the door soon enough. With the foresight of experience, this time he'd prepared for either route before his talk with Alyea. His room held enough strong, coarse liquor to get even a desert lord properly drunk.

He contemplated the jugs and bottles, trying to think of nothing in particular, and waited.

At last, a shivering howl broke through the air, a sound that Eredion suspected nobody but a desert lord or ha'ra'ha could hear. It raised the hair on the back of his neck, along with other things; he wished ruefully he'd thought to have a servant girl present.

But damn, he hadn't thought Deiq would lose control so *completely*.

"At least it wasn't me," Eredion muttered, and reached for the first of the jugs stacked neatly by his chair. "Welcome to the wonderful world of being a desert lord, Alyea."

And at least, he added to himself, setting the empty jug aside a few moments later, he was reasonably sure nobody would interrupt his badly needed bender this time. He grinned with absolutely genuine cheer for the first time in too long as he reached for the next jug.

A knock on his suite door, a moment later, brought a savage frown to his face. He shouted, "Go away! I'm busy. I'm ill. I'm sleeping. I'm not here!"

The silence hung long enough that his frown began to shift into a relieved smile; then the door opened and Wian stepped in, shutting the door behind her.

"My lord," she said coolly, studying him with eyes that seemed too large and dark for her thin, pale face. "You can't possibly be all of those things at once, you know."

"I'm about to try," he growled, taking another swig from the jug in his hand. "Go away, girl. I'm not in the mood for your games right now."

She moved forward a deliberate pace. "And just where should I go, my lord?"

"To all the hells at once, for all I care," he snapped, and took another swig.

"That's farther than I care to travel," she said. "And you're much closer."

Eredion lowered the jug to his lap and squinted at her, acknowledging that at least she'd dropped all pretense: this was the real Wian before him, cynical, spirited, and unafraid.

"What makes you think I want you?" he asked bluntly.

"You're a desert lord," she said, with an oddly twisted smile, and unfastened her dress, letting it fall to the floor. Stepping out of it brought her another pace closer. "And I haven't heard a single servant gossip about being in your bed, ever."

"That doesn't mean I want *you*," he said, aware that his breath had grown rough and his pulse faster. The bruises patterned across her body had faded into dull yellow and brown splotches, no distraction at all from an abundance of curves in all the right spots.

She took another step, her smile widening. "Stand up and say that," she suggested.

He stayed still, watching her with abruptly cold calculation. Dropping the pretenses didn't mean he could trust her; it only showed that she understood lying to him wouldn't get her what she wanted.

"And what do *you* want, Wian?" he asked. "Another protector? Another master?"

"If that's all you have to offer," she said with an indifferent shrug. "It's preferable to taking my chances on the streets of Bright Bay. I don't exactly have many friends there."

"Why *me*?"

She raked an amused glance over him from head to toe. "Why not you? You're handsome, you're rich, you're not likely to die and leave me stranded any time soon, and I'm fairly sure you won't beat me for your own pleasure." She cocked her head to one side, a wide grin spreading across her face, and slid one hand in a slow circle across her hip, stomach, and chest. "And I'm *very* curious to find out if what they say about desert lords is true."

Not bad reasoning, from her point of view; he couldn't fault it. Still, she was a complication, and he had enough of those in his life already. He drew in breath to refuse, to send her away; but the echoes of that hair-raising howl still hung in the air, and he found himself saying, instead, "Come here, then."

She settled in his lap, purring, and he put the liquor jug aside in favor of pursuing another, more pleasant method of obliterating thought for a time.

As she leaned in, he sensed a shift: artifice slid a smile without truth onto her face. He put a hand between her breasts, holding her away from him, and said, "No. Be honest or get out."

She froze, staring at him like a frightened rabbit; he stared back without flinching. After what felt like a long time, she said, in a muted voice, "I don't . . . My lord, I don't know how."

He let out a long breath. "That," he said, "is a damn good start."

Chapter Seventy-two

Song drifted through the air, from avian and human throats alike: gulls from the western harbor, immigrant mystics from much farther south greeting the dawn. Warm sunlight crept across the windowsill, down the wall, and across Alyea's upper body. She lay still, listening, eyes half-shut and not thinking of anything in particular.

Deiq lay sprawled against her, one arm under her neck, breathing evenly. She turned her head a little, listening to his pulse thud in her ear, and studied his face. His hair lay loose, scattered across his face like a thready mask; his eyes were shut, his mouth relaxed and even hanging open slightly.

The muscles of his face shifted and twitched with dreaming; sunlight brought multicolored striations to his black hair. For just a moment, she thought she saw a faint tracery of silver lines across his face, but it was gone in less than a blink.

She inhaled through her nose, tasting the aromas of sweat, paint, and dust on the back of her tongue; exhaled, watching dust swirl through the shafts of sunlight now pouring in the wide tower window. A seabird called, hoarse and loud, from somewhere nearby: Deiq twitched, his breathing stuttering towards conciousness.

Alyea lay still and watched Deiq's face; his eyes fluttered as though starting to open, then winced shut, spreading pained creases across his temples. Tension began gathering in his lean body, his pulse staggering to a faster beat.

She said nothing; waited, her breathing deliberately even, until he finally opened his eyes and met her gaze, his own murky with shame and dread.

Then she let herself smile, and watched disbelief spread across his face;

after a moment, like a sunrise lighting clouds, understanding broke through.

"I didn't hurt you," he said, sitting up, and stared down at her in bewildered astonishment. "How—what—?"

She laughed, unable to hold it back, and sat up. Her whole body felt lit with a satisfied glow of boundless health. She stretched out her arms: even the remaining tracery of healing scars and bruises had disappeared.

Deiq ran a hand up her arm, his expression so bewildered that she grinned at him like a newborn fool. "This isn't *possible*," he muttered from the back of his throat, blinking hard.

She shrugged, flexed her fingers, wiggled them in his face, and laughed again at his bemused stare.

"It didn't *hurt* you?" He seemed unable to grasp that idea.

"Not at all." She didn't remember much of what had happened once his hands closed around her arms, dragging her close; but *pain* wasn't any part of the picture: only vague images of floating in warm water, like an ocean-sized hot bath, and a sensation of being touched, inside and out, everywhere at once. She remembered a rocking sensation, like being a child in the cradle again; and a steady, attentive presence, right there with her through every moment.

It hadn't been anything like her blood trials at the Qisani; and she found herself wondering if, perhaps, the ha'rethe was doing something wrong.

Her thoughts darted around, wheeling like the seagulls still crying outside the window. Everything seemed so clear, so simple. She would go back to Peysimun Mansion and set her mother straight. She now saw exactly how to ease her mother's ruffled feathers while maintaining her own standing. She knew how to handle Oruen, saw the delicate dance she'd have to go through with him from now on. She understood Eredion's flaws and strengths, and saw how he'd been navigating the complex traceries of desert politics as they mingled up against northern negotiating styles.

Chabi was easy: she was vaguely surprised so many people had problems understanding the rules. It all made sense. Absolutely perfect sense, as though she'd been playing it for years.

Deiq was staring at her, his expression still lost and worried. "It didn't," he whispered, blinking hard. "And you're *healed*. But I can't do that! I thought you'd—" He stopped, wincing, then shut his eyes and shook his head.

She saw, in the agonized creases angling across his face, that he'd truly expected her to hate him. In a flash of insight like the one that had foretold Lady Arnil's death, she realized that he'd even been ready to kill himself to avoid hurting her; with deep compassion, she decided to keep the tone light.

"You did tell me," she said, smiling, "that you're my guardian, and that you wouldn't hurt me."

He stared at her, mouth open as though hunting for words; then lowered himself to an elbow, pulling her down, and buried his face in the curve of her neck. His hands trembled against her back and head.

"I don't understand," he murmured into her hair. "I don't *understand*."

"Hells if I know," Alyea said. His hands felt warm, solid—safe. She didn't want him to let go. "Does it really matter?"

He pulled back and stared at her from arm's length. "Yes," he said muzzily.

He traced the curve of her face with one large hand, his eyes hazing and dilating; she felt her own pulse kick up. Warmth flared through her entire body, leaving her dizzy for a moment. She barely heard his next words: "And no. Right this moment—no."

He gathered her close again, with a much more human hunger; and she matched that fierce need with her own.

Guardians of the Desert
Glossary and Pronunciation Guide

A number of the words in the southern language include the glottal-stop, which is rendered here as ^. A glottal stop involves closing, to some degree, the back of the throat, resulting in a near-coughing sound when released. Sometimes this sounds as though a hard "H" has been inserted.

Aenstone (**ayn**-stone): An Aerthraim Family-created stone composite; they hold the process secret. In sufficient quantity, aenstone blocks psychic communications, inhibits the use of psychic abilities, and weakens ha'ra'hain.

Aerthraim lanterns: Any lamp filled with the peculiar green oil produced only by Aerthraim Family; gives off an unusually white light and little to no smoke when burned.

Aesa (**ay**-sah): A common plant whose leaves, when dried and used in a pipe, produce a mild euphoria. Illegal in the north; legal south of Bright Bay.

Aqeyva (ack-**ee**-vah, alt. ahh-**keh**-vah): A combination of martial-arts training and meditation disciplines. The combat training is often referred to as a 'dance' as it involves smooth, flowing motions that have no apparent resemblance to any fighting mode.

Asp-jacau (asp-jack-**how**): A slender canine with long, thin snout and legs. Its short-haired coat tends toward fawn or brindle coloring. Its excellent sense of smell is primarily used to detect dangerous snakes and (in some cases) drugs. In Bright Bay, only royalty or King's Guard patrols may own an asp-jacau, but below the Horn the asp-jacau is a common companion animal.

Athain (ath-**ain**): Lit. translation: *spirit-walker*. Teyanain specially trained to manipulate energy and psychic forces; extremely dangerous people, and very rare. Athain are considered holy by the teyanain. While they have elaborate outfits for ceremonial purposes, in "ordinary" clothes athain are distinguished by a unique manner of braiding their hair: beginning as one braid, then dividing further into three smaller braids, usually laced with tiny beads.

Ayn (**ain**): Chabi piece representing water. Cylindrical in shape, the ayn moves like a crooked stream: two spaces in one direction, three in another. It is one of the most versatile pieces on the board.

Cactus-flute: A long, thin flute made from minor branches of the same hard-skinned cactus used for making shabacas. Produces a thin, piping sound; sometimes tied together in sets of three to produce a wider range of tones.

Callen (**call**-en): One sworn to the service of a southern god.

Ceiling tube: A skylight in the form of a wide tube lined with mirrors; developed by Aerthraim Family. The secret of their manufacture is tightly controlled; they must be installed and repaired by Aerthraim craftsmen.

Chabi (**chah**-bee): A desert game whose underlying principles, moves and strategies reflect the principles of survival in a dry, hostile environment. In chabi, different types of pieces represent wind, water, goods, and money; different areas of the board represent compass directions, fortresses, fire, air, and water.

Clee: Three athain working together; extremely rare and extremely dangerous.

Coming or going: Street-slang inquiry about a relationship; "Is she coming or going" means, more or less, "Is she your girlfriend or a temporary amusement?"

Comos (**Cohm**-ohs): One of three gods honored in the southlands. Represents the neutrality/balance/questioning energies; also linked to the season of winter, the colors white and brown, and curiosity. Callen of Comos, if male, must be castrated; women must be past menopause to be allowed out in the world at large.

Dahass (dah-**hahs**; alt., dah-**hass**): Nomadic tribes that roam the uncharted and unclaimed southlands and follow no ruler but their own leaders. They are likely the source of many of the wilder tales of southern barbarism that circulate in the northlands, as they find spreading such rumors amusing.

Dasta (**dah**-stah): A drug originally developed by the ketarches, whose use has altered significantly over the years.

Dashaic (dash-**ache**): So-called dasta tea is dasta powder turned into a thick, potent syrup. Dashaic travels better than the powder, as it runs less risk of being ruined by damp conditions, but is more difficult to produce and thus far more expensive.

Datda (**Dat**-dah): One of three gods honored in the southlands, Datda represents the negative/death/change energies; also linked to the season of high summer, the colors red and black, and the emotion of anger. Commonly called "the Sun Lord"; saying the name aloud is held to be bad luck. Only Datda's Callen may safely pronounce the holy name, but they tend to be reluctant to advertise their affiliation; everyone knows that most Callen of Datda have trained extensively as assassins and spies.

Dathedain (**dath**-heh-**dane**): Followers of the god Datda.

Desert sage: A tree-sized plant resembling ordinary garden sage, which has adapted for desert life; the leaves curl up during the day's heat into thick, needle-shaped rolls, and spread out in damp weather or at night. After a long drought, even a slight breeze will stir the dead leaves into a shivery, rattling sound. The dry wood gives off a pleasant aroma when burned, but the leaves are not edible. Often holds large nests of blood-spiders and micru.

Desert truce: An agreement to work together for mutual survival in a hostile environment; ends immediately upon reaching safety.

Devil-tree: A tree largely found in southern wastelands, with deeply fissured bark, wildly twisted branches, and semi-soft needle-style leaves; cones are bright red and poisonous to humans, but attract a variety of wildlife. The wood does not burn easily and gives off a nasty smoke.

Eki (**eh**-key): One of the Four Gods of the Northern Church pantheon; represents Wind. She is considered to be the most evil of the Northern gods, and her good nature is rarely appealed to, for her favors carry a heavy price. Her strength is that of the air and clouds. She is deceitful and often malicious. Thieves often call on her for protection.

Esthit (**ess**-thitt): A drug originally developed by the ketarches, whose use has altered significantly over the years.

Estiqi (est-**eek**-ee): A liqueur made from esthit; lowers boundaries and dulls the senses. Used to help "stuck" desert lords (i.e., desert lords resisting the transition to their altered natures) open fully to their new abilities, by allowing them to briefly relax back to "normal".

Four Gods: The pantheon of the Northern Church; Eki (Wind), Payti (Fire), Syrta (Earth), and Wae (Water). Each has a dual nature (good/evil), and the Church teaches that mankind must ever be careful not to provoke the "evil" side.

Fours: Street slang term for devout followers of the Northern Church.

Furun (**fuhr**-roon): Chabi game piece representing money. Shaped like a coin, the furun may move one square in any direction once unlocked; it may only be unlocked by a grey shassen jumping over it.

Gods'-glory Flower: A common vine in the humid areas of the southlands; sports large, funnel-shaped flowers in an infinite variety of colors and blooming patterns (morning, evening, middle of the night).

Ha'inn (properly: hah-^inn; more commonly: **high**-inn): Lit. translation: *Honored One.* Reserved for ha'ra'hain. The glottal stop between *a* and *i,* always difficult for humans to manage, has fallen out of favor over the centuries.

Ha'ra'ha (hah-^rah-^hah); plural **ha'ra'hain** (hah-^rah-^**hayn**): Person of mixed blood (human and ha'rethe).

Ha'ra'hain (hah-^rah-^**hayn**): Plural of **ha'ra'ha.**

Ha'rai'nain (hah-^ray-^nayn): Plural of **ha'rai'nin.**

Ha'rai'nin (hah-^ray-^nin); plural **ha'rai'nain** (hah-^ray-^**nayn**): One who has dedicated his or her life to serving the ha'reye.

Ha'rethe (hah-^reth-ay); plural **ha'reye** (hah-^**ray**): Lit. translation: *golden eyes.* An ancient race, predating humanity.

Ha'reye (hah-^**ray**): Plural of **ha'rethe.**

Ha'reye-kin (hah-^**ray**-kin); alt. **true-ha'rai'nin** (hah-^**hray**-nin): 1. A human who has spent so much time around the ha'reye that he or she has changed physically; no longer human, a ha'rai'nin more closely resembles a lesser ha'ra'ha. 2. A lesser ha'ra'ha who has spent so much time among the ha'reye that it is growing into greater powers. Both are extremely exceptional; at this time, only one human qualifies as the first and only one ha'ra'ha qualifies as the second.

Hai-katihe (high-kat-**tea**): Rough translation: *those who serve (intimately) a ha'ra'ha.* No longer in common use.

Iii-naa tarren, iii-nas lalien, iii-be salalae (eee-nah tar-**ren**, eee-nahs **lah**-lee-en, **eee**-beh sah-**lah**-lay): Rough translation: *We serve the gods, the gods smile on us, we survive under the glory of the gods.* Implications of submission, sacrifice, loss of selfhood in service of the divine.

Ish (**isshh**): Prefix indicating feminine/female aspects.

Ishrai (**Ish**-wry): One of the three gods honored in the southlands; represents the positive/feminine/birth energies. She is also connected to the season of spring, the color green, and the emotion of love.

Ishraidain (ishh-wry-**dane**): Women serving penance for various crimes, under the protection of Ishrai.

Ishrait (ishh-**rate**): High priestess of Ishrai.

Itna tarnen, itnas talien, itnabe shalla (it-nah tahr-**nehn**, it-nahs **tah**-lee-en, it-**nah**-bay **shah**-lah): Rough translation: *We empty ourselves into the gods, the gods pour themselves into us, glory be to the gods.* Implications of partnership, gods and man giving to one another in service of building a better world.

Jacau-drum (jack-**how** drum): A large drum, generally stationary, with a wide head; produces a deep, booming tone. Originally covered with the skin of unusually large asp-jacaus, thus the name. Today these drums are usually made with cow, deer, horse, or goat skins, depending on how rich the owner is.

Jungles: Also called *Forbidden Jungles*. An area of tropical rainforest far to the south where the majority of the surviving ha'reye and their human devotees live; outsiders are not permitted to enter.

Justice-right: The right of a desert lord to intervene in a situation and see it resolved according to his own opinion of justice.

Ka (kah): Honored (generic term).

Ka-s'a (kah-ss-^ah): Honored lady (generic term).

Ka-s'eias (kah-ss-^ey-as): Honored (mixed gender) group (generic term).

Kaen (kay-en): Honored leader/supreme authority.

Kaenic (kay-nick): Southern term for the most common Northern Kingdom dialect.

Kaenoz (kay-nohz): Rough translation: *kingdom*.

Kahar (kay-har) Pyramid-shaped chabi game piece representing wind. These pieces move in straight lines.

Kath (kath): Rough translation: *servant*. Used with a variety of modifiers to indicate occupation and status; *s'a-dinne kath* indicates a kitchen or dining hall servant; *s'a kathalle* indicates a cleaning servant. When used in conjunction with *kath*, the female gender indicator (*s'a*) does not imply a female servant, but rather the concept of serving. The term *katha village*, while in common usage, is grammatically incorrect: it should properly be *va-kathe*, "village of intimate services".

Kathain (kath-ayn): Personal servants to a desert lord; generally offered to visiting desert lords as a courtesy, and considered an essential part of a new desert lord's staff for at least the first two years. Duties range from amusing their lord with playful games to more intimate services. This peculiar word is the same in both singular and plural forms, (i.e.: *Tanavin was a kathain; The four kathain left the room; The kathain's room was small.*)

Katihe (kat-tea): Rough translation: *honorable intimacy*; obscure term rarely used in modern times.

Ke (keh): Prefix or suffix indicating masculine/male aspects.

Ketarch (kee-tarsch): Organized groups of healers in the south who focus on preserving old healing lore and researching new ways of healing.

Loremaster: Combination historian, genealogist, and researcher; as a group, one of the major political forces behind the scenes in the southlands. Every Family has (or is supposed to have) a group of loremasters resident.

Mahadrae (mah-hahd-ray): Rough translation: *chosen mother of the free people*. Proper title for the female Head of Aerthraim Family. A male leader would be *mahadran*; but that version has not been used for quite some time.

Micru (mick-**rue**): Rough translation: *small death*; a small, black and tan striped viper found in rocky desert areas, whose poison is instantly fatal to large animals. Also the call-name of a member of the Hidden Cadre.

Nu-s'e (noo-ss-^eh): Honored man of the south (female is *nu-s'a*); generic honorific in the absence of specific indicators.

Numaina (noo-**main**-ah); plural **numainiae** (noo-main-**ay**): Proper title for a Scratha Family ruler.

Payti (**pay**-tee): One of the Four Gods of the Northern Church pantheon; represents Fire. Payti's "kind" incarnation is usually pictured as a short, plump man, with ruddy cheeks and a contagious cheeriness. In Payti's "dark" incarnation, the form is that of a tall, beautiful woman with a seductive gaze that bewitches all men who gaze upon her to their destruction. Payti's strength is that of the sun and the flame.

Protector: Not all fortresses are protected by full ha'reye any longer; some are occupied by first or second generation ha'ra'hain. Those aware of the distinction tend to use the term 'protector' to refer to those ha'ra'hain bound to serve a particular Fortress.

Qisani (key-**sahn**-nee): A rocky cavern complex in the southern desert, which was given, under a Conclave decision, to the Callen of Ishrai many years ago as a haven of their own. All the desert Families contribute to supporting the Qisani. The followers of Datda and Comos also have central havens, but they are more secretive about the locations. Blood trials conducted at any of the havens are considered the hardest of all possible.

Ravann (rah-**van**; alt., rah-**vahn**): Similar to lavender in appearance and scent, but tends towards a darker leaf color, white flowers, and a slightly more acrid odor; only found south of Water's End, largely around the Aerthraim Fortress lands. Adapted for desert living, very hardy, but does not transplant well.

Reeven (**ree**-vehn): A ghost that seeks to possess living humans whenever possible; most dangerous during the dark of the moon, and generally driven away by (regional variances in the tale) the scent of lavender, rosemary, or pine. Usually strong-willed people, especially women, are seen as potential reeven after their death; the theory being that such people are be more likely to fight off the final journey into the afterlife, so as not to lose their earthly power.

S'a / S'e / S'ieas / S'ii: Respectful address designators, analogous to *sir* and madam; specific to gender, and frequently parts of complex and highly specific expressions of relationship between the speaker and the person being addressed.

S'a (ss-^ah): feminine

S'e (ss-^eh): masculine

S'ieas (ss-^eh-ahs): a group of mixed gender

S'ii (ss-^ee): neuter; generally used to address a eunuch.

S'e-kath (ss^eh kahth): Personal servant to the lord of a fortress; the best are highly trained in scholarship, politics, and combat. Extremely well respected and dangerous.

S'iope (s-^igh-o-pay): Lit. translation: *beloved of the gods*; implications of being neuter, all energy devoted to the gods. Term used to refer to the priests of the Northern Church. Disrespectful nickname: *soapy*.

Saishe-pais (say-shh-paws; alt. say-she-pays): An expression of heartfelt gratitude, indicating that the one so addressed has shown great honor in his/her actions.

Sanahair (sahn-ah-hair): Lit. translation: *shit boy*. The word ties into an obscure southern joke about kicking the person ranked just below you until there's only the chamberpot contents left to kick.

Shabaca (shah-bah-kah): A large dried gourd or cactus filled with pebbles or dried beans to make a rattle; common musical instrument in the southlands.

Shall (shawl): A temporary, portable desert shelter.

Shassen (shass-sen): Chabi game piece representing goods. Cubic in shape, the shassen moves one to three spaces in a straight line; it may never move diagonally or jump another piece, with the singular exception of unlocking the furun.

Sheth-hinn (shethh-hnn): Assassin.

Split, The: A time of great chaos and dissension, during which humanity and the ha'reye renegotiated the Agreement and much knowledge was lost.

Stibik (stih-bic): A substance developed by the ketarches that temporarily weakens ha'ra'hain and ha'reye. Usually found in the form of a white powder, but sometimes as a concentrated, corrosive oil. It is illegal to bring stibik onto the land of an active ha'rethe; an even greater offense to use against a ha'ra'ha. Stibik was banned and ordered completely destroyed years ago; the ketarches, ever independent-minded, disobeyed the order.

Su-s'a (sue-ss-^ah): Northern lady.

Syrta (seer-tah): One of the Four Gods of the Northern Church pantheon; represents Earth. In his "good" incarnation, he is described as a leafy tree in spring or summer; when provoked to evil, he takes the form of a twisted, winter-stripped tree. He is credited with creating mankind and placing them in dominion over all beasts and growing things.

Ta (tah): Prefix implying masculine aspects; usually involved in insults (see *ta'karne*).

Ta-karne (tah-carn-ay): Insult. Rough translation: *asshole*.

Ta-neka (tah-neek-ah): Insult; female version of *ta-karne*.

Tas-shadata (tahz-shah-dah-ta): Rough translation: *fool, coward, idiot*.

Taska (task-ah; alt. tah-skah): Courier and guide.

Tath-shinn: Rough translation: *ghost of a female madwoman/assassin/murderer*; implies that a woman who would kill is insane, overly male, and impossible to handle even after death. Probably originated in the lower southwestern coastline region, among the Shakain. In the upper northlands, a similar creature is called a *shia-banse*: the ghost of a woman who died while under the influence of evil.

Te (teh): Prefix indicating formality and honor; no gender.

Teth-kavit (tehth-**kah**-vitt): Lit. translation: *Gods hold you, and blessings to your strength.*

Teuthin (too-thin): Rough translation: *meeting place.* Any agreed-upon neutral ground where all are seen as equal and violence is forbidden. Generally implies the presence of nobles of some rank.

Teyanin (tay-ah-nin); plural: **teyanain** (tay-ah-**nayn**): A very old, small tribe which retreated to the mountains of the Horn after the Split. Originally the judges and law determiners of the desert, they're now considered the guardians of the Horn.

Tharr (thahrr): Rough translation: *the invisible ones.* A derogatory term used by the ha'reye and ha'ra'hain to indicate those humans who do not directly "serve" them (in essence, everyone but desert lords).

Thass (tass; alt. **thass)**: A person with great status, beyond even noble rank.

That in it: Street-slang for *involved*; politically, not personally.

Thio (thee-oh): Status.

Thopuh (thoh-poo): Lit. translation: *blood of victory.* Also the name of a style of tea production currently monopolized by F'Heing. Thopuh tea grows stronger, more complexly flavored, and more valuable with proper aging.

Tibi (tee-bee): A shallow oval bowl usually carried by travelers in the south; food is scooped from a communal bowl into one's own tibi.

Toi, te hoethra (toy, teh hoe-thrah): Lit. translation: *I swear to you I am speaking truth.*

Ugren (oo-ghren): A very rare universal bonding mixture; also used in the southlands to imply unbreakable permanence in an arrangement or situation.

Wae (way): One of the Four Gods of the Northern Church pantheon; represents Water. Wae can take any form; in his kindly incarnation he is often drawn as a great, wavering blue horse made from the coldest water of the deeps. His dark side is depicted in forms with a dark, shiny surface, like treacherous black ice—often a snake is drawn for this. Wae's strength is that of the waters, both still and quick, and the mountain glaciers.

Wailer: Street-slang for the tath-shinn.

Ways, the: A series of passages linking areas with an active ha'reye or ha'ra'hain presence. Travel through these passages generally requires the active cooperation of a ha'rethe or ha'ra'ha, and is essentially instantaneous regardless of intervening distance.

About the Author

Leona Wisoker's work is fueled equally by coffee and conviction; addicted to eclectic research and reading since childhood, she often chooses reading material alphabetically rather than by subject or author. This has led her to read about architecture, basil, coffee, depression, economics, feathers, grammar, horses, and many other random subjects.

Leona has lived in Florida, Connecticut, Oregon, New Hampshire, Las Vegas, Alaska, California, and Virginia; has experienced the alternate realities of Georgia, North Carolina, Arizona, New York, Maryland, and Italy; and believes that "home is wherever my coffee cup is filled."

She currently lives in Virginia with an extraordinarily patient husband and two large dogs.

For more information on Leona and her current projects, visit one or all of the following:

Children of the Desert series page:
http://www.MercuryRetrogradePress.com/Worlds/ChildrenoftheDesert.asp

Leona's web site: http://www.leonawisoker.com

The Writing of a Wisoker on the Loose: http://leonawisoker.wordpress.com

Free eBook

Whether you're traveling across the desert or just taking the train to work, sometimes you want the convenience of reading electronically. At the Mercury Retrograde Press website, readers who purchase the book in Trade Paper format can download the eBook version of *Guardians of the Desert*—for free. Just enter the code CHABI on this form:

http://www.MercuryRetrogradePress.com/eBookform.asp

and we will email you a download link for *Guardians of the Desert*, in whatever eBook format you choose.

Want More?

Visit the *Children of the Desert* page on the Mercury Retrograde Press website:

http://www.MercuryRetrogradePress.com/Worlds/ChildrenoftheDesert.asp

for even more background on the world of *Guardians of the Desert*.

Author updates

For information on appearances and new releases, visit

http://www.MercuryRetrogradePress.com/Authors/LeonaWisoker.asp

for announcements and news, or to register for updates by email.

Also from Mercury Retrograde Press

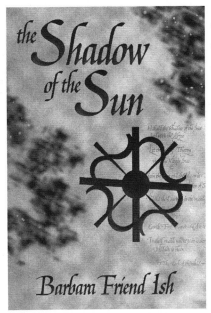

A Man Cannot Deny the Gods

Ten years ago, Ellion violated a sacred rule of magic and brought tragedy on his family. Forced to abandon his throne, exiled from the holy Aballo Order of wizards, and severed from his patron goddess, he swore never to work magic again. He retreated into music and a bard's footlose existence: living in other men's kingdoms, singing of other men's victories.

A Man Cannot Escape Destiny

But then the ard-righ, the king of kings, is murdered in an act of insurrection by a rogue wizard who follows the old gods. As the human nations teeter on the verge of chaos and civil war, Ellion tries to slip even farther away to the Tanaan realms, only to discover that they are threatened by the same enemy.

A Man Cannot Hide from the Shadow of the Sun

Now Ellion finds himself the protector of Letitia: a Tanaan princess, daughter of one of the greatest Tanaan heroines, and unwitting key to a great arcane mystery. Pursued by the rogue wizard's minions, enticed by gods he was taught to forswear, challenged by his former mentor, and tempted by the most enchanting woman he has ever encountered, Ellion must battle his faith, his vows, and the darkness his soul yearns to tap as he races to unravel the secret of the rogue's power: the Shadow of the Sun.